The
MOONSHINER'S
DAUGHTER

Center Point
Large Print

Also by Donna Everhart and available from Center Point Large Print:

The Education of Dixie Dupree
The Road to Bittersweet
The Forgiving Kind

The
MOONSHINER'S DAUGHTER

DONNA EVERHART

CENTER POINT LARGE PRINT
THORNDIKE, MAINE

This Center Point Large Print edition
is published in the year 2020 by arrangement with
Kensington Publishing Corp.

The text of this Large Print edition is unabridged.
In other aspects, this book may vary
from the original edition.
Printed in the United States of America
on permanent paper.
Set in 16-point Times New Roman type.

ISBN: 978-1-64358-488-1

The Library of Congress has cataloged this record under
Library of Congress Control Number: 2019952040

For Mom, a warrior—battle on

Acknowledgments

A n author's success is built on the backs of many. Without the help, encouragement, and hard work from the following people, I would most likely still be an IT cubicle rat working somewhere in corporate America. To that end, I would like to extend my sincere appreciation to the following individuals:

To John Scognamiglio, I am truly indebted to you for your inspiring words and the enthusiasm you express for my stories. Those moments are the fuel to the furnace of my imagination.

To John Talbot, my talented agent, you've shown nothing but rock-solid support over the years and it is so appreciated. Your dedication to me, and my writing, have enabled me to keep moving forward with my career.

Vida and Lulu, you make the magic happen behind the scenes. I am deeply grateful for your efforts, and tireless promotion on my behalf.

Kris, I am in awe of your talent. Your cover designs steal my breath away.

To Lauren, Paula, and the rest of the Kensington team, I am indebted to all of you for what you do, each and every day.

My fellow Kensington authors, Mandy, Eldonna, and Lynne, there is no doubt having you as part of my life enriches me beyond measure.

To all the independent bookstores and booksellers who strive to help authors connect to readers, you provide an important service to our communities; my profound thanks to you.

To the libraries that nurture and encourage a reading life that often begins for many in schools, and beyond, I owe you a lifetime of gratitude. Visiting the library as a child was the highlight of my week while growing up.

To all the book clubs, I am truly appreciative of your support for my work.

Jamie Adkins, of The Broad Street Deli and Market, you have created such a special place in our small town, and in my heart.

To the book cheerleaders who work so hard to diligently promote my work online through social media, I am grateful. It's because of individuals like you that word of mouth about good books has taken on new meaning. From Kristy Barrett, to Susan Peterson, Linda Zagon, Susan Roberts, Leslie Hamod, Dawnny and Denise (the dynamic duo!), and too many more to name, thank you again and again!

A very special thank-you to a fierce writer, J. C. Sasser, not only for the use of your last name, but for all those phone calls, the friendship, and so much more.

I am forever grateful to my family for always being there and supporting me. I love you all very much.

To Blaine, my devoted husband, I know no words are necessary, but sometimes they are, and this is one of those times. You always tell me "don't worry," and I do anyway, but I still need to hear that because it means you have faith in what I do. All my love, always.

We wander, question.
But the answer waits in each separate
heart—the answer of our own identity
and the way by which we can master
loneliness and feel that at last we belong.

—Carson McCullers,
The Mortgaged Heart: Selected Writings,
1971

Chapter 1

The only memory I have of Mama, she was on fire.

I'd been watching my baby brother, Merritt, digging in the dirt, when I heard a subtle pop, then a loud explosion, and the big pot Daddy and Mama were always tending suddenly burst into flames, and so did Mama. The sight made me grip hold of Merritt's hand hard enough to make him squeal.

Daddy would sometimes have to burn tent caterpillars. He'd hold a flaming end to the white cottony fuzz woven around the branches of the apple trees, and as the nests blazed, the black wormy bodies fell and hit the ground like the soft patter of raindrops. Fire always saved the fruit, but it's what took Mama from us.

Mama took off running, going this way and that.

Daddy yelled, "Lydia!" and then, "Stay there, Jessie!" to me.

Merritt had already gone back to stabbing a stick in the mud over and over, making baby noises, completely unaware. Mama beat her hands against her head; then they caught fire too.

She ran in a zigzag pattern, as if performing a strange and chaotic dance.

Daddy tried to catch her, yelling over and over, "Stop running!"

Somehow she evaded him, his efforts to help. He stumbled, twisted his ankle, and then he couldn't run near as fast, staggering after her, limping badly.

She didn't make any noise until the last seconds before she fell, when she shrieked his name, "Easton!"

The cry came long, and high-pitched, like a siren. She faltered, collapsed, everything from her head down to the tops of her legs consumed. Daddy threw himself over her, smacking his hands along her body. His movements frantic, he jerked his T-shirt over her head and pulled it down as far as it would go. If the flames singed him while he held her, he didn't act like he noticed. Puffs of smoke curled and drifted around them like tiny gray clouds while an odd stench penetrated my nose, a distinct smell that held me rooted in place. The imprint of her face came through his shirt.

I quit crying and waited for them to get up, for her to start laughing and say, *Did I scare you?*

The fabric over her face where her mouth pushed against the cloth was a perfect oval. The only movement a slow sucking in and out of the now smutty material. That spot mesmerized me.

In. out. After a few seconds, the area no longer moved. Daddy struggled to sit upright, still cradling her upper half. Her arms lay limp at her sides, hands blackened. He tilted his head like he didn't understand what happened any more than I did.

He bent close, whispered in the area of her ear, "Lydia?"

Mama didn't answer, didn't move. I remained fixated, waiting. He pulled his shirt up and away. Where she'd been creamy-skinned, she was raw, charred, peeling. Her hair was mostly gone, and only a few wispy clumps still clung to her skull, while her blouse was near about scorched off. It didn't matter though, because everything, her face, the lack of movement, was wrong, all wrong. It was as if she'd melted away, and my world turned as lopsided as the crooked bend of her torso in his arms.

Merritt had lost interest in his dirt digging and started toward them, steps unsteady as he made his way over the roots and leaves, dragging the stick along the ground.

He whispered, "Mama-mama-mama," but this was overtaken by Daddy's gasping.

He appeared to be trying to breathe for the both of them. He made noises such as I'd never heard before.

I mimicked Merritt, whispering, "Mama?"

This is what I remember. The three of us

making our distress known while Mama lay forever silent.

I was four years old when she died, according to the date on her gravestone, July 10, 1948. It was twelve years ago, and although I've tried to remember her before that terrible day, I can't. Her features before the accident are blurry, like a picture that's had water dropped on it, smearing everything so it's like looking through a frosty window. I also can't say what happened right after, what we did, where we went, who came to help us. I can't call to mind no service, or the burial. Obviously there was one because of that gravestone, which holds all I know, her name, Lydia Marsh Sasser, and the date of her death, both engraved within a heart.

New routines filled the empty gaps her passing left in our small world. Somehow, we made do. There'd be times when I'd purposefully recall what little I knew, and each image would flip by in my head, like the slide projectors teachers use in school. Sometimes there'd be moments when something from deep within would break through all on its own. Once was when I was around eleven, and Merritt and I'd gone to one of the stills tucked back in the woods where we were making sour mash. There's an odor to it, and I came to realize I'd smelled that very same thing just before Mama caught fire. A puzzle piece

14

fell into place. Merritt, who was nine, happened to bring her up as I was having this moment of clarity.

He said, "Jessie, you reckon our mama ever did this?"

My hands had gone sweaty as that one single thought dared to peek through a thick veil, surfacing through foamy memory, boldly rising up and out of my head, like the bubbles in the sour mash I stirred.

I mumbled, "I don't know, but I think it's what killed her."

Merritt stopped poking at the wood he was stacking under the boiler, my comment so out of the blue neither of us moved for several seconds. I quit stirring, and kicked at the collected logs nearby.

I pointed at the boiler, "The day she died, it smelled like that, but there was another odor too."

Merritt grew wide-eyed. "What was it?"

I shook my head, wouldn't allow that uglier fragment to emerge.

"I don't want to remember that part."

"Was I there?"

"Yes."

"What was I doing?"

"Playing in the dirt."

"And then what?"

"I don't know."

The tops of the trees overhead created lacy, waving patterns of green against a blanket of solid gray, thick, and heavy. Above the clouds existed a deep blue heaven, and a sun that shone hot and brilliant, but it was as if that world didn't exist at this moment. Trying to remember her as she'd been was like that. If I could wipe away the clouds in my head, I was sure I'd be able to bring her to mind. He'd gone back to stacking wood, and I'd gone back to stirring the mash.

Daddy refusing to talk about Mama was like trying to solve a math problem with only part of the equation. This is impossible because you've got to have all the necessary steps, and without his help I was stuck. Back then, I'd ask him about it every now and then.

"When Mama died, there was a popping sound, and then a bigger noise; what happened?"

He'd say, "Jessie, it was so long ago."

"But Daddy, she was burning, I remember it. How did it happen?"

"I wished you'd not ask them questions. Think about something else."

"Well. Why ain't we got no pictures of her?"

"I got to get to work. Don't forget to lock up when y'all leave for the bus."

There came the time when he started to get mad about it and he'd yell at me, "Jessie! I mean it! One more word about that, and you'll regret it!"

I crept away and the pan of peach cobbler I'd

16

made the night before became my temporary solace. I pulled it from the oven, grabbed a spoon, and stuck one in Merritt's hand too.

He quit after a few bites. "I can't eat no more."

I stopped but only for a second. I could eat more, and I did. I ate and ate, miserably spooning in sweet, slick peaches, soft buttery cake, while scraping the sugary golden syrup off the bottom of the pan. It was half-gone before I realized it, and then I was so sick I wanted to throw up. Had to. I went down the hall and into the bathroom holding my tight stomach. I stared at the toilet and thought how it felt when I had a stomach bug, the misery of getting sick, and the relief that followed. I got on my knees. I tried gagging. It didn't work. I remembered how when I brushed my teeth, I'd sometimes get the toothbrush too far back and it would almost make me throw up, so I tried sticking my finger down my throat. I did it again, a little farther, and retched. Again, again. Finally, the cobbler came up and a good, clean feeling followed. I felt better.

Relieved, I sat on the floor. It made no sense how Daddy acted. I was simply asking about Mama, how she died. His aggravation and refusal to talk about her fueled my strange hunger, and after I would always feel the need to rid myself of all I could, as if by doing so I could expel my own anger.

It worked for a while.

• • •

Time came and went with little change. When I was thirteen, I asked Uncle Virgil about her. He rubbed at his neck where the skin was sunburned, and it flushed even deeper after he dropped his hand.

His voice cranky, like I'd asked about the birds and the bees, he said, "Don't be asking me them questions; ask your daddy."

I said, "He don't never tell me nothing."

Aunt Juanita, who'd married Uncle Virgil a couple years after Mama died, didn't know a thing about her. I complained to her once and she waved her cigarette so dramatically, the end point flared orange and ash hit the floor.

She said, "Well, it's a doggone shame she ain't here to raise you and your brother," then narrowed her eyes at the bowl of ice cream and chocolate syrup I cradled in my lap. "Honey, listen, I can't be your mama, can't expect to take her place, but take it from me, ain't no man ever gonna want to marry no tub of lard."

She took my bowl, yet half-full, and put it in the sink, smiling a little to herself like she'd done right by me and her way of thinking. I became self-conscious about my belly, my thighs, and my breasts—because that's where she looked next. They kept growing faster than anything else. The next day she came to the house with two new bras stuffed into a bag.

"You got to start wearing these or all manner of hound dogs are gonna be showing up here at this door."

You could say Aunt Juanita was a blend of sympathy and meanness, neither all that helpful. I wore the bras, and didn't ever bring Mama up to her after that. That had left Mama's mama, Granny Marsh, who couldn't talk or do much for herself after a massive stroke. We would stop at the rest home to see her, only she didn't know we were there most times. I'd look for any resemblance, believing Mama had to have had her features.

When she died, I was relieved because I could quit waiting for her to share something, could stop hoping she'd see me and say, *By the Lord sweet Jesus, if it ain't my own Lydia.*

By the time I was fourteen, my patchy memories eventually led me to my own answers. First, Mama died while Daddy was making moonshine. Second, something went wrong, and it had been his fault; otherwise he'd talk about her. Guilt was what kept him silent. My arrival at this conclusion sent me plundering the kitchen cabinets and the refrigerator more than ever, eating till I couldn't move, followed by remorse at being such a pig, and the need to get it out. From that point on, we hardly ever had leftovers. There's only so much you can do to show frustration when you're not but a teenager. It wasn't long before I understood all the eating and vomiting did me no good. I still knew nothing about Mama, only now I'd come to a point where I couldn't stop. My resentment toward Daddy continued to bloom. I finally thought of something I could take from him, not quite like what he was taking from me and Merritt, but a way to show him how I felt.

We were sitting at the supper table, plates filled with chicken, rice, and gravy, corn bread. Daddy liked lots of pepper, and the shaker sat near Merritt's elbow.

Daddy always spoke soft, so his, "Pass the pepper, Son," wasn't heard by Merritt as he scraped his fork across his plate, mixing rice into the gravy.

I raised my voice and said, "Easton said to pass the pepper!"

It got pretty quiet. I slid a big forkful of rice in my mouth, and didn't need to look at the head of the table where he sat.

Daddy said, "What'd you say?"

The food turned gummy, thick, and I focused on swallowing. It could've been the dim light of the bulb overhead, or it could've been the fact I unexpectedly had tears, but I believe it was sadness I recognized and what drew his mouth down.

I was determined, though, and poked Merritt. "Easton said . . ."

Daddy set his fork down. "What's this about?"

Resolute, I said, "You know."

"I know? What do I know?"

"You *know.*"

The double meaning was lost. Daddy sat back on his chair with a look of consternation and a hint of impatience. I crammed in more rice and gravy, bit into the chicken, and ended up with a mouthful so big I wasn't sure I'd manage it without choking. I chewed, swallowed, and the clump sat, midway in my throat. I drank water to wash it down.

Merritt said, "Gee whiz, Jessie."

His voice held a tinge of awe.

Daddy said, "Don't you go being disrespectful now."

"It's your name, ain't it?"

"Don't you be sassy neither. There's that woodshed out back."

He'd never whipped us much, so I called his bluff, "I ain't scared."

Merritt gasped, and said, "Doggone, Jessie."

Daddy said, "I don't know what this little game of yourn is, but you go right on, if'n it makes you feel better."

"It does."

He leaned forward and I jerked back. I didn't fear him, but that abrupt movement wasn't like him. For the most part, he didn't get riled about much; it wasn't in his nature. Usually.

He pointed his fork at me and said, "Get this out

21

of your system, whatever it is, but by tomorrow, I expect you to call me proper."

"It's in my system because you don't talk about it, *won't* talk about it."

Merritt slid the pepper over, and Daddy sprinkled it over his food till everything was the same color, mounds speckled black. He went back to eating like I'd never opened my mouth.

"See?" I said to Merritt and the room.

The next day Daddy backed up our steep drive, and in the back of his truck sat a big box.

"Look a here," he said, pointing at it as he got out. "Got us a TV. We're the first ones around here to have one. What'cha think, Jessie? Merritt?"

Merritt hopped about, his exuberance making up for the lack of mine. Daddy pulled the tailgate down, and Merritt climbed into the back and pushed the box toward him. Between the two of them, they lifted it out, grunting, and straining under the weight of it, and brought it up the couple of steps to the door that I at least held open.

They pushed and shoved it into the corner of the living room, and after it was unboxed, Daddy said, "Plug it in, Son. Turn it on."

Merritt obliged; then they stood side by side staring at the glass tucked into a wood cabinet. As the TV warmed up, it made a low whistling noise that went higher and higher until the white dot in the middle of the gray screen became black-and-white slanted lines. Daddy slapped a hand on his head, and went back outside. He came in with a smaller box, and out of it he took what he called "rabbit ears." He set them on top of the TV, wiggled them back and forth, and fiddled with one of the knobs on the front. A grainy picture finally emerged of a man talking behind a desk with the letters *NBC* above him. Meanwhile, I tried to consider how a TV was supposed to make up for what I really wanted. Little did I know I would soon become enamored with a show called *The Untouchables*, and wishing for my own Eliot Ness.

The first time Uncle Virgil heard me call Daddy by his given name, he said, "Now that don't sound proper like."

By then Daddy had gotten used to me calling him that, and waved a hand like "don't bother."

Aunt Juanita pursed bright pink lips, pinched her cigarette out, and said nothing. Oral and Merritt acted as if they couldn't decide whether they should be in awe or not. I quit asking him about Mama, even stopped speaking his name unless it was absolutely necessary. Meanwhile, I remained on the lookout for possible hints of her presence. I'd noticed how when Daddy sat at the kitchen table, always on this one chair, he'd get to rubbing a finger over a couple of brown spots where a cigarette had blistered the Formica top. I

23

began to dwell obsessively on that scorched area, wondering who left the mark. Did she smoke? Maybe it was from her very cigarette from when they'd sat at the table together, smoking and enjoying a first morning's cup of coffee.

Over time I'd noted a couple of other small places about the house and my imagination ran wild. Like the circular stain on the night table in their bedroom, the one opposite the side where he slept. The small fingerprints left in the paint on the wall in the hallway, a happenstance discovery when the sun hit there a particular way, and only at a certain time of year. The day I detected them five little ovals, I placed my own fingers in each one, easily recognizing they were slightly bigger, yet too small for Daddy. I became certain the prints had to be hers, yet these were empty and unsatisfactory findings, especially when Mama's ghostlike presence was only as tangible as the wisps of smoke from the blaze that took her all them years ago.

Chapter 2

I stared at my new driver's license reflecting on how any picture could be worse than my school photo. It was early, about an hour before school, and we were in the kitchen where Daddy counted money from the haul he'd made the night before. The radio was on, and the broadcaster sounded as bored as I was as he delivered the news of the day. He droned on about the Ku Klux Klan and the cross burnings along major roads in South Carolina and Alabama over sit-ins at lunch counters. I expected to hear more about such an event, but he moved on to a race car driver who'd died at the beginning of a twelve-hour endurance race in Florida. I got up and fiddled with the knob, looking for a station with music. Uncle Virgil and Aunt Juanita had dropped by, supposedly on their way to town for corn needed at one of the stills. Sometimes this was the inconvenience of them living only two miles away.

Uncle Virgil couldn't take his eyes off the small piles of cash, and this was the real reason he was here. He had a hard time keeping a job, having worked at the feed store, and then at the factory where they made mirrors, and now he worked at a poultry farm. He had a bit of a drinking problem and Daddy said if it weren't for him needing to keep Aunt Juanita happy, it would be all he'd do. They were an unlikely pair as I'd ever seen. She came from Lenoir, and you could call that a big city compared to anything out here. The Brushy Mountains where we live are part of a spur off the Blue Ridge. She joked about how they really weren't mountains at all, more like bumps.

She sipped her coffee, leaving a pink half circle of lipstick on the cup's rim. Her nail polish matched. She wore another new dress, and kept brushing her hand across the fabric as if she liked the feel of it. Aunt Juanita was slim, and had her hair and nails done once a week at the beauty parlor. She knew better than to make any suggestions about my appearance. We'd had that reckoning a while back.

She'd said, "Jessie, I think it's high time you start taking better care of yourself."

"High time to who?"

"I'm trying to help you."

"I don't need any help."

She said, "Don't you think you ought to do something about yourself? You could start with your clothes, fix your hair."

"I don't know why it matters to you."

She said, "Suit yourself," and that was that.

My abrupt ways had always gotten under her skin.

I listened in while Daddy told Uncle Virgil about a close call he'd had with a revenuer last night. Uncle Virgil's head was in his hands. He was unshaven, hair going in all directions, as if the shock of what he'd ingested had it standing at attention. He was younger than Daddy, but looked older. When Merritt and Oral came in from outside, letting the screen door slam, he gave them both a dirty look, but neither one noticed. They were all agog at the sight of the cash stacked on the table. They sat, Oral taking the chair farthest from his daddy.

Merritt said, "Whoa. Looks like a good night!"

Oral pointed, then whined, "How come we ain't never got that kind of money?"

Uncle Virgil reached all the way across the table to backhand him, but Oral ducked, then shot a hateful look his way. Merritt propped his chin on his hand, watching with apparent adoration the man at the head of the table.

Daddy winked at him and continued on. "I believe it were Bob Stoley. I kind a played him along just to see what all he'd do. 'Course, he didn't stand a chance against old Sally Sue."

He chuckled with affection for his car, an Oldsmobile Rocket 88 modified to carry liquor in a fake gas tank, and jars of it under the back seat. He joked he could hear the goods sloshing when he took a curve too hard. Uncle Virgil laughed too, but it didn't sound natural, more like he was only doing it to go along. He kept his eye on the money the same way Oral did, licking his lips every now and then, wanting to say something. I'd seen this before, him working up his nerve to ask Daddy for a handout. I got up and poured myself some coffee, waiting to see if he would. It didn't take long.

Uncle Virgil said, "I might need me a little cut."

Daddy thumbed the bills and Aunt Juanita got to studying on her cuticles, her cheeks gone deeper pink.

Daddy said, "Yeah?"

Uncle Virgil sat up straighter. "Yeah."

"Well now."

Daddy turned to look at Aunt Juanita, who found something not to her liking on her pinkie. She was almost cross-eyed trying to see whatever it was.

Uncle Virgil said, "Yeah. I mean, it ain't like you got nothing to worry about. I got rent, and we need'n a few things."

Daddy said, "What happened to the money from that last run?"

Uncle Virgil raised his shoulders. "Like I said, there's things we need."

Aunt Juanita dropped her hand into her lap, and with exasperation said, "For heaven's sake, Virgil. Just tell him you owe people because you can't play cards worth a lick and lost it over that foolishness."

Daddy said, "Who do you owe?"

Uncle Virgil rubbed his hands together, the sound raspy and dry, like papers rustling.

"That's my business. Mama gave you this place here, while I got nothing but a damn plow and combine I ain't never gonna use. I reckon I don't quite see that as fair. Seems like maybe you ought to pay my rent now and then, and it's just how I feel about it."

It was an age-old argument Uncle Virgil liked to use to make Daddy feel accountable for his self-made struggles. It worked about half the time and today was one of them. Without hesitation, Daddy took one of the stacks and pushed it toward Uncle Virgil, who snatched it up like it was a ham biscuit. He shoved it in his front pocket, and grinned at Aunt Juanita. She rolled her eyes and sipped her coffee. He simmered down now he had what he wanted.

Uncle Virgil said, "Hell, it ain't nothing but money, ain't it what you say?"

Daddy nodded. "Sure, sure. It's what I say."

Uncle Virgil stood and so did Aunt Juanita. "All good?"

Daddy said, "All good."

Uncle Virgil went to the back door with Aunt Juanita on his heels. She motioned to Oral, who ignored her, and then Daddy got to laughing softly again. Uncle Virgil was about to step outside and he stopped.

He said, "What's funny?"

Daddy went back to thumbing the rest of the stack of bills.

He said, "That run last night?"

Uncle Virgil said, "Yeah?"

"I'll be damned, if it were Bob Stoley, he fired off a shot at me."

Uncle Virgil said, "Woowee! When's the last time that happened?"

"Never."

"I suppose he was mighty ticked off he couldn't catch you."

"He can't stand being beat, for sure."

"Maybe it was a Murry."

Daddy grinned as if he enjoyed reflecting on the danger and excitement of being chased and shot at.

His manner irritated me, and I said, "I honestly don't get the way y'all act."

Uncle Virgil said, "The way we act?"

I said, "I reckon it shouldn't bother nobody getting shot at, or thrown in jail, noooo, it's just a game is all."

Merritt mumbled his favorite response, "Oh brother, here we go again."

Five pairs of eyes turned to me, like I was a stranger among them.

I stood my ground. "Ain't it right? Nobody here thinks it matters."

Uncle Virgil put his hands on his hips and

poked his rear end out. He waggled a finger at Daddy like he was scolding him, and at that, the men and boys laughed. Aunt Juanita faced the screen door again, ready to leave now they had what they needed. I fumed. This was typical of how it went when I got, as Daddy would say, up on my high horse. Their laughter followed me down the hall as I escaped. I went into the small bathroom and splashed water on my hot face. I brushed my hair, and put a headband on to hold it back. I bent forward toward the mirror and rubbed at the two frown lines in the middle of my eyebrows. Uncle Virgil's truck started, making the small bathroom window vibrate. The sound faded, and I was glad they were gone.

I went back into the kitchen in time to see Daddy going out the back door. He would hide the money, maybe in the shed, or in the old outhouse. He didn't trust banks. His mama, Granny Sasser, had been the same way, keeping jars filled with coins and bills buried in various spots only she knew. One day he found her out in the backyard, keeled over under the clothesline, still holding on to a jar filled with cash. She'd had a heart attack and the story goes him and Uncle Virgil used that money to bury her, then searched, trying to locate where she'd hid the rest. They found some, and split it, but both contended there was a good chance more was out there,

31

somewhere. Merritt was all the time digging in the yard, like a pirate hunting buried treasure, whereas I'd come to look at liquor profits as dirty money. I wanted none of it, yet it was as if I was surrounded by its very existence, even down to the very ground I walked on.

Daddy came back in a few minutes later, held out his hand, and said, "Here."

In it was a ten-dollar bill. I made no move to take it, but Merritt did and Daddy gave him a look.

Merritt said, "Why can't I have it if she don't want it?"

He ignored that and held it out again. "Jessie. I ain't having people think I don't provide for you when you're about to bust out of what you got on."

It hadn't helped one of my teachers sent a note home saying I needed to come to school in proper-fitting clothes. If Aunt Juanita knew about that she'd have felt vindicated for her comment.

I said, "I ain't got no use for bootleg money."

"Jessie."

"What?"

"How do you know where this came from?"

"You just carried a bunch of it out the door."

"For all you know, this very bill was took out of my wallet from my other job."

"It ain't from your other job."

"Well, I suggest you stop eating then. I'm the

one putting food on the table and evidently it don't matter where it really comes from." Daddy kept on. "Them pork chops last night? I noticed you enjoyed them. I bought them with bootleg money. Yeah, you ate the hell out of 'em."

I was suddenly very conscientious of my physical form, fleshy thighs, hefty middle, and overly large breasts. I stared at a corner of the kitchen ceiling and noticed a cobweb.

He went on. "You want for things to be harder maybe. Not have that kind of food to eat. And here I go again, trying to give you money for nice clothes, but you won't take it. Instead, you want to go around without a decent thing to wear, going about looking like a hobo. You're making me look bad."

I said, "It ain't me making you look bad if people think like that."

"I work hard; that's all that ought to matter. After all, it ain't nothing but money, Jessie."

"If that's true, why can't your job in Wilkesboro be enough? Why can't you just do that, instead of using it to *hide* behind?"

Merritt sat with his shoulders hunched, head down. I didn't need to see his face to know his opinion. *Shut up, Jessie.*

"I make hundreds of dollars a night doing this"—and Daddy waved the ten dollars—"while I only make forty dollars a week being a mechanic. It don't take much ciphering to know

33

what's what. I pay bills on time, and have had that job for twenty years."

He was right. Unlike Uncle Virgil, Daddy handled finances carefully. We had electricity that didn't get shut off, that TV he was still so proud of, and a bathroom with running water, sink, tub, and a toilet. While our house was old and dilapidated on the outside, and needed a paint job, that was for appearances only. He had money to do anything, but he let it set ramshackle and run-down on purpose. While everything was nice inside, he made sure we came off as dirt poor to anyone coming up the drive, meaning if there was a raid, we sure didn't look the part of successful bootleggers. Junk was piled up in the yard. Tires, parts to tractors long gone, an old lawn mower, the rusty fender off of one of them running cars, other odds and ends.

He drove a beat-up Ford truck about town and it was what he let me and Merritt drive too. He didn't care if it got accidentally backed into a tree, which Merritt had done a few times when he was about eight and could barely see over the back seat. Sally Sue was a whole other matter. That was a hulking tank of a car and in good shape. It was so fast, he was a blur going down the back roads of Wilkes County. He kept her out of sight behind the house in an old shed.

"Can't you ask for a raise?"

He gave a short laugh. "That forty bucks is *with*

the raise I got earlier this year. It ain't nothing to be ashamed of, Jessie, what we do. Our family's been doing it a long time."

"If there's nothing wrong with it, why're we always sneaking around?"

I glared at him, and it was like one of them old Westerns, locked in a standoff, one or the other about to pull the trigger. He was about sick of me and my constant rub, like a pair of shoes that didn't fit. He stuffed the bill back in his pocket and walked back outside. A few minutes later his truck went down the drive, on his way to the job in Wilkesboro, and we had to get to school.

I said, "Maybe I'll just quit eating then."

Merritt got up, a disgusted look pulling his face down. "You ain't never gonna stop."

He went to get his books while I started thinking about me sitting at the table with my empty plate in protest. Food I would have surely cooked passed right under my nose. Mashed potatoes the way I liked, creamy with little pools of warm butter. Fried chicken on a platter, crispy and hot, and beside it, another bowl filled with rich, brown gravy. Fresh corn. Tomatoes. Warm biscuits and pear preserves. My stomach growled. There happened to be a chocolate pie sitting on the lower shelf in the refrigerator. I opened the door and bent down to swipe my finger through the whipped cream.

From behind me came, "I told you so."

Embarrassed, I straightened up and said, "It ought not to matter to you what I do or don't do."

"It don't."

Merritt went outside, and I stared at the pie a second longer before I shut the refrigerator door. I picked up my books and followed him. He was already at the end of the drive, and when I approached, he kept his back to me like I wasn't there. It was April, and still cool with the sun not giving much warmth, but suddenly, I was hot. *I ain't embarrassed,* I told myself, while knowing very well my own brother was ashamed of me because I was fat. The bus pulled up, and the doors swooshed open. He bounded up the steps and had a choice of sitting with Curt Miller, or Abel Massey, his best friends. I searched for Aubrey Whitaker, and when I saw her she slid over, patting the spot next to her. Relieved, I dropped into it, and didn't speak.

She said, "What is it?"

She had large brown eyes like a fawn, silky black hair cut in a bob and always perfectly rolled in a pageboy. She was thin as a vine. Aubrey had been my friend since we were seven years old. They'd moved here from Charlotte, when her daddy accepted a position as the minister at the Shine Mountain Episcopalian church. As we'd grown older, I began to see how different it was in her family, how they led a respectable life, with her father steering his congregation to Jesus, and her mama, sweet and kind, if a little strange. I'd sometimes wished I was Aubrey for all them reasons, but mostly because she didn't look like me. To her question, I shook my head.

She insisted, like I knew she would. *"What?"*

"Just the usual."

"You want to talk about it?"

She reminded me of the school counselor sometimes.

"Not really."

She huffed loudly and flipped her hand. When I got grumpy, she got impatient. We gazed out the window, neither of us speaking. While I usually told Aubrey everything, I'd never before talked about how I was unhappy with myself. I was afraid she'd get to thinking maybe I was right. That her time ought not be spent with the likes of me, and then she wouldn't want to be my friend, and where would I be? Trying to find a seat on the bus, and eating my lunch at a table by myself, like scary Darlene Wilson with eyes black as night, who spent most of the time hissing and talking to herself and whose mama was said to be off her rocker.

The bus finished with stops and picked up speed as it went along Highway 18 toward Piney Tops High School. Other girls seated toward the front laughed without a care. There they sat with their brilliant white bobby socks rolled down to show slim strips of legs tanned from helping with family crops and gardens. Their crisp ironed skirts and dresses made them look cool, and clean. They laughed and twirled gleaming pieces of curled hair, as carefree as leaves on the wind. I couldn't imagine any one of them doing filthy work like stirring sour mash.

My mood darkened.

Aubrey pointed at Cora McCaskill and said, "Gosh, she's got on enough makeup today."

Cora had turned around in her seat to talk to the girl behind her, and from where we sat, it was easy to see the blue eye shadow clear up to her eyebrows. She was very popular, and could get away with it. She wore new penny loafers, the copper coins glinting like she'd spent a few hours polishing them. Her daddy was one of the richest people in North Wilkesboro. He owned a car dealership and his commercials played on the TV all the time.

Aubrey stared at her intently. "Whore of Babylon."

She would think that. She wished she could wear makeup, but her strict religious daddy wouldn't allow it, and she resented anyone who could.

She repeated herself, and when I didn't respond she said, "I bet I know why she's popular."

I still didn't reply and we rode for a while with me watching Aubrey watch Cora.

I finally said, "I might go on a diet."

Her attention shifted back to me. "Huh? Why?"

Exasperated, I said, "Ain't it obvious?"

She leaned toward me, and in a hushed voice like she didn't want anyone to hear she said, "Daddy doesn't eat for days at a time on occasion, usually when he's seeking knowledge and enlightenment."

"Enlightenment."

"Yeah, you know, insight to a problem. It's called fasting."

Aubrey and her family were different, mainly because her mama came from California and was a bit of a nut ball in my opinion. She practiced something called yoga. I didn't know a soul who'd ever thought of twisting themselves into such a tangle, but her mama did and I'd watched her a time or two. Said she was exercising. She ate peculiar stuff too. I'd once seen her crack open a couple eggs and swallow them raw. As soon as I'd said it, I began to rethink my declaration. Aubrey's enthusiasm would only lock me into something I'd blurted out to get her attention.

I said, "I don't know. I'm just thinking about it."

Once you talk about a thing, it's like a commitment, and before you know it, you're getting asked, *Have you started yet?* and, *Why not?* I went back to looking out the window, wishing I'd not brought it up, unsure I could hold myself to it.

Chapter 3

The smell of steak and gravy. The sound of forks scraping plates. Even their chewing. All of it grated, as I sat with a glass of water before me, reading the *Wilkes Journal-Patriot* while trying not to stare at their loaded plates. I was looking at the front page where it showed Senator John F. Kennedy at some campaign rally in West Virginia with his brother Bobby by his side. They were interesting-looking people, but what the article said wasn't enough to keep my mind off what was going on around me. I'd somehow found the fortitude to do what I'd told Aubrey, and had survived twenty-four hours on water alone. It wasn't easy watching them eat and my attitude was a little more than sour at this point. The day before, when I'd told Aubrey about dieting, Daddy had come home that night and pointed about how he'd bought the food we were eating with that "good ole bootleg money." He and Merritt laughed while I shoved my plate aside, got up, and started washing the pots and pans. Daddy had tried to get me to sit back down.

"Jessie. Jessie, come on, I was only playing."

I kept my back to them, pictured the meat gone

green, the squash and butter beans flecked with rodent hair, the biscuits filled with mealworms. The decision was mine to own, and if Aubrey's daddy got himself enlightened, maybe I'd get answers for my own self.

This second night was harder though. I set the paper aside, got up, and began washing. Both had finished, but remained at the table. I removed their plates without making eye contact. The chair creaked as Daddy leaned back to relax.

He said, "I need you over to Blood Creek with Merritt, see how it looks while I make a quick run tonight."

At the moment, I was not enlightened. I was light-headed and irritable.

My answer was short. "I got homework."

"It won't take long."

"It'll take long enough."

He got up out of his chair, and as he left the kitchen he said, "Do as I say, Jessie."

I so wanted that one last piece of steak and I'd been thinking about giving in and eating it until he said that. Merritt's expression was gloomier than mine. With Daddy out of the room he didn't need to say or do anything for me to know he was aggravated. It showed in the way he got up from the table, the chair shoved back harder than necessary. It was different between them. All Daddy had to do was tell him what he wanted done and Merritt acted like he couldn't wait to get on it—but he had his own reasons. He'd been wanting to do the runs down the mountain and into the big cities, not just haul in supplies to the stills. Daddy was, at the moment, dead set against that notion mostly because of revenuers, and he sure wasn't going to ask me, the wretched, disagreeable daughter. It was enough we had to ride with him as deterrents now and then, and he had to hear me complain about that on top of everything else.

Merritt waited by the door as I stacked dirty plates in the sink and turned on the hot water. He tried to act tough, but with a trace of milk on his fuzzy upper lip I could only view him as my baby brother while also seeing how much he resembled Daddy with his dark hair brushed back off his forehead.

Defiant, he said, "I can do what needs doing."

"No you can't. We both got to lift that cap off, and unload the corn, and it needs to be done quick."

As we went down the back steps, he mumbled, "I don't know why you got to think you're so high-and-mighty all the time."

I ignored him. We got in the truck and I took the keys out from under the seat. I drove Route 18, then a remote dirt path with a lot of switchbacks. It ran along Blood Creek, thus the name we used for the still. We had two other locations in Wilkes County, Big Warrior and Boomer, also named for the general areas they resided. We didn't talk the entire fifteen-minute ride. I parked the truck out of sight under an old poplar. We each hefted a fifty-pound sack out of the back, balanced them on our shoulders, and began the walk in. We took a left on what could be called a trail until it dwindled away to nothing. From that point, the woods were dense, and we followed what had become familiar to us, but anyone else would swear they were lost. Certain trees appeared and we knew where to turn, then came the bend and wind of the creek, and we crossed it, carefully balancing the sacks. My leg muscles burned and went wobbly. I dreaded having to go back for the rest. It would take several trips and I was already exhausted.

I broke the silence and said, "It ain't that I'm high-and-mighty."

He was breathing hard, but had enough air to argue. "You act like what we do ain't no good. I don't see why you got to keep pushing the way *you* think. Whether you want to admit it or not, it's why we got what we got."

"You sound just like him."

"I don't care."

"You should. It's illegal."

I'd given up trying to talk to him about Mama, and instead wanted him to see what we did was wrong. He'd only been two and didn't have any recollection of her. He didn't have a feeling of loss, a sense of missing out on something important and special like I did. Merritt plowed ahead like he didn't want to hear any more. The way it was with Daddy and him, I was like a lone daffodil in the early spring that dares to find a way to poke through the frozen ground. I pondered my future as we went, like I did a lot these days. I wanted to get away from the legacy of my ancestors that was attached to me like my own skin, our last name synonymous with moonshine and bootlegging.

I didn't want to be known as the moonshiner's daughter.

As we approached the Blood Creek still, the very smell was as dishonest as a local politician. We set the bags on the ground, then squatted behind a big rock. We had us a perfect view of the ugly wooden contraption that sat festering in a stand of trees, near to a small offshoot of the creek. We assessed the surroundings. Nothing was out of the ordinary, so I nudged him and we went a bit closer. We stopped again, listening, and watching. After another minute, we moved until we were finally standing near enough that Merritt could look for what he, Oral, and Uncle Virgil set up the day before. There was a way of leaving the area so as to know if someone had been there. The easiest way was to lay a couple sticks like an X near the front of the still, and hide it with leaves. Some people tied threads so they'd get broke. He bent down and carefully swept the leaves aside. The X was still there, nothing appeared out of place, and the still was doing what it was supposed to, much to my disappointment.

We got the corn and stored the bags under the lean-to Daddy fashioned. The sun had set its edge at the tops of the trees, and the air was becoming cool. I could've used a jacket, especially in this heavily shaded area of the woods. Frogs and crickets began a steady serenade joining in with the late day twittering and calls of various birds. There was solitude here, the only thing I liked about it.

Merritt whispered, "Uncle Virgil's supposed to bring more corn."

A real family affair, I thought with sarcasm. I hoped we'd miss him. He would often show up reeking of liquor and either get into telling dumb stories about how he and Daddy were living their glory days like they were legends in Wilkes County, or he'd be moody, itching for a fight like he'd been the other day. Merritt pointed at the big box contrived from old boards and lined with copper. Blood Creek was a different type of still called a submarine. Daddy liked it best since he could get several runs of liquor off one mash recipe, and what we were checking on had been started a couple days ago. When spring hit, liquor making was nonstop. It only took three to four days for the mash to ferment, whereas in colder weather it could take up to two weeks.

We were practiced and used our hands and facial expressions for communicating. Come evening, we were always more cautious. Revenuers were known to spring from out of nowhere, sometimes lying in wait after dark.

The boiler held the fermenting mash and Merritt made another sign indicating he was ready if I was. We lifted the lid covering a layer of bubbling foam. We swiped our hands through and studied it. It was close to the distilling stage, the head thinner. I held up a finger, estimating how many days it would take before the froth would disappear. It would only be beer at that point and about 6 to 12 percent alcohol. The mash would be heated and stirred to the boiling point of alcohol, 173 degrees. Steam would pass through a thumper and into a flake stand and out what Daddy called the "moneymaker." We'd been shown how to shake the jars it trickled into, to get a bead, meaning if bubbles formed and disappeared too quick, it wasn't good for drinking yet. You want the bead to last longer. I was almost certain it was at some point during the heating process, when a fire is built underneath the boiler, that Mama had come to her end.

We replaced the lid, and made sure the X made with the sticks was covered well before we began making our way back down the path. We'd no sooner gotten started when an unexpected noise made me grab Merritt's arm. There'd been a distinct cracking sound, like someone stepped on a branch. It hadn't come from the direction I would expect, and I placed a finger to my mouth. We ducked behind a cluster of black haw to scan the darkening woods. The fading light created the appearance of someone hiding behind an oak, an edge of clothing visible. I was about to jab Merritt until I saw it was only a thick vine. I waited to see if I could detect any kind of unusual movement while Merritt cupped a hand around his ear. The creek running nearby wasn't helpful in separating noises caused by nature versus man. After another few seconds, and again, the crunch of a footstep came.

I imagined what I'd heard about all my life; revenuers had finally caught us. They would sometimes get lucky and locate a still, then lie in wait for somebody to come back just so they could arrest them. They'd surround the area, prepared to tear apart what they found, and then put the responsible party in handcuffs, or in the case of their being underage, I wasn't sure what would happen. Daddy wasn't really a criminal, more like a tax evader, but I'd considered more than once he might end up behind bars and Merritt and I would be stuck living with Uncle Virgil and Aunt Juanita. There were times I was certain it would take something like that for him to quit and I'd even wished for it, until this moment. What would the agents do if they caught a couple of kids? Make us talk? We heard a hoot, like somebody signaling to another person. I was set to holler and run. Merritt's eyes were like giant black marbles. I grabbed his arm and pointed. Something slid by the trees just to our right.

"Run!" I hissed, and before we could get our feet under us good, a figure came running, bent at the waist like he had intentions of knocking us down the way a bowling ball smacks into pins. His hat was pulled low, and the dark pants and shirt made him look like a black ghost. We ducked to get out of the way, but I was grabbed, and squeezed so hard I squeaked. He let me go and I dropped to the ground with a thud, landing on my rear end. Merritt put his fists up like he was going to punch if he could get a swing in, only the man started coughing, and remained doubled over. Then he started laughing. We knew that idiotic hooting snicker. It was Uncle Virgil, stinking to high heaven, the faint odor of peaches coming off of him. He'd been into the peach brandy he favored.

He puffed and wheezed, and in between his gasping, he said, "Law, I pitched that rock behind y'all and you both 'bout lit out of here like the boogeyman was after you."

I brushed my pants off and said, "You ain't funny. Not one bit."

Uncle Virgil, still laughing, said, "Well, well, if it ain't the old sourpuss."

Even Merritt was annoyed. "You scared the shit out of us."

Uncle Virgil said, "That there was an ambush test. Hate to say it, but the both of you failed. Gonna have to report it."

Still picking twigs and burs off my clothes, I said, "Ha-ha. So much for being discreet; for all that noise, we might as well send out invitations to where we are."

Uncle Virgil said, "Well now, I think you done turned more sour since I seen you last. It ain't possible."

The tang of his breath overtook the cool, fresh air, and I waved my hand in front of my face. His answer was to reach into the pocket of his coat, and bring out a jar. He offered it and I pushed his hand away.

"You know I don't touch that stuff."

He said, "This'll straighten you out, make you more pleasant so you can see the world right."

"I doubt that."

He tipped his head back and said, "I agree."

Merritt said, "I'll have some!"

I said, "No you ain't neither. Easton won't stand for it."

Uncle Virgil took a swig and Merritt swallowed reflexively. I'd caught him and Oral sipping on a jar, the first off a run known as singlings. It's nasty, bad stuff, not fit to drink, and they'd been halfway to being loaded. I told him I'd not say a word, long as he didn't do it again. His head hurt so bad the next day, I think he'd learned his lesson.

Merritt pointed at the still. "It ain't got but a day."

Uncle Virgil said, "That's real good. Them other two ain't far behind. It's gonna be one big steady stream out the pots and into pockets. Well, I reckon it ain't nothing left to do here. Things set like they ought to be?"

Merritt nodded while I started winding my way through the trees. They followed behind me and no one talked. I speculated on whose property we were using this time. I mean, if you thought about it, everything from start to finish stunk of wrongdoing. If it weren't for what we'd just tended to, I might could've enjoyed being out here where the dusky silhouettes of tall trees camouflaged human presence, where I could come close to believing I'd not been hunkered down near the stinking box. Slipping through the woods soundless, leaving no trace, I could even imagine, *I wasn't ever here.*

We made our way back to the vehicles and left quickly. To my dismay, Uncle Virgil followed us to the house, and came right on in. He sat down on a kitchen chair with a thud, as if his legs give out. I caught that sharp odor again, and supposed he'd been at it all afternoon. His eyes were bloodshot, and his clothes disheveled. The knees of his coveralls were muddy, like he'd fallen down at some point, and a chicken feather was stuck to the back of his shirt. He was liable to pick an argument as he was wont to do when he'd had too much. If Daddy had been here, he'd tell him to go home and sleep it off.

I said, "Want some iced tea?"

In an overly polite, mocking tone, he said, "If'n it ain't no trouble to you."

Merritt sat across from him and said, "What's Oral doing?"

"Your aunt Juanita's got him tangled up with chores. He's in a bit of trouble, you could say. Hell, we both stay in trouble."

Merritt's attention sharpened, and he leaned across the table. "Yeah? What kind a trouble?"

Uncle Virgil yawned, scratched at his belly, and said, "The kind he hates most."

I set a glass of sweet tea in front of him.

I said, "You mean he's been into the liquor again."

Merritt said, "I wished I could do that."

I smacked his shoulder and said, "No you don't."

He frowned at me. "Do too."

"You know what Easton said."

Uncle Virgil picked up the glass and drained it while Merritt leaned forward, eager to hear more, thinking he was missing out on what he viewed as fun. He waited for Uncle Virgil to elaborate.

Uncle Virgil hiccupped, then put his head

down on his forearms. "You got anything for this popskull headache a mine?"

I opened a cabinet beside the sink and got out a packet of BC Powders. He sat back, then hunched over again, like he couldn't get comfortable, and you'd think Merritt would see this as a lesson to be learned. Instead, he only looked disappointed he wasn't getting more details about his cousin. Merritt conveniently ignored my animated gestures behind Uncle Virgil's back where I made like I was buttoning my lip, hoping a lack of conversation would make Uncle Virgil leave. Uncle Virgil sat up, shook the ice in his glass, a rude way of telling me to get him some more. I poured it full again, and set the pitcher beside him, a little harder than necessary. He winced, turned a bleary eye on me, but I ignored the look. He unfolded the little wax paper packet, tipped the contents in his mouth, and took a big swig of sweet tea. I started washing the cold, now greasy plates.

After a while, he said, "Hey, sourpuss."

I kept washing and rinsing.

"Hey."

I put the plate in the drain.

"Hey, you know what? Hey."

"*What,* Uncle Virgil?"

He sniggered, his laugh grating, and making my own head hurt.

He said, "You ever heard that saying 'don't

bite the hand that feeds ya'? That's something to think about."

He had no inkling I wasn't eating, so it was kind of funny what he said.

I stopped washing a plate, and said, "When I see what a fine example you set, maybe that's got something to do with it, among other things."

Merritt made some noise.

Uncle Virgil said, "Shoot. Lemme tell you what. Blame your aunt Juanita for that boy of mine liking this fine product of ourn, not me."

"I can't see how that's true."

"Why sure. She's the one got him started on it. Used it ever since he was a baby. Teething, here come a little whisky rubbed on his gums. Started to coughing, here come a little whisky, honey, and lemon. Couldn't sleep, here come a little hot toddy. You ask me, that's why he's got the taste for it."

I waved a hand, dismissing what he said.

I said, "You don't see Easton drinking."

Uncle Virgil's little buzz was wearing off and he said, "Nope. Not the Saint."

Uncle Virgil slumped on the chair, in no hurry. It was true, many around here used whisky the way he'd described, and Daddy had him a reputation for doling it out to the elderly who couldn't afford a doctor. Maybe it was true, it might help some people, but it sure didn't make up for all the other goings-on.

Uncle Virgil burped, and said, "When did he go on his run?"

"Couple hours ago."

He stood and said, "Reckon I'll see him tomorrow sometime."

Relieved he was leaving, I held the back door open and he wobbled his way out. I waited till he got the truck cranked, then shut it. Merritt hurried to escape to his room before I could get started in on about Uncle Virgil's downfalls. I tidied around the kitchen some more, and by then it was going on ten o'clock. I stared at the refrigerator, then opened the door. There was that one leftover steak floating in gravy. Why not? It would've been mine anyway. I reached for it, then remembered why I wasn't eating. That piece of steak was stained by liquor money. I shut the refrigerator, got more water, and went to my room. I sat at the small wooden desk where the dim light of the lamp cast a yellow glow over papers I'd left spread out. I had trouble focusing on what was in front of me. English was not my favorite subject for one, especially when I was too tired, too hungry, to concentrate. I bent over the work anyway, trying to ignore my discomfort.

When the sound of tires squalling on pavement came, I got up and went to my window. Our house was set back on a hill, and although the road out front was too far away to be seen, we could hear vehicles as they passed by and when someone went into the curve too fast that was the sound we heard many a night. The clock on my bedside table said almost eleven. I pulled the curtain back, but all I could make out was my own reflection and the view of my room behind me. I reached over and turned off the lamp and looked out again, staring at the white line of gravel leading to the house, almost shining under the moonlight.

Within seconds came the low rumble of an engine, and the crunching sound of tires rolling over the shattered small stones. The Oldsmobile Rocket 88 slunk past the house, heading up the hill behind the house. Daddy didn't have his headlights on, which told me he'd been avoiding someone. I exhaled, partly relieved, partly annoyed. While we stayed at odds, I still worried he'd get in a wreck, or something else would happen. For now, another night was over, and finished. I could go back to my desk, work on the assignment half-finished, and stew over what I couldn't change. A few minutes later the back door opened, and then he was tapping on my door.

He said, "Jessie? You up?"

The strip of light below my bedroom door showed the shadowy shape of him blocking part of it. I didn't acknowledge him. A sigh, and a soft good night came from the other side before he went down the hall.

Chapter 4

The next morning I would have bet it was the same ten-dollar bill lying only inches from the gap at the bottom of the door. Sometimes I thought Daddy did stuff like this on purpose to get me riled. I picked it up. Brand-new, crisp, stiff, and perfect. To my mind's eye it should've been grimy and weather worn as the moldy contraptions that bubbled and burped their vile concoctions out in the woods. I was unwilling to fight with him this morning. I brought it into the kitchen and placed it in the tin behind the sugar canister where he'd eventually find it. Or Merritt.

He was sitting at the table asking Merritt how it went over to Blood Creek.

Merritt said, "Fine."

Without thinking, I opened the metal bread box and stared at the loaf of bread, inhaled the yeasty odor before I let the small metal door slip from my fingers, rattling as it shut. I was absolutely regretting my impulsive decision now.

Irritable, I said, "If you call Uncle Virgil showing up drunk as a coot fine. Which is why Oral didn't make it neither. Aunt Juanita kept him at the house punishing him for being drunk too. I bet that's really what that money's for. Uncle Virgil only wants it so he can hand it over to Aunt Juanita and keep her happy, and only time she's that is when she gets to gallivant around town spending it."

Daddy wore a white T-shirt, navy-blue work pants, and white socks. He smelled of aftershave and the bleach I used to wash the whites, mingled in with fresh-brewed coffee and cigarette smoke. He didn't act too put out.

All he said was, "Never did have a taste for it, myself."

I poured a cup of coffee and said, "If there'd been anybody around, we made enough noise to get their attention."

Daddy pushed his chair back. "I'll say something about it again."

Merritt said, "I can't see what's so bad about having a little taste of it here and there."

Daddy said, "I ever catch you, it ain't gonna be a good day."

Merritt, anxious I'd let on about his little escapade with Oral, gave me a sideways glance. I narrowed my eyes over the rim of the cup, letting him know I hadn't forgot.

"I need the both of you to come with me later on this evening. It ain't far where I got to go, but it's down that road where Virgil said he's heard them government agents have been seen."

These rides we went on bothered me as much as making liquor, the idea being if revenuers were on the prowl, we would appear like a family riding to the store, or off to visit somebody. No call for suspicion, no cause to question.

Merritt said, "What time?"

"Don't worry, you'll be done with ball practice. It ain't till after supper."

Daddy hesitated, but I had nothing to say, and he might have been surprised I didn't pitch a fit. He went to put on his work shirt and shoes and left five minutes later, not a word about the money he'd left. Not a word about me not eating, not only the night before, but now. Maybe this was his new way of managing what he believed were my shortcomings: ignore them.

Merritt and I caught the bus, and I sank into the seat beside Aubrey, a hint of moisture on my upper lip and brow. The bus shuddered as it moved forward and so did my stomach. She didn't act like she noticed my silence. She was more of the talker anyway, and was going on about some boy she was wild about, thinking he might like her. If she'd said his name I hadn't heard it. The bus rolled along, my gut following every curve and dip in the road. Aubrey's voice faded away. I gripped the metal bar on the seat in front of us, praying I'd make it to school without embarrassing myself by getting sick.

• • •

Mrs. Brewer, our school nurse, had seen a lot in her lifetime. Once a granny woman, she'd come from Grassy Mountain in the next county over to attend to students at Piney Tops after her husband died when his tractor flipped over on him in the middle of a tobacco field. It happened early morning right after sunrise, and she didn't know. She didn't go looking for him until he didn't show up for noon dinner. Minor ailments like fever, dispensing bandages, and the occasional aspirin for some pain here or there was how she now filled her days. She had snow-white hair and looked to be in her seventies.

She scowled at a notepad and wrote my name down with some comment off to the side I couldn't see well enough to make out. I'd only been once before, back when my stomach was cramping bad enough I couldn't sit up straight.

She said, "What ails you this time?" as if I'd been coming to see her on a regular basis.

I didn't look her in the eye. "Nothing."

"Nothing? Mrs. Hardin thought you was 'bout to pass out."

I said, "I'm on a diet."

She sniffed. "Dieting. Hmph. You young gals sure is something else nowadays. Always trying some fool notion. You got to et. Dieting? More like starving yerself. Can't be doing such or you get to feeling like this."

59

I didn't give her any response, and she said, "Wait here."

Five minutes later she came back with a tray from the lunchroom and plunked it in front of me.

"Et."

I didn't want to eat, but given her tone, and the look she delivered, I believed I'd not be allowed back to class until I did. It was a peanut butter and jelly sandwich, and a carton of milk. My belly said yes while my head said no.

She crossed her arms and said, "I hope I ain't got to tell you 'bout the gal who keeled over and died right in front of me when her fragile heart couldn't take no more of her 'dieting.' "

"No, ma'am."

"Then et what I took the time to bring."

The miracle that was simply food inside me soon eliminated the floaty spots, and my hands quit shaking too. Mrs. Brewer busied herself arranging gauze and pills in a small cabinet while I tried not to cram the food in too fast.

After a few minutes, she saw I'd finished and said, "Now. I know you got to feel better."

"Yes'm."

I was not lying.

"Good. Now get on back to class. If you want to go about it sensibly, there's something called food a body needs. I want you to drink this."

She dug around in an enormous pocketbook

and handed me a paper packet. I stared at what was scribbled on the front, in her jagged, sharp writing. "Blessed Thistle Tea."

She tapped it with her forefinger, the first knuckle joint twice as big as it ought to be, and said, "Put about a teaspoon in tea ball, bile, and drink it."

I nodded.

"Hot, cold, with or without honey or sugar, however you want. It's good for lots of ailments. Particularly the kind some of you seem to get these days with all of you caterwauling about weight. I ain't never for the life of me ever heard of such."

"Yes'm."

She shooed me out of the tiny room, and slammed the door. I held tight to the packet as I went down the hall, and stopped outside the girls' bathroom, wanting to get rid of the sandwich that burbled in my belly. The thick taste of peanut butter in my mouth almost made me gag. I'd tried eliminating peanut butter before, and it didn't work well—at all. The bathroom door banged open and here came Cora with her best friend, Stacy McKinney. I turned sideways to let them pass and they breezed by me chattering like I wasn't there. I went in, and stood over the toilet. The thought of forcing food up made me weak-kneed. This thing I did, it was hard. Today, there came a clear *don't*. I left the bathroom, and by the time I got back to class the taste of what I'd eaten was gone and I wished for more.

That afternoon after school I changed into a pair of dungarees. I sucked in my belly to button them and pulled the zipper up. I got a belt, and cinched it tight around my middle, tight as I could get it. I stood, getting a tiny bit of relief from the gnawing ache with the pressure against my innards. I'd eaten that sandwich and now my stomach rebelled, wanting more food. After two days you'd think I would give up, but I couldn't. I'd come this far, it had to matter. I fixed a quick supper, fried a few hot dogs, heated some baked beans, and popped open a can of biscuits. They ate and no one noticed I didn't. I inhaled the aroma of food like smoke off of someone else's cigarette. I brewed some of Mrs. Brewer's special tea and drank a cup of it. I hid the packet in the cabinet, behind some canned goods.

After supper Daddy got up from the table and I quickly washed the dishes, staring out the window as he backed Sally Sue out of the shed and came down the hill. Merritt went out and got in the back, sat on the fake seat concealing the jars of liquor directly beneath him. They waited on me, the engine grumbling as if it wasn't used to idling. I dried my hands, went outside, and got in the front on the passenger side.

Daddy commented, like I cared.

He said, "Got us a full load tonight off Blood

Creek earlier this afternoon. Y'all done real good."

That meant the fake gas tank was full too. The delivery would hopefully be over and done with quick, like most of them. I leaned forward to fiddle with volume on the radio, tuning into WKBC. To my disgust they were playing "White Lightning" by George Jones.

I started to shut it off, but Daddy said, "Now that's what I call good timing. Turn it up!"

I rolled my eyes and did as he asked, listening to George wail and carry on about making shine. He glorified it. Daddy's fingers tapped the steering wheel in time to the song, the radio the only sound except the slap of Merritt's baseball into the palm of his glove coming from the back seat.

We headed toward the obscure back roads where nothing except an occasional house, pastures with cows, or a tobacco barn broke up the landscape. The top of Shine Mountain rose above all others, tall enough to see as we drove south. Soon we turned onto Lore Mountain Road, where the revenuers had been spotted. Daddy obeyed the speed limit, keeping his eye on his side view and rearview mirrors. He motioned for me to turn the volume down. A sliver of the orange sunset leaked through the trees every now and then as dusk created shadows in the creases of hillsides. Sharp curved switchbacks made the road appear indecisive, as if it wanted to first go left, then right. We finally came to a little stretch of straightaway.

Daddy said, "Ain't nothing like a little evening drive."

It was like him to try and turn liquor hauling into any old ordinary pastime. I didn't bother to answer. His window was down halfway and cool air circulated inside the car. The sun was soon gone altogether, and with the veil of night over us, I leaned my head against the back of the seat, occasionally glancing at my side view mirror. At least if I had to be involved, obscurity was always comforting. We descended into one of many hollers, and as we came to the bottom of the hill I saw the flash of headlights in my side view mirror.

I said, "Somebody's behind us."

Merritt spun around in his seat and looked out the back window.

He said, "Sure is."

Daddy kept his speed, and we began to climb again.

He said, "It don't mean nothing."

He kept a look out though.

We lost sight of the car in the curves, but soon as we came to another stretch where the road went straight, Daddy said, "They's closer."

He accelerated a bit, and Sally Sue's engine responded. We went along as quick and effortless as the current of the Yadkin River. He could put plenty of distance between us and whoever was back there without really trying. All he had to do was press on the gas a bit more and that would be that. When the other car held the distance, and then came closer, Daddy kept looking in his rearview mirror.

He said, "Getting closer," as calm as if he was browsing the newspaper and had run across an article of interest.

In the back, Merritt turned around completely and started giving us second by second comments on the car's distance. All it did was increase my anxiousness. When the car was two lengths away from our bumper, Merritt announced this.

I said, "We can see for ourselves, Merritt."

Daddy said, "Got all this road, ain't no need getting so close."

He accelerated and we rounded the curve; the force of speed combined with direction pushed me against the door. I gripped the armrest and watched the headlights of the other car grow smaller. Daddy kept his foot on the gas even as we came to another curve. There was a slight squall of the tires and I saw how he wore a little smile, like he was enjoying himself. None of the runs in the past had turned into anything other than a meandering ride down the mountain, and then up the drive of someone's house, or to the back side of a store where smiling faces welcomed him and what he carried. This was different, and I worried about the speed and the curves, and the other car.

I said, "I hope they got the good sense enough to leave us alone."

Daddy said, "Maybe I'll pull over, see if they'll go on by."

Hopeful he'd do that, I said, "Yeah."

Another straightaway came and the car regained most of the distance lost and was almost as close as it had been before. They slid over into the other lane like they were going to try and pass us. Daddy let off the gas some so they could. As they came alongside, they stayed there, which made him look. Without warning, he floored it.

Merritt, his voice worried, said, "What're you doing?"

Daddy didn't answer; instead, he leaned forward and concentrated on driving, both of his hands gripping the steering wheel. The other car made an attempt to come alongside us again, and he went even faster, like they were at the racetrack everyone had been talking about lately, some dirt circle where others who were running moonshine raced their cars against one another. Up ahead the road veered off to the left in a sharp curve.

Panicked, I repeated Merritt's question. "What're you doing?"

Daddy didn't answer me neither. There was no way we could make it at this speed, I sensed it, even though I'd never ridden in a car going this fast before. The other car was beside us again.

Daddy cussed under his breath. "Hellfire and damnation, they must've been working on that heap."

I leaned forward, trying to see if I could make out who it was. "Who?"

The car swerved into us, tapping our front bumper, followed by a slight scraping of metal on metal. Sally Sue shuddered.

Daddy let off the gas a little and said, "Them damn Murrys. Sit back, Jessie!"

Merritt's fingers were clamped to the back of the seat and he said, "Whoa! They're crazy!"

Daddy said, "Hang on."

I pushed back against the seat, and thought about my room. Thought about how I wished I was there right now, sitting at my desk, doing homework. I didn't want to be here. The thought of an up close encounter with a Murry made my mouth go dry as dirt. I'd heard enough talk between Daddy and Uncle Virgil to know they weren't the sort to mess with. Willie Murry's daddy, Leland Murry, was someone I'd seen in town a few times, a big lug of a man who limped bad, was always scowling. People moved out of his way as he came down the sidewalk, elbows jackhammering up and down to accommodate his bad leg. Everyone at school did the same for

Willie Murry, him acting as if they had no right to take up his space.

Uncle Virgil couldn't stand the sight of any one of them, cussed about them all along while Daddy went mute if they came up in conversation, about like he did about Mama. The Murrys used the very first run off their stills, those singlings, which everyone knew was poisonous. Daddy said they mixed their product with ethanol. We'd heard the rumor, drink what a Murry sells, drink at your own risk. They tried to steal business from others, and between their bad liquor and stealing, Daddy couldn't hardly abide a one of them.

We hurtled down another hill, tires whining on the pavement, a fiendish roar coming from under the hood, the vibration of the car strong under my feet. The other vehicle dropped back a bit, then hit us again, hard enough to make our back end swerve. Daddy compensated, while our headlights illuminated the trees, creating a green blur as we tore down the road. I thought Daddy would lose control, yet I couldn't scream; I was too stunned to make a sound. My arms and legs were rigid, like they had steel rods through them.

Merritt whispered from the back seat, "Please, please, please."

I found my voice and squeaked out, "Slow down!"

They hit our car again, harder than before.

Daddy fought to keep it straight, but the tires went onto the soft shoulder, and the right side, my side, tilted downhill at an awkward slant. I instinctively leaned the opposite way and Daddy slammed on the brakes. There came a sensation like the trunk would meet the engine, like we'd be squashed in the middle of an accordion of metal. My hands gripped the dash as we came to a grinding halt. I couldn't look anywhere but at my lap, the slant of the car telling me the hill was really steep. I sat stunned, my chest heaving.

Daddy said, "Damn."

The other driver sat in the road, and pumped his foot on the gas, revving the engine. He did this over and over, then edged closer until their front bumper was against the side of our car, pushing us farther down the slope the way a bulldozer does a mound of dirt. The back door made a crunching noise and Merritt scooted over behind me and we began this slow slide down the embankment. The underside of the vehicle scraped over small brush and plants. Glass jars rattled and clanked under the back seat. The car caught on something, rolled completely over, and we were carried along with it, going all topsy-turvy.

Merritt made an odd sound, a deep grunt. I could hear jars breaking and the popping of glass from the windows. I hit my head right before we ended up against a tree. The car was on its roof and the only sound was dripping, and the screech of tires as the other car took off. Our headlights were out, but I could make out that Daddy and I had landed against the front windshield. My head throbbed. I put my hand up, touched the lump on my forehead.

Daddy said, "Jessie, you all right?"

"I think so."

He said, "Merritt?"

I could see his shape only a couple feet from me, looking like a rag doll. He was near the back windshield.

Daddy repeated his name: "Merritt."

The odor of gas combined with the reek of liquor was so pungent, I almost gagged. I was soaking wet where the shine had splashed all over us. It was as if I'd been baptized in it. Pieces of glass stuck to my hair, skin, and clothes. Daddy maneuvered himself around until he was on his knees, bent low.

He said, "We got to get out of here."

He crawled out of a broken side window. He reached through to help me and I grabbed his hand and crawled out.

Daddy called out again, "Merritt? Hey, Merritt!"

Merritt didn't reply. Daddy inched his way back in. He backed out, pulling Merritt along with him by his shirt collar. Finally, he was outside of the car. As I looked at my brother, I couldn't be sure, but one of his arms didn't look exactly right. It was bent off at some strange angle, and even in the dark, I could tell something was wrong. I pointed at it.

"He's hurt!"

Daddy said, "We'll get him fixed up, but first I got to see—"

We heard the sound of a car approaching and slowing down above us.

"Shh," he said, a finger up to his mouth, motioning with his hand for me to get down.

I crouched on the ground, and Daddy ducked too, shielding Merritt. We heard the sound of a door opening, footsteps, then silence. I inhaled the pungent odor of uprooted plants and freshly turned dirt. I needed to cough and instead swallowed over and over, knowing whoever was trying to see where we'd ended up might hear me. I buried my face in the bend of my arm, disregarding the painful lump to my forehead. I shut my eyes so tight, rainbow colors swirled and shifted against the backs of my eyelids. I strained to hear any noise that would give some idea of what was happening. After a few seconds, there was laughing, and then doors slammed shut. The car engine roared, a distinct sound I'll never forget. As they left, I lifted my head. My vision adjusted enough to make out the shape of Daddy, and I found he was staring at me. I wondered if he could sense my fury.

Chapter 5

Merritt was in a lot of pain.

He said over and over, "My arm's hurting something fierce."

Daddy had gone to check and see if the ones who'd run us off the road had left, and when he came back down the hill, he said, "It ain't a lot of folks on this stretch, but I know a feller 'bout a mile back or so. Maybe I can get him to give us a ride to where we can get this arm looked at."

I knelt beside Merritt, my arms crossed tight, shivering in the night air. His face was pale and he turned his head one way, then the other, clearly in a bad way. Daddy ought to do something, and quick, quit standing around jawing about this and that.

Merritt spoke through gritted teeth and said what I was thinking. "Just hurry. I can't hardly stand this."

Daddy said, "Y'all gonna be all right here till I get back?"

I said, "We ain't got no choice, do we?"

"Jessie."

I wasn't being helpful, but I didn't care. I was still trying to recover from the fright over the wreck, staggered by Merritt's situation.

Daddy motioned at the creaking upside-down car. "Listen to me. If it catches, you got to help him get out of the way. Fire tends to burn uphill faster, so go left or right, not uphill."

I pictured Mama running, burning, collapsing. I said nothing. Kept my expression free of the crazy shit going on in my head. I averted my face, his conciliatory cautioning as worthless as the liquor he made. After he left, the woods held a gloomy look, the trees like huge stiff-legged giants. I sat close to Merritt and began to hum a tuneless song while glancing now and again at Sally Sue or looking up at the half-moon rising through the tree branches.

After a while Merritt said, "Geez, quit that racket."

My offbeat humming fizzled into silence.

He lifted his head and tried to look up the hill and said, "I hope it ain't gonna take long." He leaned on his good elbow with some effort, and grimaced at his mangled arm, hand facing the wrong direction.

He said, "I can't bear to look at it."

"You probably shouldn't."

He collapsed back onto the ground.

"It ain't fitting," I said.

"What?"

"This. We could've died. It ain't fitting, and it ain't right, what he has us do."

Merritt said, "Will you quit? I don't want to hear your same old crap."

We waited on the ruined hillside, the silence between us thick as greenbrier. I tried to block his misery out. He sounded the way a wounded animal might. My stomach rolled as he suffered, and I kept wishing he'd pass out again while my outrage grew at our predicament. His hurting was about to make me start talking again, start reasoning my position despite him telling me to be quiet.

He broke the silence first. "Can't you look see if there's a jar ain't busted? I got to have me something for this pain."

"Hell no. You ain't supposed to be drinking that mess."

"Come on, Jessie. It's hurting bad, worse by the minute. Daddy gives it to old man Thompson and his wife for the arthritis. And Mrs. McAllister, she drinks some of it every morning, for her constitution he said."

I ignored him and looked toward Sally Sue. "Easton said it might could catch fire."

He flopped onto his back again, and made a whistling sound as he fought the pain.

I couldn't bring myself to study on his arm too long, and after a minute of listening to him gasping, I gave in, and said, "All right."

Soon as I stood, I had to drop back down. A vehicle approached and I rolled over onto my belly, peering through the flattened underbrush. I grabbed a hold of Merritt's good arm. He didn't pull away.

He whispered, "Shit. Hope it ain't them damn Murrys."

He stopped panting in an effort to not make any noise. The trees and surrounding brush were lit up from the headlights off to our right. I hoped it was Daddy and whoever he'd gone to get. The vehicle stopped and I went stiff with fear. Doors opened and closed, and then came the scrape of footsteps on asphalt. A soft beam from a flashlight swept back and forth, then landed near to where we hid in the scrub. I didn't move, paralyzed, uncertain who was above us.

Above us, came Daddy's voice, "Jessie, it's me."

I pushed up onto my knees, then my feet. The shape of another man was behind him, his silvery hair catching the light of the moon. Daddy hurried down the hill, and the older man followed with a flashlight held high so they could see.

When they got beside us, Daddy said, "This here's Marty Naylor, customer of mine."

Mr. Naylor spoke around the chaw in his cheek. His "how do" was soft.

I lifted my hand and let it drop, a halfhearted greeting at best.

Daddy knelt beside Merritt. "You doing all right?"

Merritt only grunted, his face chalky white.

Daddy said, "We got to get you back up this hill. Probably going to hurt."

Merritt said, "Can't get no worse if'n you ask me."

Mr. Naylor said, "We got something in the car for it; you just hang on."

Daddy helped Merritt stand and had him put his good arm around his neck. Merritt closed his eyes for a brief moment and they started up the hill. Merritt cried out only once when they stumbled, his voice hoarse with pain, the bad arm flopping like it belonged on a puppet. Daddy traversed the incline, trying to make it a bit easier. Mr. Naylor trailed him, and appeared to handle the steep slant better than me despite his age. On unsteady legs, I followed them, and before too long, we were at the top. I gasped and tried to recover while Daddy guided Merritt into the back seat. Mr. Naylor was kind enough to have brought a blanket and a pillow. After Merritt was situated, Daddy brought out a jar from under the front seat.

He handed it to Merritt and said, "Here, it'll take the edge off."

Merritt looked directly at me as he tipped the jar. He took a big swallow, and gave the jar back to Daddy. To my surprise, Daddy took a swig too, then held it out to me, but I crossed my arms, and scowled.

Daddy handed it back to Merritt and said, "Take some more."

Merritt readily obliged, and then Daddy held his hand out for the jar. He motioned for me to get in the front between him and Mr. Naylor. I slid onto the seat, glad to be out of the woods, out of the night air. Daddy and Mr. Naylor got in, and Daddy stuck the jar under the seat. I looked over at Merritt. He wore a tiny smile as he rested, his pain already seeming less severe. I turned back around, ashamed at how I could be so harsh and inconsiderate at times.

Mr. Naylor said, "Where to?"

Daddy hesitated, and said, "That arm's bad."

Mr. Naylor said, "Want to get him over to Wilkes General?"

Daddy rubbed at his chin. "I got to come up with some reason. They'll ask what happened, how he hurt it."

Mr. Naylor said, "What was it again?"

Daddy went into the account of how we'd been run off the road. He didn't say by who.

Mr. Naylor said, "Hm. Guess that would only set off more questions. Get some others involved that don't need to be. Could say it was a farming accident."

Daddy nodded. "Working on the tractor, fell off."

Mr. Naylor said, "Yup."

Daddy said, "That'll work."

Mr. Naylor drove like it was Sunday morning, not any faster than twenty-five miles per hour. It took a long time coming down the mountain.

Merritt moaned from the back, and asked, "How much longer?"

"Won't be long," said Mr. Naylor, as we poked along.

Daddy handed Merritt the jar again. I commended myself on keeping my mouth shut. Merritt slurped away while Mr. Naylor drove even slower as we made it into the more populated area of Wilkesboro. In town, some paid no mind to what Daddy did, while others relayed a different message: *We know what y'all are doing. For shame.* For that reason alone, I had never liked coming down off Shine Mountain and into town every Saturday to get groceries. For the past year or so, I'd begged not to be made to go, my humiliation like the weight I carried, easy for anyone to see. Daddy generally sold on 10th Street, where a strange mixture of preaching and prostitution existed. The ones listening to the preaching would sometimes duck into questionable establishments where Daddy's jars were kept hidden until someone came in asking for "that special drink y'all got." If I was forced to go into town, I walked behind Daddy and Merritt, stared at the ground in front of my feet. Daddy said I was going to walk into a light pole, or a wall, one of these days. He couldn't see my embarrassment. He couldn't see it, or it didn't matter.

On Main Street we passed by the federal building and post office where I'd heard the government had set up a revenuer's office for Wilkes County, and where a slew of agents had been sent to try and catch all moonshiners and bootleggers, but tracking down people who didn't want to be caught wasn't easy. No one could see that it had made much difference. From there we went across the Yadkin River into North Wilkesboro. We went by Pearson's wholesale grocery where Daddy would get milk, bread, eggs, and cigarettes on them miserable Saturdays. Finally, we came to Wilkes General Hospital.

Mr. Naylor said, "Want I should pull up to that there entrance?"

Merritt burped while Daddy stared at the brightly lit building and sucked hard on his cigarette.

He blew a stream of blue smoke out of the cracked window, and said, "Yeah. I reckon that's where we ought to go."

For the first time in my life, I believed I heard a hint of nervousness in his voice. Mr. Naylor eased up to the door and put the vehicle in Park. Daddy finished his cigarette, and got out. I scooted across the seat after him and got out too.

He leaned down to speak to Merritt, and said,

"I'm going in and see if I can find somebody to look at that arm."

Merritt, his color gone from white to an unhealthy-looking flush with eyes bright and glassy, didn't respond. Daddy acted like he was deciding something, and he finally turned and went inside where the large windows of the entrance showed him looking around for help. It didn't take long before a nurse approached. Daddy gestured toward the car, at where I waited on the sidewalk. Merritt had propped up on an elbow and grinned stupidly. I glared at him, then turned back to see what was happening.

Mr. Naylor said to no one in general, "You think she'd be a little quicker."

He was one to talk.

Merritt slurred, "It's all right. I'm feeling purty good now."

The nurse disappeared and came back pushing a wheelchair. Daddy held the door for her and in a matter of seconds she was beside the car's back door, locking the wheels. She was all business, barely sparing me a glance before she leaned down, and studied Merritt's wacky-looking arm.

She said, "When did this happen?"

Merritt was vague. "Not long ago."

She said, "What's your name?"

He wore a lopsided grin and said, "Ish Merritt, ma'am."

I wanted to be anywhere but here. It was

evident he was three sheets to the wind. Daddy shoved his hands in his pockets and paced.

The nurse said, "It's going to hurt some getting you into this chair."

Merritt said, "Naw, ma'am, it ain't. Not now."

Daddy came forward and said, "Here, I'll help him."

He motioned at Merritt, who apparently no longer had an issue moving out of the back seat. It didn't seem to bother him one bit as he shifted with Daddy's help into the chair, his arm resting in his lap, all wrong-angled. The nurse grabbed the two handles at the back and whisked him toward the hospital's door.

Daddy said, "Marty, thankee kindly. Go on home. I'll bring what I had for you another night."

We hurried to follow the nurse as she breezed by the desk where another lady sat writing in a ledger.

The nurse said, "Let Doctor Barnes know we've got a serious arm injury."

The woman immediately picked up a phone, held it to her mouth, and spoke. Crackly speakers overhead blasted, "Doctor Barnes, treatment room one. Doctor Barnes, treatment room one. Stat."

We had to walk fast to keep up, and soon we stopped at some double doors.

She said to me, "You have to wait here."

Daddy handed me a couple of dimes and said,

"Call your uncle Virgil. Tell him to come get us."

I took the change and watched as the nurse took Merritt beyond the double doors.

Daddy said, "We'll be out soon as we can."

The doors closed after them, and a few seconds later an elderly-looking man in a white coat with a stethoscope slung around his neck went through them and I took him to be Doctor Barnes. I tried to see if I could see Merritt and Daddy before the doors closed again. The hall was empty. I walked back the way we'd come, looking left and right for the pay phone. I found one a minute or so later inside a small metal box hanging on the wall. All around it were dirty messages, the names of girls who would apparently do this or that, if you called them, along with the so and so was here types of scribbles. I put a dime in the slot and dialed Uncle Virgil's number. It rang six times and I was about to hang up when Aunt Juanita answered.

She shouted an irritable, "Hello!"

That followed what sounded like a pot being thrown on the floor. I swallowed, my throat about to close up, and not allow me to talk.

She said, "Whoever this is had better speak up . . ."

I choked out, "Hey Aunt Juanita, it's Jessie."

"Jessie. What is it, why are you calling?"

I imagine it wasn't natural seeming, getting a phone call from me.

"We're at the hospital. Merritt hurt his arm."

She said, "Good Lord. You okay? What about your daddy?"

"I have a knot on my head, but Easton is all right. Our car got run off the road."

She said, "Wait a minute."

A scraping and rustling came through the earpiece as she passed the phone to Uncle Virgil. Before he spoke, he coughed, a hoarse hacking that rattled my ear. I held the receiver away until his voice, sounding like a buzzing bee in a tin can, came through.

I put it back to my ear in time to hear him say, "What happened?"

I spoke in a low voice even though I was the only one in the hall.

"Daddy and us, we were on a run, on that road where you said there'd been agents. A car started following us. It ran us off the road, and then pushed us over the side. I think we rolled a couple times. Easton said it was Murrys."

Uncle Virgil coughed again, and said, "Damn."

I waited and there came a long stretch of silence. He finally said, "Juanita said Merritt's hurt?"

I said, "Yeah. We're at Wilkes General."

"What's the doctor said?"

"Nothing yet. I'm waiting to find out. Daddy wanted you to come get us."

"Let me get dressed and I'll be there quick as I can."

He hung up without saying good-bye. I walked back the way I'd come and found two chairs in the hallway near the double doors. I sat in one of them, jiggled one foot, then the other. After a while, I noticed mud, bits of grass, and other debris from my shoes sprinkled over the shiny, clean waxed tile. This fit my general attitude at the moment, like I had no right to be sitting in this clean place operated by people who made a living by doing fine and upstanding jobs, people who were valued. Like the nurses I'd seen with their white dresses and shoes, pristine uniforms of mercy and kindness. I stared at the floor again, at what I'd left, and thought of what I'd read earlier on the wall by the phone. What was on the floor said, *Jessie Sasser was here,* without me having to write it down. I moved one foot and tried to scrape the mess out of sight. More fell and I gave up.

Before long, I began to realize how hungry I was. The peanut butter sandwich and milk was long gone. My stomach rumbled, protesting its vast emptiness. It was like my belly had a demon in it, growling at me. I only had the one dime left. I doubted it would be enough to buy anything from a vending machine, if they even had one. I got up and drifted down the hall again, passing by doors that said: "Janitor," "Men's Bathroom," "Women's Bathroom," "Supply Closet," and directions to other parts of the hospital. I found nothing, so I walked back the way I'd come, sat back down in the chair, and waited. Time slowed to a crawl, while I preoccupied myself trying to count each square of tile I could see without getting up. The doors finally swung open.

Daddy came out first; the doctor followed close behind, saying, "I can smell it, and see it. The boy is drunk."

"If'n he is or isn't ain't none of your business."

The nurse came next with Merritt, his arm swathed in a huge white plaster cast almost to his shoulder. At least it had a slight bend in it. He wasn't grinning now, his color gone gray. The doctor left quick as he'd come. Daddy evidently wanted to explain the situation to the nurse, and he gestured at Merritt.

He said, "He had a little bit of something to help him with the pain until we could get here is all."

The nurse waved a hand and said, "You don't need to explain. My own granddaddy and grandma loved to sip the fruit bitters for what ailed them now and then. Doctor Barnes isn't from around here. He doesn't understand. This young man's going to be in some pain as the days go by, but the doctor's given me a prescription for you to fill."

Daddy said, "Where do I pay?"

"We'll send you a bill. He'll need to come back—"

Daddy cut her off. "We ain't coming back."

"He'll need to get that cast off."

"I'll see it gets taken off."

She didn't say another word. She wheeled Merritt back to the entrance we'd come in off the parking lot. The nurse gave Daddy a piece of paper just as Uncle Virgil came through the doors looking like he'd been in a fight with the ground. His pants and shirt were rumpled, and his eyes bloodshot. We made our way out to his car and I imagined to her we looked like a rough lot. I considered my family, and turned inward, assessing my own self.

My conclusion, *A rough lot, to be sure.*

Chapter 6

On the way home Uncle Virgil and Daddy talked about retaliation. Merritt sat hunched against his door while I leaned my head against the window, eyes closed and listening.

Daddy said, "First I'm gonna have Troy get his wrecker and haul Sally Sue back over to the house where I can get her fixed back up."

Daddy trusted Troy Dalton because he'd go get his car, no questions asked.

Uncle Virgil said, "I can do the routes if'n you need me to."

Daddy pulled hard on his cigarette. "I'll see what calls I get. Everyone got what they needed only a couple days ago."

Uncle Virgil said, "What're we gonna do about it?"

"I got to think on it, but you can bet I ain't gonna forget it."

"Maybe I should try and find out where they got a still."

"It could be useful."

Uncle Virgil grunted. He dropped us off and since it was late, he didn't stay. Merritt wobbled inside, and immediately went to his room. I trailed after him and watched as he sat carefully on the bed, grabbed his extra pillow, and then laid back using it to prop his arm up. His mouth was a straight line, his eyebrows lowered so he didn't have to look at anyone. It was starting to dawn on him how hard it might be for the next few weeks. No ball games. Merritt held distant dreams of maybe being a major-league player, and for as much as he liked pitching, I'd seen the difference when we worked a still. He played ball, and he was good, but the way he talked about making and hauling liquor, it was like his destiny. There would be none of either for a while.

Daddy came into the room with a glass of water and set it on Merritt's nightstand. He was in a begging mood apparently.

He motioned at the glass. "It ain't gonna do me no good. My arm's already killing me again. Can't I please get me some more of that hooch?"

Daddy ignored him and I was glad.

He said, "Take these."

He dumped some pills in Merritt's hand. Merritt gaped at his palm with disappointment, then took them. I hovered in the doorway, and when Daddy went by, he shook his head, warning me against anything I might have to say. I was empty though, in more ways than one. What had happened to us fastened around me like when I tightened my belt to keep my stomach from hurting. We could've all been killed and no one would have found us for days. He went down the hall into his room and shut the door firmly, letting me know he was done for the night.

It was just as well.

I went into the kitchen. I didn't turn on the light as I reached for the refrigerator handle, the peace of the house reassuring me I was safe. I opened it and the light inside came on, throwing out a half circle of brightness around me. I visualized one of them seeing me there, ready to point and laugh. I hesitated, then grabbed the beans, hot dogs, biscuits, the bottle of milk. I shut the door, and with the light gone, I let out a sigh. I didn't think about what I was about to do. I pushed my negative thoughts aside as I lifted the tinfoil off the bowls, the crinkling sound loud to my ears. I waited a moment, then unwrapped the biscuits from the wax paper. I could see myself getting drunk off food like Merritt had gotten drunk off the liquor.

It began like it always did. I would start slow, chewing with care, until an urgency overtook my methodical approach. It happened when there came this need to fill what was barren, satisfy a void that belonged not to regular hunger, but to something else. It compelled me on, go quicker, quicker, as if my body was only this chasm, the hole in my middle always there, always growing until I was overtaken by it. Even I understood this wasn't entirely about food. No. No matter how

much I ate to try and rid myself of the hollow-
ness, to eliminate the want, I didn't know how
except to do this.

I ate the hot dogs first. There were four, gone
in eight bites. I grabbed the beans next, scooping
spoonful after spoonful. When I'd emptied that,
I grabbed the milk, and guzzled straight from
the bottle, big gulps that threatened to spill
over. I suffered one of those strange headaches
and my insides churned. I sat back, noticing the
kitchen, the mess around me. I turned my attention to my middle, which had become tight, and
uncomfortable. I got up and paced the floor,
breathing deep. I was repulsed by my tremendous
weakness. I could fix it. I started for the bathroom and stopped. I swallowed over and over,
attempting to fight the inevitable.

It was so uncomfortable, I relented and rushed
down the hall. I waited, standing over the toilet
before turning away, and instead, I turned on the
faucet and splashed my face with cold water. I
straightened up, and didn't look in the mirror. I
didn't want to see me, to look at my betraying
eyes, the ones filled with such revulsion. The food
roiled, reminding me of sour mash fermenting.
It was revolting when I thought of it like that. I
turned from the sink, dropped to my knees, and
rested my forehead against the coolness of the lid
on the toilet. I wanted to cry knowing I couldn't
stop this any more than I could stop Daddy. I was

already heaving as I lifted the lid up. I let my body do what it wanted, and finished by shoving my fingers into my throat.

I was out of control again.

From the living room window, I could see Aubrey through a slit in the curtains. Her head swiveled, taking it all in, judging how we lived. Like I was prone to do, I envisioned how she might see it, the long-standing rusty junk, weeds grown knee-high, paint peeling to expose old graying wood. I usually went to her house. When I'd been little, Daddy would drop me off to spend the day, but now I'd drive myself unless he was needing the truck. As the preacher's wife, her mama was expected to keep everything neat as a pin for any unexpected soul needing spiritual attention. Their grass was perfection, mowed like a flat-top crew cut, flowers bloomed in various beds around the yard, and it was the same inside the house.

Aubrey tapped again, and I moved away from the window, toward the back of the house. I didn't want to see anyone, not even her.

She knocked harder, and Merritt yelled from his bedroom, "Jessie! Answer the damn door, will you? Geez!"

I froze midway down the hall.

She called my name through the screen. "Jessie?"

91

I plodded back to the living room and wrenched it open.

"What?"

Her eyebrows raised. I hadn't been to school in a week, hadn't washed my hair, hadn't done much of nothing since *that* night.

She held up a little basket covered with a cloth and gave me a hesitant smile, "Can I come in?"

I held the door open, and she walked by smelling like Breck shampoo and whatever was in the basket, warm from the oven. I folded my arms over my middle, and wished I'd at least washed my hair. Or put on something other than the too-small, ratty-looking housecoat. I held it tight around my neck, the way someone much older might do, like I didn't want any part of my flesh exposed. I was back to not eating again, struggling with shame while arguing with myself over the justifiable reasons for emptying the refrigerator. There was more to that overall picture as it was. What Daddy had cared most about was getting Sally Sue, and now that was done, every night when he came home, he'd worked on her, while he and Uncle Virgil took supplies out to Boomer, Blood Creek, and Big Warrior. Another night they went on an unexpected run together in the truck. Nothing was different, nothing had changed, despite what happened. It hit me hard.

I'd declared, "We could've been killed!"

Daddy denied it. "Nah. Sally Sue's built to withstand a lot more than that."

Making and hauling shine was the most important thing to him. More important than Mama, Merritt, and certainly me. I fought to maintain an outward calm that hid my inner turmoil as I came to a realization that his take on all this was as twisted and coiled as the back roads of Shine Mountain.

Aubrey said, "We heard about Merritt. Mama baked him molasses cookies."

I said, "He'll like that. Thankee, kindly."

My hand shook as I reached for the basket she handed me, but she didn't act like she noticed. The smell was intoxicating, and I carried it into the kitchen and left it on the table. I returned to the living room, where the lack of cleaning over the past few days was obvious. The stack of newspapers Daddy had left on his chair, his overflowing ashtray, the layer of dust everywhere, was enough to make me want to hide. Then there was Aubrey herself, like a bouquet of flowers in the middle of a trash pile. I belonged because I was as dumpy as a basket of unwashed laundry.

I was sure she must have spent the past hour alone brushing her hair to get it to that high shine. Her spotless dungarees, rolled at the hems, her penny loafers without a speck of dirt, her perfectly white blouse, offset my appearance, but that was nothing new. What *was* different was the glittering excitement in her eyes. She sat on the couch and then hopped up and walked to the door to look out. She came back, sat again, and tapped her fingers on her knee. Her restlessness made me uptight, and I began gathering my thoughts about what I'd say, embarrassed at the truth, trying to figure out what sounded best. Nothing, really.

Her tone polite, she asked, "How'd he get hurt?"

I fiddled with the collar of my robe. "It was just one of them things."

She frowned, her perfectly tweezed eyebrows rose, and she leaned forward. "You ain't gonna tell me?"

I intentionally misinterpreted her question. "He broke his arm in two places; one part of the bone was stuck out. It's in a cast."

Aubrey winced, and said, "Oh. That's horrible. But how?"

"It wasn't nothing really. You know how boys are."

She leaned back, and said, "I reckon."

I stared at my bare feet, trying to ignore how dirty and miserable I'd felt since she arrived. She raised her chin with this odd, knowing look.

She said, "I know what really happened."

Defensive, I said, "I don't see how."

"Y'all were running liquor."

"Says who?"

"Zeb."

Aubrey's brother. He was a big talker, always made stuff up. She knew that better than I did. Shame and a swift anger took hold.

"No we weren't neither. Besides, how would Zeb know?"

"I can tell when you're lying, you know."

I picked at a loose thread on my housecoat.

She went on, "Gosh, Jessie. If y'all ain't careful, your daddy could end up in the penitentiary, or worse. Daddy says there's too much of this going on in the county, and he's praying hard for those who do it to turn away from it, to come to Jesus, ask his forgiveness."

My dander rose. "Running liquor ain't got a darn thing to do with it, and Zeb wasn't there, so what does he know?"

I wished I'd not answered the door.

She changed the subject and said, "When you gonna come back to school?"

Still annoyed, my answer was sharp. "I don't know."

She said, "Have you tried what I mentioned?"

I lied about that too. "Nope."

"Daddy says clarity comes from suffering."

If that were true, I ought to know about as much as God himself. She stretched her arms overhead like she was reaching for the sun, and smiled. It was out of place, considering my attitude, and our conversation.

She brought her arms down, hugged herself, and said, "I got something to tell you. You know Willie Murry?"

It was a dumb question. Of course I knew Willie Murry, and she knew it too.

She waved her hand, and said, "I know what you and your family think of his family. But listen, he's been to the house a few times, and he's been real nice to me. Ain't you ever noticed how handsome he is?"

The words came fast because she was excited, but I'd heard enough over the years to know anything a Murry said or did, no matter what others might think, couldn't be trusted. Not one bit.

"When did he start coming over?"

She said, "Him and Zeb, they've been in the same grade all along, but never really talked until this year. They've got some classes together, so I guess they're friends now."

"Oh."

"I think you've got'em all wrong, Jessie."

"You can have your opinions, I reckon."

She played with a button on her blouse, then said, "Willie said y'all tried to run them off the road."

Growing angrier, I said, "I thought it was Zeb who told you?"

My head felt like Uncle Virgil's must when he'd had too much to drink. Like it was about to pop. It was just like a Murry to turn it around. Fitting. Bunch of liars, they were that.

"Well. I overheard Willie telling Zeb."

"And you believe him? That says a lot."

She jumped up and said, "Well, fine, I guess I'll go since you're so cranky. I'll see you at school?"

I shrugged.

"Jessie?"

"Yeah?"

"Is there anything you need?"

"What do you mean?"

"You look . . . like maybe you could use some help."

"I'm fine."

She stood by the door and then focused on scratching at a peeled spot on the woodwork.

She said, "Our church gets stuff, donations like clothes. I could bring you some."

Mortified, I said, "No!"

"Why not? It ain't but a dress, maybe a skirt or two; all of it looks brand-new. I've noticed you always wearing the same old stuff. Ain't your daddy giving you money for such?"

"He's tried."

"What do you mean?"

"I mean I ain't taking none of that shine money to buy nothing."

Aubrey said, "Daddy would say that's commendable, but you got to have something decent to wear."

I clutched at my shabby housecoat, pulling it tight again.

"If you want me to bring them, I will. It would all fit; I'm sure of it."

I couldn't stand the thought of being one of the Whitakers' charity cases, but Aubrey could be like one of them little old Feist dogs, tenacious and stubborn to a fault. It would at least keep the school from sending home any more notes about my attire.

I gave in, and said, "Okay, fine."

Aubrey looked pleased I'd accepted her offer, self-satisfied, like she'd taken in a starving cat.

"I'll bring everything tomorrow."

"Fine."

She left, almost skipping to her car. She waved, but I didn't return the gesture. Aubrey had every reason to be cheerful and happy. Her life appeared very different from mine, upright and proper. I didn't bother watching her leave. I went to Merritt's room, curious if he'd heard anything we'd talked about, but he was asleep. I went into the kitchen where the basket of cookies sat innocently. *No, no, no. Don't undo what you've done.* I made myself go to my room and sat on the bed. I was tired, and convinced young as I was, I ought not to feel so old.

Chapter 7

I was watching an episode of *The Untouchables* when an idea I'd had before pushed through, distracting me so much that even though the show wasn't over, I turned the TV off and went to my room. The moon was bright and cast shadows of my lamp and books, gray shapes imprinted on the walls. I got into bed and began a deep consideration of what I'd thought of many times before, usually only when I was spitting mad. I'd never had the nerve to take it seriously. Maybe I was now because of what we'd been through, what had happened to Merritt. Fear could sometimes overtake everything. If Daddy wouldn't make a change, maybe I could.

Next morning I could hear him stirring his first cup of coffee, his spoon hitting the sides, the clinking noise soothing. The thought of going back to school didn't set well, but after remembering what I planned to do, I got up with a bit more enthusiasm and went to the bathroom. I washed my face, brushed my teeth, even had the gall to look at the mirror and study my reflection. I suffered a momentary shift of my good mood when I stepped on the scale. I stared at the number, stepped off and back on. How could it be? I was up by two pounds. Despite all of my precautions. I looked at the toilet, could already taste the acidic burn rising in the back of my throat.

There was no way around it. Resolute, I dropped to my knees and tried not to think too hard. *Be quick,* I told myself. *Be quick and you're done.* I put a finger down my throat, but my body, trained, experienced, reacted. The immediate relief was mixed with revulsion. I did it again. Again, to be sure. Afterward, I brushed my teeth once more. I kept my face averted from the mirror this time as I left the bathroom.

Back in my room I stood before my closet, glad I'd agreed to Aubrey's offer. I pulled out a dress, hurrying to cover myself. I tugged the material down, but it didn't feel right. Annoyed, I hauled it off over my head, and began to flip through other choices, a couple other dresses; all of them I'd worn for a long while. I felt as bloated as the belly of a pregnant cow and anything restricting set me on edge. Discarded items ended up on the floor, but I didn't care. Finally, I resorted to my favorite skirt, the one piece of clothing I found bearable. I pulled on a blouse that would do, and a pair of oxfords. My shoes fit, at least.

Daddy was in the bathroom, and I paused by the door. Had I remembered to flush the toilet after ridding myself of all I could? I couldn't remember. In the kitchen I had some coffee, and eyed the cookies on the table. I picked them up and went to Merritt's room where he was propped against his headboard, bored and restless. The fact he perked up at my presence said how bad he hated his confinement.

"Aubrey brought these for you yesterday. Molasses cookies her mom baked."

I set them on his nightstand.

He said, "You going to school?"

"Yes."

Daddy came out of the bathroom and into Merritt's room too.

Merritt said, "When can I go back to school?"

Daddy said, "I guess it'd be all right in a couple days or so."

Resigned, Merritt reached over, got a cookie, and began eating. I stared as he chewed until Daddy nudged me.

"You need to go to Big Warrior tonight, see how far along it is. Virgil and Oral got to make a run near to Charlotte, and I'll be going to Blood Creek."

I said nothing and he went down the hall. It was time for me to go too, and to Merritt I said, "See you later."

I got my books, went outside, and walked down the drive to wait for the bus. When it came, I climbed on, but Aubrey wasn't in her seat. Disappointed, knowing I was going to have to either stand, or pray someone would take pity on me, I searched their faces, one by one. They stared out the windows, ignoring me, even Oral. I paused by Pauline Doyle's side. She sat alone, her books in the space beside her. She hunched herself up against the window, but not before she put her hand over the seat as if silently telling me she was holding the spot for someone. She'd been my only chance.

Resigned, I braced myself to accommodate the sway of the bus as it went around the curves, and accelerated downhill. The bus driver kept looking in the mirror at me while shaking his head. If he stopped and demanded somebody give me a seat, I'd be even more humiliated. Furtive glances were tossed my way, heads dipped, hands placed over mouths, whispers, and secretive laughter; I could hear it all. I clenched the metal bar, held my books tight to my chest, as if they could somehow shield me. They made it clear I was ugly, hideous even. I wished I'd stayed home. The bus made several stops, and others found a seat without any problem. I tried to ignore that, but I couldn't. I said to myself it didn't matter. They didn't matter.

When we pulled up to the school, I hurried to the front, and as soon as the door opened, I took off down the steps, walking fast, my cheeks burning hot, my legs shaking. It wasn't the first time I'd had such an experience on the bus, but each time I did I came away knowing I was an outsider, a loner—except for Aubrey, and I was hateful to her yesterday. I would make up for it today, be nice. She was in the gravel lot where students who drove parked, Willie and Zeb by her side. So, that's where she'd been. My previous thought about being nice disappeared, and was replaced with irritation. I hurried toward the building, eager to be swallowed up by the mass of bodies milling about in the hallways.

"Jessie, wait!"

I wanted to run, but I was too self-conscious of how I moved through my world, seeing myself the way everyone else did. It was bad enough having to take Phys Ed three days a week, plus having to put on the regulated gym clothes the school handed out. They never fit neither.

Mrs. McCall, the gym teacher, was always yelling, "Come on, Sasser! Come on! You got it in you; I know it!"

I moved with an urgent purpose to get out of Aubrey's sight, to vanish. She yelled loud enough it drew attention from the other students, evident in their looks aimed at me and her.

"Jessie, stop!"

I did, but I didn't turn around. She ran up beside me, panting.

"Didn't you hear me?"

I shook my head. She looked mad.

She thrust out a paper bag, and said, "I was trying to give you this. I wanted to bring it to your house after school, but I can't now."

There was an unfamiliar, yet becoming, sparkle to her this morning.

I took it and said, "Thankee."

Her excitement, usually contagious, wasn't catching today, even though she was practically vibrating with it.

She said, "Wanna guess why?"

I side-eyed her, then Willie Murry, who leaned against a car every bit as capable as Sally Sue, with the same black color, and the bulkiness of a tank. I could tell what it was used for, running his daddy's radiator poison whisky. I could tell about Willie too. He was mean, and his perpetual spiteful expression matched how he walked down the hall in school, chin raised, almost like he dared anyone to cross his path. If they did, they'd connect with a hard shoulder or a foot placed just so. Aubrey couldn't be still and wiggled with pent-up emotion.

I said, "I can't imagine."

She grabbed my arm and said, "I'm going out for a milk shake with Willie. He asked me! And I can't believe Daddy's actually allowing it! Law, his eyes are gorgeous. You ever seen green like that?"

I pulled away from her hand. "You got to be kidding."

She mistook my meaning. "I know! Ain't it something?" She tilted her head. "You don't look like you're too happy about it."

I wasn't aware of how I looked, so I tried to smile, and failed.

She laughed, and said, "Oh, Jessie! You look like somebody's making you swallow poison," and she giggled again.

We approached the school doors, and I shoved against them hard. One side banged the wall, and Aubrey was silent as we walked down the hall toward my locker, sensing I wasn't happy about what she'd said.

I said, "Ain't a one of them good for nothing but trouble."

She shook her head, denying what I said. "Willie's nice! Mama likes him fine, and you know how choosy she can be. I know what you've said about them, but Willie, he says his daddy works for the county. He says it ain't nothing but a bunch of rumors. He said people just like to talk, stir things up."

There was no need in arguing with her about it. It was already Willie this, and Willie that.

I said, "You gonna start riding with him to school?"

She tugged at the sleeves of the light blue sweater she'd tied around her shoulders.

She sighed. "I don't know. It's too early to tell what might happen. But I really like him, and I hate waiting! I wished I could see into the future. Mrs. Aubrey Murry. Don't it sound grand?"

My only friend, head over heels for a member of a family mine tried to avoid at all costs. It was too much to take in. I came to my locker, rotated the dial on the lock, and thrust the bag she'd brought inside. She kept talking and dreaming. She was at the point of what to name their first baby. Heaven help her. I grabbed the books for my first class as she went on and on. I didn't want to hear anything more about the new life she dreamed of with Willie Murry. There was a picture of us taped inside my locker door where we sat in the backyard at her house, ten years old, grinning, the words "best friends" scrawled across the bottom with the skill of fourth-grade penmanship. She'd moved on to choosing paint colors for a nursery.

I cut her off. "He's only taking you out for one stupid milk shake, Aubrey."

Her eyes widened, and she said, "You're just jealous."

Well, that was plumb crazy. The long hall had filled to capacity as bus after bus unloaded, and without another word I stepped into the flow of bodies, like wading into a rushing river. Classes came and went, and as I was released from each, I navigated the corridor, slipping along the edges, brushing against lockers, turning to avoid the press of the others milling about. When school started each year, I always took a seat at the back of the classroom, praying the alphabetical arrangement teachers favored to get to know us by name wouldn't mean I'd get stuck in the very front. This year I'd been able to shield myself, lucky enough to have a seat at the back of every one. I had no idea how this had worked out, but it was a comfort knowing there was no one behind me. This was a new feeling that had started in the past couple of years.

Lunch came, and with it a tinge of regret for what happened earlier. She might not show up. I sat on the low brick wall near the big oak and pine tree, our customary spot. I debated if I cared or not. I looked around and it seemed the whole school had come outside to sit in the sun, enjoying a warm day. Everyone had someone with them. I was the only one alone. With my legs straight out, one foot jiggling nonstop, and my hands on either side of me, I studied the grass. I stared up at the clouds floating by. I made out a unicorn on one, a rabbit for another. More time passed. I began to sulk. Aubrey took me for granted. The fact she was pretty and well liked by most, she would never have to wonder what people thought of her, or if they talked about her behind her back. She would never have to hope for a seat on the bus. Why did she even consider me her friend?

Maybe she was beginning to see me as I really

was, fat, ugly, and uninteresting. The murmur of voices and the occasional laugh began to grate. I lifted my head long enough to look down the sidewalk and over to the gravel lot. Willie's car was in the same place it had been earlier, so they hadn't gone off grounds like some would do, although it was forbidden. With only ten minutes left to the lunch period, I resigned myself to the fact she wasn't coming. Well, fine. I nudged a ladybug crawling along the edge of the cement. It flared its wings, momentarily distracted from its mission, and then continued on. Finally, I noticed Aubrey hurrying toward me, and when she was close she was full of apologies. She sat beside me, and I was so relieved she'd not abandoned me, I couldn't speak. I don't think she noticed as she hurried to open her lunch. She began eating, taking big bites while shaking her head, and looking at her watch while I ogled her sandwich. She saw that and, without thinking, offered half.

I said, "No. Remember?"

She brought her hand up to her mouth, and she said, "Oh, gosh, sorry!"

Aubrey acted as if nothing had happened this morning. I tore my gaze off her food and saw Mrs. Brewer directly across from us, watching. I began studying the grass.

Aubrey said, "I had to go see Mrs. Adams about my test grade in science. I hate that class; I really do. Willie says—"

She stopped, then cleared her throat.

She said, "How's Merritt?"

"Okay. He might come back to school in a day or two."

I was back to watching the ladybug now making its way toward her fingers. She saw it and flicked it away. It landed by my foot. I wanted to share what was bothering me, explain why I was so short-tempered.

I finally said, "I hate what Daddy does. Really hate it."

She nodded. "Yeah, I know."

"I'm thinking about doing something about it."

She perked up and said, "You are?"

I was about to admit it, but again, I paused. She smacked her shoe on the ladybug as she waited for me to respond. I gave her a disgusted look.

She said, "Well, I hate them things. They stink! Hurry, the bell's gonna ring any minute."

I said, "Promise me you won't say a word, Aubrey."

She did that thing we would sometimes do when we were going to share a secret. She made an X on her chest, and said, "Cross my heart, hope to die."

The words came out fast, an elimination, like food. "Daddy loves his moonshining and bootlegging more than anything. I've always been of a mind it was the thing what killed Mama."

She said, "I know."

"Ain't nothing I've ever said about that, or done, has ever made a difference. He just keeps on. I feel like I ain't got no future except up on that mountain, doing that, or doing nothing. Least that's how it seems. He ain't ever said I got a choice. It's like he expects it, and that's that. I got dreams too, though. I want to do something, almost anything other than that."

Aubrey leaned in closer. "Has it got to do with the other night, y'all getting run off the road?"

I huffed. "No! Why do you keep on about that?"

"Well, I know what you said, but . . ."

"Geez!"

"What?"

"It's for all them reasons I *just* told you."

There was more, but I didn't want to explain how it made me feel second class. Point out any more of my faults and doubts. Despite my annoyances with Aubrey, she *was* still the only friend I had, and maybe I didn't want her to get to looking at me too hard.

I finally half-whispered it to her. "I just might get rid of them stills myself. Can't nobody know who really done it."

She drew back, and her voice went a notch higher. "You mean like what them revenuers do?"

"Uh-huh. Crenshaws got caught about a month ago. Not that it's common, but it could happen to us too."

Aubrey was openmouthed and I nodded firmly as if to convince myself.

I said, "Daddy might figure it out though. Ain't nobody ever found ours."

She said, "Somebody must've snitched on the Crenshaws. That's the only way anyone ever does."

The comment made me look at her. I'd taken her a time or two, shown her what we had, just two gals going down a mountain road on their way to check on some stills.

"You can't say nothing about this."

"Gracious, Jessie, I already said, didn't I?"

I said, "I know. I'm just nervous about it, I guess."

The bell rang and we walked back to the school. Inside, before we parted ways, I had to throw out one more, "Keep it to yourself."

Aubrey rolled her eyes and hurried down the hall. She waved at Zeb and Willie while I hoped I'd not made a mistake. Sitting in English class, I recollected hearing about what happened to Mr. Crenshaw. Everyone in Wilkes County knew about it because it had been one of the more successful raids anyone could recall. Revenuers and moonshiners had a strange relationship. It was all about the chase, the elusive nature of it. Cat and mouse like. They'd been close to catching Mr. Crenshaw and the ones who helped with his operation for some time. The story was there'd always be the backslapping and teasing when he'd see one of the agents in town. A "just you wait, I'll get you," and Mr. Crenshaw laughing and saying, "Not hardly."

Eventually one of the agents did find his stills, a couple large sites capable of making hundreds of gallons at a time, and Mr. Crenshaw happened to be at one of them. This, in and of itself, was of real interest to the community—how had they even found the sites caused a lot of talk, and catching him was always regarded as suspicious. Revenuers generally had a hard time because they didn't know the area all that well. They came from other parts of the state or were from out of state altogether. The back roads, trails, the hidden hollers, caves, and creeks, were like a maze and some had been known to get lost and had to have local help rescue them. Now and then they'd get lucky through their own diligence in exploring suspicious areas, or listening surreptitiously to locals, or having someone inform, and a still would be no more.

In Mr. Crenshaw's case, it was the suspicion it had been an informer, maybe someone in his own operation even. There was always somebody wanting to put somebody else out of business, especially if there was competition, or if there'd been a grudge between families. The revenuers brought their government-purchased axes and went to chopping holes into the sides of the boilers, thumper boxes, and the jars and buckets sitting full and ready to be loaded up were smashed or overturned. The moonshine flowed then, just not where Mr. Crenshaw wanted. He had to stand by and watch it all.

What was most important to Daddy was that Sassers were moonshiners through and through, but I just didn't see myself that way.

Chapter 8

Daddy had a leather-bound book with the name Sasser etched on the cover, containing entries all the way back to the days of our great-grandfather. Merritt had once said he wanted it, like a keepsake. I had said I'd burn it and Daddy had looked at me like he had no idea who I was, or how I came to be there. What I wanted to do was fitting, considering Mama. Daddy liked to thumb through the ink-smeared pages, and whether I wanted to hear it or not, he'd recite various bits of information back to me and Merritt. He'd make some remark about how our great-granddaddy had started a new still on a particular day, or how Daddy himself had been entrusted to run their biggest load ever into Tennessee when he wasn't but thirteen. He pointed out special routes, secret trails, and obscure roads so deep in the hills, nobody knew of them but Sassers. He talked about the rudimentary little maps no one could understand unless the notations were explained.

"It's important to understand," he'd said.

He'd recounted what good times they'd had back then, talked about the people involved like sharing about a family reunion. It was as

114

if he was looking to prove our history was as deeply embedded as the ancient rock face on the southern side of Shine Mountain. Showing me what I was made of, that there was no escaping it.

It's in your veins, girl.

Merritt loved hearing about all that stuff and asked questions while I viewed it like a mountain I had to climb, whether I wanted to or not.

Since I'd decided to set out and destroy the family stills, I'd already been through the readying of them several times. Each time I helped lug in corn while figuring out how to tolerate Oral, and Uncle Virgil to the best of my ability, I told myself it would happen, it was simply waiting for the right time. At the moment, however, Big Warrior was ready for distilling, and once again, with great reluctance, I'd upheld the Sasser legacy. I waited for Uncle Virgil and Oral's help, and heard them long before they came into view. Neither one was as cautious as me, Daddy, or Merritt. They argued back and forth, clanging and banging the buckets they carried, used to catch the liquor. They finally broke through the trees, and Uncle Virgil nodded at me as he tossed a few on the ground while Oral ignored my presence. They went back for more, and while they were gone, recollections of Mama came unwanted. I stopped setting buckets in place and leaned against a juniper tree, thinking of her, hating this part we were about to do. Uncle Virgil and Oral soon returned and Uncle Virgil raised his voice and pointed at me.

He said, "Ain't you gonna help? Or maybe you ain't wantin' to mess up them fancy new clothes I see you finally gave in and bought."

He said to Oral, "Get that oil burner going there."

Oral said, "I will, damn; we just got here."

I let Uncle Virgil think what he wanted. I didn't owe him any explanations, didn't want him making fun of me wearing someone else's castoffs. I started for his truck, moving easier in dungarees that fit good, paired with a plaid blouse that fit too. I peered through the trees, left, then right, listening for what didn't sound typical, vigilant and wary, my nerves on edge because of their disregard for being cautious. At the truck I grabbed as many buckets as I could hold and started back. Several hundred feet from the site, near to the start of the creek head, I could hear them arguing.

Oral shouted, "Give it here!" and when they came into view, Uncle Virgil had a jar held over his head, and Oral was jumping for it.

Uncle Virgil turned this way and that, laughing in that ridiculous hooting way of his while shoving Oral back. I dumped my load near the ones they'd brought and knew by the way they were getting more and more rambunctious, their little game was going to end badly. Sure enough, Oral jumped again for the jar, and this time, he knocked it out of Uncle Virgil's hand. It landed on the ground, and busted. Uncle Virgil changed in a split second, going from laughing to snarling.

"Sheeyut! Now look it what you done made me do, boy!"

He walloped Oral on the back of his head. I wouldn't want to be on the receiving end of the look Oral gave him before he stalked away, cussing a blue streak. He flopped down under a tree like he would spend the rest of his time sulking. Uncle Virgil kicked at the shards of glass, knocking the pieces from sight under the foliage. He acted no better than Oral, tramping around, and cussing. Finally, he went to the boiler and knelt by one of the burners. Daddy had started using oil burners a while back because they heated the stills without putting off smoke like wood fires.

I backed away as Uncle Virgil brought out a match, and flicked the end of his thumb over it. He fiddled around, adjusting the blaze, and I let go a sigh of relief when the flame caught and we weren't sent to kingdom come.

Now we'd take turns stirring until it was the right temperature when we'd have to put the cap back on and hold it in place with a big rock. This kept the cap from exploding from the buildup of steam. It really wasn't much different than a big pressure cooker. While Uncle Virgil stirred, I envisioned myself busting the still up. Over and over again I saw myself as I chopped and bashed, watching the mash soak into the ground, and me, wild and frenzied as I delivered blow after blow. My mouth filled with saliva like it would when I was standing in front of the refrigerator. I pictured Daddy discovering it, and coming home with the news, perplexed as to who'd found it, and had the nerve to defy him and what was his.

Ever since telling Aubrey, I'd been uneasy. She got to asking about it all the time, more than was necessary, in my opinion.

"You done it yet?"

I shook my head, irritated, and her mouth would go down, disappointed in my lack of gumption maybe.

Her remark was similar to Merritt's, "You ain't never gonna do it."

Like I'd been bluffing, like I was nothing but talk. I didn't understand why it mattered so much to her.

"I got to be careful. It takes time. I got to think. And quit asking me about it."

She got huffy and stormed off. After that I'd gone to lunch alone more than I cared to think about, and the bus rides for the past week were hell. Merritt started back to school and sat with his friend Curt Miller, Abel, or sometimes Oral, while I stood in the aisle, ignoring him, ignoring everyone. It was okay because I was preoccupied, obsessing, my mind restless, and I couldn't concentrate in my classes. I kept rehashing where Daddy would be, where he might want me to go, and I had to consider Uncle Virgil and Oral too. Nothing made me comfortable enough to pull it off. I began to think I was too chicken. I began to think maybe Aubrey was right.

The stills were all at the fermenting stage; at least six hundred gallons would come from them, meaning Daddy and Uncle Virgil would be busy hauling for the next few nights, collecting their cash, and, you know, breaking the law. I listened carefully to him saying where they needed to go, and recognized I might have the opportunity I'd waited for. During the runs, the both of them would be gone for hours. I had a chance. Next day I went to the shed during the late afternoon. The inside was dim; the rays from the setting sun directly behind the building seeped through thin cracks in the walls and made jagged yellow lines on the dirt floor. Like a jail cell. Daddy had just taken off in Sally Sue, and I could smell the exhaust when I went in, and got the axe. I hurried down the hill, and shoved the tool under the front seat of the truck. When I straightened up, I saw Merritt at the back door. His face was flushed and I froze. What if he'd seen me?

He said, "Ain't nothing for supper?"

Relieved, I said, "I was about to run to the store. What do you want?"

"Chicken."

I almost laughed at his choice. Back inside I took down the small tin box in the cabinet, and stuffed some money in my pocket. The truck was slow to crank, turning over a few times, but finally the engine came to life. Once on the road, I drove that old truck hard as I could, as if I was punishing it. It shook and rattled like it was about to fall apart, but held tight in the curves. Finally, I slowed down and began talking, reassuring myself I could do it, that it would be all right.

"Be quick and don't think too hard on it, do what you need to do, and get it over with. Them other two will be easier then. You only need the confidence of a first time. Afterward, you'll go into Wilkesboro, pick up what to cook for supper, go home, fix it, and maybe even eat a little. Act normal."

I fell silent. It had been a while since I'd sat at the table and I'd noticed Daddy had quit teasing me. As I washed the pots, I'd seen him looking at me, hesitating before he picked up his fork, like some measure of blame had maybe shown up. I was living on coffee and water alone, but each time I got on the scale, I wasn't never satisfied. When I looked in the mirror, I was repulsed. If I didn't do what my mind wanted, I hated myself even more.

I parked in the spot well hidden off Boomer Road, and grabbed the axe out from under the front seat. I'd chosen this one because out of the three, it was the easiest to get to. I ran for the cover of trees, then stopped after going only a short distance, feeling weak. I ignored my shakiness, and went along the familiar path. There were a few areas off to the sides where the weeds were pressed down, as if someone was going one way, and then changed their mind. It could have been deer, or maybe a black bear. I went on, my belly knotted up. I came to the last turn of the creek, and stopped. I hunkered down, peering through the underbrush, my heart hammering in my ears while I inched forward to see the area better.

When the tiny clearing came into view, I placed my fingertips against my eyelids, and exhaled slowly. I pictured myself doing this and finishing it, all the while knowing revenuers could get you if you were within fifty feet of a still. I opened my eyes, checking once more before I left my hiding spot. I edged forward, constantly looking around, and as I got closer, I discerned something was wrong. The boiler had huge holes gouged into it, while the thumper box and the oil burners were flattened like somebody had run over them. The area looked like a tornado had gone through it. I couldn't make sense of it. Someone had come and, by the looks of it, gone plumb wild.

The condition of the area held me rooted in place for I didn't know how long. I finally found the courage to walk around the damaged still, my shoes squelching through Daddy's precious mash. There was a yeasty, beer smell permeating the air. Flies and other insects buzzed about, and dotted the ground, intent on consuming what was left. They flew up as I moved through, getting in my face, and I swatted them away. There was the dread of being caught mixed with initial elation at my discovery. I began to calm down when nobody came rushing out from behind a tree.

I recounted my conversation with Aubrey, could see her telling Zeb and Willie what I'd said. But it might be the landowners, whoever they were. I didn't think it was liquor agents. No, this was recently done, and they'd have waited to catch someone before turning it into a pile of splintered wood. They'd have waited as long as it took. A lone bucket sat at the edge of the woods, and the oddity of it caught my eye. It was one of the ones we'd brought for catching the liquor, and it had been left behind, unneeded maybe. It sat upright. Beckoning. The axe handle felt slippery in my damp palms, but I was glad to have it, ready to go to swinging it if anyone jumped out at me.

I crept closer. It was something about that bucket. The smell, like that of an outhouse, greeted me when I was only a few feet away, because somebody had used it for just that, relieving themselves in it. I backed away, looking around. It was obvious they wanted to send a message. It would be just the thing a Murry would do. I cussed Aubrey. I should've never taken her to these sites; I should've never told her. Other than the pieces of wood, and metal parts on the ground, scattered about like the scene of a bad car wreck, there was nothing else to see. It was too quiet, the birds hushed, and only the low hum of the insects continued, like someone was watching and waiting to see what I'd do next. My skin was sticky while I shivered like I was cold. I had the urge to leave and quick. It was possible they could come back, or they could be watching me right this very minute.

A sudden onset of panic made me turn and run. I pushed tree branches out of the way, ducked under limbs, and my leg muscles begged me to stop within seconds. I didn't care about the noise I made and I didn't slow down until I was back at the truck. I snatched the door open, climbed onto the seat, and stuck the axe under it. Hands shaking, I turned the key, and heard the sluggish, reluctant turn of the engine. My body reacted; a sharp wave of anxiety flooded in like I'd jumped into a cold mountain stream. I swiped my damp hands down the front of my shirt, and turned the key back, then forward again. The engine chugged once, a last effort, and then the motor clicked. I turned the key to Off and sat there. I smacked my hands on the steering wheel. Heat filled the cab as I tried one more time. Clicks. I couldn't believe it. I shoved a hand into my pocket and pulled out a rubber band. I scraped my hair up into a ponytail and took the key out of the ignition and got out. I dropped it in my pocket while I stared at the old cantankerous piece of machinery and then I kicked it. I pummeled the hood with my fists. I wanted to scream and the swell of it rose in my throat, but I took hold of my anger. It would do me no good. With one last whack of my fist on the door, I began walking. I was already hot and sweaty, my temper having gotten the best of me.

I trudged along, my footsteps soft over the layer of fallen leaves from the past winter. I arrived at Boomer Road and there was nothing except me, the stretch of pebble-filled asphalt, and faded, cracked yellow and white lines. The thought of what I'd discovered, how I was going to explain myself, was beyond me at the moment. I started for home, walking along the thin shoulder, feeling vulnerable, exposed, as if I'd been caught in the very act. I kept vigilant for the sound of an approaching car, scouring the embankment in case I needed to hide. What only took about ten minutes in a vehicle was going to take more than an hour, even if I hurried. I prayed the road would remain empty and I'd see no one.

Before too long my feet hurt, and I had the

124

beginnings of a blister forming on my right heel. I stopped and adjusted my socks, and went on worrying about the incriminating evidence of the truck and the condition of the still. Daddy had said no need to go check on any of them for a day or so, and it was going to look suspicious from the start, no matter what.

By the time I was within a quarter mile of the house, the sky was pricked with pinpoints of star-light. Another few minutes and I came to the sharp curve. I was so relieved I'd made it, I stopped in the middle of the road and stared toward the heavens, breathing in the cool night air.

Small squares of yellow lights appeared from the windows of the living room and Merritt's room. That should have been a welcoming view, but instead, I dreaded going inside. I was really limping now, so I took my shoes off. A spot of blood on the back of one sock explained my hobbling gait. I began the climb up the steep drive and the closer I got, the louder and harder came the bumping from within my chest. My mouth, already dry from thirst, somehow got drier. The shed revealed the chrome of Sally Sue's bumper and then the back door was yanked open, and Daddy was there.

He said, "Jessie, that you?"

I stepped into the dim light shed by the yellow bulb near the upper corner of the back door.

"It's me."

"Where have you been? Where's the truck?"

I pointed back down the drive and couldn't find any words for how to begin the charade.

"Did you get in a wreck?"

"No. I was going to go to the store to get something to fix for supper."

Daddy motioned for me to come in. I unlocked my legs somehow, and slowly climbed the back steps. He held the door open and I slid by him into the house. Merritt sat at the table eating a Smithey Burger from the Goodwill store in Wilkesboro. He chewed and watched us like he did when he watched a good TV show.

Daddy said, "Sit down."

I sat.

"Where is it?"

I whispered, "Over to Boomer."

Daddy said, "What in hell were you doing there? I thought you said you were going to the store."

I pressed my hands together on my lap, twisting my fingers. "I decided I ought to maybe check on it, be more helpful, you know, with Merritt's arm and all."

Merritt made a derogatory noise while Daddy gave me a look that matched.

I must have looked petrified, because his features relaxed some, and that helped until he said, "Ain't none of them stills needed tending at the moment. You knew that."

"I got something to tell you about what I found out there."

He frowned, and said, "What?"

"I went like we usually do, being careful and all, but I could tell something was wrong right away. I'd seen some new leveled areas along the path before I got to it, you know, like where somebody might've been looking? There were these places that didn't look right, there in the weeds. I thought maybe bear, or deer. But now I figured that ain't it because that still? It ain't no more."

Daddy leaned toward me and said, "What the hell you mean, it ain't no more?"

I said, "Everything has got big holes in it. It couldn't have been too long ago when it happened, because the ground was still wet with what had run out. I hurried back to the truck and it wouldn't start. Battery's gone dead."

Daddy rose from the chair and paced the floor.

He faced me and said, "What else did you see?"

I shook my head. "Nothing."

Daddy rubbed a hand through his hair and down his jaw. He went to the phone and called Uncle Virgil. I expected he'd do that, only doing so was going to be like mashing the gas pedal on Sally Sue and hitting ninety miles an hour around a curve. Uncle Virgil would bring his shotgun and he'd be ready to, as he put it, "take care a them assholes."

Merritt said, "No wonder you look like you seen a ghost."

Daddy's words came fast as he explained what happened to Uncle Virgil. I'd never seen him so mad, his face tight and angry.

"It's got to be one of them damn Murrys."

My hope he'd blame a revenuer disintegrated.

He listened some more; then he said, "Maybe. Jessie was the one found it all tore up."

He paused, eyebrows raised in my direction, and my insides knotted. I mashed on my stomach repeatedly, but the pain only got worse.

He said, "Damned if I know. Something about it ain't right. Get over here. We got a decision to make."

I stared at my bloody sock, wishing I'd only gone to the store.

Chapter 9

Daddy couldn't sit still. He went from the stove to the back door, to the table and to the sink. Round and round. I didn't talk, and before too long, a truck door slammed announcing Uncle Virgil. He walked into the kitchen bringing with him an odor, pungent and tangy, his day working in the chicken houses still clinging to his clothes. I sat at the table with Merritt, tired, edgy, and feeling like I could eat every single thing we had in the fridge and cabinets. As was typical, Uncle Virgil looked to me for a glass of cold tea. I jumped up to get it, more accommodating than usual, while thanking my lucky stars Daddy hadn't questioned me harder.

Daddy said, "Might be time to go see one of them agents."

He'd never done such before, only threatened it, because those who lived here didn't like to rely on outsiders. They liked to handle their own matters, and didn't take kindly to anyone else butting in. I brought glasses of tea to the table, and sat down to listen. More than likely he'd go, but he might have Uncle Virgil do it. Daddy sipped on his tea, got his pack of Winstons

129

from his shirt pocket, shook one out, and lit it.

He said what we'd heard before. "Ain't a one of them Murrys worth a blunt nickel."

Uncle Virgil agreed. "They act like they the only ones ought to be making and running. They ain't been in it near as long as us."

Daddy said, "That's a fact. Hell, they don't even drink what they sell. They know it ain't nothing but rotgut."

Uncle Virgil said, "Heard Jerry Watkins took real sick after drinking some of it the other day. Somebody over to the chicken houses said they'd tried it. Said it tasted like poison 'cause that's what it is."

Daddy said, "Jerry's lucky he lived."

Uncle Virgil said, "I found out they been using Elk Creek for a water source just a ways down Tom Dula Road. There's a twin oak near where they go in; start there, and it ain't too far. 'Bout ten minutes north. They got several boilers going."

Daddy blew out a cloud of gray smoke and said, "Jessie, you got to be the one to go tell this agent feller."

I sat up straight.

"What? Why me?"

"They'll believe a woman 'fore they'll believe a man. They think somebody like me showing up, or your uncle Virgil, is only trying to stir up trouble. Plus, it draws attention, seems suspicious, like maybe we're talking because we got some part in it."

Uncle Virgil said, "That's the truth. Mrs. Taylor, she's been to'em several times when her and Dinky found themselves cut out of their profits by that no-account, good-for-nothing Fred Cullers. They listened to her, and that was the end of Fred Cullers' still."

Daddy tapped his ash into the ashtray and agreed with him. "That's right."

I crossed my arms. "I ain't doing it."

He said, "You will do it unless what happened up there ain't exactly like you said."

I shifted in my chair, and said, "I found it the way I said, and that's the truth."

Merritt and Uncle Virgil studied the tabletop while Daddy studied me. I reconsidered my quick answer. It would prove I'd told the truth if I agreed to what he asked.

I said, "Fine. What would I have to say to him?"

Daddy stubbed out his cigarette. "Tell'em you got information on the whereabouts of a still. They'll take it down and you walk out. Anonymous, and all."

"All right."

Uncle Virgil said, "Can't hardly believe ole sourpuss here ain't putting up more fight than that."

Daddy said, "You bring them jumper cables with you?"

Uncle Virgil said, "Yeah," and they got up from the table and went out the back door. I got up too, wanting to take a bath, tend to my foot, and fill the hole in my center growing by the minute.

Merritt, his face flushed an exceptional bright pink, said, "Shoot, wonder how long it takes them agents to find a still, even when they got directions?"

Irritable, I said, "How would I know?"

He grunted, then went to get up from the table and had a hard time keeping his balance. Maybe I shouldn't have snapped his head off. I reached out to help him and he used his good hand to push me away

He said, "I ain't that bad off."

His hand felt hot; his eyes were glassy.

I said, "Shit, Merritt, you been into the hooch?"

He said, "Hell no. Leave me alone."

I leaned forward and sniffed, and he stuck his hand out again, warning me off.

"Merritt!"

"Well, get away from me."

I waited for him to turn, and then I put a hand on his back. It also felt abnormally warm. He spun around, lifted the hand again like he would smack me. I took several steps back and raised my hands up to let him know I wasn't going to touch him again.

I said, "Merritt, I think you got a fever."

"Probably."

"You feel bad?"

"It ain't nothing. I'm going to bed."

"Get some of them BCs in the bathroom cabinet."

He said, "I already did."

He was probably lying, but if he wanted to feel miserable, what could I do about it? He clumped down the hall, holding his bad arm with his good. He'd been using the fingers that poked out the end of the cast some before, and now he relied solely on his left arm and hand. After he shut his bedroom door, I went into the bathroom, and filled the tub with water. I stayed off the scale. I didn't look in the mirror. I stuck my blistered heel into the hot water first. It hurt like the dickens, but once I got all the way in, it eased off. I stretched out, avoided looking down the length of my body. I didn't want to start obsessing about my breasts, my belly, my thighs, without clothes. I listened to the internal workings of my gut. The gurgles and protestations. I wanted to eat. It didn't have to be much. Just enough to feel less wobbly-legged. Just enough so I wouldn't need to put my finger down my throat.

I dropped lower, used my foot to turn on the handle for more hot water. The wish for food went away when I thought about talking to the revenuer, but what bothered me just as much was Aubrey. I stared at the water gushing from the spout. Maybe she was like Zeb. Maybe her mouth worked like this faucet. After a while I pulled the plug, and it was while I was drying off I heard a muffled noise. I wrapped the towel around me and opened the bathroom door. Steam rolled out and around me, swirling like white smoke. I poked my head out and listened as Merritt mumbled to himself.

I said, "Merritt? You all right?"

The mumbling stopped. No more sounds came from his room.

I shook my head, shut the bathroom door, and finished drying off. When I was done, I put on my housecoat, and carried the wet towel out to the back porch where an old rusty washing machine sat. I dropped the towel in the drum, and when I came back into the kitchen, I eyed the refrigerator, then the clock. It was almost nine. Daddy could come back any minute. I leaned against the counter, my belly crying for something. I got the glass from where I'd left it on the table earlier and refilled it with more tea. I drank and all that did was make me hungrier.

I flicked off the overhead light, liking the dark as I went toward the refrigerator, and pulled on the handle. There on the top shelf sat a white paper bag, grease spots staining the outside. I remembered Merritt eating a Smithey Burger when I came in earlier. Daddy brought them home at least once a week and it couldn't have worked out better, since there was nothing else.

I took the bag out, and shut the door, returning the room to darkness. I reached in, got one out, and set it on the table. The paper crinkled loudly as I closed the bag. I went to the kitchen door, checked to see if anyone was coming, then gave a quick peek down the hall at Merritt's door. Still closed. I was alone. I was deliberate when I put the bag back in the refrigerator. *Only one, Jessie. That's all.* I went back to the table and unwrapped the hamburger. It was slick with mustard and ketchup. I brought it up to my nose, and the smell made my mouth water while I gagged at the same time, my midsection and head in conflict. I bit into it, taking only a small bite, chewed once. Twice. I chewed some more, and fought the rising nausea. That happened sometimes, and I didn't know why. I swallowed and waited to see if it would stay down. Depending on how long it had been, sometimes I found myself running for the bathroom to get sick.

It stayed and I wanted more. This time I took a regular bite, and another, and another, until I was cramming the rest of it in, my fingers pressing against my lips as I acted on impulse, going back to the refrigerator a second time. I grabbed the bag, took it to the sink, and stood over it to eat. I was still chewing while reaching for another when the sound of our truck coming up the drive sent me rushing to the metal trash can by the stove. I spit the clump of hamburger out, knowing

I had to bury the empty wrappers. I put my hand over my mouth, fighting the need to release the pressure in my stomach as I grabbed them, and shoved them underneath the newspapers and food scraps.

I grabbed the bag with the rest of the food, opened the refrigerator door, and was putting it back when Daddy came in. I slammed the door shut as he flipped on the light. He shoved his cap back off his head, revealing pale skin that didn't match the lower part of his face.

He said, "Why's this light off?"

"I was about to turn it on. I was putting the tea up. I saw the glasses needed washing. I was going to wash them, and—"

He cut in and said, "Explain something to me."

His voice didn't sound right. I walked to the sink, turned on the faucet, got the water good and hot. I didn't like the way he spoke, low, almost ominous, like he was going to tell me something bad happened. I swished the water around and waited with my back turned.

"Tell me why this axe was under the front seat."

Shit, the axe. I'd forgot about the axe.

I faced him. He held it out, like he was wanting me to take it. I didn't move. I couldn't. Dumb. So dumb. I should have brought it with me when I walked home. I could've thrown it down a hillside on Lore Mountain Road. It would have

136

been one of them things, mysteriously gone. Left somewhere, never to be found again.

"Don't hand me no bullshit about how you didn't know about it. I ain't put it there."

There wasn't nothing else to do but tell him the truth.

"I took it with me. But I didn't do that to the still."

"You mean to tell me it's busted all to hell, and you were out there with this, and you didn't do it?"

"I didn't."

He said, "That story don't seem possible. Not when all I ever hear out of that mouth of yourn is how much you hate it. You don't never want to do a damn thing except be a pain in the ass. Swear to God, this here's lower than anything them damn Murrys would do. Worse. They ain't family."

I pressed my hands together. The hamburgers tried to climb back up my throat and I swallowed repeatedly.

Daddy said, "What a goddamn mess. My own daughter."

Trembling, I said, "I didn't do it. I didn't."

His voice was low when he said, "You know what I say to that? Bull. Shit."

Resentment took over, and I yelled, "Okay, fine! I *was* going to do it. I was going to hack it to pieces, beat the hell out of it, but *I* didn't have to. I'm telling you, it was like that when I got there."

The silence grew and the taste in my mouth turned oily and repulsive. I went to the sink and started scrubbing the glasses so hard it was a wonder they didn't break. Pissed, I splashed water everywhere as my indignation grew. Daddy went back outside and I was glad. Merritt came from his room back into the kitchen and that made me madder than I already was. I didn't want to hear him take sides. I let the water out of the sink and heard a funny scraping noise. I saw he hadn't quite made it to the chair yet and wobbled back and forth, like he couldn't decide if he wanted to sit or stand. He pitched about and I was sure he'd fall. He acted like he was drunk, and I began to think he'd lied. I bet he had a jar of it hidden somewhere, and my earlier concern he might be sick was replaced by an even hotter anger.

Feeling stupid over the axe, I snipped at him, "What's the matter with you? You're drunk, that's what's the matter. Between the two of you, it's a wonder I ain't into it myself."

He ignored me and sat on a kitchen chair. Impatient, I began wiping the counter off in a frenzied fit of cleaning. I went over to the table, scrubbing at the top, working to dispel my anger. I was only about a foot away from where he sat and heat came off him like I'd opened the oven door. I stopped wiping the table and studied him, trying to determine if something was actually wrong. He had his head down on his good arm and was making this little rocking motion with his body. His face was turned toward the wall, and he didn't look up, but I made out what he said.

"Something's wrong with my arm."

I said, "Is it hurting worse?"

He had trouble focusing on where I was, his face scrunched in pain.

He said, "I can't hardly stand it."

I went to the back door. I couldn't see Daddy anywhere.

I hollered, "Easton!"

Merritt looked like he'd been put under a broiler. I got a clean dish towel and wet it, and brought it to him He leaned back, put it across his forehead, and I caught the odor of something putrid.

I said, "Merritt, what is that smell? God. Ain't you been bathing?"

He tugged the sleeve of his pajamas up, exposing the length of the cast and a small part of his arm above it. That and his hand, really the entire sight, made me gasp. What wasn't covered up with plaster was swollen almost twice the normal size, constricted so his wrist and hand bulged, as did his upper arm. He'd been trying to get at something down inside the cast. There were long, scarlet streaks on his skin, like cat scratches. The tips of his fingers were bloated, and were an uncharacteristic whitish color.

I said, "Oh my God, Merritt, how long's it been like that?"

He placed his head on the tabletop, and said, "I don't know. It was okay; then it started itching real bad last week. I got to scratching it by sticking a coat hanger down inside, until it got like this."

His eyes were barely there slits and I was sure his fever was high when he began shivering. I went into the hall closet, grabbed a blanket, and brought it to him. He sat with it around his shoulders, slumped over and trembling. Otherwise, he didn't move. I sat on the chair beside him and hoped wherever Daddy was, he wouldn't be long. Merritt needed to go to the hospital again, or at least see a doctor.

There was an occasional miserable groan out of him and I sat with him for what felt like a long time before the screen door opened and Daddy came inside. He didn't look at us. I was about to speak, to tell him about Merritt, when I noticed he held a mason jar with the clear liquid I despised.

He brought the jar up to the light, and said, "It ain't half-bad. I can see why some got to have it." He dropped his arm, and in a curious, musing tone he said, "Wonder why it is you think you got the right to judge, to act like you ain't a part of this family."

I ignored what he said and pointed at Merritt.

I said, "Look."

Merritt lifted his head, and quickly put it back down on the dish towel, as if even that caused a lot of discomfort.

Daddy noticed and he said, "Son?"

The concern in his voice created a tinge of green inside me.

I pushed it away and said, "It's his arm. It ain't healed proper."

Daddy bent down, staring at the part exposed above the cast, and without a word he hurried back outside and returned with a saw.

He said, "I got to get that cast off."

Merritt said, "It hurts bad, worse than when I broke it."

Daddy said, "You tell me soon as you feel anything coming through against your skin, okay?"

Merritt nodded. Daddy had him turn it so his hand was palm up. He placed his own hand on top to brace it, and began sawing. Puffs of white powder fell, dusting the table and the floor. Merritt tried not to look. Daddy worked as fast as he could, and within a minute, Merritt held up a finger to indicate he'd felt it. Daddy moved down some, and after a few minutes, Merritt signaled him again. Daddy focused on the area covering the elbow where it was thicker. It took longer, and sweat dripped off his forehead, while Merritt tried not to make any noise. He unexpectedly flinched, and Daddy stopped. Wiggling the fingers of each hand between the cast and Merritt's arm, he began pulling in opposite directions, like he was splitting a melon open. It took a couple of attempts and the pain from the pressure caused Merritt to lose that high color from the fever. The cast cracked open and his arm was exposed. I smacked my hand over my mouth and nose as I glimpsed his arm. I had to walk away. I went to the sink and stared out the window. It wouldn't never be the same again.

Daddy said, "Jesus," while Merritt cried.

Chapter 10

Merritt came home and it was all I could do to look at him. Eyes dull and lackluster, it was evident he'd lost more than his arm. He would have to get used to the idea of never pitching ball again, because he was going to end up with a prosthesis at some point and would have to spend time learning how to manage that. While Aubrey's daddy always preached how shine was evil, made fools of men, and caused nothing but trouble, he'd once said the only thing it was good for was as a disinfectant. That proved not to be true in Merritt's case. He told me he tried to spill a little liquor down inside the cast, feeling certain his arm was getting infected. It burned so bad, he was pretty sure he'd passed out, and then it got worse instead of better.

Good for nothing is what it's good for.

He moved about the house as if in a fog, his world shrunk to the living room, kitchen, and his bedroom. We watched him try to eat left-handed, drink left-handed, do for himself, and it was hard. I anticipated the moment he would blame Daddy, grow angry at being crippled, tell him he'd all but ruined his life, but he didn't.

Daddy hadn't said much since he'd gone to get him. Every now and then he'd stare at Merritt's empty sleeve, folded up and pinned to his shirt. If Daddy made eye contact with me, he'd quickly turn his attention to the TV or to the newspaper. It was the closest thing to contrition I'd ever seen, and I wasn't sure you could call it that. He'd dropped the subject of what happened at Boomer. He didn't talk anymore about going to see some agent.

I began to think what happened to Merritt mattered until one morning shortly after he'd come home Daddy got to talking about buying the materials to replace the still. Merritt sat opposite him at the kitchen table, and I waited for him to point to his missing limb, to tell Daddy he wasn't inclined to listen to that garbage anymore. Instead, they conversed like it was any other day with Merritt asking him how big the new still might be, and what it would turn out. Daddy told a story about Granddaddy Sasser building a new still, how he'd made it bigger. Merritt absorbed every word, and said once he got his new arm he'd get back to shine making again.

I was dumbfounded. Where was his rage?

Merritt's infection was called osteomyelitis. It had poisoned his arm, traveling through his blood, infecting the tissues. Every time I watched him struggle to do the simplest tasks, it brought back what happened to Mama, reminded me of

144

that brokenness inside my own self. Listening to them talk about a new still, and getting back to making shine was as if the both of them had something like that infection seeping through their veins, filling every crevice and inhabiting their thoughts like a disease.

I was glad I had the excuse of school so I could get out of the house. I waited for the bus, and moments later it climbed around the curve, and stopped with a jolt. The door swung open with a whoosh and I climbed on. I searched for Aubrey, and like it had been lately, our usual seat was taken by Alice Knowles and Denise Bradford. I leaned against the pole up near the front. Even the bus driver ignored me now.

Someone said, "Jessie!"

It was Merritt's buddy Curt Miller, waving a hand, indicating for me to come to the back and sit with him. Surprised, I moved down the aisle and lowered myself into the seat.

"Thanks, Curt."

He said, "I only wanted to know how Merritt was doing."

I understood the seat was a onetime offer. He didn't have to explain. I told him about Merritt, and by the time the bus got to the school he'd gone to staring out the window, looking glum.

We stood, and when the aisle had cleared enough for me to get off, he said, "Well, let him know I asked, and that I said hey."

"I will."

It only stung a little when I overheard him reassuring Abel, "Hell no, she ain't sitting with me again. I ain't stupid."

I hurried so I didn't have to hear more. The rest of the day was the usual dreary rotation of classes, and still no sign of Aubrey. Lunch came, and I sat outside on the brick wall with no expectations. Minutes later, footsteps approached from behind me, but I didn't bother to turn and was surprised when it was her.

She came around to face me and said, "Hey. Gosh, that skirt looks nice."

I went back to studying my oxfords. I wished I hadn't chosen to wear something she'd given me. I wished I'd thrown all of it out. Before, I'd have thanked her for the compliment, and would have reiterated my appreciation. Before seemed like a long time ago.

She said, "It sure is terrible what all's happened to Merritt."

I said, "Is that what you came over here to say, or are you really nosing about because of the still?"

She was about to sit beside me, and my comment stopped her.

She stepped back instead, and said, "What?"

"You know what I'm talking about."

She shook her head. "No, I don't."

I mumbled a couple words under my breath

that would have turned her preacher daddy's ears inside out.

Louder, I said, "You can't tell me you didn't tell Zeb what I was going to do, and for all I know, Willie too. One of our stills been busted all to hell and I got blamed for it."

Aubrey's eyebrows went up and she said, "Well, from all I've ever heard out of you, I thought that would make you happy. I mean, ain't it what you wanted? What do you care if it's gone?"

"I don't care, but I said not to say nothing and you did anyway."

"Uh-uh. I didn't tell nobody what you said. Why would I do that?"

She fidgeted with her watch, not making eye contact. I was right, and my silence told her I thought so.

She threw her hands up and said, "Fine, think what you want."

"I will."

She got up to leave, and then said, "Here comes Willie. Why don't you ask him yourself since you know everything!"

He walked fast across the lawn and I wanted to run toward the school doors. Across the grass other students sat calmly eating, studying with their books set in front of them, the sun warming their backs, enjoying their day.

Aubrey smiled big, and waved, "Hey, Willie!,"

and then she leaned in and said, "Go on. Ask him."

I wasn't about to talk to Willie Murry. I got up, my arms folded across my middle, fingers gripping my waist. His gaze skimmed past Aubrey, who'd pinned her eyes on him the moment he appeared. She giggled in a way I'd never heard before, a silly little singsong noise like someone practicing scales on a piano. She had it bad, a severe crush. I was sorry for her, and offended at the same time. He stopped by her side, and I moved back by several feet.

He said, "Well, if it ain't Jessie Sasser of them famous Sassers up on Shine Mountain. So they say."

I'd never talked to any Murry and I wasn't about to start now. His hair was slicked back, and he wore rolled-up dungarees, a less than white T-shirt, and Wearmasters, the leather creased and wrinkled as an old man's face.

He said, "Heard you don't take kindly to the family doings."

Aubrey, put out by the fact Willie was ignoring her altogether, wasn't paying attention to a word he said as she thrust her chest out and postured in other ways she thought might look appealing. Aubrey's common decency had left, and she had no idea he'd confirmed what I'd suspected. I moved a little to the right so I could leave, but Willie sidestepped and blocked my way.

He rubbed a couple of fingers over a stubbly chin, and said, "Could've sworn somebody said something about some unfortunate mishap on Lore Mountain Road a few weeks back."

I moved again, and so did he while Aubrey continued to posture dramatically.

She finally poked out her lip when it got her nowhere, and said, "Willie, Jessie wants to go."

"She can go. Anytime she wants."

I moved, but he blocked me again.

Aubrey's annoyance showed in the way she said his name. "*Wil-lie,* come on, quit messing around. We only got five minutes. Let's go sit in your car."

She spun around and marched off without saying another word, black hair swinging back and forth, her back rigid. Willie gave her the briefest of looks. If Aubrey saw what I did in his expression when he looked back at me, she'd run like I wanted to do. He had hateful eyes that showed nothing because there was nothing in him, only pure meanness.

"Well, go on, Jessie Sasser. Permission granted."

He bent slightly at the waist and waved his arm, ushering me forward. Moving by him was like edging along a narrow, steep path and one wrong move would send you tumbling over a rocky cliff. It didn't help that he laughed, like he knew I was afraid, and the sound crawled up my back and into my head, making it ache. I rushed toward the school, lurching along like my legs were having spasms. Once I was inside, and out of sight, I dashed down the hall as the bell rang for fifth period to begin. I passed the small nurse's room as Mrs. Brewer came out.

She saw me and said, "Sasser. Good timing. Git yerself in here."

I had a couple minutes to get to class, so I obeyed, remembering the look on her face days ago.

Inside her tiny office, where everything was painted white and smelled like alcohol, she said, "You been drinking that tea?"

"Yes'm."

"You need more?"

"I don't want you to go to no trouble on account of me."

"Hmph. Trouble is what you just had for lunch. Tea ain't trouble."

I didn't know she'd seen me and Willie Murry.

"Yes'm."

"Heard about yer brother. Wished I'd a known. Could a hepped him, maybe."

She handed me a similar packet as the one before, and said, "You need to be drinking this. It'll help that stomach problem you got. It is yer stomach is ailing you, ain't it?"

Pale blue eyes pierced.

"Yes'm."

She said, "You ettin'?"

150

I shifted off one foot to the other. "Some."

"Some. Here you stand and I see yer body crying for it. I may be old, but I see that, and I see what you ain't able to, least not right now. You best be careful; yer gonna ruin them teeth, too."

My teeth? I wasn't worried about my teeth; I was worried about how I was all soft, and pudgy.

I stared down at myself. "I'm fat."

"Pfft. Says who? Now git. I got things to do. And drink that tea."

I left her office, tucking the packet of tea into my skirt pocket. Mrs. Brewer might be ill-natured and gruff, but I was starting to think within her was a tender, soft heart.

I walked in on Merritt tending his stump. His back to me, he didn't know I was there. He stood at the kitchen sink, with the hot water running. He cried, and swabbed and cried some more. It was what he said next that set a resolve in me stronger than anything I'd confronted before.

He said, "It ain't ever gonna be right again."

More sobbing, more words and wishes.

"I wished it never happened. I wished we could do something else."

He was in tremendous pain, his hand shaking like that of an old man as he tended the raw open wound. He beat on the counter with his good hand, making the dishes in the drainer rattle

151

while he was crying like his heart was broke. I retreated to my room and sat on the edge of my bed and thought hard about what I'd heard and seen.

The next day when I came home after school, Sally Sue was gone, which meant Daddy was off running his precious liquor to some poor soul who thought they needed it. I told Merritt I was going to Aubrey's, but I wasn't.

"You need anything while I'm out? That prescription need filling again?"

He shook his head, as he sat by the living room window, staring out like a prisoner. My mouth set, I went out and got in the truck. I drove into Wilkesboro, and parked a couple of streets away from Main Street. I watched the comings and goings of various people, imagined what errands they might be on. I sat with my hands resting on the steering wheel with a tremendous need to have someone listen to what I had to say, to tell me what I was about to do was a good thing, a worthy thing.

I climbed out and walked in the direction of the federal building and post office on Main Street. There was a small hardware store, tucked back into the alley across from it, and I stopped when it came into view, working up my nerve. A couple of people I didn't know walked down the sidewalk and they certainly didn't pay me no mind, but I felt like they knew what I was up to.

What if someone I knew did spot me and started asking questions about what I was doing in town on a weekday afternoon? Small-town talk would require they mention me in passing to Daddy if that happened, because that's how conversations went around here.

I hurried across the street, and went inside. The walls were painted pale green, and made of cinder block, and my footsteps rang out with a hollow sound, amplified by the tile floor. The sound of rapid typing from somewhere within the building matched my pulse. Down the corridor, the line of doors on each side were all shut. One opened and a man came out, dressed in a white shirt and dress pants. Like Eliot Ness.

He said, "Can I help you, miss?"

I hadn't expected it to happen like this. I'd imagined I'd speak to a receptionist first and she would usher me into a small private room, anonymity intact, and I could gather my wits about me. I grew light-headed, uneasy. My fingers curled tight as I thought about Merritt and what I'd overheard. I imagined myself walking away without saying another word. I could go back out into the warm sun, drive home, and keep pretending.

I noticed his carefully combed hair, starched shirt, and tie. He wore a look of patience, like he'd dealt with a lot of other people struggling to make a difficult decision, like he knew it wasn't easy. I forced the words out before I could change my mind.

I said, "I need to see one of them agents looking for people making shine."

He said, "I'm with the Alcohol Tax Unit. ATU for short. You can speak to me."

I pushed fear aside and let my resolve take over.

I said, "I got something to say."

He said, "Come with me."

I followed him back into the room he'd just exited.

He said, "Have a seat, Miss . . .?"

I said, "I ain't prepared to give my name. It's got to be without it."

He said, "Fine. That's not a problem. You want to go ahead, then?"

I held tight to the arms of the chair, and considered how I might appear. My ill-fitting clothes, my expression, the shakiness of my hands, my pale skin. What did he see, some lowly mountain girl unfortunate in all things, even pitiable maybe? He waited, alert and inquisitive. The clock ticked behind him while I struggled to figure out how to begin.

Finally, I said, "You ever watch that show *The Untouchables*?"

Chapter 11

His name was Nash Reardon. As I tried to figure out where to end the discussion on the TV show and where to begin telling him why I was here, the sight of him, a bona fide Eliot Ness of sorts, stole my words. He'd nodded at my question about the TV show, then asked if I wanted some water or a Pepsi. I asked for water. He left the room and I stared out the window. A few more passersby went down the sidewalk, but one person caught my eye and sent me into a panic. Daddy disappeared around the corner of that hardware store as the office door opened, and Mr. Reardon reappeared with a paper cup of water. He set it in front of me, and sat back down behind his desk.

He held the pencil hovering above the notepad. "Ready when you are," he said.

I was thoroughly spooked. He could've seen the truck. I had no idea where he'd been or where he was headed.

I stalled for time. "Do many come in here and talk about moonshining?"

He tapped the end of the pencil on the pad, and said, "A few. Not too many."

I glanced at the window. There was no sign of him, but I'd lost my nerve.

I cleared my throat. "You ever hear anything about them Murrys over near to Shine Mountain?"

He repeated the name, "Murry?"

I nodded.

"Go on."

I shifted, certain I appeared squirrely at best. He leaned back in his chair, the kind that swiveled. He moved it so he no longer faced me, and instead looked at a picture on the wall and an official-looking framed document.

He put the tips of his fingers on his right hand against the tips on his left and said, "Look. I know it ain't easy, coming in here and doing what I think it is you're about to do. But believe me, you aren't the first, and you won't be the last. Take your time."

The image of Merritt's tender red wound materialized in my head. His pain, the words he'd said echoed and then faded, my fear of being caught after the fiasco over Boomer nudging all of it out of the way.

"I'll start with them for now."

Such a chickenshit, Jessie.

"Fine."

"There's word they got a still up near Elk Creek."

"Okay."

I stalled again, tried to untangle my thoughts.

"They ain't the kind of people you want to stir up. They'll try to find who ratted on them and if they do, they'll make'em pay."

"Are you afraid of them?"

"Everyone is, mostly."

"So, why're you here?"

I had to give him a reason that didn't point to us.

"They sell rotgut. Radiator poison. I heard tell somebody died from drinking it. Lots of folks get sick. My uncle took sick. I'm ashamed to say he tends to like his liquor."

That was a good reason enough to believe I was doing this out of good cause.

He said, "Why do people keep buying from them if they know it's bad?"

"Some got to have it, I guess. It's a need I've seen, like my uncle's."

He said, "And maybe some would say you've got some stake in it. That these Murrys are cutting in on your own family's business. Maybe your kin are involved?"

I spoke with conviction, "I don't lay claim to none of it."

He tapped the pencil on the paper again.

Finally, he sat forward and said, "All right then. Exactly where is this still?"

I gave him the whereabouts, instructing him to go down Tom Dula Road, where to walk in.

"It ain't exact, but ought to be close."

Mr. Reardon took it all down and then looked up. "Anything else?"

I paused, knowing if I walked out and didn't do what I'd really come to do, I'd regret it. I'd pay for it somehow. I couldn't bring myself to do more than skirt around it.

"I got more to say; I just can't tell it all to you right now."

He seemed satisfied. "All right, well, I appreciate you coming in. If you've got good information here, and you come back and tell me more, it'll go a long way to help clean this county up. We got fourteen agents working the area, but I tell you what, folks make them hard to find. Wilkes County is known as the Moonshine Capital and I can see why. The mountains here are pockmarked with stills. I hope you'll keep your word."

I'd never heard Wilkes County identified that way before. It didn't make me proud.

"I will."

He got up and I stood too. He stuck out his hand, and I took it, and we shook, like we had us an arrangement. He opened the door, and I went out.

He said, "Thank you, miss. I'll expect I'll see you again, and soon?"

I couldn't say yes; I could only nod and hurry away, staring at the tile floor, and then the concrete of the sidewalk the entire way back to the truck. I was so uptight at the possibility I'd hear Daddy yell my name that when I got to it and it hadn't happened, I couldn't believe I'd been that lucky.

Inside the warm interior, I spoke out loud. "You chickenshit. You stinking pile of chickenshit."

I drove off, staring through the bug-spattered windshield. Familiar feelings of disappointment and disgust kept me company as I passed 10th Street where we did our shopping, mostly empty and unlike Saturdays when everyone came from all around, double-parking by the curbs, darting among the cars and trucks to visit or shop. A napkin blew across a sidewalk, reminiscent of a ghost town. I went down Route 16 and then over to 18. I didn't know how long it would take that revenuer to find Elk Creek, but once he did, a fuse would be lit under the Murrys and they'd be hell bent on finding out who done them wrong.

At home Aunt Juanita's car was parked near the back door, and my hackles instantly rose. Inside I found her busy putting food in the refrigerator.

She turned and said, "I brought y'all some fried chicken and biscuits."

It was always chicken with everyone lately.

"Thankee."

She smelled like she'd just come from having her hair permed. Her hair rested on her scalp in tight curls, the slightly eggy sulfur odor of the product they used obvious as she moved back and forth from the table to the refrigerator. She wore her favorite color, a pink dress and shoes to match.

She said, "Is that a new dress?"

"Not really. Aubrey gave it to me."

She bent forward and studied my face. "You look like you could use some sleep. You've got circles under your eyes. Did you ride with the window down? Your hair's a mess."

I reached up and began finger combing my hair. I stopped when I came away with some strands caught in my hands.

Aunt Juanita said, "Good Lord."

I went to the trash and brushed them off in it. It wasn't the first time it had happened. Didn't everyone lose a few hairs now and then?

Her brow was puckered and she said, "I hope you ain't going to end up bald. There was a woman at our church, lost all her hair due to hormones. You're too young for all that, I imagine."

"Aunt Juanita, I'm fine."

"Well, you don't look fine. You got them bags under your eyes and your hair's dull as dirt."

"Gee, thanks. You're always so helpful."

She opened up her pocketbook and got out her compact. She snapped it open and held it in front of me.

She said, "Take a good look. Truth hurts, but sometimes is necessary."

I wanted her to leave, so I glanced at the tiny

160

mirror, seeing what I was used to, pale cheeks, green eyes, confirming what I already knew. Me with pale skin and messy hair. I gave her a blank look, one that said I didn't much care.

Exasperated, she snapped the compact closed. "I try to help you, but you don't want to be helped." She was at the back door now, and said, "Why don't you let me make you an appointment with my hairdresser, at least get your hair trimmed, shampooed, and styled?"

"No," then, "thankee," came as an afterthought.

She sighed, and shook her head. "Well, it's all I can do. You don't want to be helped, then there ain't a thing more to say."

She let the door slam behind her. I had the childish urge to stick my tongue out at her back. I waited until she'd backed up, and I was sure she was gone before I went to see Merritt. His door was closed and I placed my ear against the wood. Nothing. I went back to the kitchen, opened the refrigerator, staring at the food she'd brought. To keep my mind off eating every single bit of it, I got some of Mrs. Brewer's tea, filled the tea strainer ball with some of the crushed leaves. I prepared it the way she'd directed and had a cup. It got me straightened out good enough so I could fix Merritt a plate, my stomach settled and not feeling so inside out. After what I'd witnessed, I wanted to do something for him. I selected a couple of pieces of chicken, and put a buttered biscuit on the plate. I arranged it on the table and set the fork on the left, so he could get to it. When I was done, I went to his door and knocked. He didn't respond.

I knocked again, and opened the door a crack. "Merritt?"

He was sitting and doing what he'd been doing earlier in the living room. He'd only changed rooms, and now stared out his bedroom window. There wasn't much to see out there.

I said, "Aunt Juanita brought some chicken, and all. Do you want something to eat?"

He shook his head.

"What's wrong? Is your arm hurting you?"

"You mean stump."

"Does it hurt?"

"What do you think?"

I said, "I think maybe you're starting to feel a bit different, that's what I think."

He faced me. "Feel different about what? What are you talking about?"

"Like why you're sitting here in a shitty mood. Why you lost your arm."

He snapped at me, "I'm sitting here in this house because of them dumb-ass Murrys."

I waited for him to acknowledge Daddy had some part of it too, but he only turned and went back to staring out the window.

I said, "That's only half-right, you know."

"Here we go again."

"Merritt, I heard you."

"Heard me what?"

"Earlier, when you were fixing your arm. What you said."

"Stump. Stump! It ain't a damn arm no more. Look at it."

He beat his one hand on the windowsill.

"It ain't the point. You said, 'I wished we could do something else.' It's what I been saying all along. If it weren't for moonshining, none of this would've happened. If we hadn't been hauling liquor, been on that road—"

He whipped around to face me again, filled with a wild anger and obvious pain.

"It ain't like what you're thinking, but it don't matter. You ain't to blame Daddy. It ain't his fault."

"It is too."

"Ain't neither. He wouldn't want nothing like this to happen and you know it."

"If that were true, he'd have stopped a long time ago. He don't care. He keeps going like a damn plow mule that can't be controlled."

"It's like you hate him."

"I hate what he does. What he makes us do."

"Well, I don't. I like making shine, and how about you get out of my room. Now."

"Merritt."

"Get out!"

He started coming toward me, anger making

him ball up his hand in a fist. He stopped at the tips of my shoes.

I said, "You're gonna change your mind one of these days."

"No, *you* will."

Frustrated, I stalked out of his room. He slammed the door behind me. I don't know why I even tried when it was clear he was on Daddy's side. In the kitchen I snatched up the plate of food I'd fixed. I didn't bother sitting down. I ate standing at the counter, ripping pieces of chicken off and chewing furiously. I sucked on the bones till there was nothing left. I stuffed in the biscuit I'd buttered as I opened the refrigerator. She'd brought a whole chicken. I snatched it off the shelf, and began working on the rest of it, and the other biscuits. I ate half of them plain, and stopped. What the hell. I ate the rest with jelly. By the time I was done, I felt so tight and full, I believed I might would explode. I headed for the bathroom immediately. I didn't even think about it. It was what was expected, only this time when I was done, I didn't feel like I sometimes did, that profound sense of relief. Instead, I recalled what I'd seen in Aunt Juanita's compact. A haggard face, the stringy, messy hair. I got on the scale. That couldn't be right. What I'd just done, the emptying out, it wasn't good enough. I bent over the toilet again. I repeated the action of sticking my fingers down my throat, over and over.

Finally, I couldn't bring any more up, no matter how hard I tried. I sat on the floor, breathless, wilted by the effort, my heart quivering unevenly. A click signaled Merritt coming from out of his room and I went stiff, and stared at the bathroom door. He stopped near it and I waited, wheezing from the effort. He continued down the hall and into the kitchen. My dread increased at the sound of the refrigerator door opening.

Seconds later he yelled, "Jessie, where's the chicken?"

I closed my eyes.

"Shit," I whispered.

I rose to my feet, drained. I turned the spigots on to fill the tub. I'd kept my secret for a long time, but if I wasn't careful, I was going to get found out.

"Jessie!"

I turned them wide open and didn't reply. I hoped he'd quit calling me, find something else in the cabinets to eat.

I flinched when he banged on the door. "Where's the food? You said there was chicken. Biscuits. Where'd you put it?"

I said nothing and he left, then came back and banged on it harder.

He said, "You *ate* it. I found all them bones in the trash, so you can't quit pretending you can't hear me."

I shut the water off.

I said, "Yeah, I ate it. You didn't want it. So what."

"But that was enough for all of us, Jessie!"

"How do you know? Maybe she only brought a couple pieces."

"I can count bones in a chicken and she brought a whole damn chicken."

I turned the faucets back on. He hit the door with his fist and I bowed my head. I slid down into the tub, covering myself with the water, full of shame. I began scrubbing hard with a wash-cloth, attacking my arms, belly, legs, every single part of me, as if I could wash away the fat, rid myself of the humiliation. The feeling of failure flowed over me like water as I rinsed and scoured until my skin was as raw and hot as my embarrassment.

His words from weeks before came like a nasty whisper in my ear, *You ain't never gonna stop.*

What he didn't know was what I'd eaten: a fitting meal for a coward.

Chapter 12

The still at Elk Creek was discovered by two agents in early June, nestled in a deep holler and surrounded by large rocks. The land disguised it well, and there was no telling how long it had been there. The full story was reported by the *Wilkes Journal-Patriot*, and it made front-page news. Normally they would have preferred to wait for someone to show up so they could arrest them, but maybe they wanted to send a message, because the agents made sure they had plenty of pictures showing hundreds of gallons of Murry shine saturating the ground. Nash Reardon was there, front and center, a serious look on his face, pointing to the gushing liquid, cascading from a large container like water rushes over rocks in the Yadkin River. I stared at the picture, a small hint of pride surfacing over the fact I'd had something to do with it, while imagining how I'd feel if it had been one of ours.

Daddy's reaction to all this was to comment, "Somebody's been careless or running their mouths about it. I can't believe them agents found it on their own."

I drew up at that, but then relaxed. How could anyone know it was me?

Soon after, rumors began circulating the Murrys were on a rampage. This was the topic of conversation over supper a week later, the night before school let out. Uncle Virgil, Aunt Juanita, and Oral had come over, and sat at the table with Merritt, and Daddy. I was at the stove, frying up a mess of chicken gizzards and livers, listening to them discuss how it didn't make sense the way that still was found. Daddy continued to be confounded.

He said, "Maybe them agents are getting better at learning this area. That or someone's got wind and reported it."

Uncle Virgil said, "Maybe it was the landowner discovered it."

I kept my attention on the food as I put plates on the table, placed the platter full of fried gizzards and livers in the middle. Next came a big bowl of rice, one with gravy, another with early sweet corn on the cob, and finally biscuits. For the sake of appearances, I sat and served myself along with the rest.

Merritt said, "Better get you some before Jessie gets it all."

His comment turned my stomach so the food on my plate was as appetizing as if I'd dropped it in the dirt. He poked Oral, and they laughed. I sat back, and put my fork down.

Uncle Virgil said, "Royce Murry might think it was us."

Daddy chewed on a gizzard and said, "Won't be the first time."

Uncle Virgil laughed and said, "Last time they came looking for trouble, I seem to recollect ole Royce got himself an ass full of buckshot."

There was a lot of hand slapping on the table, more laughing, and of course Oral and Merritt soaked it all in. Aunt Juanita only smiled, puffed on her cigarette, while fingering the new necklace strung around her neck, tiny glistening pearls the size of little green garden peas. Uncle Virgil had a jar of shine he kept by his tea glass and he took more from it than tea. There was an air of celebration, the Sasser swagger on display, invincible and unshakable. How could I ever feel part of this family when I didn't understand what they felt, or where it came from, that pride and honor? It would be like thinking I was beautiful and popular. It would be false.

Oral said, "I say we ambush'em before they git us," which earned him the habitual reaction from Uncle Virgil, a smack to the head.

Merritt didn't join in on this part of the conversation. He generally asked Daddy questions, but tonight, other than the little jab he'd made about me, he wasn't saying much.

When the phone rang, Daddy got up to answer it while Uncle Virgil got to messing around with

Aunt Juanita, reaching under the table to grab at her legs. She good-naturedly swatted his hands away.

Daddy said, "Hello?" and there was a pause, followed by, "You got to be kidding."

Everyone around the table fell silent.

He said, "We're coming." He hung up and in disbelief he said, "Your damn house is on fire, Virgil. That was your neighbor."

Uncle Virgil and Aunt Juanita jumped up at the same time.

Alarmed, she said, "Our house? How did it catch fire?"

She repeated the question, and pulled on Uncle Virgil's arm. He jerked away, irritated.

He said, "How the hell do I know, maybe you left the goddamn iron on, or the stove. Hell if I know, but come on, let's go!"

They moved toward the door as one, and she said, "Don't you dare blame me! You leave them cigarettes burning all the time! You left one in the ashtray, and if I hadn't seen it, it would have fell right onto the floor!"

Daddy was halfway to the truck and yelled, "It ain't time to be arguing and blaming while the damn thing's burning. Let's go!"

I suffered my first twinge of denial. Surely the Murrys wouldn't have reacted so quick. Maybe it hadn't been them; maybe it was something stupid Uncle Virgil or Aunt Juanita had done.

They tore down the drive and onto the road, the sound of tires squawking as they met asphalt. Merritt backed away from the table and stood at the screen door.

He said, "It was them; I know it."

"No you don't."

He gave me an annoyed look. "The Murry still was just found, and now Uncle Virgil's house is on fire, you don't think that's obvious?"

Hesitant, I said, "Not really."

"They might come and do something here."

I said, "No they won't! I'd bet it was Aunt Juanita or Uncle Virgil's fault. Who knows? Ain't no reason to jump to no conclusions. Could be coincidence."

Merritt eyed me, and said, "Coincidence? More like suspicious."

"It ain't all that suspicious."

He moved into the living room, his face rigid.

"Is too."

Like Merritt, I was afraid it was them. I wanted to deny it because I didn't want to accept blame, but being too adamant might also sound fishy.

Reluctant, I said, "You're probably right."

The sound of sirens rose and fell as the fire trucks made their way up and around the steep roads and on toward their house. I stepped outside on the front porch and Merritt acted like he might want to run after them, but he stayed behind me, watching. Our house sat near the crest of Shine Mountain while Uncle Virgil's was about midway down, and situated similar to us, in a deep curve that gave way to a straight section right before their drive. A trail of black smoke rode the breeze, appearing above the tree line, thick, and rolling. I was afraid of the outcome. If they lost their home, it would surely be my fault, no different than if I'd lit the match and flicked it into the house with my own fingers. When I went and spoke to Nash Reardon, I'd not thought of such consequences.

I went back inside, laid down on the couch, and stared at the ceiling. Merritt came in after a minute and eventually dozed in a chair. I got up when headlights hit the opposite wall where the front door had been left open. The room went dark again as the vehicle went around to the back of the house. Doors slammed and I went into the kitchen. The clock said midnight. Merritt appeared in the kitchen doorway.

He said, "This late, it can't be good."

Daddy walked in first, looking like he'd been working in the coal mines. Behind him came Uncle Virgil, Aunt Juanita, and Oral, all of them just as grimy as him, clothes and skin smudged and dusted with ash. Red-rimmed eyes blinked in the stark glare of the overhead light, faces pale under the smut.

My voice low, I said, "Is the house okay?"

Without answering, Daddy dropped onto his chair at the table. The rest of them sat scattered around the same way they'd been in only a short time ago, only the atmosphere was very different. I got clean glasses from the drain, cracked open a couple of ice trays, poured tea, and handed filled glasses around. Nobody spoke. My answer came from the way they acted.

Finally, Daddy said, "Stay long as you need."

His offer broke the silence, and Uncle Virgil said, "I'm gonna get'em. They gonna pay for this. I had money kept near to the bed. They got it or it's done burned up with the house."

Daddy said, "We don't know for sure it was them."

I looked at Merritt, but he ignored me.

"Who in hell else could it be?"

"It could have been anything that started it."

"You blaming one of us?"

"I ain't saying nothing other than we can't just go off half-cocked when we don't know."

"They got to be made to pay."

"We ain't stirring them up, not until somebody says something, and they will. They ain't never been ones to not know when to keep their mouths shut."

"Hell. They's already stirred up. It makes me crazy. I got to do something about it. I can see'em now, snickering behind our backs. Making us look like dumb asses."

173

"Won't be to anybody but their own, and who gives a shit about that?"

"I do."

"We'll handle them when the time's right."

"Since when did you get to be boss man of all us?"

Daddy rubbed at his face, in a tired manner.

Uncle Virgil got up and paced the floor. He said, "I got to be able to make do; I got to think about how to get along."

"We'll have us a run here before long."

"And what do we live on till then?"

"You'll get paid working over at them chicken houses."

"Hell. It ain't hardly worth my time."

"Virgil, you ain't got diddly-squat owed now with that house gone. If you eat, sleep here, ain't a thing gonna cost you one red cent. Save your money, you'll be ahead of yourself in no time."

Daddy's logic didn't set well with Uncle Virgil, and the old rub he had rose quick as his temper. He stopped beside Daddy's chair.

"You know I ain't never had what's owed me all these years."

His eyes challenged. Daddy shoved his chair back quick and the legs scraped the floor loud as he stood. Uncle Virgil stepped out of his way and Daddy went outside without a word.

Once he'd left, Aunt Juanita said, "Virgil, can't you let that go? It ain't his fault."

174

"Hell no I ain't gonna let it go. He knows it ain't right."

It was uncomfortable listening to them snipe at one another over Uncle Virgil's idea of injustices and what he was owed.

Aunt Juanita said, "Always running your mouth, ain't you got no pride?"

"Running my mouth? Pride? Hell, it ain't a damn thing wrong with me reminding him what's right and what ain't."

"He's letting us stay here."

"Like that's supposed to make it even?"

Merritt shifted in his chair, while I grew preoccupied with a scratch on the tabletop and traced my fingernail along it. Oral paid attention to his feet, ears pink like slices of bologna. Daddy came back in and tossed some bills onto the table. Uncle Virgil gave Aunt Juanita a self-satisfied look. He picked them up and counted.

He said, "A hundred bucks? I can't hardly begin to build a house with that. It's gonna cost me twelve thousand or so."

Daddy said, "You expect I'm supposed to give you money to build your house? It ain't my fault the damn thing caught fire."

"Well, by God, it ain't mine neither."

"Ain't what it sounded like when we left out of here a while ago, blaming for this and that."

Uncle Virgil shoved the money in his pocket. "It's just talk. It didn't mean nothing."

Aunt Juanita changed the subject. "It's late. Where're we sleeping?"

There wasn't much choice in a three-bedroom house and six people.

I said, "You and Uncle Virgil can have my room."

Daddy's eyebrows went up, and he said, "Good, that's good, Jessie."

Aunt Juanita said, "I appreciate it."

Uncle Virgil said nothing, still obsessed with his idea of fairness. He was propped against the sink, ankles and arms crossed, seething. I left the kitchen, went into the living room, and laid on the couch, pulling the blanket off the back. I covered up, even my head, and hoped by the light of day it wouldn't seem so bad. I was an expert at hashing over problems in the middle of the night. Worry always made sleep impossible, like I'd had ten cups of coffee. Having three more people and the one bathroom, plus I'd just lost the privacy of my own room; how would I manage myself? That compulsive need that came and went without warning?

No more talk came from the kitchen. Oral was talking a mile a minute, his voice carrying down the hall from Merritt's room. Other footsteps passed, and I heard Aunt Juanita and Uncle Virgil whisper arguing. Cigarette smoke hung in the air, even with the front door still open and the night air slipping in. I pulled the blanket away from my face. What did Daddy think about what happened? Did he think it was the Murrys or some mistake made by Uncle Virgil and Aunt Juanita? I could see the back side of his chair, a part of his T-shirt. He didn't move and I stared at that spot until I fell asleep.

The next morning, when the sun had yet to come up, I woke up with that strange awareness of others in the house. I threw the blanket off, and went into the bathroom and shut the door. I stepped on the scale, and noticed I'd lost a pound. I got off and stepped back on, to be sure. One pound. Happy about that, I brushed my teeth, and my hair. I pulled some off the bristles and threw the fuzzy clump in the toilet. I brushed some more, without looking in the mirror, and before I went out, I flushed the toilet, watching the strands disappear. I left the bathroom, and went into the kitchen to start a pot of coffee. I was startled by Daddy still sitting on his chair like he'd never left it the night before.

I said, "Didn't you go to bed?"

"For a little while."

"Oh."

I went to the sink and ran water into the coffee-pot. I got coffee out of the cabinet and scooped some into the basket. I turned a burner on, and the entire time I did all this, Daddy didn't say a word. It was like he wasn't really there. With the coffee on, I got out the packet of tea Mrs. Brewer had given me and put a pot of water on the stove to boil.

Daddy said, "What's that?"

I held up the packet. "Tea."

"What kind of tea?"

"Blessed Thistle."

"Let me see it."

"Why?"

"Just let me see it, Jessie. I don't know why you always have to be so contrary."

I handed the packet to him and he looked inside.

"Where'd you get this?"

"Mrs. Brewer, the school nurse."

"Why is she giving you this? You sick?"

"No. I ain't sick."

"What's it for?"

"She said . . . it'll help my stomach."

Daddy dropped the packet on the table and the subject, likely assuming woman issues. The coffee finished percolating and I poured him a cup. The water had boiled too, and I poured some into a mug, and dropped the aluminum steeping ball in. We sat together and he didn't say anything else about the tea.

Before long the others were up and in the kitchen. Aunt Juanita was very different in the morning, hair gone wild, and makeup scrubbed off. She'd found one of my nightgowns, and it hung off her the way a flag hangs down a pole without any wind, all folded upon itself. I tried to recall how it fit me. Not the same, definitely not the same. Oral had on one of Merritt's striped T-shirts and the same pair of dungarees he'd worn yesterday. Both boys sat at the table yawning. Uncle Virgil wore one of Daddy's white T-shirts, his skinny arms ropy with muscle and tan below the sleeves only. I pictured doing laundry till kingdom come. I got up and put pieces of bread on a pan to toast.

"Anybody want eggs?" I asked.

There was an odd dancing of eyes between our "guests."

I made it a statement. "I'll fix eggs too."

Aunt Juanita said, "I want mine fried."

Ignoring that, I cracked several open into a bowl, and began beating them within an inch of Sunday.

Daddy said, "Mr. Naylor over to Lore Mountain Road has a place to rent."

I dumped the eggs into the skillet and swirled the spoon through the pale yellow liquid, waiting to hear how that would be received.

Uncle Virgil said, "I ain't renting again."

Daddy said, "I don't care what all you do; I only mentioned it as an option, if'n you want it."

Uncle Virgil said, "Ain't but one option, in my mind."

Daddy threw his hands up, and went out to the mailbox to get the paper.

Oral, voice innocent as a two-year-old, announced, "Merritt says Uncle Easton's got money buried all over this place."

Aunt Juanita pressed her lips tight, and then did what Uncle Virgil would routinely do. She popped him on the head.

Chapter 13

Just like the Murrys' still, the house fire made front-page news. The *Wilkes Journal-Patriot* said nothing more than the renters had lost everything and more had to be done to determine the reason for the blaze. The fire chief was shown against the backdrop of flames, pointing to the house, stating the only thing they could look for was signs of gasoline and that process would take a while.

Uncle Virgil talked for days after. "Shit, we know who it was; we don't need no official ruling from them. I say we get 'em now."

Of course Daddy gave him more money to keep him from doing something irrational and Uncle Virgil took it, because as he said, it was owed him. I saw how Oral's eyes glittered and he found ways to be near the back door when Daddy went out, like he was trying to figure out where he kept his stockpile. It was apparent Oral had a hankering even stronger than the liquor held on to his daddy.

The last day of school came and final test scores were handed out, creating sighs of relief or groans of disappointment. Yearbooks went hand to hand, everyone busy getting friends to sign the bound dark green leather books adorned with a gold pinecone design. Engraved in gold as well were the words "Piney Tops High School Warriors, 1959-1960." I held mine tight to my chest, the pages without one single signature. I eventually saw Aubrey standing with a bunch of people, including Cora and Stacy, laughing, having herself a grand old time. She saw me hovering at the edge of the crowd, and I started to raise my hand, to wave her over. I hadn't told her about Uncle Virgil's house, proof the Murrys were no good, and dangerous, the sort intent on only causing trouble. She ought to distance herself from Willie, if she knew what was good for her.

Someone said something and she turned away. Everyone took turns placing their books on each other's backs, and scribbling in the sort of notes I surely wouldn't see on my blank pages. Like, "It was great getting to know you in Mrs. Walker's history class, hope to see you this summer!" Or, "Hey, beautiful, here's my number, call me and we'll get together!" At the moment, I had no idea why I'd even bothered to buy one. The longer I watched the joyful interactions, the more uncomfortable I became of how I might look, like a dog begging for scraps. I left, and when I passed by a trash can I tossed the yearbook into it. Why force myself to look through pictures of people who didn't know I existed, and the ones who did acted like they wished they didn't?

I went to my last class and sat waiting for the final bell to ring. The room was empty. Out the windows to my left were my classmates standing or sitting under a perfect blue sky, a buttery sun shining warm on their flawless world. I saw myself in their midst, a mar on their perfection, a weed in their manicured garden. The bell rang and the quiet room filled with noise, laughter, the scuffling of shoes on the slick tiles. One by one, they filed in, filling up seats, and I could smell them, wearing the scent of fresh air, mixed with starched cotton, soap, and sweat. I fingered the edges of my science book, the last one to turn in for the year. I listened to their conversations, occasionally interrupted by a burst of laughter, happiness overflowing. A pair of legs appeared by my side, feet in scuffed oxfords, skirt midway to the calves. I raised my head and encountered the obscure eyes of Darlene Wilson. She popped a wad of bubble gum, made a show of looking under my desk, and then at the science book I fiddled with.

"Yearbook?"

Self-conscious, I hoped no one paid us any mind.

"I tossed it."

Her jaws quit moving for a second.

"Trash?"

I gave one nod.

I couldn't say she smiled, but she appeared to approve.

She said, "Superfluous junk."

She plunked herself on the seat in front of me. I wanted to get up and move away.

She said, "You're like me."

I started to shake my head and stopped.

She said, "No friends. Nope."

Her lips popped on the *p*.

"Aubrey Whitaker's my friend," I argued.

"No, she ain't."

I said, "Well, I don't see you talking to anyone except yourself."

She got up, chomping on her gum faster, and said, "That's what *you* think. There is one bit of difference between us. I know *who* I am."

She sauntered over to sit in her usual spot by the windows, wearing a tiny smile. What did she know? Nothing.

When the final bell rang, I didn't wait like usual for the class to empty before I made my way out. I didn't want Darlene handing out any more of her weird wisdom. I followed the rest of the students into the hot sun, my head turning left and right, hoping to spot Aubrey. Darlene made sure I saw her watching me, that same stupid grin on her face. Exasperated, I moved toward the bus while scanning the parking lot where Willie Murry's car was parked. Just before I got on, I noticed Aubrey with him. She had her head tilted as he talked and I couldn't imagine what he could be saying, but it couldn't have been good, because she looked serious. I kept glancing at her, hoping she'd break away and come find me. She didn't. She got in his car, and I saw he didn't even open or shut the door for her.

I climbed the bus steps, and because I was earlier than usual, there were only a few students already on, and still plenty of empty seats. I chose the one Aubrey and I had always used, feeling a little sad about that. Soon others filed by talking about summertime plans of visiting relatives, swimming in the Yadkin River or at Moravian Falls, of summer picnics. I half-listened as I stared toward the front, but when Willie Murry unexpectedly got on the bus, I bent my head and focused on the rubbery mat that lined the aisle. His Wearmasters came into view and stopped. He eased himself into the seat beside me.

He said, "Give me your yearbook. I got something to write in it."

I kept my arms crossed tight.

I said, "I ain't got it."

He looked under the seat, and then beyond my lap to the small empty space between me and the side of the bus.

He said, "Don't lie. You were carrying one earlier."

I ignored that while I went to cussing in my

185

head. I could hear the whispers starting up behind me.

He said, "Fine. I'll just tell you what I was going to write. Let's see, it would've been something like, 'Watch out. There's more to come.' Yeah. That would've been it."

It was as close to admitting they'd been responsible for our still and Uncle Virgil's house as it could get. I kept my head turned so he couldn't see my fear. The seat rose and I knew he'd left. I leaned my head against the window, understanding I'd made a big mistake.

Uncle Virgil and Aunt Juanita quickly settled into a routine at the house, and soon got to acting like it was theirs. No matter where I went, they were either sprawled in the living room watching TV, sitting in the kitchen waiting on food to be put before them, or taking naps in my room all hours of the day. Daddy got up every morning and went to work, while Uncle Virgil and Aunt Juanita got up about midmorning and expected me to cook them breakfast. Uncle Virgil sat at the kitchen table, rubbing on his belly and yawning, while Aunt Juanita took about an hour in the bathroom doing herself up only to sit around the rest of the day. After her first offer to help cook, she hadn't offered again, other than to make a new pot of coffee sometimes. It didn't seem to bother either of them how it looked and it was easy enough to see why Uncle Virgil couldn't hold him a job. Sometime before noon dinner, he would go out to their car, and come back in with a jar. He'd unscrew the lid and start in on his daily dose of shine.

He smacked his lips and said, "Ain't nothing better than strong coffee followed by a little jumpin' juice."

After he had a little more, he went into the bathroom, shut the door, and then it was him in there for some time, smoking, drinking, shaving. He'd come out smelling like Daddy's Aqua Velva, and by then, the liquor was working on him, and he paced around the house raving about revenge on the Murrys. It would get on toward late afternoon, and it was clear he'd had more than enough as his voice grew louder, and he'd get to acting more ridiculous.

Aunt Juanita went along until he got like that, and then she told him, "Shut up, Virgil, for God's sake! You're giving me a headache!"

She got ahold of one jar once when he made the mistake of setting it down, and dumped it in the sink. He got mad, went outside, and came back with another. He held on to them after that like they would sprout legs and run off. He had to have a stash, jars that should've been sold, but he'd somehow managed to have kept hidden for his own personal enjoyment.

Uncle Virgil hadn't been at the chicken houses

far as I could tell since he'd been here. Aunt Juanita prodded him a time or two about getting on to work, but it was one reason or another as to why he couldn't—or wouldn't—as the days went by. Daddy went down the hall the second week they were there and banged on my bedroom door.

He yelled through it, "Ain't you got to go into work?"

Uncle Virgil hollered back, "I ain't got that job no more!"

Daddy said, "Ain't got the job? What the hell, Virgil."

Uncle Virgil opened the door and said, "I figured we'd do some runs, and you'd pay me. You're always saying how much more money you can make. Hell, what do I need that chicken-shit job for?"

He laughed at his own joke and when Daddy came into the kitchen, his expression was the exact same as when he was mad at me. I didn't need to tell him about Uncle Virgil drinking all day. I was pretty sure he knew. Later on when we sat down to supper, Uncle Virgil propped himself up on his elbows, weaving back and forth. Eventually he was slouched over his plate, slurring words.

Aunt Juanita poked him and said, "Nobody wants to be around you like this. Sit up, act right."

He went to slide his fork through some mashed

potatoes, and the food fell off. He frowned at the fork, perplexed as to where the potatoes went. He dropped it on his plate and started crying, declaring how much he loved her. This didn't set well with her, him blubbering, and trying to hold her hand.

She pushed him away and said, "Sit up, Virgil, for God's sake. Act like a man. And quit bawling. Christamighty."

Oral tossed ugly looks at his daddy while he ate, and for the first time I could recollect, I felt sorry for him and his situation, even though he acted like a little twit most times. Aunt Juanita showed her own ragged edges at Uncle Virgil being underfoot, more sharp edged, and snappish. She stabbed out one cigarette only to light another one. She took little bites of food now and then between long puffs and exasperated exhalations. Uncle Virgil eventually leaned back in his chair with a groan. Before long his head fell forward, chin resting on his chest, and he started snoring. Aunt Juanita looked relieved, while Daddy said a word I was sure I'd only heard out of his mouth once when he banged his knee against the bumper of Sally Sue. He sprang up and grabbed the back of Uncle Virgil's chair and hauled him away from the table. He twisted it to one side and dumped him on the floor. Uncle Virgil came to for a second, saw where he was, then rested his head on his arms and passed out again.

Daddy said, "Oral, Juanita, y'all grab a leg, and I'll get his arms, and let's get him to the bedroom."

They did as he asked, faces flushed with the effort or shame, I couldn't tell which. They struggled under the dead weight, but lugged him down the hall, where a solid thump signaled he'd been deposited onto the floor.

The door slammed, and before they got back to the kitchen, I pointed my finger at Merritt and whispered, "See? Now ain't that a pretty sight? You want to end up like that, you just keep talking about how much you like it. Ain't a damn thing it's good for."

He was silent, and I was satisfied I'd made a point. The rest of them came back and sat down to finish eating. Even though nothing more was said, the mood around the table relaxed. I watched them eat, counted the mouthfuls I took, and hoped the scale would be kind.

The next morning I fried bacon and listened to Daddy talk to Merritt about getting his new arm. Merritt's disposition had improved somewhat, and he was already going on about what he'd be able to do once he got it.

Daddy approved, and said, "You'll be good as new."

Merritt said, "Yeah, I'll be able to go outside and toss the ball, maybe even start back to practice, and play on the team again when I get back to school."

Oral said, "Yeah, once you get it, it'll be like nothing ever happened."

The wound was raw with a red, raised ridge and tender-looking. The flap ends of skin were drawn together above the elbow joint and stitched together. I couldn't picture him trying to cram it into that plastic cup thing in the brochure Daddy brought home one afternoon. They'd gone for a plaster mold, and fitting, and while there was soft material inside, it would seem like anything resting against that delicate spot would hurt. It made me cringe. I kept turning the bacon, the grease popping and hitting me now and then. The smell made my mouth water and I looked over my shoulder to see if anyone was looking. No one paid me any mind, so I snatched a piece and plopped it in my mouth.

I finished frying the rest of the package, and filled a pot with water for grits when Daddy motioned for me to follow him outside. Wary, I set the pot down, turned the burner off, and wiped my hands down the front of my pants. The boys stopped talking as I went out the back door behind him. He walked across the yard and stopped by the truck. He leaned against it and waited until I was within a few feet of him. My back to the house, I inhaled deep the scent of morning, a mixture of dewy grass and wild grapes. He pulled his pack of cigarettes out of his pocket and tapped the filter against the fender before lighting the opposite end. He blew smoke toward the sky and I shifted from one foot to the other, uncertain where this unexpected conversation might go.

He said, "Jessie, can I trust you?"

The question took me by surprise and the taste of the bacon I'd eaten earlier turned rancid. My mind went haywire, thoughts scattering like gunshot. He must've seen me on Main Street that day.

He said, "We got us a bit of a problem."

He was cryptic, and I was too rattled to ask questions. He tossed his cigarette on the ground, and rubbed a hand over his face like he was unsure of what to say.

Finally, he began to talk, but it wasn't what I expected. It wasn't about Main Street, or even about the Boomer still and what he thought about that.

He said, "I really need me somebody to rely on."

He waited for me to respond. I didn't know what he was after, because I already did what he expected, even though he knew I hated it.

I said, "What about Uncle Virgil, and Oral?"

"You've seen your uncle Virgil, and the way it can get with him. Him doing right is hit-or-miss, and lately, I ain't sure I can trust him to do much at all. I got to have someone I can depend on, and it ought to be you."

This was different in that he was saying he needed me. As if that was supposed to make a difference.

He said, "Merritt's arm's gonna cost a pretty penny, and with them all here, and not having a red cent to their name, I'm gonna have to do all I can to get them on their way. I got to have someone dependable, to check them stills regular, not be drunk, and screw something up."

Through the screen door I saw the faint outline of Merritt sitting at the table. Oral had Merritt's baseball and he was tossing it up in the air and catching it. Merritt watched, but turned to look outside at us every now and then, curious. Daddy wanted the best for him, while all he wanted for me was to obey him whether I liked it or not. I understood, but I didn't want to. I brought up a subject I hadn't in a while, giving up on it as something that would never happen. Since he was asking, maybe now was the time to try again.

"Tell me about Mama."

He looked away, staring into the distance, and I began to think he might. When he spoke, his voice was low.

He said, "You know I can't talk about it."

He was holding on to her, but she wasn't only his.

"I have a right to know her too. She ain't for your memory alone."

I didn't bother pleading, or even arguing. It was

193

like being lost, walking endlessly while hoping to find your way only to recognize you're right back where you started.

He repeated the question he'd asked me before: "Jessie, can I trust you?"

I walked toward the house without answering his question and he stayed outside for a while. When he finally came in, he didn't put much food on his plate, and what was there went mostly untouched. Aunt Juanita drifted into the kitchen with Uncle Virgil and they filled their plates, eating and talking like nothing had happened the night before. Meanwhile, Daddy watched me like he needed to hear me promise, or at least know I wouldn't add to his problems. Maybe I could give him the answers he needed if only he could do the same in return.

Chapter 14

By July, it was necessary to find ways to get away from Aunt Juanita and Uncle Virgil's constant bickering, so I actually did volunteer to go to Big Warrior and Blood Creek on my own. It was late one afternoon after Daddy said they needed tending.

He hesitated when I spoke up, then said, "Get your uncle and Oral to help you. There's corn to be hauled in to both."

"No. I'd rather do it on my own."

He went to the sink and rinsed out his coffee cup and gave me a look like I'd spoken in a foreign language. It meant nothing more than I needed to get out of the house, and away from them for a little while.

I was desperate enough I added, "You said you needed someone trustworthy, dependable."

Without a word, he reached into his pocket and gave me the keys. That's where he kept them lately instead of on the hook by the door. I couldn't read his expression, yet I had the feeling I was being tested in some way.

He said, "I took the last run off of both of them yesterday. Everything you need is in the back of the truck. Do Blood Creek first."

I nodded and said, "Okay."

A short while later, I parked near the old poplar, got out, and assessed what was in the truck bed that I had to carry in. I hefted a bag and began to walk. It was an uneventful journey, but tough going as I wound my way around the recent growth of catbrier and Virginia creeper, balancing the weight as best as I could. When I got nearer to the still area, everything was in place. He'd cleaned it out, made it ready. I dumped the corn, and started adding water to the boiler and got the burner going. I headed back, the only noise my footsteps and the running water of the creek. It took several more trips, and by the time I was done, the sun touched the treetops while my heart flickered like a lightbulb about to go out. Despite that, I was still glad I'd come alone. The peacefulness was worth it. If nothing else, I loved being in the woods and, most of all, being alone.

I took a minute to sit and rest, before I added in the cornmeal that had been ground at a mill, special, so it wouldn't create too much heat. I stirred out the lumps, then added in the rye. I had to let that sit for a bit, and while I waited I perched on a small boulder, combed my fingers through my hair, discarding the silky strands that came out. I wondered if it was common to lose so much.

Before long, it was time to separate the mix

into other buckets, so I could add malt. All this was blended back together into the boiler and I sprinkled some remaining malt on top. I sat down again, waiting for cracks in the foaming top to appear. By the time that finally happened, I was limp as a dishrag, and dreaded the long winding walk back to the truck. I finished by adding yeast; then I heaved and pulled on the large square piece of wood to cover everything. I sat on the boulder again, resting and staring at the still, feeling nothing much about what I'd just accomplished, by myself. In about three hours, what I'd done would be fermenting, and in three days, if all went right, it would be ready to distill.

I began walking to the truck, and had to stop several times to catch my breath, leaning against various trees for support, seeing pinpoints of light dancing in front of my eyes. When I got like this, it was a sign I needed to eat, but my ordinary rituals were off because of Uncle Virgil and everyone at the house. Although more food was cooked, they always ate most of it, leaving very little behind. Last thing I could remember eating was the piece of bacon I'd snuck on the sly.

The final time I had to stop I leaned against a big oak, rubbing a hand across my forehead where my hair clung. It was dirty work in the summer, and my clothes were covered with brambles, leaves, and splattered mud from the creek water. I pushed off the trunk when something moved near a tree to my right. I saw a man, one eye covered with a black patch. That same side of his face had an unsightly scar, the skin mottled, and lumpy. His clothes were dirty too and he wore a long-sleeved plaid shirt, even though it was warm, and a leather hat, showing a line of sweat where a piece of rawhide circled the crown. He had a shotgun pointing straight at me. He had to be the landowner.

His voice demanded, "Who're you?"

I stammered, gave him a flimsy answer. "I-I was only taking a walk out here. It's such a nice piece of land."

The one eye narrowed. He spit tobacco juice and wiped his mouth.

"Walk?" he said. "Pretty dirty for just walkin'."

I said, "I fell, took a little tumble."

He said, "Hm. What's yer name?"

"Jessie."

"Jessie what?"

"Jessie Sasser."

He lowered the gun. "Sasser," then moved it so the stock end rested on the toe of his boot.

He repeated my last name, "Sasser," like he'd heard it before, then said, "Well, now."

I wanted to go, but he kept on talking.

He said, "What's back thataway?"

"Nothing."

He stepped closer. "You sure about that?"

I nodded. "Yes, sir."

"No illicit activities?"

"No, no, sir."

"Things is changing; revenuers gonna see to it one way or the other. Guess you could say I'm helping to oversee it."

"You work with them?"

"You might say it that a way."

He looked like he belonged to the Brushies, not the government.

I said, "You know Nash Reardon?"

"I don't talk about who I know or don't."

"Well, I was just out walking, and I'm leaving now."

He said, "I know this area pretty good, and I know it ain't the best place for a casual walk. What you reckon goes on in them woods there?"

I grew more fearful, believing he already knew what was back there.

He cut a new plug of tobacco and said, "Maybe you can help."

He shared what might have been a smile, except the scarring on his face twisted it into that expression of pain.

"Help? How?"

He shoved the new tobacco in his mouth, and brown spittle lined his lips. "You might have some information to share."

I said, "I don't know anything, and if I did, I wouldn't share it."

With that pained smile, he said, "Fine. If you're so inclined one of these days, I'm over there directly," and he pointed to a completely different area I'd never been. "Over yonder is a small shack. An undercover hideout, you could say. You change your mind, well, that's where I'm staked out. About two miles northeast."

I said, "It don't interest me none."

After delivering an assessing glance, he then said, "You can't run in both directions."

He went back the way he'd shown me, and anxious to put distance between me and him, I ran for the truck. Once there I cranked the engine, appreciating how the new battery made it dependable. I headed down the path and out onto the highway just as the sun was giving up its hold on the sky and sinking below the trees. I rolled the window down, eyes on the road ahead and the darkening sky above, thinking about the stranger and the last thing he'd said, like he knew Nash Reardon, maybe even knew me, but I couldn't figure out how. I'd not given my name when I'd told Mr. Reardon about the Murrys. Maybe this man with the eye patch saw me that day, coming out of the building. That was the problem in a small town; nobody missed nothing.

I rounded a few curves, and caught the glow of lights in my rearview, a car right on my bumper. It was as if it had materialized from out of nowhere, like a spirit. It had the low, sleek hood of a runner's car, and my first thought was it belonged to the man in the woods, but I knew it was more likely a Murry if it was anyone. I pressed on the gas, accelerating from thirty-five to forty-five. It was as if I'd made no change in speed at all, as if the car had attached itself with an invisible link. I was immediately taken back to the night we were pushed off the road.

I didn't know how to drive like Daddy, who knew when to go faster or when to let up. He could do a one-eighty in the middle of the road, called a bootleg U-turn. It would get a vehicle pointing in the opposite direction, with a balanced measure of speed and a spin of the steering wheel in seconds flat. I didn't know how to do that, much less how to take the curves when accelerating. I only knew how to drive normal. Not like a bootlegger. My hands gripped the steering wheel, while the rearview showed the car remained close. I could hear the sound of its engine above the wind whistling through my open windows, a deep, rumbling noise like thunder filling the cab. I pushed down on the gas and my speed climbed to fifty. I came up on a curve and had to apply the brakes, and as I slowed down, the car moved into the opposite lane, until it was almost alongside me and took the curve with only a slight squeal of the tires.

The bend in the road straightened out, and I slowed down, my speed barely above twenty, hoping they'd pass me, tired of fooling around. They dropped back instead and I didn't know if I should stop and pull over, only if it was a Murry I surely didn't want to come face-to-face with one of them alone. I began to think about the coincidence of them being on this road just as I was leaving. Like I'd been spied on.

My headlights revealed wrinkled tree trunks, steep drop-offs, and occasionally twin golden orbs belonging to wildlife frozen at the edge of the woods. The driver didn't let up, and before long I came to our road. It was worrisome I'd been followed this far. I turned onto it, and my chest went hollow, emptied of blood when they did too. I came to the sharp curve, and what I'd been expecting happened. The car sped forward, swerved in front of me, but instead of slamming on brakes, they whipped into the drive and roared up the hill to the back of the house. I stared in dismay at the rear lights as they disappeared into the shed.

A slow, growing heat of anger came over me. That was Daddy driving Sally Sue. Fuming, I pulled the truck in behind the house, parked, got out, and slammed the door hard enough the hinges protested. I stalked back and forth in front of the truck's hood, all the while glaring into the night, waiting on him to show up so I could give him a piece of my mind. He came down the hill, footsteps swishing through grass that needed cutting, and materialized from the gloom, lighting a cigarette. Nobody inside had thought to turn on the outside porch light and the night covered us like a black blanket. My eyes adjusted enough to make out his white T-shirt.

Angry, I said, "Why'd you do that?"

"To prove a point."

"What? How you could scare the living daylights out of me?"

He said, "You think that was scary? What if it had been one of the Murrys and they started giving you a hard time, and run you off the road?"

"I'd have stopped the truck before they could do that. Locked my doors. When they got out to mess with me, I'd have hit the gas and got away."

"And you think that would've worked?"

"Yes."

"You pulling a stunt like that wouldn't do nothing but piss them off but good. Let me tell you something. If they'd seen you alone, they'd have made sure you would remember it. They'd have got you, one way or another. What you reckon they would've done then?"

I didn't want to think about that, but I also didn't want to admit he was right.

Daddy said, "You got to learn how to drive and be on the offense, not helpless. You didn't know what you were doing, slowing down, speeding up. That would've only made them think you were playing around. They'd have got you, girl, they'd have got you, and all hell would've broke loose."

He was scaring me, but I didn't let it show.

I insisted on my way of thinking. "I could've gotten away if I needed to. Besides, I could tell I wasn't in danger."

"That was because it was me. Not them. I've seen what they'll do. I've dealt with them sons a bitches a long time. I'd bet money they set fire to your uncle's house, and it's not the only thing they've got a mind to do."

"I would've come straight here."

He said, "You wouldn't have made it. I saw them go by on Highway 18 just after you left. Had you been a little later, you'd have seen'em too. They were out scouting around, looking for trouble. I parked close to where you were, and waited. You got to learn to drive better'n that."

What he was aiming at was me learning to drive like a bootlegger, something Merritt wanted. Far as I was concerned, I had no need for it. He was about to say more when we heard a shuffling noise near the shed where he'd parked Sally Sue. He grabbed my arm and pulled me to the other side of the truck and we ducked behind it. Someone stepped onto the gravel and went across the drive toward the house. Daddy motioned for me to stay put and began to creep toward the shadowy shape of a man. The space between them shrank until Daddy was almost on top of him and the man suddenly spun around, lost his footing, and stumbled.

He put out a hand to steady himself on the back-porch rail, and said, "Shit, I didn't see you there."

It was Uncle Virgil.

Daddy said, "What the hell you doing out here?"

"Thought I heard something."

"Heard something? Like what?"

"Don't know, something up yonder."

"Behind the shed?"

Uncle Virgil cleared his throat. "Damn, I reckon. Somewhere near there."

I had a good idea what he'd been doing.

Daddy waved a hand at me and said, "Let's go on in the house."

Inside the kitchen light was too bright, and there was a pile of dirty dishes in the sink. If I didn't get something to eat, I was going to be in a bad way, but I wanted to wait until everyone went to bed. I could at least drink some of that tea, and I went to the cabinet and got the packet out only to find it was empty. I'd had at least enough for three or four more cups. Aunt Juanita came shuffling in, wearing my housecoat, and another gown. She had on a pair of slippers, new ones I'd never seen before, and she sure hadn't come here with them. Even Daddy stared at her feet.

She yawned, motioned toward the sink, and said, "We done ate supper."

I waved the packet in the air. "Who drank my tea?"

She turned to me. "Oh. Was that yours?"

I wadded the paper up and threw it in the trash.

Daddy said, "Virgil, what was going on outside?"

Uncle Virgil said, "It weren't nothing, I reckon. Just thought I heard something is all."

Daddy said, "Hm."

Uncle Virgil wobbled, put a hand on the table, and said, "What? You think I'm lying?"

Daddy said, "Why didn't you take the shotgun?"

"Hell, I don't know. I just didn't."

"You've always carried one."

Aunt Juanita went and took Uncle Virgil by the arm. "Come on, Virgil. Let's go on to bed."

Daddy said, "You notice anything behind that shed?"

He was thinking what I'd been thinking.

Uncle Virgil pulled his arm from Aunt Juanita's grip.

He said, "Nothing worth my time."

Daddy said, "Good. That's real good."

Uncle Virgil said, "I'm going to bed."

Daddy said, "You need to get out tomorrow and see about getting a job."

Uncle Virgil mumbled, "Shit," before he

stumbled off down the hall, with Aunt Juanita trailing behind, her voice low and angry, questioning. My bedroom door slammed. I went over to the sink and scrutinized the clutter they'd made and left for me to clean up.

Daddy said, "He ain't never had the motivation to do nothing except get a jar and bend his elbow."

I turned on the hot water. I squirted dish soap, and gritted my teeth, my insides feeling so hollow, I was sure air could blow straight through me. I gripped the cabinet edge to hold myself still, fighting a dizzy spell. Daddy didn't notice my distress because I had my back to him.

Daddy said, "I'm taking Merritt down to Charlotte tomorrow. They got that arm of his ready."

Wishing he'd hurry up and go to bed, my voice clipped, I said, "All right."

He said, "You want to go?"

It hit me wrong, partly because he made it sound like a regular outing, like we were going grocery shopping or to get a fountain drink, and partly because I was about to collapse.

I said, "Why in the world would I want to be part of something like that? He's gonna be a cripple the rest of his life all because of you."

Daddy said, "Jessie. Watch your mouth."

"Who cares what I say? It ain't ever mattered before."

"It matters."

"I sure can't see how."

Daddy walked by me and went out the back door and disappeared into the night. The shed light came on and I was certain he'd be out there a while. I didn't care if what I'd said made him mad or offended him. I eyed the refrigerator as I turned off the kitchen light and pulled the door open. My hands trembled. So did my legs. I quickly gathered up what I could hold, sank onto the floor, and pulled the food around me like treasure. The ritual took over. I wasn't thinking anymore. I only attempted to fill the void, working myself into a frenzy, restraint gone, and the rapid mechanical-like movements of hand to mouth became the only things that mattered. I forgot everything except the urge to keep going. I forgot about Daddy being outside, about the fact that Uncle Virgil, Aunt Juanita, Oral, or Merritt could walk in at any moment. I was in my other world, my body demanding more, more, and more. Comfort came, those spontaneous moments when I experienced something akin to euphoria, and I built onto it, layer by layer. Words circled, my mind whispered, *It isn't enough, it isn't enough* . . . until the kitchen light came on, and I was caught.

Chapter 15

Motionless, I sat on the floor, waiting for whoever had turned on the light to speak.

Aunt Juanita said, "What in God's name on earth?"

My hair hung in my face, hiding my shame as I considered the new slippers only two feet from me. *So clean,* I thought, white with pink roses on top, polished toenails peeking out from the opening. I felt her staring down at me, but I didn't look up. Food surrounded me in a little pile. The empty plate, the bowl, smears of jelly on the counter, the milk that had dripped on the floor, it was all there where she could see and know what I was. Pig. My hand was over my mouth, holding in the partially chewed food. My chest rose and fell. Each second was a year. Daddy came back in at that moment and saw me on the floor with Aunt Juanita hovering nearby.

His voice raised, he said, "What's going on now?"

Aunt Juanita said, "Hell if I know. I come in here to get a glass of water, and there she was on the floor, cramming food into her mouth like nobody's business."

Daddy said, "Jessie?"

How would I explain? This would most certainly appear . . . peculiar. I was sure I would choke if I tried to swallow. I put my other hand up, the need to be sick hitting me without warning. I rose to my feet, fought off the bizarre dizziness, and with both hands over my mouth, I left the kitchen. I shut the bathroom door and locked it. I spit out the wad of food into the toilet, and fought down the yearning to get rid of everything I'd had. I could hear them. They were both out there, whispering, making comments I couldn't understand. Daddy knocked on the door.

"Jessie."

All I had to do was convince them it was because of all the work at the still, lugging supplies, the back-and-forth. Tell them anything. Don't let them know. I couldn't let them know. Without thinking, without any plan on what I'd say, I unlocked the door.

"What?"

Daddy jerked his thumb toward the kitchen, then at me. "What're you doing?"

"Nothing."

Aunt Juanita had recovered from her initial shock evidently. "Eating on the floor like a dog is what she was doing."

I raised my chin. "No, I wasn't."

"Sure appears thataway to me."

Daddy said, "Juanita. It ain't helping."

She put her hands up and said, "Fine. I've tried to in the past. Been on the receiving end of that smart mouth of hers. Can't nobody tell her nothing. She knows it all."

She went back to my room and slammed the door. Daddy exhaled, and I chanced a look at him. He had bags under his eyes, new lines in his face. He shoved his hands in his pockets and to my mortification began to try and reason why I'd been doing what I'd been doing.

"Is it . . . you know . . . a, uh, certain time?"

"*No!* I was hungry is all."

I followed him back into the kitchen. My belly protested at being so full and felt distended, like my insides were being pushed out. In the kitchen I hurried to get rid of the evidence. I picked up the wrappers, the scraps, everything off the floor. I wiped the counters clean and washed dishes. Daddy sat at the table smoking a cigarette and paying bills, as if already on to other matters. I wanted to go to bed, but I needed time in the bathroom. I wiped my hands on the dish towel, my pulse rate ticking like a time bomb.

I said, "Good night."

"Jessie."

I stopped, my back to him.

"It ain't natural."

Innocent expression fastened on like a Halloween mask, I faced him and waited.

"Earlier. You, there on the floor like you were."

211

"Everyone's making it out worse than it was."

"It didn't look right; you didn't look right."

"That might have had a lot to do with what you did, riding my bumper and scaring me half to death."

"I told you why I did that. I know how they are; they'll keep on till they're satisfied."

I didn't want to talk about any of this, and I reckon it showed.

Daddy stubbed his cigarette out and said, "Go on to bed, Jessie."

Dismissed, I left the kitchen, went into the bathroom, and shut the door. I ran the tub full of water to help hide the noises I might make. As it filled, I dropped to my knees as if praying, and gripped the toilet. It took nothing to get started, but I left everything.

In a way, I almost didn't care if he heard.

The next morning, Aubrey came tearing up the drive in her mama's car unannounced right after Daddy left with Merritt to go into North Wilkesboro. She knocked on the front door, and soon as I opened it, she pushed her way into the living room. It wasn't yet ten o'clock. Uncle Virgil, Aunt Juanita, and Oral were still in bed, because getting up before dinnertime was not possible for them. Aubrey's hand worked on the tail end of her red shirt, twisting and untwisting it.

She said, "How're you doing?"

It wasn't right how she avoided looking at me directly.

"I'm fine. What're you doing here?"

"Just seeing what you're up to."

I said, "It's early yet. I ain't doing nothing."

She twisted the shirt some more and then stopped.

She said, "I came to tell you something. You best be careful."

I'd been feeling hot, and now I turned cold. "Why?"

She said, "Is your daddy and Merritt here?"

I didn't explain where they were, I only pointed at the front door, and we went outside.

Out on the front porch, she said, "Willie's daddy claims to know how that still of theirs was found."

I had to work at keeping my voice level, uncaring.

I said, "Oh yeah?"

She said, "Yeah. I overheard him tell Royce, 'It was the Sasser girl,' when I was with Willie the other night. He looked right at me when he said it too. He knows we're friends."

My knees went rubbery, bones too, every part of me sinking, folding, collapsing.

She said, "I thought I better come and tell you. It wasn't you, was it? I mean, he acted pretty sure," and then it was like she was studying me,

213

like I was one of those tiny glass slides stuck under the microscope in science class. It was unnerving.

There were plenty of people who might want revenge against the Murrys aside from revenuers wanting to clean up the county. They had enemies up and down these mountains and beyond.

It could've been anyone, and I said as much, and then I said, "He can't prove nothing."

"So you *did* say something?"

Maybe she was fishing on their behalf for information. She'd already shown she couldn't keep what I told her to herself. I remained steadfast to my lie.

"I didn't say nothing."

Voices came from inside the house. Aubrey stared at Uncle Virgil and Aunt Juanita shuffling by on their way into the kitchen, up surprisingly early for them.

She lowered her voice and said, "What're they doing here?"

"Don't you read the paper?"

"Not unless Mama says there's something about a sale."

"Their house burned down. Didn't Willie tell you?"

Aubrey said, "Why would he bring that up?"

I picked at the porch rail where paint was chipping, and said, "Why wouldn't he? He likes to brag."

She said, "You're saying his family had something to do with it?"

"That still of theirs made front-page news, and then the house where my uncle lives burns down, and you don't think there's nothing suspicious about that?"

It was Merritt's argument, and he'd laugh if he could hear me. She shook her head, and her hair caught the sun, glossy as oil. I wondered if Aubrey knew how pretty she was, that she could have her pick of boys in school, yet she was enthralled with the likes of Willie Murry. Such an unlikely pair.

I said, "You don't want to believe it because of Willie, but he pretty much admitted it."

"He did not!"

"He sure did. He got on the bus and asked for my yearbook. Said he would have written: 'Watch out. There's more to come.' "

"That could mean anything."

"It was a threat they're going to do *more,* Aubrey."

"Prove it. Show it to me."

"I ain't got it."

"Then what you're saying is good for nothing, far as I'm concerned."

"Don't be dumb. You know what he meant."

"I don't know nothing."

"Why don't you ask him, see how he acts?"

Aubrey's face grew redder by the second, and

she tossed her hair. I'd seen her do this a million times when she was ticked off.

She said, "I ain't asking him nothing."

"Because you know I'm telling the truth. I can't believe your daddy lets you have a thing to do with the likes of him. They're sorrier than sorry."

Her lips stretched out into a thin straight line.

She said, "You best quit acting so high-and-mighty, Jessie Sasser."

She stomped down the steps and turned back to face me, her voice raised. "Don't forget what you told me. How you wanted to bust up your own family's stills. Willie says you ain't nothing but a traitor, anyway. He said nobody goes against their own."

I hurried down the steps, my voice loud, indignant. "Traitor? You're the one who talks too much, Aubrey Whitaker! Some friend you are! I *knew* you'd told him!"

She rushed to her car and got in. She even rolled the window up while keeping her face averted as if the sight of me repulsed her. This was it for our friendship. The End, like in books. I didn't even care. She cranked the car and was out onto the road faster than a revenuer giving chase. I inhaled leftover exhaust, and felt a headache coming on. I wanted to throw myself on the ground and have a good old-fashioned temper tantrum. Instead, I climbed the steps to the porch, and debated whether to go in or not. From the kitchen came the raised voices of Uncle Virgil and Aunt Juanita already arguing about something. Oral appeared from out of nowhere, mashing his nose against the screen, giving him a strange, piglike appearance.

He said, "Boy, ain't it something?"

"What?"

"How you can hear everything so good, even when you ain't tryin'."

He gave me a calculating look. I pulled the door open, and he stepped backward, grinning.

My voice threatening, I said, "What is it you heard?"

He said, "Her. What all she said."

"You ain't heard nothing."

"Right. Just like she ain't asking Willie Murry nothing."

I advanced on him and his smirk grew.

"Traitor," he whispered.

The raised voices of his parents continued with the persistent drone of a beehive.

I said, "Big deal. You heard a couple things."

"Yeah, well, maybe I won't say nothing, but maybe I will."

The little shit was actually threatening me. He and Merritt had been watching too much *Dragnet*.

He said, "You keep quiet and I'll keep quiet."

Hands on my hips, I said, "Me? About what?"

"That money your daddy's got hid. I been searching around. Found twenty dollars tucked away, and I aim to find more. I think a pot of gold is behind that there shed, directly."

"That's stealing, Oral."

"No, it ain't. Finders keepers."

"It ain't for you to find."

"Your daddy owes my daddy; you heard him."

"You let me catch you snooping around, see what happens."

"What happens is I'll tell'em what you were going to do, like she said, *to your own family.* I'll tell'em you been talking to them agents and it was 'cause of you our house burned up. Hey, and come to think of it, maybe it wasn't them Murrys who messed up the still neither."

He lifted his chin, confident. I couldn't speak I was so mad, and could only stare after him as he sauntered into the kitchen. Uncle Virgil and Aunt Juanita paused at his appearance, and then picked back up on arguing again. I followed to see what he was about. I didn't like him thinking he could manipulate me, agitated at the realization he'd heard it. I poured myself a cup of coffee, slopping some of it on the counter when my hand wouldn't hold steady.

Aunt Juanita touched the pearls, and said, "You'll have to rip them off my neck."

She was really good at making dramatic declarations.

Uncle Virgil said, "I'll buy you more when we get straightened out."

"We ain't never going to get straightened out. Not when you can't keep a job."

"I got started off on the wrong foot; it ain't like I ever had a fair chance to begin with. If I'd had what's owed . . ."

"Jesus! Don't start on that again."

Oral grinned at me, nodding ever so slightly, as if to say, *See?*

Aunt Juanita glared at me and said, "We're outta milk and coffee," and walked out, the bedroom door slamming seconds later.

Uncle Virgil said, "Damn it all. She knows just how to piss me off."

Oral said, "Why don't we just do what you talked about?"

Uncle Virgil went to hit him and Oral ducked, then made the mistake of laughing. Uncle Virgil sprang up, and Oral scooted around the table while Uncle Virgil cussed a blue streak. He reached across and grabbed Oral's arm, and yanked it. Oral howled while Uncle Virgil delivered several smacks, not caring where his hand landed.

He let him go and said, "Boy, when you gonna learn to keep that trap of yourn shut?"

Oral rubbed the spots where Uncle Virgil's hands had landed while giving me a dirty look, like I was the one who'd beat him. Uncle Virgil dropped back onto the chair while Oral glared at the tabletop like he wanted to kill something. Daddy and Merritt had taken the truck, and wouldn't be back till late, but I needed to get out of the house, away from everything and everyone. It wasn't even dinnertime yet and I was tired enough to want to go back to bed.

I said, "Uncle Virgil, can I use your truck to go get the coffee?"

He reached into his pocket, handed his keys to me, and said, "Get me a pack of Luckies too."

I hated having to get the money out of the tin behind the sugar canister with them sitting right there. I washed a glass or two, while waiting on the both of them to become preoccupied. Soon Oral was busy picking his nose and Uncle Virgil had his head on the table like he was about to go to sleep. I dug out a five-dollar bill. There was another five and three ones, and with them two around, I needed to keep up with what was left. I went out the back door wishing I was going somewhere other than Pearson's grocery. As I drove down from Shine Mountain, I imagined going past Wilkesboro, North Wilkesboro, and on to sights unseen. Going someplace where no one knew me, didn't know a thing about me, away from the worry.

At the store I got the coffee, Uncle Virgil's cigarettes, and was about to approach a clerk when I saw Mrs. Brewer holding a jar of mayonnaise only a few feet away. She was dressed different, wearing a pair of men's overalls, shabby and stained, a work shirt, and a big floppy straw hat with a bandanna around her neck. She saw me too, and approached.

She nodded a greeting, and said, "Sasser."

"Hey, Mrs. Brewer."

She gave me the once-over. "You need'n some of that tea."

"You ain't got to keep giving it to me. I'm fine."

"Like hell."

I was sure I looked the same as I had in school, but she thought different.

She said, "My house ain't far. Pay for that and let's go."

She marched to the front of the store, slammed her bread down, and tossed some money to the clerk. Hands on her hips, she glared about while the clerk developed the same clumsiness I did under heavy scrutiny. After Mrs. Brewer got her change, which was all dropped by the nervous clerk, I paid for the coffee and cigarettes. On the latter she gave an evil glare, and I shook my head denying they were mine. She waved me out the door.

She said, "Hm. Follow me."

I obeyed. She lived in a nice small house, old but kept up. It was painted pale green, and had a tin roof gone to rust, a yard full of flowers, and a beautiful braided grapevine off to the right, the vines crawling along the old wooden frame. The root coming out of the ground was as big around as my thigh.

She got out of her old clunker of a car, pointed at her house, and said, "It was my grandmother's. I was borned in this here house."

She had a small, well-laid-out vegetable garden, and there were chickens running loose in the yard. There was a one-eyed cat sitting on the rail of the porch who arched his back in greeting as she went up the steps. Mrs. Brewer stopped and stroked down his spine before motioning me inside.

She pointed at the cat and said, "That's Popeye."

Inside the kitchen were what looked like dried herbs hanging in the corners, and her walls were painted light yellow; the cabinets, white metal. The sink was against a wall and had two legs holding up the front. There was a flowered curtain hiding what was below it. She had an old Philco refrigerator, and on the stove was a dull copper teakettle, and a cast-iron frying pan. The kitchen smelled like sausage, and biscuits. I sniffed again, and my mouth watered. She went to a small wooden box, almost like a miniature dresser. It was situated below a window, and she pulled on one of the handles and slid out a wood tray. She took out some dried-up plants and brought the cluster to a worktable near the sink.

She took down a big knife off a hook and began chopping.

She pointed with the knife and said, "Sit."

I sat at the small kitchen table, troubled, but curious at the same time. "What're you doing?"

"Jes' choppin' this here. It's the plant what makes the tea. Pulled leaves from it the other day. Read the dregs in the bottom of my cup, and they said I'd see you. How you doin'?"

"I'm fine."

"Somethin's done knocked you off-kilter."

I shook my head.

"You ettin'?"

I said, "Yes."

"Naw, you ain't neither. You got to et, chile."

Her voice had gone from being prickly to soft. I watched her while she kept working, and for once admitted a tiny truth.

"I eat too much, then feel sick."

She said, "Start with small meals."

"I shouldn't eat at all. I'm too fat as it is."

Mrs. Brewer set down the knife and said, "Come on with me."

We went into a small bedroom off the kitchen. It was her room, with a peach-colored crocheted bedspread, a dark maple bureau, and one of those mirrors that sets on the floor with legs, same wood as the bureau. She pulled me toward it, and with her hands on my shoulders she set me in front of it.

"Look."

I turned my head away and said, "I know how I look."

She took hold of the sides of my head, and gently turned it back to the mirror. "Look."

I didn't like a mirror. My heart pumped harder, and then trembled. I put my hand there.

She said, "It beatin' funny?"

I dropped my hand and didn't answer.

Her voice was soft when she said, "All I'm saying, child, you ain't fat."

I didn't need confirmation to know what I'd seen before. A mirror doesn't lie.

She said, "Bones. You ain't nothing but bones. I'm telling you the truth."

I raised my eyes to meet hers reflected in the glass. It was apparent she believed what she said, but I couldn't.

Chapter 16

She was an old woman with bad eyes. She was wrong and plainly couldn't see I was bloated as a dead coon on the side of the road. No one could tell me different.

Back in the kitchen, Mrs. Brewer said, "I seen gals thinking they's fat when they ain't. Getting peculiar ideas."

"It ain't what you say," and I pinched the flesh around my middle, jiggled it to prove I had meat on my bones, more than enough.

She shook her head and said, "Any old body can do that."

I let the skin go, unwilling to accept what she said. "You're being nice is all."

She said, "I ain't nice. I'm only wanting you to see straight."

She scraped the freshly chopped tea into a small container.

She said, "Take it. It's enough to last a while. Be sure and drink it every day."

She acted as if it would change me somehow from the inside out. I didn't see the need.

I said, "What does it do?"

"Don't worry none 'bout that. Trust me when I say it's good fer you."

Trust. That little thing everyone wanted or needed. I straightened up, wanting to seem capable, and strong. At sixteen, I could look after myself. I didn't need anyone helping me, and I sure didn't need anyone else telling me what I ought to do. She shook it at me, meaning I should take it. I only did to avoid argument. It was exhausting having to conduct myself a certain way for everyone else's benefit and getting even more difficult to manage my compulsive needs.

"I'll come check on you in a few days. You up on Shine?"

I didn't respond, only thanked her for the tea, and left. I backed out of the driveway and didn't look to see if she'd followed me or stayed in the house. On the way home I brooded over what she said, what she claimed, and what I knew. She denied being nice, but that's all it was, although why she felt the need to help me was a mystery. Back on Shine Mountain, I parked the truck, and picked up the container with the tea, lifted the lid off, and sniffed it. She said it would help, but I couldn't see how.

I heaved a sigh and got out. As I started for the back steps, there was a chopping sound on the hill near the shed. I set everything down, walked close enough to see Oral making good on his word, shovel in hand, digging furiously.

Near him were two holes, overturned patches of soil like a dog had been digging at random. He paused only for a second as I approached, then went back to work.

I said, "Oral, what in tarnation you think you're doing?"

He stopped again, his dark hair stuck up like a porcupine's from a recent haircut.

He said, "What's it look like? I'm doing what I said I was gonna do."

"Stop it, right now."

He grunted, and tossed clods of dirt off to the side. "I ain't stopping."

He jumped on the edge of the shovel, and it went into the ground easy.

"You ain't gonna find nothing."

"I might."

"You think you can dig up his money and he's not going to know?"

"Oh, he ain't gonna know. See, I'm gonna put this all back 'cause I got that nice chunk of grass there I cut out when I got started. I'll just set it on these holes, and nobody will be the wiser. Long as you don't blab, ain't nobody gonna know. I ain't got to learn you again about what all I heard, do I?"

I pictured myself grabbing the shovel and walloping him with it. I left him stabbing the earth and mumbling as I trudged my way down to the house. I picked up the items I'd left on the steps, entered the kitchen, and confronted a completely different and unexpected situation: Aunt Juanita bent over the sink, gripping the faucets, and Uncle Virgil directly behind her, pants around his ankles, red-faced and puffing.

He yelled, "Get the hell out!" while the traumatic look on Aunt Juanita's face had to have matched mine. I dropped everything and smacked my hands over my eyes. Mortified, I rushed back outside, but didn't know where to go, what to do. I jerked the truck door open, slid inside, feeling dumbfounded. I turned the key. The gauge for the gas tank said it was almost empty, so I couldn't go anywhere. I was stuck. I rolled the window down to let some air in, and shut my eyes tight, trying to get that image out of my head. I sat that way for several minutes.

"Hot damn!" came from somewhere up the hill.

Off to my left Oral came running out from around the back of the shed. He had something in his hands, and as he passed the truck he didn't see me watching him. He clung to a jar, holding it like a treasured object.

He went into the house, the back door slamming, yelling, "Looky here!"

If Uncle Virgil and Aunt Juanita weren't done with their hanky-panky, I was prepared to see him come flying out of the door like I had, but he didn't. I got out of the truck, listening. With them, it was always fighting, loud talking, doors slamming. It was too peaceful. I entered the kitchen and no one was in there. Down the hall my door was shut, while Merritt's and Daddy's were open. I crept forward, and when I got to my bedroom I heard muttering.

Uncle Virgil said, "Holy shit, Son."

It was the first time in my life I'd ever heard him call Oral something other than "boy" or "stupid."

Aunt Juanita said, "How much is it?"

Uncle Virgil said, "Well, let's see."

There was the sound of a lid being unscrewed, a rustling noise, and I could picture him rearranging a pile of money like cards, laying them down on the bed one by one, counting it out.

Uncle Virgil finally said, "About two grand."

Aunt Juanita said, "Oh my God. What're we gonna do?"

Uncle Virgil said, "We're gonna let this little mole keep working; that's what we're gonna do. There's more where this come from, and we're gonna get what's due us."

Oral said, "It ain't no telling how much. I been watching him on the sly. It ain't gonna be hard to find more."

Aunt Juanita said, "What about Jessie? Where'd she go?"

Uncle Virgil said, "Good question."

I scurried back down the hall, through the kitchen, and outside. I went straight to Uncle

229

Virgil's truck, opened the door, and made like I was just climbing out. The three of them stared at me through the screen. Did I look innocent enough? Uncle Virgil came out, followed by Aunt Juanita and Oral.

He said, "Girl, you white as a sheet, like you done seen something you shouldn't. You seen something?"

I thought he meant Oral's find until he reached down to grab Aunt Juanita's backside. She lightly pushed on his shoulder, almost playful, smiling. They all wore silly little grins, an irregular occurrence but it appeared the money had tweaked their outlook. Oral's threats kept me silent, only this moment was too much, even for him. For once in his life, his daddy liked something he'd done, and it made him bold.

He said, "She ain't seen nothing, right, Jessie?"

Uncle Virgil gave him an odd look, and said, "Huh?"

Oral believed his daddy was talking about the money.

Oral said, "Nope. Not a thing."

Uncle Virgil's gaze shifted from me to Oral and back again. Oral was like a rooster with the itch to crow first thing in the morning. He was going to have his moment, determined to hold on to it for as long as he could.

He laughed and said, "She's gonna act like she's blind."

Uncle Virgil said, "What in the hell you talking about?"

Oral hesitated. He reminded me of Uncle Virgil, angling for his best opportunity, a way to utilize the moment afforded him to get what he felt was his due.

Oral finally said, "She ain't one of us. She's a traitor is what she is."

Uncle Virgil was getting impatient.

He took a step closer to Oral and pushed him. "What do you mean, boy?"

Oral said, "She won't talk 'cause she's already been talking."

Aunt Juanita said, "To who?" and Uncle Virgil said, "Yeah, to who?"

Oral said, "Some revnooer."

Uncle Virgil half-laughed, half-snorted, and I took advantage of his doubt. This was Oral, after all.

I said, "He only *thinks* he knows something."

Oral said, "I know one thing. She's the reason our house got burned down."

Uncle Virgil gaped in disbelief at me while Aunt Juanita drew herself up, and said, "By God, I sure hope not!"

Oral said, "That's right, and it ain't all neither. She was gonna ruin Uncle Easton's stills. That friend of hers said so. They got in an argument about it."

Uncle Virgil went stone-faced, like when

231

Daddy reminded him he needed to get a job.

He said, "That a fact? Well, shoot fire, maybe your daddy was right about you all along. He didn't believe you that night the truck broke down."

I said, "I was telling the truth."

Uncle Virgil said, "Sure. Sure. How about the rest of it? What about our house, you cause that? Did you go to some revenuer?"

Aunt Juanita said, "I bet she did. She's always acted uppity, like she's better'n everybody."

It felt like ages before Uncle Virgil said, "I tell you what. You ain't gonna say a word because way I see it, your daddy's owed me all along, and even more so now. What's fair's fair. We're gonna get what's ourn, and you're gonna keep quiet about it."

I despised Daddy making shine. It and the money that came from it was fouled, not only because I believed it caused Mama's death, but because it was also the source of every problem we'd ever had. Yet somewhere deep within me, an angry injustice at what they thought they could do, a tiny spark that ignited, began to burn.

I hunkered down in the living room, steering clear of the kitchen where Aunt Juanita and Uncle Virgil parked themselves, speaking so low I couldn't make out what they said, which was bothersome. I missed my room, wished for a haven. I had nowhere to go, so I sat on the couch, with the TV off, staring at the wall or toward the window. Every now and then movement caught my eye, and it would be Oral grinning at me every time he passed by the living room door. It was infuriating. When I heard Daddy's truck, I got up and moved the sheer aside to get a better view, wondering what Merritt's new arm would look like. He got out, sulking, and pale-faced. I'd thought it would resemble a hand, and instead, there was the flash of silver, the shape of a hook.

Merritt stood different, crooked, one shoulder dropped lower in an awkward pose. He bent his body like he wanted to get away from the harness attached to him, not that much different than what you'd put on a mule or a horse. Daddy said something, but Merritt ignored whatever it was and made his way toward the house. They came up the steps, and once inside Merritt wouldn't meet my eyes. I didn't mean to stare, yet I couldn't help it. Here was Merritt, supposedly made whole again with something no better than attaching a board to his body by all appearances.

I said, "Does it hurt?"

He headed for the kitchen without answering me. Daddy and I followed, watching as he sat down at the table, refusing to look at anyone or at the hook. Uncle Virgil, Aunt Juanita, and Oral studied the new contraption with expressions of surprise, like it was some strange device laid on the table for them to examine. Uncle Virgil reached over and took hold of the hook and lifted it. Merritt let him, like he didn't want to associate with it, like it didn't belong to him and he knew not a thing about it.

Oral said, "How you supposed to do anything with that?"

Daddy said, "Oh, it's gonna work good, right, Merritt? No different than your thumb and other four fingers. Doc said it was like a pincher."

Merritt sat stone-faced.

Daddy said, "Here, show'em how it works. Might as well start getting used to it. Doc said the more you practice, the easier it gets."

Merritt used his left hand and turned the hook a certain way, then did a funny shrug of his shoulders to get it to open and close. It made a clacking sound, like knocking two spoons together. He worked on grabbing the edge of the newspaper, lifted his shoulder up and down, per-forming all manner of gyrations to grip it. It was a process. Shrug, click, shrug. After a minute, he pinched the edge of the paper with the hook. As Daddy watched Merritt go through these movements, he'd mimic him, going one way, then the other, like he wanted to do it for him. Aunt Juanita and Uncle Virgil sat slack-mouthed, the same way they did when watching a movie on TV. Merritt flipped the paper over, which I guess was what he'd been attempting to do, and once he'd accomplished that, his eyes trailed around the table, reading expressions.

Oral, confused, said, "But what else can you do?"

Merritt said, "This."

He lifted his right shoulder, and the strap that was wrapped around his left dropped off and hung by his waist. He grabbed it with his left hand, yanked it back over his head, pulled the other part that kept the wooden arm attached to his stump off. He'd removed the arm in much less time than it took him to try and grab the paper. He discarded it on the table like it was a pile of junk he'd found on the side of the road. He got up, and went to his room, and shut the door. Daddy rubbed a hand over his face.

He said, "It's gonna take him some getting used to it. The doctor said it's a matter of practice, just like in baseball."

Oral said, "It's like a pirate's hook."

Uncle Virgil said, "I bet it gonna cost a pretty penny."

Daddy said, "It don't matter. He needs it."

Uncle Virgil said, "Least you got plenty of money, huh."

Daddy had been staring after Merritt, and now he faced Uncle Virgil.

He said, "It always comes to that with you."

Uncle Virgil said, "Well, I got reasons," and

then he leaned over and tickled Aunt Juanita. She let out a ridiculous-sounding giggle.

Daddy said, "So I've heard. Over and over. It's why you need to get out and get you a job."

Oral said, "Or a shovel."

I really had to marvel at how he was so good at opening his mouth, letting crap just fall out of it. He sure lived up to his name. Aunt Juanita gave an imperceptible shake of her head, but Uncle Virgil made some god-awful noise as if he'd let loose a demon, and when he jumped out of his chair, it startled all of us, except Daddy. He sat with his arms folded, observing the chaos as it unfolded. Uncle Virgil whipped his belt off in a split second and grabbed Oral by the arm almost in the same motion. Oral's eyes bulged with alarm and then fear. I believed Uncle Virgil might wrench it clear out of its socket when he jerked him from the chair. He began thwacking Oral with the belt while Oral screamed and begged for mercy.

"Please, Daddy! Shit! Daddy, quit, stooopppp!"

Aunt Juanita pulled on Uncle Virgil's shirt, yelling at him to "stop! Virgil, ain't no need for this!"

Uncle Virgil's arm went up and down like a piston, faster and faster as his anger won out over reason. It wasn't a whipping. This was a beating.

Oral was beside himself with pain, and in

between the screams came, "I'm . . . gonna . . . tell . . . it!"

Uncle Virgil released his arm, and as soon as he was free Oral whipped around and tried to punch him. Uncle Virgil raised his arm, threatening to start again, and Oral bolted out the door. Uncle Virgil flopped into a chair, letting the belt hit the floor.

Daddy said, "Damn. Was that necessary? And what's he talking about a shovel?"

Uncle Virgil kept his wits about him enough to say, "Shit if I know. Maybe he wants me dead."

Chapter 17

Oral didn't come back that night, or the next day. Aunt Juanita and Uncle Virgil were unconcerned as they sat at the table on the second morning, a Sunday, drinking coffee, and yawning. I mean, the gall they had to face Daddy knowing they held on to his money. The sun was up, leaking through cracks in the curtains, offering warmth, and the kitchen could've been cheery but for the inhabitants of this one.

Daddy said, "Reckon we ought to go look for him?"

Uncle Virgil was disinclined to move.

He said, "He can take care of himself."

Aunt Juanita nodded. "He goes camping sometimes. Better check the fridge and make sure he didn't sneak in here last night and get him some weenies to cook over a fire."

Daddy wasn't buying it. "Unlikely he's camping after that ass whupping you gave him. He went out of here like a scalded dog."

Neither one of them reacted, something that stood out to me.

Uncle Virgil said, "He'll show up when he gets good and hungry."

"What if he's in trouble? He could be hurt."

Aunt Juanita nudged Uncle Virgil. "Virgil, you yourself said he can get into more trouble than ten young'uns stuck in a room together. Maybe you ought to go see if you can find him."

Uncle Virgil raised his hands like he was under arrest. "A pain in the ass is what he is."

Aunt Juanita sniffed, and said, "Wonder where he gets that from."

They fell silent. I pulled the oven door open, and retrieved a pan of biscuits, my mind half on the conversation, half on the aroma that filled my nose and caused my stomach to growl. I was drinking that newfangled tea Mrs. Brewer kept plying me with, but to me, it only increased my urge to eat. I pressed the top of a biscuit and wished the kitchen empty. I visualized splitting each one open, laying on butter thick and creamy, spooning fresh peach preserves Daddy brought back from Mrs. Naylor in North Wilkesboro (who always got a jar of his shine for her cough, so she said), and at the same time, the thought was repulsive, sickening even, as the other part of my compulsion resisted.

I was so into my thoughts, I jumped when Aunt Juanita said, "Jessie, you gonna bring'em over here, or stand there petting on'em?"

I took the pan to the table and set it down, then went and leaned against the stove. I sipped on more of the tea and tried not to watch them eat.

My stomach groaned long and loud, and I set the cup down so I could press on it. Merritt came into the kitchen at that moment, his empty shirtsleeve flapping loose, drawing Daddy's attention.

He said, "Son, where's that new arm?"

"It ain't comfortable. It hurts."

"You got to get used to it and it ain't gonna happen if'n you don't wear it."

Merritt sat and lifted a biscuit using his left hand. He did a fairly decent job prying the top off. He ignored what Daddy said, a peculiar thing since he generally hung on to every word. Aunt Juanita and Uncle Virgil filled their plates, but Daddy didn't.

He got up from the table and said, "Big Warrior ought to be ready. What're you doing, Virgil?"

Uncle Virgil took his time spreading butter on his biscuit like he was painting a masterpiece, while still chewing on the previous one. It was obvious he didn't care to lift a finger, not when he had that bundle of Daddy's money hidden away. I detected an argument coming and turned to look out the window only to stare in shock at the figure on the back steps. Oral sat hunched over, the back of his shirt torn. He shook like it was freezing, but I'd already seen the outdoor thermometer and it was in the mid-seventies.

Still watching him, I said, "Y'all, Oral's out here on the back steps."

Chairs scraped the floor; they rushed outside.

I went out, and circled around so I could see Oral's face. He didn't move, even as Uncle Virgil grabbed him by the shoulders. Oral's mouth was bloody.

He said, "Boy, what's done happened to you?"

Aunt Juanita bent down and said, "Oral, honey?"

Oral shrank from Uncle Virgil, and didn't speak.

Uncle Virgil shook him, demanded an answer. "Who done this?"

Daddy said, "I bet I can guess, but let him tell it, if he will."

Oral put a hand up to his mouth, and wiped. His fingers came away with the blood that had caked there.

Aunt Juanita said, "Honey, open your mouth."

Oral turned to her, his face bruised and puffy. He opened his mouth, and revealed he was missing a front tooth, and his lip was split. Uncle Virgil grabbed at Oral's hands and examined his knuckles.

He dropped them like he was disgusted, and said, "You didn't even get in one lick to them sons a bitches who done this to you?"

Oral tucked his hands into his armpits. He had nothing to say, a rarity. Uncle Virgil's face flared as if his insides were boiling, and he clenched and unclenched his hands like he might tear into Oral again. Aunt Juanita intervened and got hold of Oral by the arm.

She said, "Come on with me. We'll go rinse your mouth out with salt water."

Uncle Virgil smacked a fist into his hand, and said, "He ain't got to say it. I know who's responsible, and by God, I ain't putting up with it."

Daddy said, "Hang on now, Virgil."

"What? You think I'm gonna let this go?"

Daddy said, "We got to think about how to handle it, not make things even worse."

Uncle Virgil said, "They done run you off the road and look at what happened to him," and he pointed at Merritt, who hovered nearby, absent-mindedly rubbing his stump. "They ruined a still, burned our house down, and now they done something to my boy here, bad enough he's done been struck dumb."

Aunt Juanita stopped pulling Oral into the house and turned to Uncle Virgil.

She said, "Virgil! He ain't dumb; he's scared!"

Oral was knock-kneed and trembling again; his chest heaved up and down like he might cry. Aunt Juanita glared at Uncle Virgil, while Daddy continued to try and persuade him to his way of thinking.

Daddy said, "You ain't got to list it all out; I know what they done. They want control is what it is, and they're just trying to force us out. Let them agents handle it. That way they'll end up in the penitentiary, and we won't be having to look behind us all the time. Get'em put away and we'll be done with'em."

Uncle Virgil tramped around the yard, kicking at his truck tires, the grass, and anything else he felt needed to feel the bottom of his boot.

Daddy turned to Oral and said, "Oral, was it them?"

Oral's answer was to lift his shirt up. In the middle of his chest was an angry puckered, blistered letter, a crude *M*, like they'd laid a smoking-hot piece of metal against him four separate times to form it. It stood out against the white of his skin, jagged red lines like on a peppermint stick. Air whooshed out of Uncle Virgil like someone had punched him in the gut, his rage building at the sight. Seeing what they'd done took my anger away for how Oral sometimes acted, and softened my attitude toward Uncle Virgil and Aunt Juanita too. Without a word, Uncle Virgil started for his truck, and Daddy followed him. He grabbed Uncle Virgil's shoulder, but Uncle Virgil wrenched it away and kept going.

Daddy stayed on his heels, and said, "Virgil, listen to me now. Don't you go do nothing crazy. Ain't no telling what'll happen if'n you do."

Uncle Virgil stopped and faced Daddy.

He said, "Shit fire, Easton. Look at my boy. A

damn *M* burned onto him, for crissake. Look at Merritt over there, a cripple the rest of his life." His voice dropped low as he walked toward Daddy, and said, "And it ain't all, is it? Is it? What about—"

Daddy started for him like he might hit him. He cut him off: "I'm warning you, Virgil. You don't get to talk about that."

Uncle Virgil tipped his head back and said, "It ain't been forgot about."

"No, it ain't. I think on it every single day."

Uncle Virgil shook his head. "We need to snatch that youngest one of theirs, that little shit Willie, give'em a taste of their own medicine. See how they'd like an *S* burned onto his ass."

Daddy said, "I ain't part of no craziness, Virgil. I ain't. We been doing this all along now, ain't never hurt nobody."

Aunt Juanita said, "Listen to him for once, Virgil, for God's sake. What he's saying makes sense, or somebody's liable to get themselves killed."

Before Uncle Virgil could respond, there came the sound of a vehicle and everyone quit talking when Daddy put a finger up to his mouth. He went toward the corner of the house. He stayed partially hidden behind the camellia as he tipped his head past the leaves to peek at who it was.

A door creaked loud, slammed, and somebody called out, "Hey, anybody here?"

I recognized the voice.

I said, "It's Mrs. Brewer from school."

I went by him and saw Mrs. Brewer beside her old clunker of a car, hand up to her forehead blocking the sun.

She said, "Sasser, you look'n' a mite peaked."

Daddy came behind me, and I said, "She's the school nurse."

Daddy said, "What is it you're wanting?"

Mrs. Brewer narrowed her eyes at him; then she addressed me. "Said I was coming to check on you, here I am."

I said, "Yes'm."

Daddy said, "Check on her for what?"

Mrs. Brewer moved her mouth like she might have a bit of chewing tobacco tucked down in her lip.

She gave him that singular look of hers, and said, "Her well-being is what, case you hadn't noticed."

Daddy shoved his hands in his pockets, like he didn't quite know what to make of that.

He said, "You know anything about burns?"

Mrs. Brewer turned her head slightly and squirted a thin brown stream out of her mouth with the precision of a toad squirting poison, affirming my previous thought she dipped.

She said, " 'Course I do."

He motioned for her to follow, and led her around the back of the house. Uncle Virgil, Aunt

245

Juanita, Oral, and Merritt were right where we'd left them, every one of them wide-eyed like they'd expected to see a Murry come round the corner.

Daddy said to Uncle Virgil, "Let her look at him."

Uncle Virgil nudged Oral, and said, "Show her."

Oral lifted his shirt again, and Mrs. Brewer squatted down and studied the mark left on him.

She stared up at Uncle Virgil and said, "Shoot. He's done been branded. Who does such?"

Uncle Virgil said, "It don't matter about that. What can we put on it?"

"Honey."

Aunt Juanita said, "Honey?"

Mrs. Brewer nodded. "Smear it on, put a light dressing on it, and it'll help keep it from getting infected, reduce scarring."

Aunt Juanita looked relieved, and nodded.

She said, "Okay."

Mrs. Brewer tilted her head at me, and said to Daddy, "I want her to come with me fer a bit."

Daddy studied her, then said, "Why?"

She didn't answer him, and stomped off around the house. I went after her, not waiting for him to tell me I could.

When we got to the front yard, she pointed at her car and said, "Git in."

"Where we going?"

"Just down the road."

Mrs. Brewer drove slow, so slow I thought it might take us all of an hour to get down Shine Mountain. We finally made it, and headed down Boomer Road toward Wilkesboro, except she turned off on another road that put us going back west again. After another ten minutes of nothing but the wind making noise in the car, she eventually turned down another road, paved, but bumpy all the same from where the asphalt was worn out. After we'd gone about a half mile, we came to an old gas station, a flat-roofed building painted white, trimmed in red, and the kind of pumps you didn't see anymore with glass tops that showed the orange-colored fuel inside. She didn't pull up to one; instead, she parked at the side where two pale green doors said: "Women" and "Men."

She got out, leaned down to the open window, and said, "Wait right here."

I said, "Okay," but she was already headed around the building.

I sat in the car, a light breeze ruffling strands of hair, tickling the side of my face. Strangely relaxed, I didn't want to think about what was going on at the house; I just wanted to sit here quiet. After a few minutes, she came back carrying a brown bag, and two sweaty bottles of Coke. She got in and whatever was in the bag smelled really good. She handed me a Coke, and something wrapped in a corn husk. I set the bottle down in the floorboard, and held the strange bundle. She unwrapped hers and revealed something like moist corn bread.

She said, "I want you to eat that one, and I'm going to eat this one."

Why she was giving me food I had no idea.

I shook my head. "I ain't hungry."

She said, "Yer telling me a story."

I set it on the floorboard along with the drink, crossed my arms, and leaned against the door, looking out the window. I felt like I might faint from the scent.

My voice weak, I said, "Why do you give me that tea? It ain't helping whatever you think I need helping with."

She sighed. "It is; you just ain't letting it. Hair's coming out most likely too. Heart's beating odd."

I did look at her then, at those pale blue eyes that said she already knew what I'd been experiencing.

She said, "You need to et, put some meat on them bones. You just don't know how to go about it. Something's messed you up, and it don't matter what it is, but I seen this before, and it can be fixed. Now, here. Pick that up, and try it. It's the best thing you ever gonna have."

She took a bite and showed me what was inside. Beef and cheese coated in a red sauce.

I said, "What is it?"

"Tamale."

I repeated the strange word. "Tamale."

She nodded toward the building and said, "Mr. and Mrs. Hernandez help pick apples, pears, and peaches. Mr. Long runs this here gas station part-time, and he's also got fruit orchards, and when they ain't picking, the Hernandezes help run this place, and they cook these, and sell'em. They're from Mexico."

I said, "I ain't ever had me a tamale before."

I leaned down and got it off the floorboard. I unwrapped the papery husk and nibbled a corner. Sensations overwhelmed, and my stomach felt like it was going up and down. I put my hand up, covered my mouth, fearful I'd get sick.

She said, "Chew it slow. Take your time."

I did as she said, swallowed, sipped on the Coke, tried not to think. She changed the subject.

"What was going on back there? What hap-pened to that boy?"

I'd taken another nibble, but at that question I couldn't help but think about how Uncle Virgil was so hotheaded he was liable to do anything. What if our own house got set on fire? The image of Mama ablaze and running under the trees came to mind, and I lost my appetite altogether. I put the tamale down.

She said, "Never mind. It's more important you et."

I was ashamed of what she'd seen. It meant I'd

have to explain about a lot of other things, but I found myself wanting to tell her, at least a little bit of it.

I said, "You know what Easton does?"

She stopped chewing and said, "Who's Easton?"

My stomach growled while I tried to ignore it. Little black dots came and went, and the imaginary ones were about as bothersome as the real gnats. I kept my hands in my lap so I wouldn't swat at them and seem crazy.

"My daddy. Easton."

She said, "You call him by his given name?"

I shrugged, then nodded.

She said, "Hm. Reckon you got your reasons. He works up there in Wilkesboro, is that right?"

I mumbled, "That and he does . . . other stuff some might question."

She kept eating like she hadn't heard the last part. I picked the tamale back up, and little by little, I nibbled and nibbled some more. She finished hers while I conducted war, battling the craving to eat it in one gulp and then want more. I finally ate all of mine, then stared at the door for "Women." My breath came faster, my eyes watered, and I started swallowing over and over. She saw my distress and started the car.

She said, "That'll go away here in a minute or so. Breathe slow; don't let it get you. You got a monster in you thinks it's the boss. You got to show that it ain't."

She reversed and pulled out of the dirt parking lot while I tried to do as she said. I closed my eyes, my hand clamped on my mouth. The fact Mrs. Brewer was a nurse took away some of my embarrassment at my behavior.

She said, "Sip on that cold drink."

She drove back the way we came, and when we got to the road to go to Wilkesboro I realized we were going to her house after we passed by Pearson's. We went by the federal building, and to my amazement, the man I'd seen in the woods, eye patch unmistakable, came out of the same door I'd gone in, shambling along the sidewalk, and my thinking he was a revenuer was confirmed. He talked to himself and I watched him in the side view mirror until he turned a corner.

We pulled into her drive. By then, my stomach had calmed down some, and the need to get rid of the food I'd eaten had subsided. She got out of the car, and motioned for me to follow her around back. She had nicely cut grass, surrounded by a white painted wood fence. There were birdhouses mounted on posts everywhere and about five or six old gourds hanging like decapitated heads from an old rusted pole, the preferred home for martins. I could hear singing and chirping as the birds fluttered about the tops of pitch pines, chestnut oaks, and sourwoods. A small shed sat in the corner of the lot, one end of the rusted tin roof a bit lower than the other. She'd painted it light green like the house, and had buckets and old clay pots with flowers sitting around it.

She had a padlock on the door, and reached into her coveralls. She retrieved a key, unlocked it, and gave a little shove. Sunlight flooded in on shelves filled with jars holding canned goods. She motioned at me to come in, and shut the door. It went dark for a second until she pulled on an old string and an overhead bulb clicked on. She slid some jars aside to reveal others with a clear liquid that shimmered like diamonds. Others held fruit and were colored pale pink, to red, and to a darker color.

I understood what I was seeing, yet I asked her, "What's in them jars?"

She confirmed what I saw. "Shine and fruit bitters."

I said, "Where you get it from?"

She said, "Shoot, child, I make it my own self."

Chapter 18

Uncle Virgil said Oral had been struck dumb, but after seeing Mrs. Brewer's personal supply of shine, I fit that description.

She said, "Been making it my entire life."

You just never could tell about people. She dusted off a few lids and eventually selected four, held them up to the light, and then handed them to me to carry. She motioned me back outside, slammed the door shut, and locked it again.

She said, "Put'em in there," opening the trunk to her car, and pointing to an old wooden box.

I did as she asked, and she tugged an old quilt over the top, reminding me of Daddy hauling shine to his customers.

She said, "Amos Cox in Traphill gets some, and the Wootens down to Cuddle Creek. They say it ain't nothing better'n a little of that pick-me-up to set them right in no time." She said, "Maybe you ought to take you a sip now and then, get that internal furnace of yern stoked."

I drew up, and said, "Never."

She spit, and while I wasn't willing to participate in a discussion on it, she got to telling me how she had her a little still set back in the woods behind her house, how she liked to go out there and tend to it, like it was a hobby. Mama's image came out of nowhere, like a fiery comet streaking across the sky. Death leaves a stain on you, a dent in your soul. That's how I felt about Mama's presence, like she'd stained my insides, left a dent in my soul. What might Mrs. Brewer think if I told her Mama had been burned alive, and how I was almost 100 percent sure my very own daddy was at fault because he loved making shine a little too much? I wanted to point to Merritt's missing an arm, Uncle Virgil and Aunt Juanita's burnt home, and Oral, with that ugly *M* scorched into the tender white skin of his bony birdlike chest. Our still being ruined was the only good thing that had resulted from any of it, but bad always outweighed good by a far cry. She felt very different about it than me. She saw shine as a simple tonic for certain ailments. She didn't hold to the idea it was nothing but trouble, and caused a mountain of grief. It hadn't cost her like it had us.

She said, "I reckon I need to get you on home so you can quit listening to an old woman's prattling."

She drove just as slow as when we'd started out, occasionally stopping so she could check on areas where she had her some ginseng growing, or "sang" root as she called it. She said she'd dig some up and what she didn't dole out to those in need would be sold in town come fall. By the time we got back to the house it was late afternoon, and I hadn't spoken a word since I'd rejected her idea of me sipping on shine.

As I got out, she said, "Your daddy, I know what he does. A man's got to do what he thinks best to provide for his own. I'll be back in a few days."

Her car rattled down the driveway, and I was left feeling out of sorts about my time with her, about how she seemed to know what I needed, while appearing to condone what Daddy does. The front door was shut, so I went around back noticing how quiet it was, like old times before Uncle Virgil and all them came here. There was no TV blaring, no yelling, no doors slamming. The trucks were gone; no one was here. The phone rang and I hurried inside to answer, only it stopped as soon I reached for the receiver. I scanned the table and the kitchen counter for a note to say where they'd gone. Nothing. I went down the hall to see if Merritt and Oral might be in the bedroom. It was empty. The phone started ringing again.

I hurried down the hall, picked it up, and said, "Hello?"

Silence.

I repeated, "Hello?"

Nothing. I hung up, and a few seconds later, it rang.

I answered, "Hello!"

Crunching noises came through like somebody biting into a bone. I hung up, and when it started again, I believed someone was playing a game. This time when I picked it up, I didn't speak. Heavy breathing, then the sound of someone snickering in the background, confirmed what I'd thought. I slammed the receiver down, and when the ringing started once more, I counted to twenty before I picked it up. Without bothering to listen, I set the receiver down on the counter. Who else could it be but a Murry? The idea one of them was dialing our house line felt like they were right here with me, able to see what I was doing. I wished I was still with Mrs. Brewer, or that someone would come home, even if it was Uncle Virgil and Aunt Juanita.

I walked to the shed while chipmunks raised a fuss, and two crows communicated from the trees as if tracking my progress. I sat on Sally Sue's bumper, and after several minutes passed I went back down to the house, and stared through the door at the receiver lying on its side. I went in and down the hall and, as was habit, ran my fingers over the fingerprints on the wall before stopping at Daddy's bedroom, calling to mind the memory of Mama. It went like this some-times, as if her spirit begged for acknowledgment from me, or maybe it was only me believing I needed to know her, although I couldn't explain that longing any more than I could explain Uncle Virgil's for shine.

I opened Daddy's bedroom door, but didn't go in. I hesitated at the threshold, taking in the double bed covered in an off-white bedspread, the lamps on the nightstands, the water stain visible even from here, the dresser where a handful of change sat in a small porcelain dish, the journal, a pack of cigarettes, and a bottle of aftershave. What wasn't there, had never been, was the ghost of her, some distinguishing fact of who she'd been. I hated when I got in this yearning state, like the hunger I fought against, and the uglier side of it.

I shut the door, and went to my room. Aunt Juanita was real particular about herself, but since they'd been here, I'd learned she was a slob when it came to housekeeping. The room was a mess. The bed wasn't made; the entire area smelled like an old cigarette from the overflowing ashtrays on my dresser and nightstand. Clothes they weren't wearing were tossed all over the place, including the floor. I kicked them out of the way, picked up the ashtrays, and took them to the kitchen, where I dumped them out in the trash can.

Back in the room I pushed the curtains out of the way so I could open the window. Setting in a corner on the windowsill was a tight roll of money, held by a rubber band. I picked it up, rolled off the rubber band, and counted five hundred dollars. Daddy's money, I was sure of it. A vehicle drove around the back of the house and I hoped it was him and Merritt. I made a split-second decision, went back to Daddy's room, slid the drawer open on his nightstand, stuck the money inside, and shut it. Let him find it, and wonder. It might draw his attention to what was happening, and while I didn't like how it was made, I believed I hated stealing even worse.

Back in the kitchen I found out it wasn't Daddy and Merritt, but them. Uncle Virgil instantly changed the atmosphere from calm to turbulent, milling around, too agitated to sit. Aunt Juanita saw the receiver on the counter, and put it back in the cradle.

Uncle Virgil hollered like I was hard of hearing, "Where's your daddy at?"

He waved a pint jar in the air, half-gone, lending reason as to why he was yelling.

"I don't know. I just got home."

Uncle Virgil went back to his pacing and ranting, while Oral was extra-quiet, watching his daddy surreptitiously. Uncle Virgil spun around, and handed him the jar.

He said, "Have you some of this. It'll put hair on your chest. Let's hope it does and covers that shit up."

Oral gave his daddy the sort of look intended to send him to an early grave but took the jar. He tipped it up and the tendons in his scrawny neck rippled as he took a swallow, then another, and another. Uncle Virgil tried to snatch the jar from his hand, but he ducked out of his way. It was like watching TV with them around. I sat down at the kitchen table, my chin propped on my hand, to see how this was going to play out.

Aunt Juanita said, "Shut up, Virgil. It ain't his fault. And you better hope the same don't happen to you after what you done today."

Uncle Virgil said, "Like hell it ain't. If he hadn't run off, it wouldn't have happened. It's all right, though. I done took care of it."

Oral drained the jar and slammed it on the tabletop, wiping the back of his hand across his mouth.

Uncle Virgil gazed at it with a sad expression and said, "Shit if he ain't done drank it all."

Oral, mouth twisted, eyes bright and shiny, worked his mouth over words he wasn't brave enough to say, even with all that liquor in him.

Aunt Juanita said, "You're a fool, sometimes, Virgil. You could've waited like Easton said, waited until the time was right."

"Hell, he ain't never gonna do a damn thing nohow. You'd think after what happened to him years ago, he'd be the first one to want to give'em what's long overdue."

Oral, emboldened by shine, said, "I'll shoot'em next time I see one of'em."

Aunt Juanita reached over and grabbed his arm.

She shook it and said, "It's bad enough your daddy's acting like a fool; you don't need to start too."

She let go of him, and Oral, wearing a devil-may-care grin, revealed the gap where his tooth had been knocked out, like that oddball character on the cover of the *MAD* magazine I'd seen in town.

Aunt Juanita said, "If anything else happens, Virgil, I'm going to Mama's. I ain't sitting around here worried sick over what they might do next. One more instance and I'm leaving, and I might not come back."

Uncle Virgil looked like a puppy that's been kicked. "Aw now, honey pie . . ."

"Don't 'honey pie' me! I mean it, Virgil, dammit!"

It was a wonder she hadn't left already, but there was money involved, and Aunt Juanita was inclined to stick around if for no other reason than her share of the benefits. I was wary of what Uncle Virgil meant.

I spoke up, and said, "What do you mean, you took care of it?"

It was like he'd forgot I was there. He flinched in surprise and turned toward me.

"Huh?"

"What you said a minute ago, said you took care of it. What did you mean?"

Uncle Virgil turned walleyed as he tried to

focus on something solid. The sharp scent of shine came off him like he'd bathed in it, and he swayed like he was on a ship.

He scratched at his head, and repeated what he'd said. "Huh?"

Aunt Juanita said, "Oh, for crissakes, Virgil, how much have you had?"

He whirled around, stumbled a bit, and said, "I'd a had more if little dipshit here hadn't drank the rest of it!"

Oral whined, "You told me to!"

Uncle Virgil was never going to recollect what he'd said. The moment was lost in his pickled brain forever. Daddy's truck pulled up and Uncle Virgil weaved his way over to the back screen door.

He said, "Hey ho, there's the king of the castle. Let's see what all he thinks about it."

Aunt Juanita said, "Virgil, you don't need his approval for nothing you've done. You're a grown man. You acted out of necessity. You're only pro-tecting what's yours, and that's your family."

Uncle Virgil stopped in his tracks.

He turned to her as if it was only dawning on him he had a reason. "Yeah, that's right."

Aunt Juanita shook her head in despair. He went outside, fingers hooked in his belt, standing wide-legged like he'd been on a horse. Uncle Virgil's confidence was riding moonshine high. Daddy and Merritt got out of the truck, their faces sweating like they'd been climbing a few hillsides.

They came in and Daddy sounded tired when he said, "We couldn't find anything. They got them other stills hid good."

Uncle Virgil said, "It ain't necessary nohow."

Daddy said, "What do you mean it ain't necessary?"

"I done took care of things."

Daddy, in a low voice, said, "How?"

"I went to see them agents myself. Told'em everything they needed to know."

Daddy said, "What is it you know? You don't know shit. Wait, you went talking to them smelling like you done been soaked in alkihol?"

"Hell, we can't be waiting on you, that's for damn sure."

Aunt Juanita said, "That's right or maybe we'd still have some place to live."

The phone rang.

I said, "Somebody's been calling here."

They talked over me and the ringing.

Daddy said, "I wished you hadn't done that."

Uncle Virgil said, "Why the hell not?"

The phone jangled again, and Aunt Juanita flapped her hands at me in an aggravated manner. "Ain't you gonna answer it?"

I said, "Why? It's been ringing on and off since I got here. Nobody says nothing when I pick it up."

She marched over, snatched the receiver off the cradle, and yelled into the mouthpiece, "What?"

She listened, head bent, and after a few seconds she said, "Don't you dare be saying that!"

She dropped it and it hit the counter, fell over the edge, and dangled in midair. Daddy and Uncle Virgil quit arguing. Merritt came over and sat at the table with me, while Oral had put his head down onto his folded arms. He'd turned a little green, but his mama's reaction got his attention. He straightened up in order to see what was going on.

She whirled around and said to Uncle Virgil, "Some man" —and she pointed at the phone like it was the person she meant— "he said things to me, nasty things."

Uncle Virgil grabbed her arm. "What do you mean, 'nasty things'?"

Aunt Juanita pulled away, and shook her head. "I can't repeat what he said. It was vile. He told me he'd best not catch me alone, if that gives you any idea."

Uncle Virgil's entire body puffed up like he'd taken in a bunch of air and couldn't let it out.

He grabbed the phone up and screamed into it, "I'll kill you!" and slammed it down.

His face was splotchy and he pointed at Daddy.

He said, "Getting them penitentiaried is too good for'em. Ever since Elk Creek, hell, even

before then, they been acting the fool. Don't
know when to quit, never have." Uncle Virgil's
gaze drifted over to me. "It ain't helped matters
none when somebody round here thinks they're
smarter than everyone else. Thinks they know
more than the adults."

I rose taller in my chair as Oral turned a nasty
grin on me.

I said to no one in particular, "Some funny
stuff's going on up the hill there," wiping that
irksome smile off his face.

Aunt Juanita made a hissing sound and looked
as if she could've knocked me into next week.
They hadn't considered I could turn the tables.

Daddy said, "What in the hell you talking
about, Virgil?"

Uncle Virgil hesitated while Aunt Juanita and I
had a stare down with one another. I didn't blink,
and I was ready to tell Daddy about them taking
money, ready to deal with the consequences of
what happened if I had to. Aunt Juanita broke eye
contact with me and waved a hand at him.

She said, "Oh, hell, he's drunk is all. He's
running his mouth, crap coming out of it like a
broken sewer line. Ain't it right, Virgil?"

She said his name low, and hard. Uncle Virgil
rubbed his cheeks, then tugged on the end of his
chin. He was at the back door, and I saw how he
wished he could walk out, go on down the road,
leave all this behind.

She said it again, a higher note tacked on the end, a warning. "Virgil?"

The money situation had ahold of him bad as Aunt Juanita.

He put both hands up and said, "You know what? I don't reckon I'm drunk enough just yet."

He went out and opened his truck door. I could see him from where I sat, unscrewing the lid off another jar he pulled out from under his front seat. Daddy exhaled and turned to me and I braced myself for his questions.

He said, "Where did you and that Brewer woman get off to?"

Relieved, I said, "Down to some gas station where we ate tamales."

Merritt said, "What's a tamale?"

I said, "It's this cornmeal-wrapped thing, shaped like a tube, with ground meat in it, some kind of sauce too."

Merritt licked his lips as if he could taste it, and I was about to tell him how good it was except Oral made a horrible retching noise.

Aunt Juanita yelled, "Oral, dammit, don't you dare puke in here! Get in that bathroom!"

He got up, took one step toward the door, lost what he drank and then some right there on the floor.

Aunt Juanita wrung her hands. "Dammit, what a mess!"

Oral darted down the hall, hand over his mouth,

while Daddy motioned at me. With dread, I stood.

He said, "Come on with me."

Merritt, giving a disgusted look at what Oral threw up, said, "Can I go too?"

Daddy shook his head. "Not this time. Help your aunt clean that up best as you can."

Merritt slumped, turned a surly eye on Daddy, while I was sure this was it. The moment of reckoning, the moment when Daddy would say he needed to get to the bottom of all that was happening.

I said, "What is it?"

He went outside without answering, and I dragged my feet as he led the way up the hill. We passed by Uncle Virgil stretched out under a pine tree, head against the trunk, the jar of moonshine resting on his belly. It wasn't until he saw where we were going that he struggled to sit up.

Daddy stopped for a second, and said, "Your boy's done got sick in there. Might want to go see about it. You ought not let him drink."

We came close to the shed, and I waited for him to show me the peculiar areas. Instead, he tossed me the keys to Sally Sue.

He went to the passenger door to get in, and said, "You drive."

Flabbergasted, I said, "What? Why?"

"Just do as I say."

I tossed the keys onto the seat on his side, and said, "No."

He picked them up, and said, "What is wrong with you, Jessie?"

"Nothing, except I ain't wanting to drive this car."

"Why not?"

I didn't answer.

He said, "Why you got to be so stubborn about everything? Why can't you do as I ask for once without being hard to get along with? It ain't no better time than now for you to learn, considering."

"I got my reasons."

"You don't know everything there is to know."

"Maybe that's because you won't tell me."

"Fine. You want me to tell you about your mama, then get in the car."

His sudden agreement stunned me. This time when he tossed the keys back to me, I caught them. I wondered if he'd seen my hands shaking and, if he had, could he guess why. This time, it had nothing to do with my eating habits, but pure excitement and fear, one equivalent to the other, wondering what he'd say. I got in the driver's seat. I didn't know where we were going, and it didn't matter. He was going to tell me about my mama, and that was all I cared about.

Chapter 19

I'd always known Sally Sue was a beast of a car. Riding in her was one thing, but behind the wheel the power beneath the hood became evident. We bumped down the drive until we were out on the road, where I lapsed into driving like Mrs. Brewer, intimidated by the vehicle. The usual puny beating of my heart, generally reminiscent of a finger lightly tapping, changed to something more like a big fist pounding against the wall of my chest. My stomach galloped along too, both dueling for my attention.

Daddy, oblivious of the internal commotion caused by his words, said, "You'll get used to the feel of her quick enough. Head on over to Lore Mountain Road."

I gripped the steering wheel tight, and ran my tongue across dried lips. I was only going about twenty-five miles per hour, but Daddy said nothing. After a few miles, I gave it more gas, and you'd have thought I'd mashed it to the floorboard as the car surged forward.

Out of nowhere, he said, "Your mama drove this car."

He spoke like we were in an ordinary conversation, like he'd been talking about her every day, while I tried to grapple with that small tidbit of knowledge.

"She did?"

He stared straight ahead, his voice quiet. "She drove it better'n me."

"What do you mean?"

"She ran our liquor. Got so good couldn't hardly nobody in Wilkes County beat her when it come to hauling. Not any revenuer, and definitely not a Murry."

I'd been so intent on what he said, I'd unwittingly pressed on the gas more, and my speed rose to fifty. I let off some, while I digested she'd sat right where I was, Daddy maybe riding shotgun alongside her. I tried to imagine it, and couldn't. But I didn't want to hear she was a part of what I'd turned against out of respect for her. I didn't want to hear she'd done the very thing I'd decided was evil and caused most of our problems, what I'd fought against, at least to the best of my ability. It rubbed me all kinds of wrong, and my anger soared with this new information. I was in denial.

I said, "I don't believe you."

"It don't surprise me none. It's why I ain't ever told you, but I've always wondered would you hate it as much if you knew your mama not only hauled liquor, she made it too."

The sun slid behind the line of trees along the

road and the evening air grew cooler, but what he'd said disturbed me to the point I went hot all at once, and had to swipe my forehead. Silence filled the inside of the car, neither one of us willing to speak anymore. While I didn't want to believe it, given the bits and pieces of memory I had, and the few that had slipped through on occasion, maybe it was true.

Down the mountain we went, and when we came to Lore Mountain Road, Daddy said, "Turn here."

I did as he asked, still silent, still stewing.

He said, "What's your speed?"

Without waiting for me to answer, he leaned over to check the speedometer.

"Get her up to forty at least."

I pressed the accelerator and the car responded, a forward sensation that reminded me of riding waves at the ocean. We'd only ever been once, sometime after Mama died. Daddy woke me early one morning, told me to get in the car, put Merritt beside me on the front seat, along with a pile of blankets, and then drove for hours. I slept off and on, and when I woke in the early afternoon, we were in this strange place with no trees, only tall golden grasses that waved in the breeze on a light brown sandy hill.

Daddy parked the car on the side of the road, and we walked down a rough wooden walkway, across another small sandy rise to face an endless expanse of blue-green water, with an edge of white foam that came toward us, then retreated. There was a different smell to the air. Instead of fertile, pungent soil, and comfortable dry breezes scented with the pine, cedar, and wildflowers I was accustomed to, there was a different sultry odor, one that was seaweed-scented, briny with an overlying fishy odor carried on warm, moist wind. I could hear a flock of birds overhead, calling to one another in a high-pitched cry, all of them white with varying colors of gray and black on their wings. They swooped and sometimes rode the wind, suspended against a blue sky before settling on the strip of sand.

Daddy waved an arm at the water, and said, "It's the Atlantic Ocean. Wanna swim in it?"

I shook my head yes, and we'd spent the rest of the day doing just that, him tossing Merritt up and down in the waves, and showing me how to ride them. Although we'd never been back, I never forgot the sensation of being weightless as the swells of water came and went. We left once the sun rested on the edge of the water, turning the sea orange as if a fire burned just beneath the surface. It was a real good memory.

I came to a bend in the road and automatically slowed down, but Daddy said, "You're paying too much attention to the curve right in front of you. Look beyond the hood; let your brain and

271

reflexes tell you how to go in and out of those turns."

I tried what he said on the next curve. The car responded and the tires didn't even squeal. My fear of having a wreck dwindled as I maneuvered the next one, and the next, smoother each time. He didn't say anything more about Mama, and I was too intent on driving, making sure I didn't make a mistake while realizing after all this time the one thing he thought to tell me first was how she'd made and hauled liquor. What I had wanted him to say I didn't know, but it wasn't that. Maybe he could've told me how they met. Maybe he could've told me how much she loved me and Merritt. There was a lot he could've said, anything other than what he'd chosen.

At the end of Lore Mountain Road it came to a T, and he said, "Turn around and let's go back. It's getting on dark."

I found a wide enough area on the side to do a three-point turn without too much problem, and went back the way we came.

We were almost back at the house when I finally said, "Why would she want to do that, of all things?"

"She did it all her life. Her family, they had their reasons."

"I sure can't see no good reason."

I'd made my own sacrifices is the way I saw it. I'd done what I was told even though I hated it. I'd fought against it at every opportunity, yet here I was finding out she'd been as involved in shine making as much as him.

He said, "Like I said, you don't know all there is to know."

He was quiet after that, and a few minutes later I pulled into the drive, and drove up the hill to the shed.

I put the car in Park, and when I pulled on the door handle, he said, "Wait."

He shifted on the seat and reached into his back pocket for his wallet. Tucked behind his license he took out what I thought was only a creased piece of paper, and instead it was a black-and-white photograph. He held it out to me. The damage from carrying it the way he had for years and years made it difficult to make out the woman's features clearly. With the interior light on, I brought it closer to my face in order to study it.

She'd paused in a pocket of light, captured by a heavenly sunbeam. She leaned against a car, the very car we sat in, newer, but one and the same. She held a cigarette in an elegant manner, one hand gripping an elbow, the other by her face, fingertips hovering near a high cheekbone. Her light-colored hair caught by a breeze had lifted about her face to frame it, and she smiled big at whoever took the picture. By her feet were clay jugs. Lots and lots of clay jugs. She had a booted foot propped on one with a look I could only describe as pride.

He said, "That there's your mama. I took that picture right before she was set to haul that big load down to Charlotte."

I locked in on the image, searching for some expression caught in that millisecond in time that would tell me who she'd been, what she thought, where life had marked her. He got out, then bent down to speak through the passenger window.

He said, "She really was the best of the best. I loved her."

I stared at the picture, dumbfounded by him sharing it, and telling me he'd loved her. I'd never understood his silence about her. Behind him hung a honey-colored moon balanced on the dark points of the treetops as if tacked in place. The more he said, the more trapped I felt by the differences between me and her. When I didn't respond he offered something that didn't have to do with moonshining.

His voice dropped into a lower tone, and he said, "Your mama? She didn't have a mean bone in her body. She never raised her voice or had a cross word for nobody. She had friends up and down this mountain and beyond. She thought before she spoke, and it earned her a lot of respect. Even that son of a bitch, Leland Murry, respected her. He showed it once, after she died."

What did he do? Tip his hat at the car carrying

her casket? It didn't matter. What mattered was everything else Daddy said, and how it was like he'd used her as a weapon against me, pointing out her disposition and how she navigated her world different from me.

How she was what I wasn't.

I said, "Why are you telling me now? After all this time? After all them times I asked?"

He hesitated; then he said, "It ain't easy for me talking about her, for one. And second, I seen something happening to you. I realize you ain't had nobody to talk to all these years. Daughters need their mamas. I've always been too busy to worry it was anything more than you being how you been all your born years, but I'm thinking maybe it's more than that."

"How I've been?"

"Tetchy, funny about eating, moody most days, never smile, strange habits going on, and such."

I compared her image to my school and driver's license photos. Mama's eyes twinkled, whereas mine appeared dull; she looked happy, and I generally looked pissed off. Uncle Virgil had rightly given me the name sourpuss, if I wanted to be truthful. What I learned so far about her made me defensive and grumpy, and now Daddy was thinking too much about my quirks and behaviors. I wanted him to get mad, wanted his attention directed away from why I was the way I was. I didn't want him trying to figure me out.

I said, "I bet she wouldn't have tried to outrun them like you did that night. She wouldn't have had to prove nothing."

That did it. He started to walk away; then he stopped.

He faced me and said, "There's a lot you don't know, Jessie."

I said, "Well, you're sure right about that."

He didn't respond. He strode down the hill, and stopped briefly by Uncle Virgil again, who made no move at all to indicate he knew Daddy was there. Daddy shook his head and went inside. The moon had been released by the treetops and was well on its way toward the crest of Shine Mountain. I considered what he'd said about Mama, yet I had trouble with his vision of this mild-mannered woman who appeared easygoing, content, and filled with happiness. All I had was that one image of her running as fire embraced her upper half. Her falling and how she'd called out Daddy's name. The way I'd imagined her didn't match with what Daddy said, or with the person in the photo. After a while I walked down the hill kicking at the ground here and there.

When I got close to Uncle Virgil, he startled me when he said, "There's a reason he won't talk about it."

I stopped. "Because he's guilty, that's why."

"That ain't it."

The aroma of shine came off him strong like

and the fact he could talk at all was miraculous.

"Then why?" I challenged him. "I remember some of it, you know. She was near a still. She got burned alive. Don't you think I ought to know the truth?"

His eyes glittered in the dark, and he took a good healthy swig again before he replied.

His answer was my second astonishing revelation of the day: "Yeah."

I moved a step closer and he shook his head, waved an arm to stop me.

"I done told you long time ago, it's 'tween you and your daddy. He'll get round to it one of these days. Maybe. Don't count on it. Can't count on nothing from nobody. That's the most important thing I can tell you."

I left him mumbling to himself. Trudging downhill, I thought about Mama being a moonshiner and a bootlegger. It made my gut burn, and my head hurt. I rubbed at my scalp, and when I brought my hand down, it was like I'd run it through a cobweb. I wiggled my fingers, releasing strands to the wind. I reached up and finger combed my hair, and more came out. I didn't know why this was happening, but I clapped my hands to get rid of the hair before I went inside and found Merritt and Aunt Juanita eating. She'd managed to fry ham, and boil some potatoes with butter. Oral was sitting at the table, but eyed the ham and potatoes with a sickly expression.

She pointed to the pot and pan on the stove and said, "There's some left. You're looking right puny; better eat."

I got a plate, plucked a piece of ham out of the frying pan, scooped potatoes out of the pot, and sat down. I tried to catch Merritt's eye. He was using his left hand to eat, and I had all good ideas he wasn't ever going to want to use the hook arm. Aunt Juanita pushed her plate away, and lit up a cigarette.

She blew a stream of smoke toward the ceiling, then said, "Where'd you and your daddy get off to?"

"Just riding."

She leaned forward, about to say something more when Daddy came into the kitchen from his room. His frown was so deep his brows met, giving him a hawklike appearance. He waved a handful of money in the air, looking at each of us.

"Anybody want to tell me where this five hundred bucks come from?"

Aunt Juanita shoved her chair back, and took her plate to the sink.

She tossed out a nonchalant, "How should I know?"

He said, "I found this money in my night table. Somebody knows how it got there."

He looked at Oral first, then Aunt Juanita's back.

She said, "I don't know why you're so upset. You found money. So what?"

She came back to the table and snatched my plate away before I'd eaten one bite. As if I cared. I fiddled with my fork, absently drawing circles on the table.

Daddy was like a hound in pursuit. "Well, I sure as hell didn't put it there."

Uncle Virgil reeled into the house at that moment. "What's all the commotion? Could hear you all the way up the hill there."

Daddy held up the cash so he could see it.

Aunt Juanita said, "It ain't got nothing to do with us, right, Virgil?"

Daddy said, "You know anything about this in my nightstand?"

Uncle Virgil reared his head back, and scratched his chest, ogling the money.

He said, "How much is it?"

Aunt Juanita had gone back to scrubbing the hell out of a plate. Nobody said a word.

Daddy, his voice filled with suspicion, said, "Sure is some strange things happening around here."

I piped up, "I'll say."

Chapter 20

First chance I had, I went to show Merritt Mama's picture. I waited until Oral disappeared into the bathroom again, still suffering the aftereffects of what he'd drank.

At Merritt's door, I was cautious. "You busy?"

He fiddled with the hook on the prosthesis, sulking. His body still slanted in that new manner to offset his missing limb, and all of this said he was too aware of his life gone off course. He kept opening and closing the hook with his left hand, while turning it vertical, then back to horizontal. I took his silence as permission.

I said, "I got something to show you; it's—"

He interrupted me and said, "This thing"—and he nodded down at the prosthesis—"it's supposed to work by me adjusting it, then pulling on this here strap thing, and making this move with my shoulder, but when I put it on, I can't ever get it to do right."

I said, "You ought to practice."

He said, "Easy for you to say."

I thumbed the edge of the photo and he said, "What's that?"

"What I came to show you."

I held it out. He set the prosthesis down and took the photo with his left hand. He studied the picture, frowning down at the image.

He said, "Who's this?"

Chills raced up and down my back as I spoke. "Our mama, Merritt. It's her."

At that, he brought the picture up again, even closer, his brow knitted.

Another minute went by before he said, "Dang. She was right pretty, wa'n't she?"

I said, "Yeah, I think so."

He nodded, and said, "You look like her some."

My mouth dropped. "What? How?"

He studied me, then the picture, as if deciding on what he saw.

He said, "Shape of her eyes, her mouth maybe. I don't know. I just see some of her in you."

I reached for it, searching for the likenesses he'd pointed out.

I shook my head. "I don't know."

He said, "People all the time are saying I resemble Daddy, but I ain't ever been able to see it when I look in the mirror."

I said, "You ain't gonna believe this. She made shine and hauled it too."

"She did?"

"That's what's in them jugs around her feet. Daddy said she was about to haul it down to Charlotte."

"Wow, that's cool!"

"No, it ain't, Merritt."

"Like hell. Who else's mama did such?"

I replied, "Exactly."

Merritt's voice turned hard. "Ain't a damn thing wrong with it."

"Except it killed her."

"You don't know that for sure."

I didn't feel like fighting over it, so when Oral entered the room I didn't pursue it. His color was so washed out, his freckles were like tiny splats of brown dirt on his face. He collapsed on his back on the bed. I was always mixed up about him. On the one hand I felt a bit sorry for him, while I also felt he got what he deserved. He'd taken his T-shirt off, and the *M* on his chest was raised up, blistered, and raw. Honey glistened in spots, making the wound look slick. He lifted his head and stared at the letter stamped on him.

When he kept on, I said, "What're you doing?"

He said, "Watching to see if any hair's growed on my chest yet."

"It's just a saying, Oral."

Disappointment fell over his features, and he let his head drop back onto the bed.

He said, "Oh."

He took so many things in a literal sense, it was a wonder he'd ever passed his grades in school.

He sat up and noticed what I held. "Who's in the picture? Is it a nekkid lady?"

I said, "No! It's our mama, your aunt Lydia."

"Lemme see it."

I hesitated, but then handed it to him. It bothered me, her picture in his hands. He might do something just out of spite.

He said, "Is that shine in them jugs all around her feet?"

Merritt said, "It sure ain't sweet tea."

Oral popped his jaw in an annoying manner while he ogled the picture.

After a minute, I said, "Give it back."

He acted like he didn't hear me. I moved closer, my hand out, but he turned away, and positioned his fingers at the top, like he'd rip it in half.

My breath caught. "Oral."

Merritt said, "Hey, give it back; it's the only one we got."

Oral paid him no mind.

He said, "It's gonna cost you."

I narrowed my eyes at him. "I'm warning you. Give it back."

He smirked. "Five hundred dollars, it's yours."

"You're such a little shit."

"Maybe, but I'm a smart little shit."

Merritt caught Oral off guard when he walloped his arm with his prosthetic, hard enough to make him drop the photo. The picture fluttered to the floor and I grabbed it.

Oral exclaimed, "Ow! Sons a bitches!" while Merritt stared down at the wood arm like he was seeing it for the first time.

He held it up and turned it this way and that in wonderment. "I ain't never thought about how it ain't got no feeling to it. I mean, I can sometimes still feel my fingers, you know?"

Oral, rubbing on the area Merritt hit, said, "Well, I sure can't feel mine now. What'd you go and do that for?"

"Because you can be such a pain in the ass."

Oral sat back down on the bed, a sullen look on his face, and I could see that peanut brain of his working overtime at being ganged up on. I left the room and went to lie down on the couch, my head starting to throb. With the lamp on, I studied Mama in the photo, staring at the jugs around her feet.

Late in the night when all should've been quiet, I woke up to Aunt Juanita and Uncle Virgil arguing. Their voices rose and fell, vibrating off the wall and sounding like giant bees. After a while, footsteps came down the hall and the shape of Uncle Virgil appeared in the living room doorway, with Aunt Juanita right behind him, whispering. They came into the room, and with the light still on they could see I was awake.

I sat up and said, "What do you want?"

Uncle Virgil came closer and said, "You went in the room today?"

"It's my room."

Aunt Juanita nudged him and said, "Which means yes."

He said, "That money, we need it."

"What do you want me to do, steal it back for you?"

Aunt Juanita bent down so her face was close to mine and pointed her finger under my nose.

She said, "You listen to me. This is all your fault. We wouldn't be here but for you causing trouble. You need to get us that money. It's the least you can do. And it ain't stealing when it's owed us. And if you can't get it back, you need to replace it somehow. Maybe from up on that hill there."

"I ain't about to dig up my own daddy's money for you. You got your little mole to do that, remember?"

Aunt Juanita clenched her fists, and Uncle Virgil gripped his head like it was about to come off his neck. She made a frustrated movement, throwing up her hands as she turned to leave.

"You can't reason with her, Virgil. She's too hardheaded. Always has been."

"Damnation," was all he said.

They went back down the hall, Aunt Juanita sounding as if she was scolding Uncle Virgil, her voice going up and down. I turned off the lamp, and flopped onto my back again. I had almost drifted off when the back door squeaked open and closed softly. I got up, crept into the kitchen, and looked out the window. In the moonlight, a tall, dark shape headed uphill, then toward the shed.

It had to be Uncle Virgil. I eased the door open and watched as he disappeared around the back of it. Aunt Juanita's constant harping must've compelled him to go back outside in the pitch dark, the time of night when the most common critters moving were possums, raccoons, and rodents. I put him in the category of a rodent.

I shut the door, and went back to the living room to decide who was worse of a traitor, me, for what I'd planned to do, or them stealing from their own kin. My thoughts came to a stop when the back door opened. Uncle Virgil went scooting down the hall faster than normal. There came the click of my bedroom door, the low murmur of voices, then silence. Finally.

I'd been out with Daddy a few more times learning to drive Sally Sue. One of those times he taught me how to do the bootleg U-turn.

I almost refused when he began explaining what I would do, and why I would do it, but he said, "Your mama, I'm telling you she could whip this car around on a dime."

I quit protesting and learned. On that particular trip, he'd made a comment that buried its way into my head where it echoed loudly.

He'd said, "You're a natural, like she was. You got a feel for this car, an ability like she had. Shoot, you might come to be as good at driving as her."

I didn't know what to think anymore. I was getting so confused about all of it.

One morning, Uncle Virgil and Aunt Juanita acted subdued, communicating through odd looks mostly. Oral wasn't behaving right neither, sitting at the table, and picking at his scabby wound, while not talking much. Highly irregular, all of it.

Daddy, talking to no one in general, said, "I'm going to get Big Warrior going, got corn to haul in."

Uncle Virgil nodded, and Aunt Juanita said, "That's nice," like Daddy had said he was going to Sunday school.

Daddy said, "Jessie, how about you come with me? I could use some help since your uncle Virgil's going looking for a job today."

My initial reaction was to balk, to throw up barriers and tell him no, but out of the blue, I found myself in this weird place, like I had to allow him a tiny bit of loyalty against the wrong being done by Uncle Virgil behind his own brother's back, while also struggling with what I'd learned about Mama.

I sighed, and said, "All right."

Uncle Virgil rubbed his hands together, and said, "Yeah, heard about some possibilities up near to Adley."

Daddy said, "Good, good."

Merritt didn't bother to ask if he could come

with us. He'd given up on Daddy letting him do much of anything right now. The both of them were already butting heads over Merritt's refusal to use the prosthesis on a regular basis. Daddy thought more harm would come to him, as if the loss of his arm made it impossible for him to function in the world, like a baby bird with a broken wing.

He'd said, "Son, you're at a disadvantage right now."

Merritt adopted Oral's behavior and sulked.

Daddy and I went outside and, as had been his custom of late, he tossed me the keys. We rode with the windows down, going south on Highway 18. We had the radio off, not talking, just riding. It felt good, although I wished I'd put my hair into a ponytail. It was flying around my face, and every time I reached a hand up to brush it behind my ears, I came away with a few strands I released out the window, floating off my fingers like threads in the wind.

Daddy said, "Why's your hair coming out like that?"

"Everybody loses a little bit of hair."

"Not like that."

"It's nothing."

He went back to gazing out the window, slouched in the seat, falling silent once more. I turned onto the small side road off Highway 18, and after a few miles there was the familiar curve where a pathway sat tucked away. The tracks were hidden, barely visible unless you knew how to find them. I put on the brakes, turned, and soon the shade of the trees cooled the air. Undergrowth scraped the bottom of the truck as I maneuvered a section and the truck jostled us back and forth. We bounced over ruts and roots until I finally came to a stop near a thicket of mountain laurel. I parked and we got out. We hefted bags of corn out of the back, one apiece, and began walking in, him in front, me trailing after, struggling a bit with the weight of what I had. This was when Daddy offered me another tidbit about Mama.

He said, "She liked coming to Big Warrior best."

I tried to stay calm, but the "why?" came out as a shocked little gasp.

He gave me an assessing look before saying, "The creek was closer, and she could cool off in that area that pools sorta deep at that one end."

He shifted the corn on his back. Here he was, dropping bread crumbs while I was starving to know her. I wanted to understand everything and as fast as possible, not unlike the way I ate sometimes. Closer to the site, Daddy set down his sack of corn, and motioned I should do the same. Silent, we observed the surrounding woods from the left to the right. Big Warrior Creek ran fast, and the water rushing over the rocks muffled the birds calling out to one another overhead. We waited several minutes before advancing a few feet, and waited some more. We did this a few more times, until finally, the still was in view, where all looked fine.

Out of the blue, Daddy whispered, "Got something I'm needing you to understand. It's about your mama, an arrangement I made after she was gone."

I whispered back, "Okay," sounding calm, but in a turmoil over what he'd said.

He said, "Let's get the still going, and we'll talk about it."

I nodded, and he held his finger to his lips, then pointed at the site, indicating he would go the rest of the way first and for me to wait until he gave the all clear. I nodded. He proceeded with care, head swiveling. He got to the point of no return, that critical fifty feet, and finally, he was right at the boiler. He faced me, and went to lift his hand in a signal, when movement in the woods beyond stopped me. To my horror, the man with the patch over his eye stepped out from the cluster of bushes behind the still. He held a pistol, wore a strange smile. The urge to yell a warning rose in my throat, but it came instead from the expression on my face. Daddy spun around to face the man as I ducked into the underbrush. Peering through leaves and branches, I watched in disbelief as the very thing we'd avoided all our lives began to unfold. The man kept the gun aimed at him, but Daddy made no move to run. Then, Nash Reardon and another agent came forward.

The man with the eye patch said, "Well now, look a here who done got caught finally after all this time."

The man's comment explained why he'd acted like he had that day when I told him my last name was Sasser. He knew Daddy somehow.

Nash Reardon said, "Easton Sasser?"

Daddy still didn't respond.

The man with the eye patch said, "I recognize him; it's him."

He took the patch off, exposing what was beneath it, an empty, pink eye socket. Daddy had no reaction and acted as if he was in another place.

The man said, "Remember this?"

Daddy ignored him, his expression passive, staring straight ahead. He moved slightly, trying to face me, but both Nash Reardon and the other man closed in tighter, like they thought he might try to make a run for it.

Mr. Reardon said, "Good stuff, Smith. Let's get on back to town, and get the process started for his day in court."

The man called Smith pulled the patch back over his eye. Mr. Reardon motioned for Daddy to follow him, while Smith and the other man stayed behind and began hacking at the still.

Daddy came within twenty feet of me. He didn't dare look at where I was hiding, and there was nothing I could do except watch as he went by. Once he and Nash Reardon were out of sight, I didn't move while the pounding and banging went on. Like before with Boomer, the distinct smell came as Daddy's shine gushed out and onto the ground. They left soon after. I remained, head down, bewildered and shaken by what I'd heard and witnessed. I didn't feel vindicated like I thought I would, and all the anger I'd held on to for years suddenly seemed petty.

Chapter 21

I remained in the hiding spot for some time, tears free-falling off my jawbone. Finally, knees cramping, I had to stand. I rose from my crouched position, stiff-legged. I stepped into the clearing, waited, and listened. Blood rushed to my deadened feet, the way the water rushed over the rocks nearby. I left, moving slow while sniffling. I stayed off the usual path just in case, so it took a while before I made it back to where the truck was parked. I was too nervous to go to it right away, and I hid behind a tree, staring at it, noting it was well hidden. We'd not seen anything odd when we first got there, and I couldn't imagine how they'd found the still. Wary and skittish, I tried to decide when to take a chance. I had to get home, had to figure out what to do. I half-ran, half-stumbled to the truck, opened the door, and slid in. I dug the keys out of my shirt pocket, panting in the manner of a dog during the summer, apprehension making my hands tremble as I gripped the steering wheel. I cranked the truck, reversed, and went down the path fast as I could without wrecking.

On Highway 18 I relaxed some, but kept my

eyes on the rearview. An occasional car whizzed from the opposite direction, but there was no one else on the road. Before long I was back on Shine Mountain, and going at a speed fast enough to make the truck doors rattle like they might come off the hinges. I rounded the curve to the house and pulled into our drive. Around back, I noticed Uncle Virgil's truck was gone, him still off looking for that job. I dreaded telling everyone about Daddy, and believed Uncle Virgil would go clear off his rocker once he heard. He'd take off out of here on a revenge mission, but it was telling Merritt that would be hardest. I went in the back door, sickened by the thought. He sat at the table alone, apparently mad, and upset.

I said, "Where's Aunt Juanita and Oral?"

With a strange glance, he said, "Gone."

"What do you mean gone?"

"They're gone and they ain't coming back."

I sat down at the table with him, and waited for what else had gone wrong today.

He said, "Soon as you, Daddy, and Uncle Virgil left, Aunt Juanita said, 'I ain't sitting here waiting on more trouble to come. I've had about a bait of it. You tell your uncle he can find me at Mama's.' "

I said, "But how'd they get there?"

"She called her mama. She picked them up an hour later. I think she had it planned."

I sat back on the chair. It was a surprise, then

again not. She'd threatened it. I stalled, unsure how to begin about Daddy.

I said, "Uncle Virgil will go after her, job or no job."

Merritt lifted his shoulders like it didn't matter all that much to him. He got up and looked out the door into the backyard. "Where's Daddy?"

Merritt scanned the backyard before he spun around, and said, "Where's he at?"

I couldn't hardly speak right when I said, "Come sit down."

His voice angry, he said, "Is what you're gonna say got anything to do with the way you look?"

I could only imagine. Eyes wild and hair stringy. Pale-faced. Sweat making my clothes droop like they were hanging on a clothesline.

I said, "Daddy got caught by revenuers."

He went still, mouth open in disbelief, and I went to studying the streaks in the wood of the cabinets, the tabletop where someone's greasy fingerprints showed up. That made me think about Daddy getting fingerprinted. I could hear Merritt fighting not to cry, a muffled noise like he'd swallowed wrong.

My voice low, I offered the details. "He did like he always does. He went first, and as soon as he was close enough, they came out of the woods where they'd been hiding and waiting."

"How'd they find it?"

"How do I know?"

My voice was higher pitched, sounding like I ought to be blamed even when I shouldn't. Everything was tangled as a briar patch.

Merritt said, "It's because of you, and you know it."

Worried, I said, "What do you mean, because of me?"

"You've always talked about how you hate it. Wishing Daddy would stop. Oral told me about you wanting to mess up our stills. He said you're the reason their house burned down. I didn't want to believe him, but why would he make that up?"

Shame flushed my face while Merritt stared at me like I wasn't anybody he wanted to know.

I said, "It's true, I did want to stop him from making liquor, but I didn't have nothing to do with him being caught. I bet that little shit didn't tell you what him and Uncle Virgil were doing, did he? I bet he didn't open his mouth about that. Come with me."

He shoved his hand in his pocket, his expression defiant.

He said, "What for?"

"You won't believe me if I told you, so you got to come see for yourself."

I led the way out the back door, up the hill, and around to the back of the shed.

Once there, Merritt said, "I don't see nothing."

I could see what he couldn't, funny little disturbed areas in the grass, subtle, but there. I went to one area, and pulled on a section of grass. Up came a chunk at least one foot by one foot, like pulling a cap off someone's head. I got on my hands and knees and moved the loosened soil. It was easy. I lifted out a jar, held it up for Merritt to see. Empty.

I said, "They've been stealing Daddy's money."

Merritt looked incredulous, angrier.

He shouted, "And you didn't say nothing? You might as well have been stealing it too, Jessie!"

"I tried to fix it! Remember when Daddy found that five hundred dollars? Remember how Oral said I could have Mama's picture back for five hundred dollars?"

He shook his head. Nothing I could tell him would make a difference, but I told him anyway.

"I found that money in my room, hidden on the windowsill. I was the one who put it back in his nightstand. I should've told him, but I figured putting it there would make him suspicious something was going on and he'd find out himself."

He didn't say anything for a minute; then he said, "You tried to fix it without taking blame for it; that's what you did. Now what're we gonna do?"

He was right. I hadn't had the guts.

I said, "I don't know."

Later on the phone rang. What if those same

297

calls started up again, as if the caller was sensing we were here alone, and vulnerable?

I picked the receiver up, hesitated, then said, "Hello?"

Daddy's voice came across the line, "Jessie, it's me."

I sank against the wall. My throat closed up. I shut my eyes, and for the first time in as long as I could remember, I addressed him in the way I'd not done in years.

I said, "Daddy," and started to cry.

He said, "I know, I know, but listen. I need you to listen. Jessie? Stop crying; it ain't gonna do no good."

Which only made me cry harder, even while I tried not to. After a few seconds I managed to say, "I'm okay. Go ahead."

He said, "In my drawer is that money, that five hundred dollars. I'll use it for bail, get to come home for a bit. There will be a court date, but you and Merritt ought to know, it might be I'm going to have to spend some time in here."

I gripped the receiver when he said the amount for bail. Coincidence?

I felt a little flicker of hope, and whispered, "Okay."

Another voice in the background said something, and Daddy said, "I got to go."

The line went dead. I turned to Merritt.

His mouth was thin and determined, him ready

to do whatever Daddy asked. "What'd he say?"

I said, "He talked about posting bail. It's five hundred dollars."

I went down the hall to Daddy's room, encouraged I might redeem myself, if only a little bit. Merritt followed, watched as I opened the drawer. The money wasn't there. Merritt made a derisive noise as he left. I found him near the shed furiously scraping at the ground. Just plain furious, really. I joined him without saying anything, and when we took a break, he walked away and stared off into the woods. At first I dug with hope, but as the day went on, I began to lose it when nothing was found.

Later that afternoon, I was surprised to see Uncle Virgil's truck coming up the drive. He climbed out and didn't bother looking up the hill. He went inside and I glanced over at Merritt, but understood from his silence, I was on my own, far as he was concerned. I started down the hill, and heard him following some distance behind me. Uncle Virgil was in my bedroom, and I watched from the doorway as he opened and closed the closet door, the drawers on the bureau, moving faster and faster as he discovered Aunt Juanita's things missing. Merritt was a silent spectator behind me, yet I could feel an energy coming off him that made my spine tingle.

Uncle Virgil said, "Where's her stuff?"

I said, "Merritt said she's gone to her mama's.

299

Her and Oral both. Said to tell you that's where you'd find them."

"I will be damned. I knew it!"

"There's something else too."

"What." His voice was flat, guarded. With his hands shoved into the pockets of his ragged coveralls, grass stains on the knees, I pictured him up on the hill where we'd been, doing what we'd been doing. I couldn't help but wonder how it was that he could be brothers with Daddy. The only common thing I could see between them was their last name.

I said, "Daddy got caught by revenuers earlier today. They done took him down to the court-house jail, and that's where he sits. He needs bail money."

Uncle Virgil took a step backward, and sat on the bed. "You shittin' me?"

I shook my head.

"Sons a bitches."

"We've been up on the hill, trying to find the money, and there ain't none left. None."

He said, "Well hell."

"You ought to give it back, that and the five hundred dollars that's gone missing."

Uncle Virgil shook his head, his voice rigid. "We had us an agreement, remember?"

"I didn't agree to nothing."

"Why, sure you did."

Frustrated, I said, "He's stuck in there!"

"The odds was against him, and he got caught. It was bound to happen to one of us, one of these days."

Uncle Virgil leaned in so we were eye to eye.

"You tell your daddy I consider us even steven now. Tell him I'd stick around, but I can't get put in that there penitentiary. She'd never let me back in the house."

He jingled his keys once, glanced about the room, then walked by me into the hall where Merritt hovered.

He stopped, and said, "You want to come with me? I reckon I can do that much for him. Look after his boy."

The offer obviously didn't extend to me, and the only way I'd have gone with him was if he'd offered to pay Daddy's bail. Merritt appeared to consider it for a second.

He finally shook his head and Uncle Virgil said, "Suit yourself."

Out the door he went, cranked his truck, and tore down the drive. We didn't speak about Uncle Virgil or what he said. We went back outside and up the hill, back to the futile effort of finding even a dollar bill. We dug the rest of that day, and again the next morning. All we found were three more empty jars lying in knee-high weeds, discarded like trash. We began to dig random holes, stopping and starting over and over.

Finally, we quit. Filled with dread, and feeling sick nonstop, I waited for Daddy to call again, and when the phone rang late the next day, I almost couldn't get up to get it.

Distressed, I answered with a shaky voice, "H-h-hello."

He said, "Jessie. Why ain't you done what I told you to?"

I was at a loss for what to say.

"Why ain't you come here yet to put up the bail?"

I blurted out, "We can't find any money."

I heard the intake of his breath and held my own. I waited, knowing he'd get to asking me questions I wouldn't be able to answer.

He said, "I, myself, put it there, so it has to be there."

I almost whispered, "No."

"What?"

"It ain't!"

He didn't say anything for a few seconds; then he said, "Somebody's took it. Listen, near the shed . . ."

I confessed, "Uncle Virgil, maybe Oral, they might've been digging around the shed some."

"You saw them?"

"I wasn't sure what they were doing."

There was a long silence and I could hear a clanging noise in the background, a gate being shut.

Finally, in a low, tight voice, Daddy said, "Put Merritt on."

I motioned at Merritt, and he snatched the phone from my hand, and where I hadn't hardly been able to speak, he had plenty to say. "It's her fault, everything that's happened. She wanted to ruin our stills, Oral said he overheard her friend Aubrey and her arguing about it."

He stared right at me as he said this and he wasn't finished. "For all we know, it's why they run us off the road that night. Why I lost my arm, and can't play ball no more. The reason Uncle Virgil's house burned, and Oral got branded. I bet it's why you're in there."

I shook my head. It wasn't true.

I said, "It ain't true," to the room.

Merritt listened to whatever Daddy was saying, responding with a, "Yeah," before he put the phone on the counter. He walked out of the kitchen, his back rigid with anger. I picked the phone up and put it up to my ear.

I said, "Daddy—" but he cut me off.

He didn't sound like himself when he said, "Damn, Jessie."

The line went dead again, not because he had to go this time. That much I knew.

Chapter 22

I was up on the hill, stabbing at the dirt again, searching in vain, when Mrs. Brewer showed up, waving a newspaper in the air over her head. Her white hair in a chaotic swirl, her mouth a thin line, I could tell she was distressed. I threw the shovel aside and walked down to where she stood by the driver's door, her apron covered with cherry-colored stains, splotchy and uneven, like she'd wrung a chicken's neck, or spilled some of them fruit bitters she touted as a cure-all. She handed the paper to me and on the front page of the *Wilkes Journal-Patriot* was a picture of Daddy with Nash Reardon. One of them had evidently snapped it right after he'd been caught. I studied the lack of expression on Daddy's face, flat as a dinner plate, his hands clenched into fists the only sign he was upset by what was taking place. She stabbed at the page with a knobby finger, crooked as an old tree branch.

She said, "Saw this and it like to have stopped my ticker. I'll tell who it otter be, it otter be one of them low-down good-for-nothing Murrys, that's who. Them and all their good-fer-nothing kind."

She looked down at the photo, made a sound of disgust like she might spit on the ground.

I said, "It's them who's been causing all the trouble we've had, like what happened to my cousin."

"That boy I seen the other day with that *M* burned into his chest?"

"Yes'm."

"They must've gone to them revenuers."

"I don't know. I think it was them that destroyed the still near to Boomer."

I didn't elaborate as to what everyone else thought happened.

"Who all's here?"

"Me and my brother."

Merritt had only come out of his room once since he'd spilled everything to Daddy the day before, and then it was to rummage about the kitchen for something to eat. It was tough because of his one arm, and I thought about helping, but I didn't. I let him do for himself. He was going to have to learn anyway. After Daddy hung up on me, I'd kept myself preoccupied straightening out my room, putting it back in order while trying not to think too much.

I said, "You want some coffee?"

She nodded. "I wouldn't mind me a cup."

We went into the kitchen and the pot I'd made earlier was still on the back of the stove, and hot. I poured, then set the cup in front of her. She sat fanning herself, while sipping the hot liquid. It was into August already and the day was warm, but would get even warmer. I opened the paper to read the article. It was brief, stated what I already knew. I skimmed by that page, wondering what people thought, especially those who knew him well. I absentmindedly scanned articles, not really paying much attention until I came to the community news where I saw another photo that made me pick the paper up for a closer look. It was of Aubrey and a few other classmates I recognized standing behind some tables set up on the lawn of the Shine Mountain Episcopalian church.

The caption said: "Students of Piney Tops High School hold church yard sale to raise money for the purchase of new sports equipment for their school."

In the background leaning against a tree behind Aubrey's table was Willie Murry wearing his customary unfriendly expression. His attention wasn't on her though. He was clearly eyeballing Cora McCaskill, who must be her new best friend. Even in this fuzzy black-and-white photo, I could see the want in Willie Murry, not unlike what Uncle Virgil had for the liquor. I was certain Aubrey was going to find out the hard way Willie would be about as difficult to nail down as a cockroach on the run after a light is switched on. I missed the old Aubrey, her energy, her presence by my side giving me a boost of confidence. I'd trusted her to keep my secret though, and she'd turned right around and betrayed me to Willie. Whatever she felt for him had been stronger than our connection. Did she even regret it? The picture said no. The picture said she was doing fine. I tossed the paper aside.

Mrs. Brewer said, "Where's your aunt and uncle?"

I didn't want her knowing we were on our own.

I gave a flimsy answer: "They'll be back."

Secretly I hoped not.

She pointed at the paper. "It's plumb ridiculous. Man minding his own business while the government thinks they got a say in what's what. Folks round here been making shine all their lives. Born doing it, like me. Ain't no different than selling jam, you ask me."

I didn't agree. I'd seen too much bad come out of it. People didn't get upset over the sale of jam, and the like. People didn't get run off the road. People didn't get branded. People didn't get killed.

I said, "Uncle Virgil said the odds was against Daddy."

"How's your daddy holding up?"

"Okay, I reckon. We ain't had the chance to talk much."

I picked up my coffee cup and sipped at the bitter brew. The cramping in my middle was uncomfortable because I'd not eaten much these past few days and I was drinking it black like her, trying to conserve sugar and milk. I thought I should talk, but I didn't want to get into all the sorry details of how we'd fallen apart as a family. What my family thought about me, how Daddy's own brother stole off of him, then abandoned us, or how my brother evidently blamed me for all the bad that had happened, including losing his arm.

She stood as if to go, and I did too, but had to grab the edge of the table to steady myself.

She said, "Dizzy?"

Mrs. Brewer missed nothing.

"My foot went to sleep."

She said, "I brung something for y'all to eat. Figured you wasn't doing as I said."

I followed her outside and she retrieved a plate off the back seat. Whatever it was, it was covered up with a dish towel. She handed it to me, lifted a jar of honey, and another of homemade straw-berry jam. She shut the door and we went back into the house, the smoky odor of sausage teasing my nose the entire way. In the kitchen I set the plate down and took off the towel. I was right. It was sausage biscuits on one side and peach jacks on the other.

She said, "I don't know any boy who ain't always ready to eat. You want to get your brother?"

308

I hesitated, then said, "Sure."

I went down the hall, pausing outside his door before I knocked. A heavy thud came, like he'd thrown a shoe at the door.

I said, "Merritt, there's—"

He yelled over me, "Leave me the hell alone, Jessie!"

Mrs. Brewer was right behind me.

She said, "It ain't surprising he's upset."

"He ain't the only one—"

The door jerked open with Merritt ready to give me what for, until he saw her.

Mrs. Brewer calmly said, "You want something to et?"

Merritt's manners required him to speak, and with a crimson face, he said, "Yes'm."

We went into the kitchen and sat at the table. Having Mrs. Brewer here was comforting, and if I could've forgot about Daddy sitting in a damp jail cell, I might would've enjoyed her company more. She offered the plate to Merritt and he took a sausage biscuit and one of the peach jacks. When she passed it to me, I didn't dare refuse. I decided on a peach jack. She said a blessing, and then the two of them proceeded to eat while I eyeballed the pastry, as my stomach flip-flopped. I broke off a small piece and stuck it in my mouth, where it sat on my tongue. I sipped on coffee and was finally able to swallow. I waited a moment or so, and that was all it took. My brain

309

got the message something was happening, and I was able to take another bite, and another, and before long, I'd finished it. I scrutinized what was left. I could've eaten all of them. Meanwhile Mrs. Brewer and Merritt finished their biscuits and had moved on to having themselves the jacks.

In between bites, she said, "Judges, sometimes they're fearful somebody'll run and they won't never catch'em again, but maybe it'll work out all right if your uncle will vouch for him."

Even if that were possible, Uncle Virgil wouldn't vouch for nobody but himself. Merritt quit chewing and his forehead wrinkled.

He said, "We can forget about that."

Mrs. Brewer said, "What do you mean?"

Merritt's demeanor changed. He scowled at his plate, and jerked a thumb in my direction.

He said, "Uncle Virgil took off with all of Daddy's money. We could've had bail if it hadn't been for her."

Mrs. Brewer sat back on the chair.

She said, "He stole from y'all?"

He nodded.

She said, "Why, shoot! Ain't no call to take from your own."

Merritt leaned forward, doing like he'd done with Daddy, filling in Mrs. Brewer. He started with Uncle Virgil, Aunt Juanita, and cousin Oral leaving, and how it was just as well. He cast rotten looks my way when he described how I'd seen them taking what belonged to us and said nothing. His belly full, he was talkative, and Mrs. Brewer listened, picking at the edge of the table. He went all the way back to the evening we got run off the road, and went from there. He even told her about how everyone at school thought I was peculiar, and how I'd only ever had one friend, and now had none. I tried to think of some way of explaining it all away that didn't make me sound so terrible. I couldn't think of how to defend myself. Finally, he was done.

I whispered, "There's reasons why it ended up like it did."

Merritt said, "Ain't no good ones."

I got up from the table and went out the back door.

Mrs. Brewer said, "Jessie?"

I didn't stop. I wasn't going to try and explain, or listen to Merritt making snorting noises each time I brought up how he had it wrong, what I'd done was because of Mama and her horrible death, how I'd turned against making shine because of it, and partly because of Daddy. It was rude to leave so abruptly, but who cared? If everyone already had such a crappy opinion of me, why not add rude to it?

Merritt said, "She just feels sorry for herself."

My insides bubbled like a still about to cap. He was wrong, all of them were wrong, about

311

everything. I marched up the hill to the shed. The field behind it was pockmarked with dark holes where I'd been violating the land, punishing it for all my troubles. The shovel was leaning against a post as well as the pick I used to loosen the soil. I grabbed the pick and began stabbing at the earth repeatedly, working out my anger and, yes, maybe even a tiny bit of sorrow for being misunderstood. Mrs. Brewer had come after me. She stood by the shed, but I didn't slow down.

She said, "You wanting to tell me your side of it?"

I raised the pick overhead and brought it down hard.

"No'm."

"I know you mean no real harm, child. Things just get out of hand sometimes when you think you're doing the right thing."

I couldn't handle that sympathetic tone, the soft way she spoke like she believed I wasn't all that bad, even without having heard me say a word in my own defense. I wanted to tell her how it happened. How I'd come to my conclusions and why I was the way I was—except I didn't know for sure if I understood it myself. I slowed, wondering how I would even start to unravel what was like a knot of strings pulled tight, how to begin to justify myself.

I leaned into the handle, spoke to the ground. "It's because of what happened to Mama I'm like

I am, and that's why Daddy's like he is. It's why I hate making shine, and why I think like I do. Am I crazy?"

Mrs. Brewer said, "Shoot, no. You're confused is all. You got to figure it out, and when you do, it'll be fine."

I shifted position, my arms and legs feeling fragile as twigs.

I said, "I ain't figured out nothing yet."

"Sure you have."

"Ma'am?"

"Last time you and I went and ate them tamales, you called him Easton. You calling him proper now."

She started down the hill, then stopped.

She said, "You know, I seen her about town some years ago."

"Who?"

"Your mama."

Those two words caught me off guard.

I whispered, incredulous at this news, "You did?"

She nodded, and said, "Here and there, sure, I seen her. I'll tell you 'bout it next time."

Encouraged, I said, "I thought I'd never know what she looked like until Daddy finally gave me a black-and-white of her."

She said, "That's good. Every girl needs to know about her own mama. Now, listen, I got to get on to the house 'fore it gets dark. My eyes at

313

night, they ain't so good. You and your brother, you're welcome to come stay with me. I don't like the idea of y'all up here alone with all that's going on."

"We can't leave. If Daddy calls, he'll wonder where we are."

She said, "Well, that's true. I'll keep a check then. Keep them doors locked."

She went down the hill and waved at Merritt, who stood on the back steps, the empty sleeve of his T-shirt moving ever so slightly in the breeze. Thinking on what he'd done, I got angry all over again. To me, at this moment, he was no better than Oral, or Uncle Virgil. I went back to work, determined to find something, anything.

Before long, I was jittery and limp and had to stop. What I'd done had brought me not one jar, not even that one-dollar bill. The sky had lost its light, like a rainbow fading. I rubbed my sore hands together and gazed at a purple-edged horizon, pinpricks of brightness winking and a quarter moon tilted against the deepening night sky. The wind lifted damp hair off my neck, and as I listened to the forlorn hoot of an owl, I stayed long enough to watch dark descend over us, turning the mountains black. I'd never felt so alone before and realized the hollow feeling wasn't always hunger.

Chapter 23

Somewhere between the croaking of tree frogs and the chirrup of crickets came the raspy sound of someone walking across gravel, then a scraping sound beneath my bedroom window. This was followed by mumbling. I sat up in the bed, and stared toward the darkened glass, at the white sash sitting halfway. I threw the covers off, and soon as my feet hit the floor there was a thump against the kitchen door. I stepped into the hall as Merritt opened his door too, and stuck his head out.

He whispered, "You hearing that?"

I put my finger to my lips, and motioned at him, much like we did when we were getting close to a still. We tiptoed toward the kitchen. Through the curtains at the back door I saw a shadow, the moon creating just enough light to reveal the form of someone hunched over. Subtle clicks came from the doorknob. Merritt punched my arm.

He said, "They're trying to break in."

I mumbled, "Get Daddy's shotgun."

He scurried down the hall while I kept an eye on the door. They were getting brave, turning careless even, making more noise as if the darkened house signaled no one was up to hear. The doorknob wiggled; then came more rattling as they tried to pick the lock. Merritt was back and carrying the gun in his left hand.

He whispered, "You ain't ever shot it much. You even remember how?"

Aggravated, I took it and whispered back, "Yeah, Merritt, I remember."

I'd only ever done it twice before, but he sure couldn't with one arm.

He said, "It's got buckshot, and I'd shoot at that spot right there. Scare'em off."

I cocked the gun, then hesitated. I wanted to know who it was. I inched forward.

Merritt became agitated, and his voice pitched higher. "What're you doing? Shoot the darn thing."

I said, "Wait, I want to see who it is."

"Why? We don't need to know!"

Whoever it was began hammering their fists on the door, and the kitchen was suddenly illuminated by two or three flashlights. I didn't know how many of them were out there, but they aimed the flashlights at the windows and it was almost as good as having the overhead light on.

Someone called out in a singsong falsetto, "Yoo-hoo, anybody home?" followed by snickering.

Then came a high-pitched whistle, like when you want to get someone's attention. My hands shook as I brought the gun up and pulled the trigger. It recoiled and hit my shoulder hard, making my arm go numb. I pumped it and waited. There was a fist-sized hole in the wall beside the door frame. I'll say this, shooting a gun inside a house is completely different than shooting one outside. The noise was tremendous and the sounds that followed were muffled, as if my head was underwater. I couldn't see the person anymore, and had a split second of dread I might've hit him. When the shadow of whoever it was reappeared at the door's window, I let the air out of my lungs.

His fist smacked the wood, and my fear turned to anger when he yelled, "Ain't none of you Sassers worth a shit!"

If my ears weren't still ringing I'd have bet it was Willie Murry, but the voice came through fuzzy, so I couldn't be sure. The hollering and laughing went on like a party. Somebody threw what sounded like an empty can against the glass.

Merritt leaned over the sink at the kitchen window and I said, "Get back; they'll see you!"

He had no more stepped away when the window shattered and glass blew everywhere, showering us in sparkling pieces that left tiny nicks on our arms and faces. We dropped to our hands and knees and scooted back into the hallway.

Someone muttered, "They's hiding," and I worried they'd try to break in again.

Another voice said, "Virgil Sasser, that you in there? We gonna see to it you Sassers stop taking what's ourn, one way or the other. This is your warning. We're gonna see all them stills you got destroyed. We're gonna find'em all; you watch and see."

Merritt suddenly stood and before I could stop him he shouted, "You ain't stopping us from nothing!"

I pulled him back down, thinking, *How stupid.* This was it. They would tear down the door to get us now. They didn't know it was only me and him, and I sure didn't want them finding out. There was more howling, and carrying on.

Someone said, "Kill them lights!"

We were suddenly in the dark as they shot out the back-porch light. The small scratches on my face and arms stung as perspiration snaked down my face and arms, and Merritt lost the boldness he'd had only seconds ago. He grabbed my arm with his hand, breathing hard like when he'd play ball for hours on end. On top of the darkness came silence, and the longer it went, the more uneasy I became. I could picture them, squatting by the foundation, surrounding the house, figuring out a way to get in. After a few seconds, my eyes began to adjust until I could make out the shape of the table, chairs, the white of the refrigerator and stove.

I said, "Damn."

Merritt hissed, "What?"

I held up a finger as I slipped quietly toward my bedroom. What if some blame fool came in through my open window? In the doorway, I stared at the raised pane of glass, saw the trees moving ever so slightly in the breeze. The only sound at the moment came from the same frogs and crickets I'd heard earlier. I crept closer toward it, and paused. There came a scraping sound, like boots toeing the foundation. I dreaded the thought of seeing someone's fingertips gripping the windowsill. The scraping kept on, but even worse was the silence. Where were they? What were they doing?

Nobody's head inched into view; no one tried to climb in. Eventually, I leaned the gun against my bed, and moved quickly to slam the sash down. I locked it at the top. I immediately stepped away, shrinking at the thought of someone shooting like they had earlier and how close Merritt had come to getting hit. I left my room and saw him near the kitchen, watching the back door. I had to motion dramatically to get his attention. I raised my shoulders in question. He did the same back to me. We didn't know where they were, what was going on, or what they were doing.

I moved closer to him and whispered, "I ain't heard nothing."

He said, "I know. I don't like it."

"Me neither."

We waited, and even the littlest of noises gave us a start. An hour went by, and I got to feeling like they were gone. I couldn't say why I felt like that way, except that I didn't think they'd sit out there quietly. I figured they were the sort to keep trouble coming long as they had the chance. We waited another thirty minutes or so, and by now, it was almost like it had never happened.

I said, "I think they're gone."

Merritt shook his head. "I don't know."

"Ain't but one way to find out."

"You can't go out there, Jessie! What if they're waiting to ambush us?"

I said, "That's too much trouble for them. They ain't wanting to fight directly. Ain't you ever noticed how everything they do is sneaky? What about what happened at our still? They snuck out there and tore it up. And what about Uncle Virgil's house? They're chicken. It ain't like them to show up like they did tonight unless Willie Murry's behind it. I bet it was his idea, and probably a bunch of his crazy friends."

Merritt acted like I was the one who was crazy, flailing his left arm about. "You keep on lying about how you ain't the one who tore up our still."

"I didn't."

He gave me a skeptical look, but I also saw a weakening, and puzzlement more than anything.

"But you wanted to."

320

"Yeah. But I didn't."

It was getting to where it didn't matter if he believed me or not. The hole in the wall allowed warm air to come in and the curtain at the back door flapped lazily every now and then, like a hand beckoning us closer. I opened the door.

Merritt said, "You see anything?"

I stepped outside. There was a slight sheen coming off the windshield from Sally Sue in the shed up the hill, the murky depths of the woods beyond the house, a sky dotted with stars, nothing out of the ordinary anymore. Merritt's shape filled the doorway.

I turned and spoke to him in a hushed tone, "They might come back. We ought to leave."

"Where're we gonna go?"

"Mrs. Brewer said we could stay with her."

"But what about Daddy? What if he calls?"

"I'll try to get a message to him. Hurry up and get your stuff together."

In my room I grabbed what I'd need for a few days, plus Mama's picture from where I'd propped it on my desk. We'd go to Mrs. Brewer's, but not for long. I was afraid if we weren't here, we would come back and find our house burned to the ground like Uncle Virgil's. Back in the hall Merritt held a bundle wadded up against his chest. He'd attached his discarded prosthetic arm. I said nothing about it. In the kitchen I went to the back door, my brain and ears attempting to separate the common from the unusual. Like before, it was quiet. I took the set of keys off the hook by the door, and out in the yard, I waited again, listening and watching. I could still hear them hooting and hollering in my head.

I said, "Let's take Sally Sue instead of the truck."

"Why?"

"I don't know. It just seems like the thing to do. She's faster."

He mumbled, "Only when Daddy's driving."

I locked the back door and we trudged up the hill, and tossed our things onto the back seat.

After the car was started, I said, "I got to get a job, get some money together, and help Daddy."

He snorted. "A job."

"Yes, Merritt. A job."

"It don't make no sense. Daddy's always said ain't no job can make money like making and running shine."

"Like I'm about to start doing that."

"Mama did."

I ignored that and pulled out from under the shed. Out on the road I guess you could say I was showing off a little when I floored it and quickly gathered speed. And I guess you could say I felt a little bit proud when Merritt said, "Dang," as I rolled the steering wheel, left, right, left again, the road in front of us captured by the headlight beam. We made our way down Shine Mountain, and I was able to keep Sally Sue tight in the curves, like Daddy had taught me. Merritt was quiet, watching what I did with a keen eye.

We came to the bottom of the mountain, and made it out onto the road without me sending us off the side into some deep holler, when Merritt ventured to say, "You could do what Mama done."

I wanted to wallop some sense into him, but I can say this one thing about me and Merritt. We'd never hit one another even if I did think he couldn't much stand me most of the time.

I said, "I ain't likely to take up something I hate, Merritt. No matter how good the money is. I might as well go out and be a prostitute, or something."

"Well, damn, Jessie. That's like saying that's what Mama was doing."

"You know what I mean."

"You just said it was like being a prostitute."

"I'm only saying it's illegal. It ain't right."

"It ain't nobody's business but ourn. We ain't harming anyone."

"Sometimes I wonder, Merritt, if you ain't about as dumb as Oral."

He sat back, and said not another word the entire drive to Mrs. Brewer's. When we pulled into her driveway, of course the house was dark and I got to feeling bad about springing in on her so late. I knocked on the door, and hoped she wasn't hard of hearing. I knocked again and a light came on in a back room. I could see it through one of the three little windows in a row at the top of her front door. I went on my tiptoes and saw her coming, wrapping a housecoat over a long nightgown. She saw me through the little window and yanked the door open.

"What's happened?"

I'd never heard Mrs. Brewer sound like she did right then, her voice thin and frail, and I hoped I wasn't bringing trouble to her doorstep by coming.

She held it open and we went inside.

I said, "I'm sorry to wake you, Mrs. Brewer, but we got trouble up to our house. Someone tried to break in. They shot the kitchen window out."

She said, "They went to shooting, jes' like that?"

I said, "I shot first, just as a warning. I only wanted to scare'em off."

Mrs. Brewer said, "Shouldn't been there they didn't want to get shot at. Got my own gun for such as that, and I don't hesitate in using it neither."

She nodded to where an old single-barrel sat propped near the door, looking like it had taken care of plenty of varmints. Without a word she clomped off to the kitchen, and we followed. She flicked the light on to reveal even more roots and herbs drying here and there than last time I was here. She pointed for us to sit at the kitchen table while she bent down in front of the old woodstove, struck a match, and had a blaze going in no time. She slammed the door shut, then ground some coffee using a hand-cranked box. She filled an aluminum pot with water, put several scoops in the basket, and set it on the stove. She retrieved a large white opaque bowl out of the drain in the sink. Aunt Juanita had talked about how all her milk glass was gone from the fire. Mrs. Brewer's bowl was milk glass too, and when she opened a cabinet there was more of it. She tossed in flour, lard, salt.

Out of the blue, she said, "You gon' have to fix it."

Her fingers worked the lard through the flour and salt. She sprinkled in some water, and kept going. My stomach was hollow and I tried to remember when I'd eaten last.

Her words were a contradiction to the calming effect she'd been having on me, and I said, "Fix what?"

"You gon' have to get their respect, and you gon' have to do it quick."

"I don't care about them."

"You got to, or else they'll drive you and him"—and she nodded at Merritt—"off'n that mountain and all your parents ever had will be for naught."

"Maybe that's for the best. Maybe it's what I want."

Merritt stiffened, and anger made his voice shake. "Well, it sure as hell ain't what I want."

I said to Mrs. Brewer, while pointing at his missing arm, "Even after that, he still thinks making and selling shine's not a bad thing. Even after all the bad that's happened. Ain't nothing good from what I've experienced, but according to him, I don't know nothing."

Mrs. Brewer said, "He can't help it. It's in his blood, and I reckon it ain't in yers, simple as that. Ain't a thing wrong wantin' to do somethin' different."

I raised eyebrows at Merritt, like, *See?* Only Daddy's words came back to me, *It's in your veins, girl,* like an echo.

Then she said, "It still don't mean you ignore what's been done to yer family. No, you got to fix it, like I said; then you can move on. If you don't, it'll come to you all of a sudden like, the things done wrong to you and yern, and how you chose to let it go. It'll eat at you, and won't be nothin' can be done about it then. It'll be too late."

"I don't see what I can do."

"There's always a way. Trust me, you got to figure it out all along, like you been doin'."

She rolled out the soft dough and cut thick biscuits using the top of a large glass. She placed them on a pan, warped with age with one end higher than the other. She stuck it in the oven and checked the time. It was going on 5:00 a.m.

The coffee finished perking, and as she poured us a cup, she said, "I reckon now's as good a time as any to tell y'all what little I know 'bout your mama."

Chapter 24

Mrs. Brewer's knobby fingers encircled her mug, and as she blew steam off the top, I waited somewhat impatiently for her to tell us what she knew. In the seconds before she spoke, it got so quiet, I could hear the ticking of the pan inside the oven as the metal adjusted to the heat, like some small creature tapping to get out. She stared at me a long time with an intensity like she might've changed her mind.

Finally, she said, "You know, she truly wa'n't big as a minute. 'Bout like how you are."

I sat up straight. If this was how it was going to start off, it was going to be real hard for me to believe anything she had shared.

I said, "Why do you keep saying things like that?"

"Like what?"

Merritt would surely point out what a pig I was and how I didn't need them biscuits I was starting to smell. He'd tell her about the chicken Aunt Juanita brought and that I ate all at once. He'd tell her in that tone of voice he got, like I was an embarrassment he had to tolerate.

Confused, I said, "That I ain't big, especially when my clothes ain't ever felt right."

This was the truth. My clothes were cutting into me this very minute.

She shook her head ever so slightly, and said, "I reckon not, chile. Not when they're two to three sizes too small. I know your daddy's got to have given you money to buy new things."

Aside from what Aubrey had given me, I'd been wearing what I had in my closet and drawers long as I could recollect. There was nothing wrong with them although my jeans might have been a little worn, my skirts and dresses a little too short, and flimsy.

She crooked her finger and said, "Lean forward."

Hesitant, I did as she asked, and felt her grab at the collar of my shirt. She pulled it up, and when the material was released, I sat back and waited.

She said, "Ain't a wonder you 'bout to bust out of them. What you got on is at least two sizes too small."

Merritt said, "Daddy's tried to give her money, but she don't never take it."

Mrs. Brewer studied me. "Why's that?"

I said, "I ain't using that money."

Merritt said, "She goes to school like that—"

Mrs. Brewer held up her hand and Merritt stopped talking.

She said, "Let me tell y'all about yer mama.

Some years back, I seen her as I was comin' out of Pearson's. She stopped to talk to Mrs. Turnbull, who was in a state. Y'all wouldn't know Mrs. Turnbull; she's been gone from here for some time now. Now, I couldn't hear what all got said, but I seen how yer mama listened, then she took Mrs. Turnbull's arm and went back into the store. They come out a minute later, and Mrs. Turnbull was beamin' ear to ear. That mama of yours sure was a kindly lady. She went with me oncet to help someone. This young gal by the name of Callie Monroe got herself in a family way. I reckon her husband wasn't wantin' no kids and I could see why. They were right poor. Lived in a shack with a dirt floor, and it ain't about that, but more about how there was barely any food in the place, and about how he was. It ain't fittin' to bring a young'un up who's gonna start off life half-starved, likely gettin' beat within an inch of his or her life near 'bout every day. She was petrified of him, and had tried to take care of matters herself."

I shifted on my chair and glanced at Merritt, who flushed red, but all Mrs. Brewer did was point her finger at him, wagging it to make a point.

She said, "He needs to hear what lengths a woman will go to when she's afeared of a man, and he's near 'bout a man."

She went on. "Yer mama sat by Callie while

330

I did what I could, trying to patch up all that damage she'd done to herself. It was too late though, but yer mama held her hand even after she'd slipped away."

"How'd she end up going with you to help that girl out?"

Mrs. Brewer said, "Well, now. I believe that gal was actually related to her somehow. A cousin maybe. She'd called me to come see about her. She didn't care none for the husband of hers, it was pretty clear. His name was Lucas. I don't know why I recollect his name. Funny what one recalls, ain't it?"

I nodded. "Like what I saw."

Mrs. Brewer said, "What you saw?"

I nodded. "Mama. What happened to her."

Merritt butted in and said, "You weren't but four," and he turned to Mrs. Brewer. "She thinks she knows. She don't."

Angry, I said, "Yes. I do."

Mrs. Brewer ignored him, and said, "You mean when she died?"

I nodded again, closed my eyes, seeing her in flames.

I said, "She burned to death. I saw her catch fire. She started running. Daddy went after her, pulled his shirt over her head, but it was too late. He won't talk about it, or her. Never has."

Mrs. Brewer said, "Such as that would be hard to take for any of us, but mostly for family.

331

'Course it wasn't never mentioned directly, how it took place, considerin'. There was always a bit of gossip, which ain't ever helpful."

"No'm."

Mrs. Brewer said, "Tell me what you think caused it."

"They were making shine. I think the still blew up. Daddy's always so careful. It wasn't because of something he did. I think somebody shot at it."

I went to studying the fine thin lines of gold swirled into white Formica, at how I could follow one of those lines and it would lead nowhere, the patterns random, without direction and coming to a dead end. I felt like this, like I didn't know which way to turn, how to move forward. Like I was stuck at a dead end.

Merritt said, "I think it was an accident is all."

I said, "I ain't so sure about that."

He shrugged as if to say, *See how she is?*

She sighed and said, "Yer mama was good at makin' the shine now. I do know she had that reputation, and she got real good at runnin' it too. She was interested in doing the fruit bitters like I do. She was supposed to come get my recipe for the cherry one. It made me real sad to know she'd passed."

It got quiet for a minute or so; then she said, "When's the last time y'all talked to your daddy since he landed in that god-awful place?"

I remembered how he'd sounded, and my voice cracked. "A couple days ago."

Merritt sounded glum when he said, "I wished I could see him."

Mrs. Brewer said, "I expect visitors are allowed."

He appeared hopeful while I figured Daddy, he wouldn't want to see me, not after I'd heard that disappointment in his voice, sharp as stepping on a nail while barefoot. Mrs. Brewer got up and got the pan of biscuits out. She set them on the table, and the smell was intoxicating.

Mrs. Brewer said, "Git you some of that butter and honey. Got it from my own hive out yonder."

I picked up a biscuit. Food was the last thing on my mind. I had no idea what it was I wanted anymore.

Mrs. Brewer called down to the facility and found out we could go see him between the hours of 1:00 and 6:00 p.m. on Sundays, and it happened to be Sunday. She said she'd drive us later that afternoon. Considering Merritt and I had been up most of the night, sleep was needed, so we sprawled out in her living room on the couch and in a chair, but I felt no better when I woke up. As we went to her car, I motioned at Merritt to sit up front. I wanted to be in the back seat so no one could see my face, see the guilt overwhelm me as we came closer.

What was it like inside where they had him? Damp walls maybe, dim light from only a tiny window, if that. Visualizing it only added to the dread. The parking lot held a half-dozen cars. Mrs. Brewer parked under a big elm tree, and as soon as we went in, the interior immediately depressed me. An old man, gray-haired and stooped over, wore a striped jumpsuit. He was working in a hallway to our right, putting on a fresh coat of beige paint, the color as flat as my own mood. He was in no hurry, his slow and methodical movement replicating the ticking of the clock directly over his head, as if he'd been mesmerized by the sound.

There was a constant clanging of thick gray metal doors. Whistling, yelling, and even laughter came from somewhere deep within the building. I smelled disinfectant above the sharp scent of body odor, and the paint. We had to check in, state who we were, and who we'd come to see. We had to sign our names, declare our relationship to the incarcerated. We were studied from behind a glass partition, as if by being here we too ought to be behind bars, as if our association to the one inside meant culpability by the very fact of knowing of him.

A guard said, "You're early for visiting hours. Go with him, and he'll take you where you can wait."

Another short, squat-bodied guard led us down

a short hall and into a room with a few chairs lined up in crooked rows.

He said, "I'll come get you in a bit."

I was in a panic internally, while outwardly I worked to keep my face neutral, and my hands still. I sat on them until I lost feeling and then sat with them pressed into my thighs. Merritt's left leg bounced up and down, and Mrs. Brewer picked up a newspaper left on a table and began reading. It felt like it took a long time before the guard returned and motioned at us to follow him. We went by the old man still painting in the hall, practically in the very same spot. Walking through this building seemed a long ways away from Shine Mountain, from that curve in the road and the driveway that led up the hill to our house. I wished I was back on the mountain, not here. Even while I resented making shine, I'd recognized the beauty that surrounded me as I made my way to Blood Creek, Big Warrior, and Boomer, back before it was ruined. There was peace in the way the creeks wound and curved across the land, trickling softly beneath the birch, oak, and pine, and where sunlight speckled the ground. I felt settled there, the slow, warm days soothing, hiding me away from the rest of the world. The quiet calmed anxiety.

Out of nowhere, I considered what Mama might have thought of Daddy being in here. Would it have changed her mind about what they did?

Would she have been ashamed, or would she have been defiant? The guard opened another door and motioned us inside the new room as flat and plain as the one we'd left. Mrs. Brewer, Merritt, and I sat at a table against a wall. There were other tables placed about, some empty, some with people already in the process of talking, sharing baked goods that had been brought, and checked by a guard. Some still waited, like us. I felt so out of place, like we had no business being here. It made me realize that, to my knowledge, Daddy was the first Sasser to ever be penitentiaried, and I had all ideas he was ashamed.

I waited uneasily, and tried not to fidget. When the door opened and he came into the room, everything dropped away like being in a tunnel and getting sucked backward very fast. I grabbed hold of the edge of the table, to stop the lightheadedness and the shakes I could feel coming on. My breathing erratic, Mrs. Brewer turned and watched me with concern.

Merritt jumped up as Daddy got closer, and the guard who led him to our table said, "Hang on, son."

The guard spun Daddy around and unlocked the handcuffs they'd put on him for the walk from wherever he'd been kept to here. His chin touched his chest while this happened. I was right. He was mortified they did this in front of us.

The guard tapped his back and said, "Sit in that chair. Keep your hands on the table."

They acted like he'd committed murder. Daddy looked so uncomfortable, and out of place in this environment, like the wild animals kept in cages at a zoo. He had on a gray jumpsuit with the giant word "INMATE" on it. His complexion matched the color of his clothes. There was a number over the pocket on the front. Inmate 3568, it said. He hadn't shaved, and I wasn't sure he'd showered. His hair wasn't brushed back like usual, but hung limp on his forehead. His eyes were as blood-shot as Uncle Virgil's would get when he'd been on a binge. He dropped into the chair opposite us, sitting with his hands between his thighs at first, until the guard made a rapping noise on the wall behind him and pointed at his hands. Daddy placed them on the table. After that, he didn't move. He didn't look at us. I started having trouble, getting dizzy, like I was twirling. It was distressing seeing him in here, and seeming nothing like himself.

Mrs. Brewer cleared her throat and said, "I brought some of these biscuits I made this mornin', thinkin' maybe you'd be hungry."

He ignored the biscuits and said, "How come you're with them?"

She said, "They come to the house early this morning afore it got light. There was some trouble up to your house."

Daddy turned to Merritt, not me. It was like I wasn't there actually. It wasn't anything specific, just this sense I was being ignored.

He said, "What was going on?"

Merritt didn't go into any detail. "The Murrys showed up yelling and carrying on. It didn't last long."

Mrs. Brewer tilted her head at me, as if encouraging me to say something. Agitated, I shook mine no, while Merritt leaned forward with a plan all his own.

He said, "We're gonna get you out of here. We're gonna get some money, somehow, and get you out of here."

I frowned at these words he spoke. At this very idea of his. How were we going to do that? If we both got jobs and worked day in and out, it wouldn't be enough, and it wouldn't be in time.

Daddy gave him a small wink. His voice subdued, he said, "I know you would, if you could, Son. Maybe it ain't worth it though. Maybe I'm right where I need to be."

Merritt shook his head over what Daddy said; then he got upset.

"No. No you ain't neither! It ain't right. You didn't do nothing. You don't deserve to be here."

That's when Daddy finally acknowledged I was even there. It was the way he did it, a subtle turn, and by what was in his expression. I wished I could've vanished. I wished I hadn't come. I understood in that moment how he felt about me, and what he thought about what he believed I'd done. He believed I'd betrayed him, had set him up to be caught. He believed I'd purposefully not told him about Uncle Virgil stealing his money. He thought the worst and I understood I'd become someone he didn't know, and didn't want to know. He stared at me like I didn't belong. Like I was an outsider, a stranger in his midst.

He said, "Some here think different. I'm sure of it."

Mrs. Brewer, disturbed by this statement, shook her head ever so slightly. Abruptly, I stood, left the table, and went toward the door.

I told the guard, "I'm done visiting."

He opened the door, let me out into the hallway, pointed to another guard standing at the door to the waiting room we'd been in.

He said, "Go wait in there."

The other guard let me in, and motioned at the chairs for me to sit. I got the distinct sense nothing happened here without one being led, directed, or told what to do. I sat down to wait on Mrs. Brewer and Merritt. It didn't take them long. I barely had time to start thinking about how Daddy acted when they came into the room. Merritt's mouth was thin, and his face was colored that deep red again like it got when he was either mad or embarrassed. Mrs. Brewer was frowning, but she wasn't angry, only troubled.

She said, "You ready to go?"

I got up and we left, no words spoken among us, not while going to the car, and not while going home. I felt downright sick. Worse than ever. I sat in the back seat and didn't care if I ever went back. For as horrible as it was, I was overcome by sadness, the unfairness of being misunderstood. Mrs. Brewer was right. I was going to have to fix it, only I wasn't sure how.

When she pulled into her driveway, Merritt was already opening the door, but she said, "Wait a minute."

He let go of the door handle, and though we'd never had us a mama to give us a talking-to, I sensed something like that was about to happen. She reached over and opened the glove compartment and pulled out a little tin of dip. She pinched some, and stuck it down in her lip. Merritt watched and then reached his hand out for it. To my surprise, she let him have it, and he set it on the seat so he could get a pinch using the fingers on his left hand.

She said, "Like this," and proceeded to show him how to get a little bit and tuck it down inside his lip against his gum.

She said, "Now you got to learn how to spit, and be accurate. Don't try it in my car though."

She glared at him, but he only mumbled a polite response around what he had: "No'm."

She relaxed against the seat, and said, "I know

that visit back there was hard. Ain't a thing easy about seein' your own daddy in such a place. It ain't gon' be easy movin' ahead without him for the next little while. But listen to me now, and listen good. You two ain't got nobody but one another. Family is family, no matter what. You two got to get over this difference between you, and that's what's got to come first. He's your brother, and she's your sister, whether you like it or not. Nothin's gon' change that. You can make this easy on yerselves, or you can make it hard, but y'all know this already. It's time for the both of you to come to a different understandin'. It's the only thing's gon' work, and get you through it. You got to help one another, not work against one another."

She opened her door and sent a spurt of tobacco juice off into the yard. Then she heaved herself up out of the seat, and shut the door. Merritt didn't move and I didn't either. I could see him working his mouth over the tobacco wad, getting used to it being there.

I said, "What's it taste like?"

He said, "If you want to know the truth, it tastes like shit. Mixed with mint."

He opened the door and spit the wad out in the dirt.

I said, "I'm gonna say it again; then I ain't saying it no more. If you don't want to believe me, that's okay too. I set out to ruin Daddy's

341

stills, but I didn't. If I could do everything all over again, I wouldn't have said nothing to Aubrey. She told Willie, and he must've told his family, and that's how it all got started. They're about half-crazy, and you know that good as I do."

Merritt got that mad look on his face again and his jaw muscle rippled as he clenched it.

He said, "Maybe. Either way, even if it wasn't you who ruined the Boomer still, the Murrys doing what they been doing is because of you, even if indirectly. What you say don't account for you letting Uncle Virgil and that little shit, Oral, take Daddy's money."

He got out and slammed the door. I stayed in the car for a while, knowing that putting all this back right was going to be a lot harder than I'd ever imagined.

Chapter 25

A couple days passed and I decided it was time to leave Mrs. Brewer's house.

I said, "I need to get back and make sure nothing's been done at home, like what happened to our uncle's house."

Merritt said, "Yeah, we need to get back."

It was about the only thing he'd agreed with me on in months, maybe years. He'd already been nodding his head toward the door, sending a silent message he wanted to go home.

Mrs. Brewer said, "Maybe I ought to go too. If only for a few days, just to be sure there ain't nothin' out of sorts."

I was reluctant to drag her into our troubles, especially since dealing with the Murrys was dangerous, reckless, and they didn't care about hurting someone. She didn't wait for our approval or disapproval. She said, "We'll go in the morning. It's getting on late, and y'all need a good night's rest."

This was the sort of mothering we weren't used to and Merritt and I stared after her as she went into the kitchen and started cooking supper.

He said, "I kind of like her."

I said, "I do too."

The next day we went back to Shine Mountain with Mrs. Brewer trailing behind us in her car and when the house came into view it was obvious something was wrong. We came around the curve, and I immediately saw the black marks on the white siding where somebody had taken black paint and put "A traitor lives here," the words seen clearly from the road.

In another spot there was, "Stay away if you know what's good for you."

I pulled into the drive and we sat in the car, staring at the damage. Mrs. Brewer got out of hers and came over to my open window.

I said, "They ain't getting away with this."

Merritt nodded.

She cautioned me, "You need to be careful now. Can't act out of anger. Them's only words. Don't let them git in yer head, make you go and do something rash."

I glared toward the house and said, "I'm tired of them thinking they can do what they want, stomping all over us like nothing can't never be done about it."

Merritt, his face pale, appeared like he was half-afraid and I couldn't blame him. He'd already paid a price, and so had the rest of my family. I drummed my fingers on the steering wheel while I considered the painted-on words. Who was my real enemy here? Maybe not the shine as I'd always thought.

I whispered, "It ain't right what's happened. None of it."

Mrs. Brewer said, "Bunch a bullies is all they are, always have been. That daddy of theirs, he's a terrible man. Acts like he ain't never knowed right from wrong all along. Him responsible for their raisin' was bound to produce a bunch a nitwits. Can't say as I knew nothing much 'bout their mama. She died when that Willie boy wa'n't but two years old. Heard tell she fell and cracked her head on a rock. Bottom line, nothing but trouble is what they are, and probably ain't worth your time."

I squinted up at her, and said, "Maybe not."

I drove Sally Sue up behind the house and parked in the shed. Mrs. Brewer parked in the back too, and when we started down the hill, we saw *jailbird* painted near the back door where I'd blasted that hole into the wall. I pointed, my finger shaking with rage at the message there.

"Just look at that."

Mrs. Brewer was calm.

She said, "Y'all got some white paint you keep around?"

Merritt said, "Up on the shelves back in the shed there. I'll get it. I'll take care of what they done."

She nodded at him while I thought, *Painting's not the answer.*

345

He said, "And there's some plywood out there too. I'll fix that hole by the door too."

Merritt wanting something to do was good, even while I doubted his abilities. I said nothing, and we went inside and I told Mrs. Brewer she could have my room and I'd take Daddy's.

She'd brought a small bag and said, "Thankee kindly."

No sooner had I gotten my room back that I was loaning it out again, but in this instance, I was happy to do so.

I said, "I just got to move a few things out of there, and then it's all yours."

I quickly grabbed some clothes, and dumped them on Daddy's bed. I took Mama's picture out of my back pocket, and decided I'd prop it on the dashboard of Sally Sue. I stuck it in my back pocket again and went out to the kitchen. Having Mrs. Brewer in the house was nice, and for reasons I couldn't explain, it felt like she belonged here. She stood in the living room staring at the TV.

She said, "I ain't ever had one, but I reckon it's right entertainin'. I mostly listen to my radio, gospel songs, and some preachin' now and then. When nothin' like that's on, I turn it off and sit and listen to Mother Nature."

Merritt came out of his room carrying his prosthetic arm.

She saw it and said, "Let me see that thing."

He handed it to her and she went to studying it, while pulling on a strap here and there.

She finally said, "I knew this man who had him one a lot like this after the power takeoff on his tractor took his arm. After a while he could near 'bout do anythin' with it. He got so fast at switchin' that hook around, you know, upright or sideways depending on what he was wanting to use it for, he operated it like a Wild West gunslinger."

Merritt stared down at the hook with a hint of new interest.

He said, "I ain't worked it much since I got it."

She said, "It don't take long you keep at it. No different than breathin'. It gets natural like. He 'bout wore his out, but he wouldn't get him a new one. He said he'd got so attached to it, he liked it good as his old arm."

Merritt was transformed by this information, and he eagerly fastened it on and began working with the straps and the hook. An hour or so later when I was sitting in Sally Sue situating Mama's picture in the vent on the dash, I saw him twist the hook, place a paintbrush in it, and carefully begin to cover the ugly words.

We got word Daddy had been to court and was given a year instead of the three to four he could've received. This was because he'd never been in jail, and never caused no trouble. Even the judge said he hated it, but had to give him some time. This was what we heard through connections Mrs. Brewer had. It was still possible he'd be sent to Atlanta, but for now there he sat, and it had been real apparent how much he hated it, and how much he blamed me. Merritt called him as often as he could, but I never asked to speak to him and Daddy didn't ask about me either, far as I could tell. From the incident on Lore Mountain Road, and all that had come about since, I recognized I *was* the cause of it getting worse, even if I hadn't been the one to initiate it. I had gone and seen Nash Reardon, and the Murrys did what they always did, came back harder, and wouldn't quit.

The guilt I carried grew heavier as time went by. I began to realize sometimes it's necessary to make a sacrifice. What I needed to do was obvious; it was only that I didn't want to. But if I didn't, I'd have to live with it, like Mrs. Brewer had said, and I began to understand how that could be even worse. Daddy would be coming back home and I'd have to face him every day and Merritt already couldn't hardly abide my presence most of the time. All the worrying over this had me slipping in and out of the bathroom often, doing what I needed while wishing I could empty my brain the way I did my stomach. Mrs. Brewer said nothing, but every time I came out she was in the kitchen making me something to eat to replace what I just got rid of.

What she didn't know was I was pretty good at what I did. I could go in and out of the bathroom in less than a minute, like I'd been in there for natural reasons. It was like a tug-of-war between us. One afternoon I came out of the bathroom and found her right outside the door.

Without commenting on what she suspected, she said, "Come on in here. Sit."

I sat at the table while she made up some concoction, pinching this and that from some of the many little bags she'd brought along, all of it going into the steeping ball. She didn't talk. After she poured hot water over it and let it set for a minute or so, she set it in front of me.

She said, "Drink it," and nodded to herself, like she was sure it would set me straight in some miraculous way.

It was a pale gold liquid, and the steam rising up smelled like peppermint. I sipped, and found it tasted like that and was sweet.

"What is it?"

She countered that with, "Honey, and some other special things just for what you got."

I sipped again, and said, "I like it."

"It ain't for you to like. It's to help. Finish it all."

I did and it settled my stomach, taking away the discomfort.

After a week with her there, and without me

even realizing it, we were in this routine. I would occasionally feel normal hunger, did my best to eat typical amounts, drank the tea, and kept food down in a more consistent manner than I had in years. I felt better, stronger. Out of the blue, she repeated what she'd said before.

She said, "Don't let it get you. You're strong, you're capable, and it ain't nothing you can't do. I believe that."

I was beginning to believe her too, but I still felt fat and longed to empty my stomach.

School was starting soon, and while I was feeling better, I wished there was a tonic I could drink to help me deal with my feelings of shame and worthlessness. Everyone would know about Daddy, and I tried to think of anyone else in this same predicament and couldn't come up with a soul. Being talked about was nothing new, or hearing the little snickers behind my back, but Merritt wasn't used to it. Not only would he have that to contend with; it would also be the first time anyone saw him with his prosthetic.

In Daddy's room I stretched out on Mama's side of the bed with the journal. I'd been studying the entries, and I was finding out some right interesting details. Daddy had never mentioned any secrets, but there were a few in here. Not only with relation to making shine, but how to get it down Shine Mountain quick as possible, and into the hands of his customers. I'd never asked how it was possible, didn't know there were secret trails. They came by way of people who had allowed my granddaddy and daddy access through their land, by the use of their private roads. They were paid in shine and it was all highly intriguing, and explained how he and Mama beat the Murrys on this run or that. It really wasn't about speed, but about outsmarting them, which they'd done time and again, evidently.

He also had a list of regulars, and a separate list of people getting it from the Murrys. He worked to win the Murry customers over, letting them sample what he had for free. He'd made notes where he'd left his goods and indicated if they'd taken him up on buying his. I was beginning to find all of it fascinating. I had no idea how he'd got the names, but there was a mark beside some and a note indicating they were new, and when he'd started to supply them. There were mysterious entries too, like the one updated with a note that said: "MM showed up, no delivery," and another that said: "MM along Lore Mountain Road."

M could mean "Murry," but since it was "MM," I had no idea who it was.

The very, very best things I found were entries written in a feminine scribble recording the amount of liquor run into this or that town, or the measurements of corn, malt, rye, and yeast, and even pages with recipes for shine mixed with other ingredients she was evidently trying out, and couldn't quite get the taste of these new liquors to her liking.

There were notations like "try three parts sweet tea with peach juice to only one part liquor next time."

And: "Too bitter, add honey or maybe some sugar."

Deep in my soul I believed it was Mama's handwriting, not only because of the style, but because it was right alongside Daddy's handwriting and abruptly stopped after the day she died. I had another piece of her right here, in my hands. I remembered telling Daddy I would have burned it and how he'd looked at me. Little did I know what it had held, and it would have been like setting a flame to her all over again. I would've destroyed something I'd wished for all along, an actual part of her I could see and touch. Like the photo.

I hugged the journal to my chest and whispered, "I'm sorry, Mama."

I set it down by my side, my fingers resting on the scratched leather. I let that solitary image of her settle in my mind, the carefree smile, windblown hair, booted foot surrounded by jugs of shine. What I'd been pushing away started to come together, and while I was afraid, I also began to recognize what I ought to do, not only for Daddy, and Merritt, but for myself. I didn't know if I could make shine, or be good at running it, but I was beginning to understand I wanted to try, that by doing this, I could make it right with us.

I knew some parts of what to do, but I'd never been responsible for each and every step, all the way to distilling. I'd watched Daddy enough to believe I could. I knew how to gauge the strength of it, how to, as he put it, a "get a good bead." Delivering it was a whole other matter. His comments about Mama being the best gave me plenty of reason to doubt myself. I slid off the bed, and took the journal with me. I went into the kitchen, and even though Uncle Virgil, Aunt Juanita, and Oral had seen me take money out of the tin, I held out hope something might be left in there. An oversight on their part in their eagerness to leave. I was surprised to see there wasn't eight dollars in there, but twelve. Daddy had probably taken some, added more back in before things went the way they did with him. I put the money back in the tin, feeling good it was there.

Mrs. Brewer was in the living room with Merritt and they were watching a movie we'd seen before called *The Defiant Ones*.

I went in and sat in a chair, and after a minute, I said, "I've been thinking."

Mrs. Brewer turned to me, curious, while Merritt remained fixated on the movie, though I was pretty sure he'd seen it at least three times already.

Mrs. Brewer said, "About what?"

"I've been studying this journal," and held it up.

Mrs. Brewer said, "What's in it?"

"All kinds of stuff. Entries dating way back to when our granddaddy started making the shine. Earliest one is 1899. He would've been thirteen. He took a hundred gallons over into West Jefferson."

That got Merritt's attention.

He said, "What're you studying that for? It don't hold nothing that interests you."

I ignored him, my attention on Mrs. Brewer. "I've been thinking I ought to try it, like Mama did."

Mrs. Brewer sat up, and nodded like she approved.

She said, "Well, see now? That don't surprise me none atall."

Merritt laughed like I just told the funniest joke, then abruptly quit like somebody slapped their hand on his mouth.

He said, "It sure surprises the hell outta me."

I ignored him, and said, "I'm gonna need help."

He grunted. "You ain't lying about that."

Mrs. Brewer waved in irritation at him, and said, "Your sister's having a revelation; she's coming to grips with something real important."

354

Merritt rolled his eyes in my direction and shook his head.

I already knew where it had to be. Big Warrior. The site Mama had preferred with her clandestine little pool, and, of course, where Daddy had been caught. I planned to get what we needed from the only still left, Blood Creek, no matter how long it took. I would set it all back up at Big Warrior. I was certain the agents wouldn't come back, because for them they'd caught the owner, and sent him to jail. They could move on, focusing elsewhere. I told Mrs. Brewer my ideas.

I ended by saying, "It's in here. It ain't ever been about being fast; it's been about outsmarting them."

She said, "Exactly right, child."

It was apparent Mama had been proud of what she did, and if she had been, how could I disrespect that? While I still wanted to find out what happened to her, maybe that wasn't the important thing right now. Maybe what mattered was for me to feel like less of an outsider, more like I belonged, a part of something. The only way I'd ever know would be to try and do what I'd fought against long as I could remember.

Chapter 26

The next day both Merritt and Mrs. Brewer ended up helping, and by midmorning I could see it was going to take us a good while. Merritt got to grumbling as he struggled to help tear the still down. Of all three we'd had, Blood Creek was the biggest in size, the submarine boiler being the most challenging part of it.

He said, "We ain't never gonna keep track of what's what."

He spun his hook around and grabbed hold of a board and yanked. He was still clumsy, but was getting into a bit of a rhythm, although this was demanding work even when you had both arms and hands.

"If we stack the pieces in order, it'll help."

"I don't see how. It'll move around in the truck. Maybe we ought to mark it in some way."

Mrs. Brewer was listening to us, and she went over to the base of the tree where she'd set her pocketbook and big paper bag. She got to digging around inside the pocketbook and brought out a small knife.

She said, "I'll make notches in the wood like so on these here pieces. Just stack the others by me," and then she showed us what she intended by etching a round hole in one with a quick couple of twists. "That'll be the bottom pieces. Then I'll make two of 'em fer the sides. Rest of it we can see what it is."

Merritt said, "I ain't never known a woman to carry around a pocketknife."

She said, "That's 'cause you ain't knowed me good till now."

We went back to work, and by dinnertime when the sun was its highest, we had everything ready to move. It was going to take us all afternoon to get it down the path and into the truck, but Mrs. Brewer insisted we eat.

"Can't do the work if'n you're hungry."

She pulled out three tomato sandwiches wrapped in wax paper, fried chicken legs, and three bananas from the paper bag. Merritt and I sat on the ground, while Mrs. Brewer sat on a stump Daddy used to use. We ate fast, and when we were done, we began carrying out the dismantled still. The walk was as tough as I remembered, and took as long as I'd suspected. Merritt grew more irritable as the afternoon wore on. He shifted his right shoulder around like the leather harness bothered him. The last was the copper from inside the still, what Daddy had said was expensive, but an investment.

Merritt said, "We ain't got time to get all this to Big Warrior tonight."

The sun was setting, and Mrs. Brewer said, "Let's go on to the house and that'll be the part we do tomorrow."

I said, "I wanted to at least get it dropped off there today."

Merritt said, "Boy, look who's gung ho all of a sudden."

Mrs. Brewer said, "It ain't going nowhere."

It was two against one, so I gave in. As I was sitting behind the steering wheel, tiredness took over, and my back ached. We made it home, and even though Merritt had painted the areas white where those words had been written, I could still see them in my head as we pulled into the drive. I parked the truck at the back of the house and we slid out, emitting a few moans and groans. Mrs. Brewer was moving pretty slow, and I worried about her as she walked carefully down the hill, having developed a slight limp. We followed her, discussing what to have for supper.

Mrs. Brewer, in that motherly way I loved about her, said, "I'll fix us some more of that ham. If'n y'all got some rice, we can have that along with some red-eye gravy, and maybe some biscuits?"

I nodded while at the same time digging my key out of my pocket to open the back door. and noticed it was already ajar. I froze, knew it had been closed when we left. I signaled them, my finger to my lips while motioning at the open door. I gave it a push, and it creaked. I didn't move for a few seconds, waiting to see if anything happened. The final rays of sun stretched across the kitchen floor, and there was the scent of cigarette smoke in the air, a disturbing fact that turned the quiet of the house into something sinister. Mrs. Brewer and Merritt followed me as I crept down the hall. On edge, I approached the door to my room first. When I nudged it open, I immediately noticed the black painted words right above my bed. The shock that someone had been in here and had done this made me stumble backward into both Mrs. Brewer and Merritt.

"What is it?" she said.

I pointed at the wall where it said: "Your next." There was another sentence that made me shake with anger. It said: "You get what you diserve." I pushed my way by Mrs. Brewer and Merritt and went out into the yard. My heart flapped wildly and I thought about what we might have to do— again. I didn't want to leave here and I didn't want them thinking they could make us. Mrs. Brewer came outside, and stood by me.

She said, "Chile, don't you let them get into your head. Don't you let them get you so stirred up your thinking goes askew. Remember, you can outsmart them. Don't forget it."

It was that word. "Outsmart."

I said, "Oh no."

As I ran back inside, Mrs. Brewer called after me, "Jessie?"

Merritt was in the kitchen about to say something, but I shook my head, and went by him, tears already coming, certain of what I would find. In Daddy's room I could tell somebody had been lying on top of the bed. It had been made neatly when I left earlier and now the covers were all messy, muddy prints left at the foot of it and an indentation on the pillow. This was where they'd been, whichever one of them it had been. Merritt and Mrs. Brewer came up behind me, peering over my shoulders.

Daddy's window was open, the curtain dragged to the outside. They'd climbed out when they heard us. I went to the dresser, already knowing the journal was gone. My head started to pound. Somehow, what had been in my family for all these years, this one thing I'd finally found an attachment to, a connection with, was gone, lost forever. They'd managed to get their hands on not only family history, and record keeping, but all the secret paths, trails, and back roads. The customer lists with notes beside them. Mama's very own recipes.

Merritt said, "What is it?"

I couldn't answer. He came into the room and I couldn't look at him.

He said, "They done got our journal?"

I nodded once, staring at the floor, at the scuff

marks, and scratches. He was so mad he groaned like he was in pain, but it was anger coming out of him.

He said, "Shit, Jessie!"

Mrs. Brewer shuffled closer and said, "That book had important family history and whatnot, but listen now, Jessie. It ain't your fault they come busting in here and stole it."

I was beside myself. "They'll know how we did things. It'll only get worse. That's how they are."

Merritt said, "We might as well forget it. They done got the best of us."

Mrs. Brewer said, "Have mercy! Listen to the two of you. Ain't never suspected y'all for quitters."

I didn't say anything, but Merritt did.

He said, "What good's it gonna do when the most important thing we had is gone?"

She said, "What about all that work today? Shoot, no. We ain't wastin' all that time doing all that we did by coming to pieces, and moping and gripin'. It ain't allowed. Now, come on, let's go on into the kitchen, and the both of you sit while I fix us something to eat. We'll talk about it."

She left the room while Merritt paced, twisting his hook, around and around. I was sure he'd blame me, point back to how it was all my fault.

He said, "I can't believe they took it."

My voice glum, I said, "I can."

I fought the urge to cry. In my mind I pictured

Mama's handwriting, the slant of the words, the softer bend of her letters with her delicate loops, the absolute beauty of it. I'd lost that extra little piece of her I'd only just got.

He said, "I remember how to make it."

"I do too. It ain't the point. It's the record keeping Daddy and Granddaddy did. Mama too. It near about makes me want to throw up."

"It ain't ever helped you before. It ain't gonna help now."

I stared at him in surprise. I didn't think he knew.

He said, "Yeah. I been hearing you do that for years now."

It was embarrassing. I saw myself through his eyes, and didn't much like how it might appear to someone who didn't understand. I imagined he thought of me as pathetic. I couldn't even begin to explain it, and I didn't try.

He said, "I'm going to the kitchen."

I followed after him, drained and limp. Mrs. Brewer was busy at the stove, frying, and she already had some rice and peas boiling too. I set the table and poured tea. After that, I propped myself at the counter and watched her slide the ham around, and stir what was in the pots. It was like she'd been here, doing this, forever. I was glad to have her. Merritt waited at the table, fiddling with his hook, putting the fork in it. He brought it up to his mouth, practicing how to eat right-handed again. I acted like I wasn't paying him no mind because he might stop trying. Soon it was ready, and we sat down. My mind wasn't on food. It was on what Daddy would think if he was here and what would the Murrys do now they had that information? It was like going inside their house, sitting with them, and spilling all our secrets.

I rolled the peas around on my plate and said, "I ought to go see Daddy, tell him what's going on."

Mrs. Brewer put her fork down and said, "It's not a bad idea."

Merritt was working on balancing rice on his fork held by the hook, and said, "I want to go too."

I said, "I might ought to go alone."

The rice fell off his fork, and he frowned in aggravation. It might have been because of what I'd said, or because he was hungry and struggling to eat. Probably both. Mrs. Brewer, who hardly ever smiled, gave me her version of one.

She said, "It couldn't hurt."

I remembered how he'd acted last time.

I said, "He might not want to talk to me."

Nobody denied that. Merritt repositioned the fork and ate a mouthful successfully while Mrs. Brewer cut a bite of ham. There wasn't much talk afterward.

The next morning all of us were up early. We

363

had the leftover ham with a pan of biscuits. We drank strong coffee, but where I'd been feeling good before, the old ways were wanting to creep back in. I hadn't had much sleep and was unsettled, thrown off balance. I tried to make the prospect of making and running shine a goal, a new focus. I got the twelve dollars from the tin, knowing despite everything, we had to somehow move forward.

I said, "We'll get the still going, and I'll go see Daddy after we do that."

Silently, we went out to the truck and crammed into the front seat. It took the morning to transfer what we'd piled into the back and out to the Big Warrior site where we began the process of reassembling it. One of the first things we did was to get the flake stand up and water going through it, to be sure there were no leaks. By using Mrs. Brewer's marks on the wood for certain pieces, and being familiar with the rest of it, by noon we had the boiler put back together and attached to the flake stand by the arm. We set the cap on, and all of us studied it. It was exactly the same as how it had been set up at Blood Creek, best as we could tell.

The corn I'd brought in with Daddy and had left behind the day he got caught hadn't survived the critters. The bags were chewed through, and most of it was scattered around, eaten, or in the process of trying to grow.

I said, "I'll have to go get more."

Merritt said, "We'll start to fill it with water and get it heating."

They began taking the buckets we'd brought with us to the creek, while I made my way back to the truck. The entire morning had been strange, the sky gone gray, and sullen. I drove with the windows down, noticing the mountains had the appearance of a season passing, the leaves no longer that fresh brilliant green of spring and early summer. They were turning dull, as if they were exhausted, too tired to show their color. It wouldn't be long before we'd see yellows, oranges, and red coming into them at the higher peaks. I kept going over possible ways to begin my conversation with Daddy, but what it came down to is I didn't know what I'd say to him about the journal being gone. I dreaded the trip, and wanted it over with.

Just before Highway 18, I made a turn onto an old dirt road called Summit Pass. I was going to where he'd always bought corn and barley from a local farmer who had a small grain mill set up in an old barn. There were several trucks there, the repetition of driving in and out creating a barren circular area in front of the building. I parked and went inside a small side door beside the big sliding front ones. Inside it smelled exactly like you'd expect, the rich scent of grains, saw-dust, and something like wet burlap. I spoke to a man missing a few teeth about needing some bags of corn and barley, and he took off to get what I needed and loaded it into the back of the truck.

As I handed him some money, he said, "Got to feed them cows and hogs good, ain't it right."

I said, "That's right."

Daddy had said it was what he'd always told them he used the corn for, though they might've known better. Still, it was easier than buying several hundred pounds of sugar from a store. That would definitely draw suspicion.

The transaction went so easy, by the time I got back to Big Warrior, my disposition had improved. Mrs. Brewer watched and nodded her head as we got the mash ready, testing the water temperature. Merritt turned off the heat when it was ready, and then we added in the corn. This was the part where I used to get bored when I'd been at a still on my own. We had to stir the mixture, until the temperature dropped; then we'd add in the barley. Then we had to keep stirring now and then until we could add in the yeast. It wasn't boring with Mrs. Brewer. She kept us entertained with stories and told us one about how she'd been a young girl and saw her uncle get caught by a revenuer while hiding under his house.

Merritt asked, "How'd they know where to find him?"

"He run into the yard, and crawled underneath the house, and was layin' there in the dirt beside his old hound dog. I had watched him do all of that, and thought it was a mite curious. Mama and Aunt Cornelia, Mama's sister, they was inside cooking. Well, you know, I was a young'un, and curious. Right when I got down on my hands and knees to study on him underneath there, the revenuers showed up. They was strangers, so I didn't talk to them.

"I hollered, 'Hey, Uncle Hobart, ain't you gonna come out here and talk to these men?'

"He tried to wave me off, but one of'em stooped down too, saw him, and that was that. Uncle Hobart always said when he got out he was going to tan my hide. I remember telling Mama I hoped they'd keep him a long time, which earned me a whipping anyway. 'Course, he got out, and did nothing of the sort, and by then I was making shine, and doing what he'd been put in the penitentiary for."

In the late afternoon, we were done and we put the cap on.

As we left, I said, "If the weather goes on like it is, shouldn't take long to get the first run."

Mrs. Brewer nodded. "It ought to be ready afore Labor Day."

I said, "That means I can deliver some before school starts."

Merritt was bringing up the rear and he said,

"Never in my entire life did I ever think I'd hear that."

I thought about it, then said, "Me neither."

The next day Merritt took the truck and went back to Big Warrior to check on it. Once he was gone, I tried to tamp my nerves down about going to see Daddy. Mrs. Brewer had offered to go too, but I wanted to do it alone.

She said, "Well then, I'll go on to my house, see about Popeye, and my mail. Call me when you get back; let me know how it went."

After she was gone, I went to my room and stared at the words we'd not painted over

Mrs. Brewer had said we should, and I'd said, "No. Leave it like it is."

Merritt shook his head like he thought that was just plain crazy.

I said, "It's a good reminder, don't you think?"

In my opinion, there was nothing more motivating than the messages those Murrys left.

Chapter 27

At the jail, I was led to the same room and told to wait. I'd never been inside any place I could remember where sound echoed so much. The shouts, whistles, doors slamming, keys rattling, chairs scraping, hands smacking walls, loud voices talking, reached a level where I only wanted to leave, get back to Shine Mountain where the loudest thing might be a creek, leaves rustling, and birds calling. I didn't know how Daddy managed in here, but I figured I was about to find out. I waited, and as the minutes went by I went from sitting to standing, to peeking out the small window on the door. After about twenty minutes, the guard who'd led me into this room came in.

He said, "You're the only one who came?"

I nodded.

He said, "Well, you best be on your way then."

I said, "What? Why?"

"He asked who came, and when I said, 'Looks like your daughter,' he said he wasn't up to seeing anybody."

Stunned, I said, "He won't see me?"

He said, "It happens. Adjustments and all."

I gripped the keys in my clammy hand. Even while I had the bad news about the journal, I'd planned to tell him what we'd done at Big Warrior. What I'd decided I ought to do. I'd come to tell him I was learning, and that I was wanting to be different, not salt in a wound, not contentious, a solid part of the family, doing what Sassers had done for decades. There was a little guilt mixed in it, but now it seemed I was too late.

I said, "Can I pass along a message to him?"

He said, "Sure, but I can't guarantee he'll read it."

He gave me a small piece of paper, and I jotted down: "Please call. I need to talk to you before you leave." I hesitated at my signature. Should I put: "Your daughter"? Should I put: "Love"? I ended up simply signing it: "Jessie."

He barely gave it a glance before he said, "Okay. Sorry 'bout that, kid."

Kid. How old did I look?

Once outside, I stared at my reflection in the windows of the building as I walked by, and caught a glimpse of a girl with flyaway hair, and bad-fitting clothes. I looked like I was about twelve, but mostly like I didn't belong anywhere, a misfit in my own right, no different maybe than nutty Darlene Wilson. I drove home, the turns here and there mechanical, and when I pulled behind the house, I didn't know how I got here. I sat in the front seat for a minute, deciding what I needed to do next. Merritt was still gone, and Mrs. Brewer had said she would come back later on tonight.

I had the house to myself, an unexpected moment of opportunity. Inside, I opened the refrigerator. I went back to all the times I'd done this and what it had gained me. Nothing. I'd never felt good during, and I surely hadn't felt good after. I shut the door, and went outside, tried not to think about my stomach, the internal upheaval, my gut as disturbed as what was taking place around me. I wanted reconciliation with Daddy and Merritt, and I wanted to be free of the Murrys. To not have their name never mentioned in relation to us in any way. I walked up the hill to Sally Sue. I got in and stared at Mama's picture long and hard. I wanted her kind of happiness worse than anything.

I didn't say a word to Merritt about Daddy declining to see me. We were at Big Warrior when Merritt asked how he was doing, I was vague, lied a little, and said he was mostly worried about being sent out of state. I stewed over the idea the news might make Merritt go back to being how he'd been when he'd discovered the hook wasn't up to his idea of a new arm.

He said, "All the more reason to keep going. For him. I want to see him before he has to leave, though."

All I could do was nod.

We were hunkered down by the spout Daddy always called the "money piece" and watched liquor dripping into a jar. Every now and then I could tell Merritt watched me, but I only paid attention to what came out. These first drippings seemed pure as water, but were toxic. This was called the foreshots, and couldn't be used. It was poisonous. It made me think of the Murrys and how no one, not anyone's family member, had ever come back on them when it was known their liquor was bad and had most likely dispatched a loved one off to heaven before their time. I figured it was because everyone knew how they were, how it wouldn't be good to tangle with them, which made me all the more uneasy about what I was about to do. It was as if I was deliberately stepping into their path, my fists raised, ready to throw the first punch. We could quit, let the Murrys have it all, but I couldn't see myself letting that happen any more than I could've seen myself running liquor down this mountain a few months ago.

I said, "Mrs. Brewer said she knows some who'll want to buy. I might be able to sell some in town too, at that spot where Daddy went."

Merritt nodded, then said, "I'm going too."

I weighed this in my mind, thinking about how it might seem with Merritt and me riding together in Sally Sue. It might appear suspicious, but riding around and even driving Sally Sue had always made me feel like that anyway. Everyone knew Daddy was in jail, and to be sure his young'uns wouldn't be up to no good after he'd set such a bad example.

I said, "Okay."

To that, he acted surprised.

I said, "We're gonna have to switch off and take turns until this is done."

He nodded and said, "I'll stay first."

"Maybe we should both stay. In case someone comes."

"I don't care."

"Since it's our first liquor batch and all."

"Don't go and try to make it special."

"It is though, ain't it?"

"It's just a regular thing, what we're supposed to be doing. What our family's done all along."

"I know that, Merritt."

"You ain't ever acted like you knew it. What's changed?"

He was starting to irk me, but I gave him the best answer I could.

"Me."

He didn't say a word. We sat around watching the liquor trickle out with an easy quiet that felt like a truce had been declared.

After a while, I said, "When we get home, I'm gonna go call Mrs. Brewer, tell her to come stay at the house, if she's inclined."

He said, "Yeah, okay."

373

● ● ●

A few days later, she sat at the supper table with us, sipping from a jar we'd taken out of Big Warrior, and said, "Now that's mighty fine. Y'all done real good."

It was the Saturday before school, and after we ate, Merritt and I climbed in Sally Sue. She was loaded down with jars and jugs under the special back seat.

Mrs. Brewer said, "I took a few of them jars and added in some apple slices and a little honey. Folks seem to like that."

I said, "Long as it'll sell, I don't care."

She leaned down, rested her forearms on my opened window, and studied us with an intensity I'd only seen when she was upset about my eating.

She said, "Y'all know where yer going?"

I nodded. "Yes'm. We'll try Tenth Street first because there's a place Daddy always went on Saturdays."

She said, "Be careful. Keep yer eyes open on the road."

"Yes'm."

She straightened up and we pulled away with Merritt grinning ear to ear. The wind blew the hair off his forehead, and he even had his hook arm resting on the edge of the door, no longer trying to hide it. The sun was bright and we were heading down Shine Mountain with Sally

Sue loaded up. It was a good day. I wondered what Daddy would think if he could see us. We got to Wilkesboro and drove through to North Wilkesboro, and as I went toward 10th Street it didn't escape me the looks we were getting.

Merritt said, "They're staring at us like we're from outer space or something."

"Who cares, I'm used to it."

I could imagine what they said, what they thought: *That's them Sasser kids. You heard about what happened to their old man, didn't you? Ain't it shameful? What you reckon they're doing?*

We poked along, going about ten miles an hour, being polite and stopping so some could cross the street. There was an atmosphere like a festival, almost. People went in and out of various stores, while some men stood around in sweat-stained coveralls talking, dusty hats shoved to the back of their sunburned heads, their booted feet propped on bumpers. They each enjoyed a chaw of tobacco and would occasionally spit. I puttered over to the alley where Daddy had done pretty good, and parked. We were underage, so we couldn't walk into some of the places he'd supply. There was a beer joint, pool hall, and a woman who had on so much makeup, I was sure she might be one of them women Uncle Virgil and Daddy had joked about being "a lady of the night."

I said, "We'll wait till we see someone getting ready to go in, and see if they can pass along a message."

He nodded, and we both watched the crowd.

Merritt suddenly pointed and said, "Hey! Daddy has sold to him. I remember him."

It was Mr. Denton, who owned a pool hall, and Merritt gave him a little wave. Mr. Denton was on the heavy side, not fat, but solid, and as he came toward us, it was like watching a bulldozer with the blade lowered and clearing a path.

He came up to Merritt's window and said, "Why, if it ain't the Sasser brood. What'cha'll doing here today, got some shopping to tend to?"

Merritt said, "You could put it that way."

I said, "Yeah."

Then there was silence. We weren't real good at the conversating part leading into what we were really shopping for—customers.

Mr. Denton rubbed at his neck, stared up at the sky, then said, "Listen. Damn shame is what it is, what happened to your daddy. If there's anything I can do, you let me know."

I said, "There might could be something."

Merritt said, "If you're thirsty, that is."

Mr. Denton's expression went from unsure to attentive.

Mr. Denton said, "I'll be danged if I ain't about parched. Come right on around to the back."

I said, "We'll see you there."

I pulled out and turned right at the next corner. Mr. Denton waited in a graveled area and pointed to a spot where we could park. A scratched and beat-up wooden door painted dark blue hung crooked off the back of the building. There were aged brick steps leading inside, and an old loading dock off to the left. It looked like an old warehouse. He held up a finger for us to wait, and disappeared inside. I turned the car off and we sat barely moving, both of us too nervous to talk. After a minute or so, I was clenching my fingers around the steering wheel and Merritt got to spinning his hook, round and round.

I finally said, "Hope he ain't setting us up, Merritt."

He said, "Maybe we ought to get out of here. We get caught with all this hooch, they're liable to stick us in a detention center or something."

I started the car, about to put it in Reverse, when Mr. Denton came back out with another man I didn't recognize, someone younger, maybe in his early twenties or so, his skin scarred by acne. He was dressed well, carried himself like he was busy, busy, busy, with a quick pace, and lots of hand gesturing. This was it. He'd done informed on us.

Merritt said, "Go!"

I said, "I ain't running now. It's too late. Mr. Denton's done told him all he needs to know."

They came down the back steps, heads together,

conspiring against us, maybe hoping to turn us in and keep some anyway.

Mr. Denton said, "This here's Mr. Lewis. He's a mite thirsty too."

I sat with the engine still running, trying to decide if it was a trap. Mr. Lewis took in how the both of us appeared like we'd been working in the sun all day. He didn't move, and I got to thinking he probably needed to see the evidence before he could arrest us. I was stuck in place and couldn't move if I tried. Merritt's hook clicked repeatedly.

Mr. Lewis turned to Mr. Denton and said, "It ain't nothing but two young'uns."

Insulted, I said, "I reckon I'm old enough."

"You don't appear to be."

"Well. I am. You wanting any or not."

"I want a sample first."

"Fine by me."

I got out, and so did Merritt.

Mr. Denton said, "Let's go inside right there," while Mr. Lewis stared at Merritt's prosthesis. I got a jar out from the back and we went inside where it was cooler, and dimly lit. In a small circle, we waited while Mr. Denton unscrewed the cap and sniffed. He sipped, and rolled it around in his mouth and swallowed.

He passed the jar to Mr. Lewis and said, "I'll hold my opinion till you have a sip."

Mr. Lewis sniffed too, then had a little taste.

He gave Mr. Denton a look I couldn't discern. He sipped again, put the lid back on real slow, and handed the jar to Mr. Denton.

Mr. Denton said, "Well? What'choo think, Glen?"

Mr. Lewis said, "Who'd you get that last run from?"

Mr. Denton studied us, then said, "Murrys. Near about threatened me if I didn't take some."

The mention of their name sent a chill down my backbone and Mr. Lewis rubbed at his cheeks, creating a rasping noise.

He said, "You still got some of it?"

Mr. Denton said, "Yeah, folks is drinking it, but complaining. Hang on."

While he was fetching it, Mr. Lewis said, "Corn, not sugar?"

I nodded, and said, "Yes, sir."

He nodded and said, "The good old kind."

Mr. Denton came back with another jar. It was grimy like it hadn't been washed, while our jars sparkled, and the shine in them did too. He opened it and sniffed and pulled his head back sharply before he handed it to Mr. Lewis, who lowered his head and sniffed, and made a face. I held my hand out, and he gave it to me. I knew right away what was wrong. I handed it off to Merritt so he could get a whiff of the Murry poison.

I said, "We only use the heart. No foreshots,

heads, or tails. That there's been proofed with all three probably and anyone who drinks that is gonna be sick with a popskull headache or worse. I can smell the acetone. We proof with water."

Mr. Denton said, "I ain't ever buying from them again."

Mr. Lewis said, "Their shit ain't never been any good."

I said, "Anyone lives to tell about drinking that is lucky."

Mr. Lewis said, "I want some of what they got."

Merritt said, "Ain't nobody never took sick drinking ours, not unless you just drank too much."

I said, "We got about a hundred gallons of what you just tasted. I'll cut you a deal, sell it a dollar cheaper a gallon than what they charged you."

Mr. Denton's smile went as wide as it could get. "That's a mighty fine proposition."

He stuck his hand out, and I shook it. He shook with Merritt too, after an awkward right, left, right fumble. Mr. Denton bought half of what we had, and Mr. Lewis bought the rest. When we were done unloading they handed us a total of two hundred dollars in cash. I'd seen more money than this piled up on our kitchen table when Daddy was home, but I'd never understood how it felt to see something through to the end, and then to be rewarded. I'd never been proud of anything I'd ever done until this moment.

I smiled at both men and said, "Thankee. I thankee kindly."

We promised we'd make a delivery once a week, same as how Daddy had handled it. Mr. Lewis happened to be scouting out for potential customers in New York too. He had relatives who conducted matters similar to the way we operated down here.

He said, "Hope you can keep up with the demand."

Merritt said, "Sure."

I said, "No problem."

We walked back out into the sun and sat in the car.

He said, "We might need us some more stills."

I said, "Yeah, and if we sell cheaper we could put certain folks out of commission."

Merritt nodded and grinned.

He said, "I can't wait till I call Daddy."

There was so much to tell him, so much we needed him for. I wasn't bothered about fending for ourselves; it was mostly about the Murrys. It troubled me how we'd manage them, but despite that, it might have been a hint of happiness I felt right then, and even the problem of the Murrys couldn't overshadow it.

I said, "I want to go buy some school clothes, some new shoes."

Merritt said, "It's about time."

Chapter 28

After tugging on a new skirt, and buttoning up a new blouse, I thought of facing my classmates. Having something new to wear might make a difference in how I looked outwardly to others, but really, I was no different than the same old house only with a new coat of paint.

The lady helping me said, "You ain't big as a minute."

It was the exact same thing Mrs. Brewer had said about Mama, but I couldn't get by the vision I'd held of myself for long as I could remember. I stood in front of the mirror, attempting not to judge, not to see what I always saw, the plain, fat, and dumpy girl with sad eyes. I tried hard, but it didn't work, because I still didn't care for what was reflected back.

The saleslady came by the changing room a couple times and said, "You all right in there, honey?"

"Yes'm."

I studied the way the clothes fit, struggling to decide what was real and what was only in my head, maybe an illusion, maybe the truth. I saw a big girl, one that defied the "you ain't big as a minute" comments. The new clothes made a difference in how I presented myself, if nothing else.

I came out of the little changing room and told the saleslady, "Can I get me some dungarees, maybe a couple more blouses, and another skirt, and a dress?"

"Why, sure, honey."

She left to get what I wanted and Merritt drifted over from the other side of the store after buying what he wanted.

He said, "You don't look the same."

I stared down at myself, and said, "I don't?"

I went back into the dressing room and came out wearing what I'd had on, the too-soft, threadbare skirt, yellowed blouse, and scuffed shoes. With the old clothes, the other me came back and inhabited my body, the uncomfortable, heavy, and stick-to-the-shadows me. The saleslady came back with the other items.

She said, "You want to try these on?"

I shook my head. I was done with shopping, decided I really didn't like it, but was glad to have gone through with it. We went up front to pay. After we left the store, everything wrapped in tissue paper and placed carefully in big bags, we went to the Goodwill store and got a couple Smithey Burgers to eat on the way home. I ate one, and before I could think twice I told Merritt to please eat whatever was left.

Monday morning came and a case of the nerves hit. I stood over the toilet, the temptation to drop to my knees like giant hands pushing on my shoulders. I turned away, knowing if I relented I'd never get past this curious behavior, never figure out how to stop. I ought to be proud is what I told myself. We'd sold our first batch of shine, made enough money to buy ourselves some school clothes, get groceries, and had money for bills. I had even washed my hair the night before and tried rolling it. I took the rollers out this morning and brushed through the light brown loops hanging near my collarbone, hoping a bunch of it wouldn't come out. Of course some did, so I tied it back in a loose ponytail, and went into the kitchen. Merritt came in a minute later, walking stiff-legged in his new dungarees, cuffed at the bottom, and wearing a white-and-blue plaid shirt. He'd used Daddy's hair tonic, and that familiar odor, fresh and sweet, brought him straight from the jailhouse and into the kitchen with us. We sat at the table while Mrs. Brewer, who'd shown up on our doorstep at the crack of dawn waving around a bag filled with links of sausage and eggs, set three full plates on the table.

She sat down, and said, "Now, don't y'all look nice."

Merritt's face had gone the color of putty, him worried about everyone seeing his prosthesis for the first time.

Mrs. Brewer said, "Maybe I ought to be ashamed of myself, but I'm glad I'm not going back. I got my pension, Social Security, and that special little something on the side. I don't need to do it; I was just doing it to keep from being lonesome."

She gave me the odd little smile that really wasn't.

Without any real thought, I said, "Why don't you come stay here for a bit? Bring Popeye."

She hesitated, her fork in the air as she thought about it.

She said, "I reckon I might could do that." And without hesitation, she said, "I'll bring my shotgun too, you know, just in case."

Knowing she'd be there when we got home eased my mind, but once we got to school that sense of well-being disappeared. Aubrey's brother, Zeb, followed close behind Willie and his voice carried clear across the school lot.

Zeb was yelling, "Hey, Willie, where you been?"

Willie ignored him, coming straight for us, and when he was close enough, he slowed down and fell into step beside me.

He said, "Sure is some interesting reading I've been doing. Hey, how does your old man like his new accommodations?"

We picked up the pace, and I said to Merritt, "Don't stop. Don't say nothing."

Willie stayed on our heels while Zeb wasn't far behind.

Willie said, "Hey, cripple. Bet you can't even wipe your own ass. Does she help? Hey, Hook Boy, she wiping your ass for you?"

Zeb laughed too loud, and too long. "Ha-ha! Tell'em, Willie! That's right; hey, cripple, does she help?"

Willie spun around and used his finger on Zeb's chest like a bird pecks for seed.

He said, "Shut up, dumb ass. And tell that nitwit sister of yours to stop calling me all hours of the night."

Zeb's laughter sputtered, while Merritt's face darkened with a combustible combination of anger and embarrassment. Heads down, we aimed for the doors. I was angry too, but couldn't think what to say to shut Willie up. A swarm of students unloaded from the buses and Cora McCaskill stepped off our old one. Willie called out and almost ran to her side. His expression molded into the same smitten look in the paper a few weeks back, and she blushed from the roots of her hair down her neck. Aubrey came zipping out of one of the doors at the front of the school like she'd been watching. She came to a standstill when she saw him take Cora's hand.

I said to Merritt, "Perfect, come on," and without waiting to see if he followed, I began closing the distance to Willie and Cora.

Merritt mumbled, "What're you doing?"

I didn't answer and fell in behind them doing my best to listen to what Willie had to say to Cora while watching Aubrey's reaction to the hand-holding. She was fit to be tied, eyebrows cinched together, mouth turned down. She had on red lipstick, a brilliant crimson slash like a bleeding cut against pale skin. She must've snuck a tube to school and put it on after she'd gotten here.

Willie was saying, "Cora, you sure are looking right pretty this morning."

Cora had her head down, and Willie sniffed at her neck. She giggled.

He said, "Boy, you sure smell good too."

She said, "Stop it now. You know I don't like it when you do that, least not in public, William."

William was stumbling over his own two feet as he fawned over her. He continued to adjust, to adapt and conform to her sense of social decorum, doing as she wanted, a different person entirely. Aubrey never stood a chance of having that kind of hold. Willie held the door open as Cora sashayed through; then he grabbed her hand again. She extricated herself from his grip to go into a classroom. Once she was gone, he rolled his head on his neck like he was loosening up tense muscles. She'd made him nervous. I couldn't imagine anything or anyone making him that way, but evidently Cora McCaskill did. He had a weak spot, and it was her.

Merritt said, "Danged if he ain't gone head over heels."

We parted ways, and he maneuvered the hallways sticking close to the walls like I would, the hook held tight against his body, shielded with his left arm. He avoided the lines of students moving like cars on a road, half going one direction and others going the opposite. I saw Curt Miller and Abel Massey, the way they whispered to one another, their eyes on him. I was getting the idea it was going to be a tough year for him. Behind me came a voice I recognized as easy as my own.

"Hey, Jessie," Aubrey said.

She chomped on a piece of gum, eyes darting about.

I said, "Hey."

She said, "You look different."

Merritt had said the same thing, but I had no comment for her since I didn't know what she meant, a compliment or not.

She said, "How was your summer?"

The entire town knew what happened to Daddy, yet here was Aubrey asking as if nothing had happened.

"That's kind of a dumb question."

"Oh. I guess you're still mad."

I wasn't really mad; it was more about knowing I couldn't be friends with her, not when she couldn't see how she'd been a part of what happened. I no longer trusted her, felt like she'd used me to try and win points with Willie. Like now, using me as her excuse to keep Willie within her sights. He leaned against the lockers near Cora's classroom, talking to another boy I didn't know.

She said, "Are those new clothes?"

"Yes."

"Nice," she said, and when she noticed Willie about to move on to his class she rushed away with a, "See ya," over her shoulder.

Next came a desperate wail out of her. "Will-ie! Waaaaitttt uuuup!"

He didn't stop, already long gone so to speak, yet she refused to accept it. She snatched hold of his hand and he pulled it out of her grip.

I went to my first class, where Darlene Wilson sat a couple of seats away. She stared in my direction, sometimes nodding her head like she knew a secret. She truly was strange, so I reckoned I wasn't leading the way in that category. My other classmates poured into the room, some a bit taller, some with new haircuts, and new clothes, yet something was different this year. It wasn't them; it was me. I was no longer concerned about the hubbub that came with being a part of something, like the Fall Festival already being discussed. The chatter about who should join various clubs, and activities. The talk of a great football season, and who might be Homecoming Queen. I was focused on how to keep the Murrys from causing us more trouble, and keeping the one still going. We had to get more liquor made, and down to Mr. Denton and Mr. Lewis.

I gave a sly peep around the room, wondering what they would think if they knew I hauled moonshine, knew how to do a bootleg U-turn, could tell by the bead what was good liquor and bad.

Word got around quick Sasser shine was still available. Most folks thought after Daddy went to the penitentiary that was it, there would be no more till he got out. When it was discovered that wasn't so, Merritt, and I were busier than ever. Mr. Denton called, and said Mr. Lewis wanted more and so did he. Before we knew it, Daddy's customers were leaving notes and messages at various watering holes along 10th Street, and then the phone started ringing. I tried to keep up with who wanted what, while Mrs. Brewer said she could help with the supply. She went home for a few days, fired up her own still, increased the amount she usually made, and came back to the house, her old car creaking up the drive, so loaded down with shine the back end scraped the gravel at one point. She used corn like we did, and added her fruit so we had all kinds of bitters.

We'd been doing as Daddy had done, hiding the money, but not in the backyard. That made me nervous, and although we'd not seen or heard from Uncle Virgil and Aunt Juanita, I wouldn't have put it past them to sneak over here, from wherever they'd disappeared, just to dig some more. Instead, we'd found places in the house. The freezer, for instance, where we'd wrapped some in newspaper, and marked it as "Steak," something we rarely ate. We'd shoved some in the back of a drawer in the kitchen that held dish towels. Stuffed some into the back side of the TV set, rolled up with rubber bands.

I said to Merritt, "I sure hope we don't forget where all we've put it."

He said, "Me neither."

We got word Daddy was to be sent to Atlanta, and Merritt was beside himself about getting to the penitentiary to see him.

He said, "I ain't been since that first time, and I been wanting to tell him how good things is going along. We ought to let him know, ease his mind so it won't be so hard on him being away for a year. Ain't you wanting to tell him?"

I said, "Sure."

I didn't see how it would make any difference to Daddy what I did or didn't do. I was sure he'd made up his mind I was no better than a Murry; he'd made it pretty clear, I thought. Mrs. Brewer stayed at the house the Sunday afternoon we went.

She said, "I'll cook us a chicken for supper and it'll be ready when y'all get back."

I was nervous about this visit, but Merritt didn't notice my silence. He talked with excitement, holding on to a little notepad he'd taken to writing in, not quite like the journal, but a way to keep up with what we'd made, what we'd sold, who was buying, where, and how much. We couldn't learn the secret trails, so those customers were doing without. I wondered if the Murrys had tried to use them, or did the customers remain loyal to Daddy? It might spark trouble for them, but there was no way to know if it had or hadn't.

I parked the truck and we got out, the afternoon sun warm and pleasant, a façade compared to the emotional tornado ripping around inside me. I let Merritt take the lead and followed behind him, fighting the internal chaos and a bad case of the nerves.

After we'd signed in and were shown to the visitors' room by the same guard I'd seen the last time, I said, "I think I might go wait in the truck."

Merritt sounded incredulous. "What?"

A door clanked and footsteps came down the hall.

I said, "Yeah. I'm gonna go sit in the truck."

I got up as he said, "But why?" while the guard said, "What's going on here?"

"Nothing. I'm just gonna wait outside."

Merritt said, "But Jessie, don't you want to see him before—"

The guard said, "You have to sign out. You

392

can't come back in. Can't have but one visit per week."

I turned to Merritt, and said, "It'll sound better coming from you. He wouldn't believe me anyway."

The guard called up to the front, and another one came to lead me back down the hall to check out. I heard Daddy coming, the shuffling and clanking of his chains, but I didn't stop. I kept going, staring at the set of doors that led me away. I figured I'd made the right decision when he didn't call out. He was probably glad to see me leaving. It would be a year. Maybe he'd be ready then. Maybe I would be too.

Chapter 29

After the visit, Merritt didn't tell me what was said between them, and I didn't ask. Every now and then I'd catch him looking at me like he had a question, but it never came out. I could picture the conversation for myself, could imagine Daddy's skepticism over my newfound willingness and loyalty. Maybe he needed evidence I wasn't playing a game, and the only thing I could offer as proof was persistence. Keep doing it, and maybe once he was out, he'd come to realize I was dedicated and as invested as any Sasser before me, and certainly as much as Mama had been. If I had to admit it, I was actually dumbfounded by my change of heart, and I'd had many a conversation with myself already.

Just what was it that had changed within me? It had been seeing Daddy in that place, seeing his hopelessness, and knowing if anybody belonged in a cell, it ought to be a Murry, not him. It had been finding out about Mama, her talent for hauling, the respect she'd had, her pride in what she did, her resilience. Those things motivated me, made me want to fix what I'd had a hand in causing. I'd realized I'd acted like I'd been born to some other name, some other family, with no allegiance. I didn't want to admit Willie Murry might have been right about what he'd called me. It had started to sink in I *was* acting like a traitor, going against what my own mama believed in, participated in. I had a strong feeling if she'd been around, I'd have had a different opinion from the start.

On a Saturday morning, in early October, I was preparing to go to Big Warrior where Merritt had been tending the still overnight, watching a boiler that was at capacity, our biggest run yet. He'd been excited by the idea of spending the night out in the woods like Daddy and Uncle Virgil had done many times before, watching over our commodity, shotgun by his side just in case.

We'd thought about whether it was smart or not, thought about a Murry showing up, and Merritt said, "Anyone comes along, Murry or whoever, I'm shooting, no questions asked. Besides, for this to work, we're gonna have to do stuff separate sometimes."

It was true, so he took the truck and had been gone since last evening while I'd already been to Wilkesboro this morning to scrounge up enough Ideal Ball jars without causing suspicion. Who would have ever thought buying sugar in bulk or purchasing too many jars at once would alert revenuers? They kept track of purchases from stores, and store owners were uneasy about selling too many to one person, scared they'd come under scrutiny. That meant I'd had to buy a case or two at one store, then go to another and purchase a case or two, and so on. Everyone talked about canning when I bought the jars.

"Got you lots of 'maters and beans to put up, I reckon."

"Sure do."

At home, I opened the trunk to get out the jars, and felt the hair go up on the back of my neck. I turned and saw the revenuer, Smith, through the early morning fog standing by the road like he'd come up out of the holler. It brought to mind the image of Mama, little gray tendrils of smoke curling and disappearing in the air around her, and the silence after she'd collapsed. A memory I didn't want to have, and I shut my eyes. When I opened them, he was gone. Shivering, I studied the spot where he'd been, questioned if I'd actually seen him. He and Nash Reardon could easily track what we were doing if they had a mind to. Maybe they already knew and maybe they were getting ready to shut us down, send us off Shine Mountain. Merritt would be sent to some reform school, and I'd be forced into a girls' home. I set the crate down, rushed inside, the door slamming behind me. Mrs. Brewer was at the sink wiping the insides of the jars she'd brought. Popeye slept on one of the kitchen chairs and my hand shook as I reached out to pet him. He'd had a calming effect on me usually, but not today.

She said, "Child, what is it? You look like something done walked over your grave."

I straightened up, and Popeye gave a low growl in protest that I'd stopped.

I said, "I saw . . . someone."

"Who?"

"I thought I saw one of them men who arrested Daddy. The one with a patch on his eye."

Mrs. Brewer wiped her hands and said, "What? Where?"

"Out by the road."

We went outside and down the drive. I walked over and stared at an area where the early morning dew was disturbed, revealed by the long, darker green stripes through the grass as if someone had walked through it.

I said, "I wonder if that's the first time he's been here."

"Ain't no telling. Could be they've decided to circle back around to check on family doings. I'll ride with you. Ain't no better deterrent than a crotchety old woman."

We loaded up the rest of the jars she'd been washing, tucking them safely away under the special back seat. As we went down the drive, the spot where I'd seen him no longer fogged in, the mist rising, and the sun coming out, it seemed more like a dream now than something real. The idea this revenuer might be watching the house, watching our comings and goings, was troubling. I remembered something after we got going down the mountain.

I said, "He knew Daddy."

"Did he?"

I nodded. "The day Daddy got caught, he said to him, 'Remember this?' and pulled his eye patch off. The other revenuer, Mr. Reardon, had asked, 'Easton Sasser?', and that other revenuer had said, 'I recognize him. It's him.' "

"Your daddy must've had some sort of run-in with him before. Sounds like he's got a grudge."

I hadn't thought about it in the horror of seeing him get caught, but she was right. What Smith said was curious now, like he blamed Daddy for his injury.

We made it to Big Warrior without any incidents. I carried one case of jars and Mrs. Brewer carried another one. Merritt was pacing back and forth, agitated, and he'd put an old bucket under the spout to catch what was already coming out.

"What took so long? It's been ready to go!"

I set the jars down, and said, "There was a revenuer close to the house."

Merritt grabbed a jar, moved the bucket out of the way, and positioned it under the spout.

"Who was it?"

"That man with the eye patch who was there

398

when Daddy got caught. Smith, I think, is his first name."

"What'd he say?"

"He didn't say nothing. I saw him; then he was gone."

"You didn't say nothing? You didn't ask him what he wanted?"

"I didn't have time, Merritt."

Merritt huffed like I couldn't do anything right. If I'd said he'd made me think of Mama, the way the fog was wrapped around him, he'd think I was, again, being peculiar.

Mrs. Brewer said, "Land sakes, you two got to quit that bickering. It ain't serving no purpose, atall."

"Jar's full," I said.

We began the process, working like a silent machine. Merritt put the jars under the spout, filled them, and handed them off to me. I placed the lids on, and handed them to Mrs. Brewer, who wiped them down and set them in the crate. We'd figured out we could make liquor faster by adding a couple more burners, allowing us to distill 700 gallons of mash into around 115 gallons in about six hours. At one point when we took a break, Merritt went over, selected a jar, sipped some from it, and handed it to Mrs. Brewer.

She took a little drink, smacked her lips, and said, "Shoot. It just gets better'n better."

She held it out to me, but I shook my head. Merritt grinned, and motioned at her he'd take it. He took another sip, then set it by his foot, and while Mrs. Brewer didn't seem to think anything about it, I did. I remembered how him and Oral thought it high times and fun to get drunk. He went back to moving jars under the spout, taking a sip now and then. I don't know why it aggravated me, but it likely had to do with how Uncle Virgil acted when he got drunk, and Oral too. It didn't take long before he got to singing, the jar now half-gone. I couldn't make out the words, but the song had something to do with mountain girls and love. It was highly entertaining, and irritating at the same time. As the flow of shine slowed down, I carried the crates to the car.

When I came back and picked up the final one, Mrs. Brewer said, "Appears I'll be driving us home."

I said, "If you take the truck and him, I can go on and make them two deliveries nearby. Tomorrow, when Merritt's got his head on right, I'll go down to Gastonia and Kings Mountain to them other customers we picked up a week or so ago."

Merritt stopped singing and said, "Hey, hey, I'm goooood, doing fiiiiine."

He sounded like he was talking around a mouthful of mashed potatoes.

I said, "Yeah, we can see how you are."

Mrs. Brewer said, "Give me that jar."

He went to grab it with his right hand, forgetting the hook, and knocked it over. What he'd not drank drained out and onto the ground. Merritt glared at the hook and a fury took over him, unexpected and sudden. He began beating the prosthesis on the ground, hammering it up and down, and clods of dirt and debris flew. We watched in shock as he lost control. He grunted, sounding like a wild animal, while his movements were harsh and volatile. He was going to ruin it, or at the least, it would be damaged in some way. He quit banging it on the ground, and went to beating on it with his left hand, snorting with an unspent rage, saying something I couldn't make out.

I started toward him, and Mrs. Brewer grabbed my arm, and shook her head. "He's fine. He'll remember how he acted. He's done got soused, but he ain't so far gone he won't remember."

Merritt finally gave out, and collapsed on the ground and didn't move. His chest rose up and down, heaving with the energy he'd spent. After a minute or so, he sat up, legs straight out, his forehead almost to his knees. He made a pitiful sound, like a wounded animal. I went over to him and knelt by his side. I put my hand on his back, and he didn't do what I thought he'd do, jerk away, or spit out an insult. He seemed broken, and I got a lump in my throat when I thought about how much he'd loved playing baseball, and how he'd probably felt at school, and how he'd not been acknowledged by his two best friends.

I said, "Merritt?"

His breath deepened, and he did move away then, as if to escape my hand. I let it drop.

Although he was still mumbling, and slurring his words, I was able to make out the same thing he'd said before, "It ain't ever gonna be the same."

Mrs. Brewer leaned on a large, knobby stick she'd been using to help steady herself around the still site, and she said, "Ain't no harm in him letting go of them bad feelings, best as he can. Come on, son, get up."

Merritt said, "Leave me here."

I said, "Don't be dumb."

He said, "I wanna sleep. Tired."

I said, "You can sleep in the truck. Get up."

He rolled over onto his belly, and pushed himself up on his knees. He looked up at me, and Mrs. Brewer, as he wobbled to and fro. He frowned at the realization he'd only made it halfway.

He looked behind himself and said, "Oops. My feet are back there."

I almost laughed, but instead, I went to one side, tucked an arm under his, and Mrs. Brewer leaned down to grip his other, and between the two of us we helped him the rest of the way up. We staggered to the truck, and it was tough going.

It took a lot longer, and once we were there, I was about give out, and poor Mrs. Brewer's hair was hanging out of her usual bun, and she was panting. Merritt tilted his head to the sky, exclaiming how pretty it was. He tried to focus on Mrs. Brewer. He asked her for confirmation of his observation of the world around him, his gestures broad and inclusive.

"Ain't it pretty?"

Mrs. Brewer said, "Very. Get in 'fore I collapse myself, right here on this ground."

I said, "I'll see y'all back at the house in a little while."

She gave me a keen look and said, "Be careful."

Once the sound of the truck faded, it got real quiet, and I worried about how noisy we might have been with Merritt acting like he had. Maybe it was only because of that the woods seemed so eerily still. It was my first run on my own, and not having Merritt riding shotgun was strange. I missed Daddy too, more than I'd have ever thought. I wondered how the revenuers had known about Big Warrior. None of our stills had ever been found to my knowledge, and while we believed the Murrys could've known about them, no one had bothered us until Boomer was destroyed. It always came down to someone talking, like I'd done that day in Mr. Reardon's office. I had to believe the Murrys had done the same.

I lowered myself onto the front seat of Sally Sue feeling like I belonged there. I reached for the key in my pocket and started the car up, a calm contentment settling in as the vibration of the engine met my hands on the steering wheel. I put the car in gear and rolled down the path, carefully avoiding the deepest ruts, and as I pulled out onto the road, I marveled at the way it all felt right.

Everything went wrong less than a minute later.

Chapter 30

It was a private road, a route identified in the stolen journal, a new path I wasn't used to yet, but remembered because there'd been a note saying it was a shortcut around Shine Mountain and just off Lore Mountain Road. As I drove, I wasn't worried, but I should've been. The way it happened reminded me of when Daddy fell in behind me. In much the same way, the car came from out of nowhere. I'd learned a little more about driving during my time with him, but, as it came closer, and the front end tapped Sally Sue's back bumper, my stomach plummeted, and I began to doubt my abilities. I pressed on the gas and Sally Sue responded to the additional fuel. I came to a curve and there was another tap to the back end.

I sucked in my breath and expelled it with a forceful, "No!"

Acid rose in back of my throat, bitter, like when I made myself get sick. My gaze shifted from the rearview to the side view to the path ahead as the car swerved out and back behind me again. Suddenly, it passed me. I immediately let off the gas, and hoped they'd keep going. In the twilight, I could tell it was a car like Sally Sue, felt certain it had to be a Murry, maybe more than one. They'd obviously been reading the journal and learning our routes. Daddy's warning rang in my ears.

They'd have got you, one way or another.

I began repeating the same thing over and over.

"Dear Lord, please don't let them get me."

Their taillights shone bright red like I'd imagined the devil's eyes might. The car stopped and sat dead center of the road. The driver's door swung open, and I swerved, attempting to get around whoever this was. I had to slam on my brakes to avoid hitting him as he put himself in my path. Stunned, I sat with the engine idling, staring at the man I knew as Smith. I figured it was best to stay put and put the car in Park. Maybe he'd let me go.

He strolled over to my window, and said, "Well, if it ain't Miss Sasser."

I said, "What's wrong?"

He leaned back, looked down the length of Sally Sue, and said, "You hauling?"

I said, "Do I look like I'd be doing that?"

"Could be. Family thing is what I reckon."

I said, "I guess you revenuers are getting smarter, or luckier."

He sucked at his teeth, and said, "Well, now. I ain't working in that capacity at the moment. I'm here for another cause. Righting wrongs, I reckon you could say."

The eye that wasn't covered with a patch was the palest of greens, rimmed in black. Familiar.

He yanked my door open and said, "Get out."

"If you ain't here working for Mr. Reardon, you ain't got no call to have stopped me."

He waved a hand and said, "Who ever said the law always plays by the rules? Get out."

He had the advantage. I got out, thinking about the jars and jugs under the back seat. He opened the back door and my mouth went dry. I twisted my hands as he pulled the seat forward, exposing the wooden box built beneath it.

He said, "Open it."

I didn't move.

He said, "I already know what's in here. Been watching your brother since last night. Watched y'all load it up."

"If you know what's in there, you open it."

"Nothing but sass. Reckon you suit your name."

He yanked the lid up exposing what was inside. The jars twinkled and shone like crystals, catching what was left of the daylight.

He said, "Now, ain't that a pretty sight? Let's see how it tastes."

He opened a jar and sipped, and emitted a thoughtful, "Hm."

He set it back in the crate, then lifted it out, and

handed it to me. He waved his hand indicating I needed to follow him. He went to his car, and opened the back door. The vehicle was different from ours but a bootleg car nonetheless, I was sure of it. It was a Ford coupe, the more typical model for a running car. Maybe they'd started using it to keep up, or as an undercover car, because I sure couldn't figure out why a revenuer would have one.

He said, "Stick it in there."

"Are you gonna let me go?"

He was noncommittal, and said, "We'll see what happens."

I wasn't going to argue. If we were going to lose this haul of liquor, if this was what I had to do in order for him to let me off, fine.

By the sixth case, I was uneasy about how it would end. I thought about unscrewing a lid off a jar myself, guzzling the contents, hoping I'd pass out and when I woke up he'd be gone, but that didn't seem smart. While I loaded his car, he went to pouring shine out of the jugs around one side of Sally Sue. The fake gas tank was full too, and I considered he might damage it if he started rapping on it. He whistled through his teeth while he released our carefully crafted liquor, turning the dirt from light brown to dark. Finally, I had carried the last crate and put it in his car.

I said, "Stealing liquor? Ain't it odd for a revenuer?"

My comment gained no reaction.

He said, "Stand back."

"What for?"

"Girl, you don't seem to realize you ain't in a position to ask questions."

I asked another one anyway. "You arresting me?"

He snorted. "Like I said, I ain't working in that capacity at the moment."

He was taking matters into his own hands like he had his own rules.

"Mr. Reardon wouldn't approve."

"He ain't the boss man tonight."

He reached into his pocket, pulled out a book of matches, flicked the end of his thumbnail over the head of one.

Alarmed, I said, "Don't," but he tossed it and it landed on the liquor-soaked ground.

The shine he'd poured from the jugs was as good as gasoline. A fiery line snaked halfway around the vehicle, and when I started for the car he grabbed hold of my arm.

Frantic, I pointed, and said, "Mama! I got to get Mama!"

He said, "Girl, you done lost your mind. Your mama ain't in there."

He didn't understand. It was the picture I had of her tucked into the dashboard. It would be like she'd been burned all over again. I bucked against the hold he had on my arm. I jerked, hit, and kicked, frantic to get to the open window of the driver's side. The fire was only getting started. I had time.

I screamed at him, "Let me go! Let me go, please! I got to get her picture!"

His hand slipped from the hold he had on me and I stumbled backward. He snatched for me again, but missed. I ran to the other side where there were no flames. I yanked the passenger door open, grabbed Mama's picture off the dash, and hesitated, staring at him through the open windows. Curiosity and another expression altered his scarred face, something akin to satisfaction, as if he was about to witness what most people would turn away from. He didn't move. He waited to see what would happen, what the fire would do. He licked his lips.

Like fingers wriggling and twisting, the orange and red flames reached past the window on the other side and he appeared consumed by the blaze. His eyes glistened in a way I didn't think came from drinking the shine. I was sure he was . . . crazy. There was a sloping hill behind me, and it dropped into a deep holler. I considered taking that first step, wondering if I would make it down, if I could escape, but I was too late. While I was trying to figure how to take the first step, he ran around the car and grabbed my arm again. I felt dumb, believing I could have gotten away. He jerked me along, his fingers tight around my wrist, pulling me away from Sally Sue, and toward his car. I stumbled after him, clutching Mama's picture.

He shoved me down into the passenger seat, and said, "Try anything stupid again, see what happens."

He got in on the driver's side, turned the key, and as soon as the car started, he accelerated, and whipped it around to go back the way we'd come. In the side view mirror, I noticed the flames growing higher on the one side of Sally Sue. I couldn't watch, and I shrank against the passenger door.

He said, "You looking 'bout like death warmed over."

I didn't respond and he went to whistling as he drove. After a few minutes, I was sure we were heading back to Big Warrior. We came to one particular area where I'd normally turn if I was going the way I was used to, a two-tire rutted path that appeared to go nowhere. He went by that, and around a curve to turn onto a narrow dirt road. We began to climb, the car rocking back and forth, the jars rattling, and he stopped when we came to a crest.

He said, "Get out."

"Where is this?"

He didn't answer. He got out and opened the back door to retrieve a shotgun, a hatchet, and one of our jars of shine. I wondered if he was

411

going to shoot me like a dog gone sick and needed putting down. Maybe he intended to chop me up afterward. I got out, and considered I ought to run. He sort of smiled, like he could read my thoughts, and aimed the gun at me.

He stuck the hatchet into his back pocket, and said, "Walk," and nodded toward the woods.

I wasn't as strong as I could be, my arms felt feeble, and my legs shook. I was weak-kneed from working at the still with Merritt and Mrs. Brewer, and then from stacking crates in Sally Sue, and again into his car. I did as he said and entered into the shadows, where the air was cooler, the woods silent. As I walked, the area grew more dense, and what little bit of sunlight left penetrated through and littered the ground with fragments of bright gold here and there.

On occasion, he said, "Go left," or, "Go right."

This went on for several minutes until I figured out we were coming up the back side of Big Warrior, and the way I knew this was by recognizing the mound of rocks that encircled Mama's pool of water. We'd come in from another direction.

I stopped and said, "What're we doing here?"

He said, "You sure do ask a lot of questions."

He reached into his back pocket, and handed me the hatchet. "Get to work."

Incredulous, I stared at him, then the still we'd only put back together again.

"Go on, take it down. Now that your old man's where he belongs, and that chickenshit uncle of yours took off, time to put a final end to the Sasser operation. Cleaning up, that's what we're doing."

I was too slow.

His demeanor changed over my stalling, and he waved the shotgun and yelled, "Hurry it up! Get on with it!"

I hefted the hatchet in my right hand, stepped over to the still, hit one side, and the blade stuck in the wood. I wrenched it out and hit it again. It made a hollow sound, empty, the way I felt at the moment. I thought about Merritt and how we'd worked together earlier in this very spot along with Mrs. Brewer. The image of Sally Sue with the fire beginning to touch the driver's door came next, and I was filled with sadness. My different attitude was still surprising in ways, yet I understood it. It had been a reckoning a long time coming, my sorting out my anger at Daddy, along with the satisfaction of finally learning some things about Mama. My middle turned into a solid knot, while a hurt I'd not recollected before, a deep melancholy, caused tears, and blurry vision.

Not that Smith noticed. He sat down, his back against the trunk of a tree, and got to sipping on that jar of liquor like it was water. It wasn't all that odd for a revenuer to taste what he'd been responsible for discovering, yet something about him was beginning to make me question who he really was, and while I whacked and beat on the still, my thoughts circled back to him bringing up Mama. He worked his mouth as if he was trying to figure out how we'd made it. I used the back side of the hatchet to pound the sides of wood we'd only just put together. I tried not to think about my dry mouth, how exhausted I was, or what might happen once I was done.

After a few minutes, I broke my silence with a question.

I said, "How do you know so much about us, about my mama?"

Moving with care, he set the jar down beside him. He reached for a pack of cigarettes in his shirt pocket, shook one out, and stuck it in his mouth. He struck a match and lit the end of the cigarette, and blew out a plume of smoke. He was stalling, or maybe just taking his time. Maybe he wasn't going to answer me at all.

Then he said, "See this?"

He pointed at the eye patch. Some thought must've flitted through his mind, because he suddenly laughed, then stopped, and gave me a dark look. The scarring over his cheekbone and down his neck didn't help his countenance as it was, but whatever thought he'd had altered him such that a hint of fear crept into my gut. He removed the patch to reveal a puckered, pink empty eye socket. The hatchet suddenly felt like it weighed too much. I wanted to sit down, yet I wanted to take off running at the same time.

He said, "You ain't wanting to look at me. I'm used to it by now. This here's 'cause of your mama. If it hadn't been for her, I wouldn't have lost this eye, got these scars. What she done messed me up but good."

He pulled the patch back down.

Startled by his admission, I said, "What do you mean, she was responsible?"

"Had me a gal, and was gonna get married, have a family."

Confused, I said, "I don't know how any of that's got to do with my mama."

He drank some more and didn't speak.

I wasn't sure he would offer anything else, and I was about to turn away when he said, "It didn't go like it should've. I'd caught them at a still, your folks. You were there. You remember any of it?"

I shook my head, still trying to follow where this was going, wanting to understand what it meant.

He said, "The day your mama died."

I wasn't completely sure what he meant. I offered the only thing I'd known all my life.

I said, "I saw her burn. Daddy tried to help her, but it was too late. That's all I know."

He said, "Yeah. Well. I reckon you could say

415

I was there in a different capacity. Sort of like now."

He wasn't making sense, and I must've looked confounded.

He said, "As a Murry."

Chapter 31

His lips spread in a creepy smile before he sipped from the jar again. All the while he watched me, his single eye like a brilliant green marble, and now I understood why the color had been familiar. Willie Murry's eyes were that very same shade of green.

"Surprise," he said.

Daddy's warning all those weeks ago came to mind, about getting caught alone with any of them. I began to believe I might not make it out of this. He was somehow involved in what happened years ago and surely he wouldn't let me walk away knowing that. He could shoot me, and there were plenty of places to toss my body. Lots of critters could come along, drag me away, and my bones would then be picked over by buzzards. It would be as if I'd never been.

He said, "Didn't think you could turn any whiter. Reckon I was wrong."

I said, "Your name is Smith. That's what Mr. Reardon called you."

"Yeah, he thinks I'm Robert Smith. Name's Martin Murry."

417

I thought back to the MM in our journal, and some of Mama's entries.

He pointed a finger and said, "Get on back to taking that still apart, and don't be causing me no problems. Like her."

"I don't know what you mean."

"No, I don't reckon you would."

This parleying back and forth wasn't useful. I was beginning to think he, of all people, had the answers I'd wanted all my life. I got up the nerve and asked the question I wanted to understand the most.

"Was it you caused my mama's death?"

"I was acting in an official capacity."

"Which means you did."

He said, "She should've done like I told her and maybe I wouldn't have had to fire off that shot."

I remembered the ricocheting noise before the explosion.

"You caused the still to blow up."

He pointed at his eye, at the scars. "And paid for it too."

"Not like she did."

"Hell. This here cost me aplenty."

He jabbed a finger again toward his face. Maybe it was the liquor working on him or pent-up years of anger, but he became more disturbed as the seconds went by.

He said, "I lost that gal I had. She couldn't even

418

look at me. Wouldn't. We was getting married until I turned up like this."

He grabbed the jar and drank some more.

I said, "I don't see how killing someone is the same thing."

He said, "I might as well have died far as she was concerned."

I said, "Seems to me you got your justice. My mama's dead and my daddy's sitting in jail. You ask me, all you Murrys ought to be locked up, not him. He ain't never killed nobody."

He started laughing, but it was more like hoarse coughing, and he abruptly stopped. He pointed at me, and made stabbing motions to emphasize each word as he spoke with anger.

He said, "Tell you what. It ends when there ain't no more Sassers running shine down that mountain. Like cleaning house, you could say."

He pointed at the still. I went back to hammering on it, letting the hatchet rise and fall, striking the sides, creating a racket. He sat back down, went back to drinking while I kept a subtle watch. I had to get away, however I could. I hoped if he ended up drinking all of that jar, it would at least make it difficult for him to run after me if I suddenly took off. I beat on the still, taking a piece from it now and then and setting it on the ground. He glared at me as I worked, and I began to think the more he had, the madder he was getting. I was wound up, anxious, and afraid.

The longer this went on, the shakier I got. What if I didn't have the strength if an opportunity came my way? I quit pounding, and wiped my forehead.

He immediately said, "Why're you stopping? Ain't nobody said stop. Did you hear me tell you to?"

I said, "I ain't feeling good."

As soon as I said it, my stomach rebelled, as if I'd sent it a silent message. I retched as a spasm of nausea hit my middle.

He said, "Puny as you look, ain't no wonder. Get it over with; then get back to work. You ain't done till that still ain't no more. Then we'll see what comes next."

That made me so scared, I couldn't handle the sick I felt. I bolted to the edge of the woods, my hand clapped over my mouth.

He hollered, "Hey! Don't you go no further. Take care of whatever's wrong with you right there!"

He acted repulsed as I threw up while clenching a tree trunk. I heaved several times, then faked the need to do more as I scanned the woods, hoping I'd see a possible way to run. I would be taking a risk getting lost, but it was better than waiting to see if I would live through this. I was willing to take the chance. He'd almost finished the shine off, and was about to have another cigarette. It was now or go back to the still and lose what might be a last chance. I took off running straight into the brush, zigzagging through the trees.

His voice was hoarse when he yelled, "Hey! Get your ass back here!"

A shot rang out, and whizzed by me. I plunged downhill, wheezing, the rasping noise filling my ears. My legs wanted to give way and I was sure I was likely to die from this effort, and save him from having to kill me.

Somewhere behind me came, "You'll be sorry! There's gonna be hell to pay," and it rattled me he sounded even closer.

Propelled forward by the idea he was, I scrambled up the hill, and as I reached the top, I glanced back and saw him starting up, his furious yelling echoing over the hills.

"You wait till I get hold of you!"

I hoped I was headed in the same direction, the way we'd come, but I wasn't sure. Another blast and a tree by me was hit. Splintered wood coated my hair and clothes like snowflakes. I dodged thick patches of sweet shrub, and sumac. I slipped behind huge oaks, maple and birch trees, putting whatever protection I could between me and him. I prayed I'd end up somewhere I recognized. My mouth tasted metallic like I'd bit my tongue while my lungs felt as if they were on fire. The ground leveled and there was his car hidden by a copse of shrubs. I don't know how I'd managed to get back to it, but it didn't matter.

I ran over, pulled the driver's door open, and saw the key in the ignition. It was the first mistake he'd made since this began. I mumbled a thank-you to Jesus, got in and cranked it up.

He showed up at the edge of the woods, and when he saw me sitting in the driver's seat he raised the gun. He was furious, his face almost purple, his expression contorted from effort, anger, or both. I put the car in Reverse, and didn't look at him again. I went backward as fast as I could without wrecking until I came to a clearing and backed into it. A shot dinged against the side of the car. I was afraid he would try to hit the gas tank and my end would come, just like Mama, at the hands of a Murry. I put the car in Drive and plowed over weeds, small trees, and bushes, almost hitting a huge pine tree. I followed the single set of tire marks flattening the brush. I tore down the path, sending dirt and dust into the air. I glanced in the rearview, saw he'd lowered the gun, grateful he was no longer shooting. He shook his fists in the air in a rage.

I made it to the road, realizing by God, I'd stolen a Murry's running car. I could've laughed except the realization sank in. What now? What would happen? Martin Murry had told me a lot. I wished Daddy was at home more than ever. Not only would he know what to do; his presence would have made me feel safer; all of us would be safer. I drove fast as I dared, the headlights shining on the road in front of me, occasionally catching a pair of glowing eyes. I fought nausea, swallowing over and over. There was no time to stop. I came to our road, rounded the curve, and saw the house, saw how the windows were lit with a warm, soft glow. I went up the drive. This car was so much like ours, if Mrs. Brewer happened to see it out the kitchen window, she wouldn't think anything was wrong.

I got out, bone weary, shaky, a rising moon before me and stars that shimmered. I stumbled across the dewy grass, climbed the back steps, yanked the door open. Popeye brushed against my legs and gave a single meow. Mrs. Brewer, God bless her, stood at the stove cooking supper. She was about to speak, and instead dropped the fork she'd been using to turn pork chops, making hot grease splash on the stove top.

"Lord, child, what's done happened to you? You ailing? What's wrong?"

I said, "We have to leave again and quick."

"Leave? Why?"

I went down the hall, she and Popeye in pursuit.

I said, "We have to go back to your house, and we have to go now. We can't stay here."

"Now hang on a minute; what's happened?"

"That revenuer, he ain't who he says he is."

Shocked, she said, "Revenuer? You saw a revenuer? Which one?"

"The one out here this morning watching the

house. I thought his name was Smith, but it's actually Martin Murry. I'll tell you about it, but we got to go. I took his car."

She wiped her hands on her apron, and said, "You ain't making no sense, but all right, all right."

I entered Merritt's room and he was laid out on his back, mouth open, snoring, sleeping off the effects of shine.

I shook his foot, and said, "Merritt! Get up!"

He barely moved.

"Merritt! Come on, trouble's coming!"

It took me another two attempts before I could rouse him and then he grumbled, "Go 'way, Jessie!"

I said, "You don't want to be here when Martin Murry comes!"

He sat up, and said, "Huh? Who?"

"There ain't time to talk, and you ain't gonna remember it anyway; now get up! Get some clothes and come on!"

I left him half falling off the bed, while I went into Daddy and Mama's room. I could hear Mrs. Brewer gathering her stuff, Popeye meowing loudly, not liking the commotion. I wondered if it might be the last time I'd be in here, because if Martin Murry was like the rest of his family, we might not have a home to come to. What would Daddy think? Would he see it as my fault as well? I grabbed some clothes and shut the door, then met Mrs. Brewer in the hall. She held a paper bag and Popeye was draped over her other arm.

I said, "I'll drive the truck."

"Wouldn't it be better for you to drive Sally Sue, leave the truck here?"

"I ain't got Sally Sue."

"But how'd you get here?"

"I took his car," I repeated.

Mrs. Brewer became even more alarmed while I thought we'd already taken too much time, though it couldn't have been more than five minutes. I tried to figure out how long it might take him to get here, if he came at all. I had no idea what he intended, only that I'd left him stranded, bested him. Merritt stumbled out of his room, his hair stuck up on end, shoes resting on top of the clothes over his good arm. He had his prosthesis, thankfully, still strapped on.

I took his things, and said, "Hurry, Merritt, get your shoes on!"

I took everything they had along with mine and ran outside. I threw it all into the back seat of Mrs. Brewer's car. She came out of the house carrying the paper bag, grease stains starting to leak through.

She handed it to me, saying, "Can't let these pork chops go to waste."

Merritt clomped outside, shoes on the wrong feet. He stopped when he saw the car, gaping at it in confusion.

I said, "Let's go."

He said, "Wait, whose car is that? It ain't—"

I said, "I'll tell you after we get going; come on!"

I got in the truck and cranked it while Mrs. Brewer dumped the protesting Popeye onto the back seat of her car. I took a second and reached into my back pocket. My fingers encountered the edges of Mama's picture. It had survived the escape and not been lost in the woods. Relieved, I followed Mrs. Brewer down the driveway while Merritt gnawed on a pork chop he'd gotten out of the bag on the floorboard. The smell from it caused a quarrel between my belly and my head.

I said, "You ain't gonna believe what happened after you and Mrs. Brewer left."

He gave me a look, and said, "I can believe just about anything way things have been lately. And whose car is this?"

I proceeded to tell him about the man with the eye patch, how he'd blocked me in the road. I explained he was a Murry in reality, a revenuer with fake name. I dropped the bombshell about his involvement with Mama's death. I talked fast, everything gushing out like a boiler left unattended. When I got to the final part about getting away, and him shooting at me, it sounded like something out of one of the *Untouchables* programs.

Merritt chewed vigorously on the pork chop as he listened.

After I was done, he said, "Holy cow"; then he said, "I ain't ever heard about no Martin Murry. He's got to be lying."

I said, "I know, but why would he say that?"

Merritt said, "True."

In Wilkesboro, ours were the only vehicles rumbling along under streetlights and by darkened houses, like cats slinking through neighborhood alleys. Sidewalks were empty, buildings unlit, hustle and bustle absent. I wished we were back home, sitting around the table, eating, and planning the next haul. A sense of lonesomeness crept in, and settled somewhere deep inside me. At Mrs. Brewer's house, we parked, and got out. Popeye ran onto the porch as she fished around in her bag for her key to open the door. The cat was the only one acting like he wasn't anxious, his tail whipping about like a flag.

"Maybe I ought to call Daddy," I said, wondering if he'd even take a call from me.

Probably not, but he'd talk to Merritt.

Merritt said, "What can he do all the way down in Atlanta?"

"I don't know. I was thinking he should know about what's going on."

The idea of Merritt talking to him was decided before I even had a chance to bring it up.

He said, "I ain't telling him."

427

Mrs. Brewer opened the door, and after she'd turned on the kitchen light she turned and said, "Tell me what happened."

I filled her in and she sat very still, hand over her mouth, listening carefully.

When I was done, she said, "I'll tell you who you ought to be talking to; you ought to be telling that revenuer feller, Mr. Reardon."

For her to say that was considerable.

Chapter 32

Nash Reardon's office hadn't changed, but he had. His tie was crooked and he was swilling coffee as if his life depended on it. His shirtsleeve had some sort of orangey-pink stain on it. Maybe ketchup. A gray haze lingered in the air, even as he lit another cigarette. I sat in the same chair thinking he needed a good swig of moonshine for himself. If what Mrs. Brewer believed was true, a little bit of it might set him straight. His eyes were red like he'd been losing sleep. I was here before school while Merritt waited impatiently in the truck. He'd suggested coming in, but I'd told him I would mess up if he did. I was already beside myself as it was. I pressed my hands into my lap, had to clear my throat before I could speak.

I said, "I got some information," and he put the cigarette in an ashtray and picked up his pen.

He said, "Good. Good. I've been waiting on you to come back. That information you gave me the first time is one of two busts we've made this summer. That makes you a reliable source."

He mashed the button on his pen repeatedly while he waited. Mr. Reardon appeared to be under pressure, like a boiler about to blow, not calm like when he took Daddy away.

I took a deep breath, and said, "I reckon I'm gonna give you my name this time. I have to in order to say what I gotta say."

I expected a reaction out of him, but he only waited for me to go on.

I said, "I'm Jessie Sasser. My daddy is Easton Sasser, the man you and them others caught a few weeks back."

He didn't seem shocked, or even remotely surprised. He only nodded, and wrote something down. My name most likely.

I said, "I ain't in here 'cause of that; it's about a Murry."

He said, "They causing trouble?"

"They've always caused trouble. You have no idea."

He said, "Okay. Well then, go ahead."

"The man with the eye patch and the scars on his face?"

He nodded, and said, "Agent Robert Smith."

I nodded. "He got burned a long time ago."

Mr. Reardon said, "Yes."

I couldn't tell if he knew more than that or not.

I said, "He ain't who he says he is."

His expression became guarded, and he replied with, "And just who is he supposed to be?"

"Martin Murry. He's one of them."

"How did you come to know all this?"

"He's been watching our house—"

"That's not out of line, considering."

I said, "He told me himself."

"How'd he come to do that?"

"I was driving Daddy's old running car. Can't no Murry stand anyone else hauling liquor on Shine Mountain. They'd been trying to get a hold on it for years."

Mr. Reardon got up and began to pace around the room. "Were you hauling?"

"No!"

Maybe that was too loud, too guilty-sounding.

I shifted on the chair. "Of course not. I told you before, I don't lay claim to it."

"It tends to be a family thing, like with them. I'm beginning to think it's why you came in here the first time. A retaliation of sorts."

I said, "It wasn't that."

I was getting flustered. I had to get him back around to why I was really in here.

"It was my own daddy I came in here to tell you about, only I got scared and told you about the Murry still instead."

"Inform on your father? Why would you do that?"

"On account of what happened to my mama a long time ago. I've always thought she died on account of making shine. I didn't know until a couple days ago I had it wrong. It was Martin Murry who caused her death."

431

He sat back down, and said, "Your mother was killed by my agent who isn't who I think he is?"

I nodded. "I was four years old, but I remember it. She was standing by a still. It blew up and I never knew why until that agent you think is Robert Smith told me only yesterday he'd shot at it. She was burned. It's how he lost his eye, got them scars of his. I been blaming Daddy all along."

He said, "I'm sorry, Miss Sasser, but this is all sounding a little far-fetched."

"I'm telling the truth."

"Let's back up a minute. What happened after he stopped you?"

"He made me go with him."

"What reason would he have for doing that?"

"That grudge he's carrying."

"What happened then?"

"He took me to our last still, told me to tear it apart. Said he was 'cleaning house.' He had a gun. I figured I wasn't going to get out of them woods."

Mr. Reardon got up again, and started pacing. "You say he's Martin Murry, and he was involved in your mother's death, and intending to maybe kill you too."

"Like I said, he's got some sort of grudge. He'd been planning on getting married back then. It didn't work out, he says because of his scars and all."

He paced some more, and while I'd been sure I'd feel better after telling everything, there was a heaviness instead, a weightiness that grew with each tick of the clock on his wall. He reached for the phone on his desk while looking at his wristwatch.

"Miss Sasser, my apologies, but I need to make a phone call."

I was being dismissed, and I rose from the chair. He didn't believe me.

I said, "Ask him. Ask him what happened to Lydia Sasser back in 1948. See what he says. Ask him who Martin Murry is."

Mr. Reardon began dialing, and said, "Yeah, I'll do that."

I said, "I'm scared. My little brother's scared. We can't even stay at our house. You go inside, and you'll see for yourself. They've painted words in some of the rooms. We painted over the ones outside, but you can still tell."

He stretched the phone cord across the desk in order to open the door for me. I hesitated before I walked out.

He said, "Phil Walker, please."

My voice pleading, I said, "Mr. Reardon, I got more proof."

He put a hand over the mouthpiece, gave me an impatient look.

I spoke fast as I could. "There's an Oldsmobile Rocket Eighty-Eight on the side of Little River

Road. If it ain't burned up totally, it'll be close to it. That was my Daddy's car, what I was driving when he stopped me. And on Shine Mountain Road, in the curve just after Little Pine Creek, is our house. There's another car parked in the backyard. It's his. It's a 1940 Ford coupe. I took it when I got away from him. He'll come for it."

"Is that all, Miss Sasser?"

"We're staying with Mrs. Louise Brewer in Wilkesboro."

He said nothing, but he hadn't shut the door on me either. He appeared deep in thought until the person he wanted came onto the line.

He spoke, "Phil! Thank you for taking my call."

He shut the door then, and I rushed down the hall. Outside I pulled my sweater tight around me and walked to where I'd parked the truck.

Merritt was waiting, and before I'd even shut the door he said, "It must not have gone too good. You got that pasty look again."

I said, "I don't know if he believes me. He shooed me out the door so he could make a phone call after I told him his supposed revenuer isn't who he thinks he is."

Merritt said, "You have to wonder, where's Martin Murry been all these years? Why ain't nobody ever said nothing about him?"

I said, "I don't know."

Another mystery.

I headed for Piney Tops and got there as hallways filled with students along with the usual laughter and talking and locker doors slamming. Aubrey was finally beginning to realize Willie had slipped from her hold, but she wouldn't give up. She stationed herself strategically only to have to watch him make a commotion over Cora. She glared into a compact, her back to them while reapplying lipstick she didn't need. Meanwhile Zeb, and some new friend, a boy who didn't act much different than him, competed for Willie's attention. The new boy was Dylan Todd and I could hear him above all else. Loud, obnoxious, he'd turn and poke Zeb seeking approval for when he did something.

Cora and Stacy mostly ignored the three-ring circus going on about them. Cora had evidently set some rules about Willie fraternizing with her at school, and he obeyed, hovering though, in case she noticed him. Aubrey had formed a new alliance with a girl named Marissa Blaylock. Aubrey chattered near Marissa's ear while the other girl bobbed her head nonstop. That was all Aubrey needed. Somebody to listen to her and agree. Maybe our friendship had been destined to end anyway. I felt different this year, changed because of what I knew about Mama and what I'd decided to do, while Aubrey still acted the same.

There was something else above and beyond all

this. It was how after Willie made a commotion the first day in the parking lot, I'd become invisible, even when I passed right by him in the hallways. After how he'd acted last year, and what took place over the summer, it stood out. I was sure it had been him and his buddies at the house, shooting, scaring us, and it had to have been him who came back and spray-painted those threats. For one, Willie had never been able to spell worth a lick, and second, someone like Royce, or Leland Murry, would've been more apt to do something like what had been done to Oral, or like burning down Uncle Virgil's house. For as bad as it had scared us, what Willie and his cohorts had done wasn't at the level of the elder Murrys. It had been more like fun for them. Cutting up. Being stupid.

The reason for his change of behavior was Cora, and what I saw as an unexpected opportunity. When the bell rang to let us out at the end of classes for the day, I found him standing just outside the front entrance.

I marched up and said, "You reckon Cora McCaskill would give you the time of day if she knew the real *William* Murry?"

I saw a nervous twitch, a minuscule jumping of his upper lip, but it was the worry that flickered briefly across his face and told me I'd said something that mattered. He tried to act cool, bluff his way out like he didn't care.

He said, "Shit. What do you know about anything?"

I said, "Plenty. Like how your family ain't nothing but sorry, and ain't never been nothing but that. Especially that murdering brother of yours, Martin Murry."

The worry turned to alarm.

"What do you know about him?"

I shifted my books, and said, "What does it matter, but boy, could I share lots with her. About how you and your family really are, what you like to do during your summer vacation."

A hint of the old Willie Murry I was most familiar with peeked through, delivering a bottomless, cold stare. Threatening a Murry was like praying to the devil. On his feet were new Wearmasters. He wore stiff new jeans too, meant to impress a certain girl, I was sure. He didn't like standing there with me, and his gaze roamed about the schoolyard to see who might notice.

He looked down at me, and spit out a question. "What do you want?"

"What belongs to my family."

He leaned in, and said, "What the hell you talking about?"

"You know exactly what I'm talking about. What you took right out of our house. I reckon I could add 'thief' to what I could tell Cora."

The timing couldn't have been better, because she came out the entrance with Stacy, heading toward the bus I used to ride. Like a special radar frequency suddenly switched on, he spotted her, and his manner became urgent as he walked away.

Over his shoulder, he said, "Hell no. I ain't doing that."

I decided to call his bluff.

I said, "Oh. Okay."

I too made a beeline for Cora, and he reached out and grabbed me. The commotion behind her caught Cora's attention and she turned around, and saw the death grip he had on my upper arm. She had a thing for Willie, not as bad as Aubrey, but it was there in the way she frowned at him, the way she noticed his hand holding on to me. She stormed off, and Stacy had to run to keep up. It was true, he wasn't bad-looking, but he certainly was bad. Willie's fingers dug deeper into my arm.

I flinched at the pressure, and managed to say, "Your true colors are showing. I'm going to tell her all about you Murrys. This won't stop me."

"All right! Fine!" he said, and he pushed me away.

I wanted to rub the spot, but I wouldn't allow him to see me do that.

I said, "It better not be ruined, neither."

He said something I couldn't make out as he raced away. When he reached Cora's side, she shook her head, denying him for what she'd seen between us. Cora had laid down the law, and it surely wasn't something he was used to. A sick longing pulled his mouth down. At least one thing had gone in my favor for the day. I spotted Merritt walking across the lawn alone, his shoulders rounded like he'd had a rough day too, and I hurried to catch up. I decided not to tell him about my encounter with Willie and what I'd said. I wanted to see if Willie would keep his word. We walked together to the school's parking lot where the truck was parked.

I said, "What's Curt or Abel up to?"

He snorted, and didn't respond.

"Have they talked to you?"

"Curt said hey, but that was about it. Abel ain't said a word. All they can do is stare at this thing."

He held up his prosthesis.

Damn them.

At Mrs. Brewer's house, I switched off the truck and said, "Why do you reckon Daddy never reported what happened to Mama?"

Merritt stared out the front windshield, digesting the question, turning his hook round and round.

He said, "We ain't never wanted the law interfering with family matters."

"I know, but he never did anything against the Murrys neither."

"You don't know that. Maybe he did. Daddy never talked much about that time."

With a hint of sarcasm, I said, "Yeah, tell me about it."

We walked across the yard and I loved how the colder air carried the smell of whatever she was cooking. We were safer here, hidden away, protected. Up on the porch Popeye snaked his body in between our legs, his way of telling us he wanted to be petted. I bent down to rub his back and he let out a throaty, *Rowr.*

Merritt went inside, and Mrs. Brewer called from the kitchen, "How'd it go?"

I followed him in, while Popeye hopped on the porch rail to watch a bird, tail switching back and forth. I liked Mrs. Brewer's house, and although it was small, she had three bedrooms. I was in the one she called "the green room," because it had the green throw rugs on the wood floor. The rugs matched the leaves in the flowery wallpaper. The bed had a white bedspread and green pillows. The lamp had a green shade. Merritt was in "the blue room," decorated similarly, only with blue throw rugs and shade. Mrs. Brewer's room was pink. I stopped by my room and dropped my books on the bed.

Back in the kitchen Merritt was telling Mrs. Brewer he didn't think the revenuer believed me. She had a pot of rice bubbling, and stirred a skillet of milk gravy. My stomach tightened and my mouth watered. She had a tendency to cook exactly what we would eat that night, and no

440

more. I wondered if that was habit, or if she only did it because of me. Maybe wanting to prevent me from doing what she knew I might do. She studied me as I came in.

She said, "You okay?"

I nodded, and sank onto a kitchen chair, my cheek propped in the palm of my hand, watching as she went back to cooking. The day had been tiring and worrisome, from seeing Nash Reardon to contending with Willie. She poured the gravy into a bowl and set it on the table while my stomach fought with my head. The bowl of rice came next, a plate of corn bread, and another of fried okra. Last was a baked chicken.

She said, "Y'all go on and wash up; then let's eat."

Merritt went to the kitchen sink, stuck his one hand under the stream of water, while I headed for the bathroom. I avoided the mirror, avoided even a glance at the toilet. I washed my hands, staring at the rust stain from the faucet drip. My belly urged me to fill it while at the same time I considered telling Mrs. Brewer I couldn't eat. I was sure it would only make her worry, and fuss. I went back into the kitchen and sat at the table.

After a quick blessing, she said, "Fill yer plates; I know you got to be hungry."

Merritt obliged, his plate running out of room while I only put small amounts on mine as the bowls were passed my way. My fork hovered, while I tried to decide what my stomach would do, rebel or not. After they started eating, I pushed the food about on my plate.

Mrs. Brewer said, "That still I got, it ain't big as what y'all had, but it'll make fifty gallons easy."

Merritt, his voice hopeful, said, "Why, sure, that's right."

She said, "Jessie, what do you think?"

I put my fork down.

I said, "How're we gonna haul it?"

Mrs. Brewer said, "In the back of my old car. Right there in the trunk. Shoot. Won't nobody never suspect a thing."

Chapter 33

Nothing escaped her because she knew me, but I thought I was smart, thought I could hide what I'd done like I always had. My new clothes, unlike my old, fit comfortably, but that made no difference as to how I felt, or my state of mind. She did like always, and kept me busy after supper. I washed up the dishes, and then we sat round the table while she and Merritt enjoyed a slice of coconut cake. We talked about making shine in her still. I only nibbled on the slice she'd given me, while drinking the special tea. The peppermint taste was nice, and I considered I might be all right. We put our plates in the sink; then we listened to the radio for some time.

When a commercial came on, I excused myself and said, "I'll be right back."

I went into the bathroom. She had a scale. I stepped on it, and clapped a hand over my mouth to hold in a cuss word. The walls in her house were thin, and I didn't want her coming to see what was going on. I'd somehow put on five pounds since the last time I'd weighed myself. *I can't let this happen.* I was locked in place, staring at the number, feeling like I'd betrayed myself, when Merritt knocked on the door.

"Hey, Jessie?"

I cleared my throat, aggravated, and with irritation I said, "What!"

"Mrs. Brewer needs help."

I said, "Just a minute."

"She said hurry."

I stepped off the scale, and yanked the door open. "What is it?"

He waved his prosthesis toward the kitchen, and said, "She can't open some jar, and I can't get a grip on it neither. I tried."

I pushed by him, irritated. In the kitchen she held a jar of homemade bread-'n-butter pickles, gnarly fingers attempting to twist the lid with no results.

I said, "You wanting to eat pickles *now?*"

She said, "I get a hankering when my stomach's upset," and gave me that look like she used to at the school.

I took the jar and tried. It was tight. I got a butter knife, and tapped the edge, and tried again. The seal broke with a snap, and the lid came off.

She plucked an olive-colored slice out, plopped it in her mouth, and said, "Here, try one. Made 'em myself."

"I'm already full."

She said, "Don't see how."

Merritt said, "Lemme try one."

Mrs. Brewer offered him the jar and the both of them crunched and smacked their lips enthusiastically, making my mouth water.

I said, "Okay, one."

She tipped the jar and I put a piece in my mouth and chewed. It *was* really good. She ate another, and so did we. A couple minutes later, my stomach settled.

She said, "Pickles been around hundreds of years. Always good for what ails you, particularly the belly."

I sighed. She was trying so hard to keep me from doing what had become natural, ordinary, far as I was concerned. While it didn't necessarily make me feel better about myself, it was a need I couldn't describe, a need once fulfilled that enabled me to function. It was as if in doing this I cleared my head the way I cleared my stomach of its contents. We returned to the living room where the radio was tuned in to a news station, but I didn't pay much attention to what was being said. Even though she'd prevented me in that moment, all I had to do was wait until they were asleep, only she left her bedroom door open after we went to bed. She'd not done that before. I leaned my back against the headboard, eyes on the bathroom door.

Popeye hopped up, and positioned himself on my knees. His warmth came through the covers, as did the contented vibration of his purring. I petted him, letting my fingers settle into his fur, and he began kneading the covers and I finally drifted off. Mrs. Brewer evidently got up at some point, eased my door almost closed, but not enough to keep the rich smell of sausage frying and coffee perking from slipping into the room the next morning. Popeye was still on the bed, half-asleep.

Remembering what took place yesterday, I got up and dressed quick. I went to the bathroom door and Merritt came out of his room.

"You using it or not?"

I backed away, motioned him to go on in. I returned to the bedroom, made the bed with Popeye still on it. He flopped on his side and stretched, even as I lifted the mattress and tucked in the sheet. Merritt came out, hair wet, and headed for the kitchen. I had to do it. I wouldn't ever get it off my mind unless I did. I went in, shut the door, turned the faucets on full. I went to my knees, clutched the toilet bowl like a long-lost friend. A fullness I couldn't stand blossomed in my midsection. It was over and done fast. I stood, shaking, yet relieved. I brushed my teeth, and winced at the shooting pain when I rinsed with cold water. I dared to peek at them, remembering what Mrs. Brewer had said. I hoped what I'd felt as a sharp, quick pain didn't mean they were about to fall out of my head. In the kitchen, I had to confront her, and breakfast.

I said, "I only want coffee."

She turned from the stove and said, "Do I look like I was born yesterday? Et."

I told a little white lie. "It's my, you know—"

"All the more reason to put something in yer stomach."

She stuck a plate with sausage, scrambled eggs, and toast in front of me.

I blanched and she said, "You got yerself all stirred up this morning."

Her gaze whittled away any excuse I was about to make.

"Yes'm."

I picked up my fork and, after the first bite, regained some appetite, but couldn't bring myself to eat all of the food. *Five pounds.*

She sat and sipped at her coffee, then said, "It ain't easy to get past it, but you can do it."

Merritt listened, shifting his gaze from her to me while crunching on a piece of toast topped with the eggs and sausage.

He said, "Get past what?"

Mrs. Brewer said, "Women things."

Like Daddy, it was enough for him. "Oh."

She said, "You reckon we ought to check on your house when y'all get back this afternoon? It would be like them good-fer-nothings to burn it down too."

I worried over Martin Murry. He might gather up Royce and Willie, even bring in Leland Murry.

The house would look normal, their cars would be hidden, and they'd pull some sort of ambush on us.

I said, "Maybe tomorrow?"

She said, "Fine by me, only a suggestion."

I drove to school the next morning, speeding the whole way. Merritt noticed, as I leaned forward in the seat like it would make the truck any quicker.

He said, "I sure ain't in no hurry."

I understood his feelings; I really wasn't neither. My speed came from nerves, came from the worry over what Willie Murry would or wouldn't do. Did he go home, and get angrier over my threat? Would he bring the journal, and if he had, had he done something to ruin it? If he had, what would I do about that? I had no idea.

I pulled in, barely slowing down enough to make the turn into the parking area, and Merritt said, "Geez, it ain't like we're hauling, Jessie."

"Sorry."

I searched for Willie's car to see if he was here yet. The lot was too full to know without checking each row and we only had five minutes before the first bell rang. Despite that, I took my time walking toward the school, keeping an eye out for any sign of him.

Merritt said, "What're you looking for?"

"What?"

"You keep looking around."

"Oh. Just Aubrey."

"I thought you two weren't talking no more."

"We ain't. I'm wanting to avoid her is all."

A girl from Merritt's class approached us, long brown hair swinging side to side in rhythm to her step. She had a sprinkle of freckles across her nose, cinnamon-colored eyes.

She gave me a little smile, then said, "Hey, Merritt."

Merritt choked out a greeting: "Hey, Lucy."

She walked with us, and said, "I'm real sorry about your arm. Does it still hurt?"

Another strangled noise and some more words fell out. "Sometimes. Not so much."

She said, "Would you want to be in our school play?"

Merritt snorted. "I ain't no actor."

Lucy sounded like she'd been practicing what she'd say. "Oh, but you'd be perfect, Merritt. We're doing *Peter Pan*: you could play Captain Hook. It's a major part!"

She took hold of his arm, the one with the hook, and said, "You can't say no. Come on, please! Jerry Stephens, Molly Campbell, and Ricky Tyndall are in it too."

"I don't know none of them."

"They know you."

"Yeah? How?"

"They watched you play ball. Said you were good."

"Oh."

"Ricky said he bet you could learn to pitch left-handed. He does."

That perked Merritt up more than anything I'd seen in a long time.

He said, "Yeah?"

She nodded quick, and said, "Yeah. Here. I got a copy of the script. I ran a mimeograph for you this morning. See? You have lots of scenes."

He stared down at the pages in her hand, and the poor girl acted as nervous as Willie around Cora. Merritt must've noticed it had taken an effort for her to ask, because the pages in her hand shook, and I was going to feel terrible for her if he didn't take them. He hesitated, then twisted his hook, shifted his right shoulder, and pinched the pages.

She said, "Wow, that's pretty neat how you can do that."

He went crimson, rattled the pages at her, and said, "Well. Maybe I'll think about it."

She actually squealed, and clapped her hands.

She said, "Come on. I want to introduce you to them."

She waited, shifting with nervousness from foot to foot until he said, "Okay."

I said, "See ya this afternoon."

He nodded and followed her inside.

Other students poured into the parking lot, and while I hadn't made any specific plan about

Willie bringing our journal back, I decided to wait for my old bus to come. I hoped when Cora exited, Willie would appear like magic like I'd seen him do even before the tip of her shoe had a chance to touch ground. The buses always came to the front and I waited there on the sidewalk as the first one pulled in, and then another. The third one was ours, and my senses went on high alert, like one of those emergency broadcast messages we occasionally received on our radio or TV. I licked my lips and thought about ducking into the closest building. I had no idea what he would do, or what I should do. Maybe if he saw me waiting it would make him madder than he already was. Maybe he'd do something to embarrass me.

Cora came down the steps of the bus with Stacy right behind her, talking. Cora walked with her head down, eyes cutting to the left and to the right, expectant, waiting. She strolled along, taking her time. The sound of tires squealing on the small street alongside the school parking lot made everyone stop and look. The top of a black car could be seen zipping in and around the other vehicles searching for a parking place. It was Willie's car, and I couldn't have been more rattled than if he'd sprung from behind me. As he approached, I tried to act like I was waiting for someone else, clenching my books to keep from shaking. He slowed down like he was having a mighty hard time deciding on something. Then he was beside me, and he stuck his hand behind his back, pulled out what he'd had tucked in the back of his belt. He held out the journal.

He said, "The old man said I had to give it back anyway."

I didn't understand. I took it, and before I could speak, he left to be by Cora's side. Dumbfounded, I laid my hand on the cover, stunned I actually had it back.

I overheard Cora saying, "William? What was that? What did you give to her?"

Willie didn't bother to answer. I tucked the journal in between my books and entered the school. Going down the hall, I didn't skirt around the edges, didn't crouch against the walls. I went just like everyone else, among them, the nothing-ness within me not quite so deep.

After school let out that afternoon I waited in the truck for Merritt. I flipped through the pages of the journal, studying Mama's handwriting all over again, as an unfamiliar sense of content-ment settled over me. Merritt climbed in and I waited with excitement for him to see what I had. He was about to say something, but then he saw what I held; his astonishment was worth all the fear of threatening Willie Murry.

He said, "How'd you get that back?"

"I told Willie yesterday I would tell Cora McCaskill what he was really like if he didn't return it. He brought it today. I'm not sure he would have except he said his daddy told him he had to return it."

"Why would he make him do that?"

"Geez, Merritt, if anybody could figure out why a Murry does what they do, not a soul would have any problem with'em."

"True. Still peculiar though."

"I'll say."

I handed it over to Merritt and he began to flip pages while I started the truck and pulled out of the parking lot.

Every now and then he'd point to one, and say, "Wow, all them gallons hauled in one week!" or, "Did you know Granddaddy Sasser had him one of them turnip stills? Wait. I think he had three."

It was like a history book, only it was filled with our past. That word, "our," quick and unexpected came natural, and I accepted it without any bitterness, actually feeling like I belonged, once and for all. All the way to Mrs. Brewer's house, our moonshine, our stills, our routes, ran through my mind. We turned onto the small side road that led up to Mrs. Brewer's, and as we came along through the cover of trees, I saw a car parked out front.

Merritt said, "I wonder who that is?"

I shook my head. "I have no idea."

I turned into her drive, and parked. The car had a government tag on the front, and when we went

453

in, Nash Reardon was sitting at Mrs. Brewer's table, drinking coffee with her. She motioned to a chair for me to sit.

She said, "He's come to tell you something, Jessie."

Chapter 34

Mr. Reardon appeared more like he had when I first met him, calmer, tie knotted in place, but still looked like he'd not had any sleep.

He said, "I found the two cars."

I set my books down, and sank onto a kitchen chair while Merritt inspected him much like I'd seen him study his baseball cards.

I said, "Did he come for his?"

"Eventually. We staked out the area, and the man you identified as Martin Murry came out of the woods from behind your house."

I said, "That's who he is."

Mr. Reardon nodded, and said, "I know."

"Where is he now?"

"I hoped he'd do something to give us reason to arrest him. We didn't have to wait long. He went to the vehicle, pulled up the back seat, took out a jar, and started drinking. He was hauling a load when he encountered you."

Mr. Reardon waited for me to respond. I could've laughed at the idea of Martin Murry drinking our shine right in front of Mr. Reardon, and I had to control my expression.

I said, "He drank the entire time I was with him."

Merritt fidgeted and Mrs. Brewer gave him the fisheye.

Mr. Reardon said, "Well, he sure didn't act like the man I knew. He started ranting about how he'd lost everything because of your family. How your family was finished. When he got in the car, intending to drive off, that's when we got him. He tried to tell us he was confiscating the vehicle as evidence, but I'd heard enough out of him to question him. I took him into Wilkesboro, and we got the full story there."

I began to have hope this was all going to be over, and I said, "Did you ask him about Mama, what happened that day?"

"I did. He seemed surprised I knew her name. I didn't tell him how I came by it. He said he was only doing his job, that he'd told her to move away from the still, and she'd not listened, had the nerve to laugh. In his words, she said, 'The day I ever listen to the likes of a Murry is the day I'll die.' He pulled the trigger, and well. You were there."

I nodded. "But we've never heard about him."

"Martin Murry's grudge also has to do with an arrangement his own daddy had with your father. After your mother died, your father went to Leland Murry, said he wasn't a killing man, but that there needed to be reparation for what

456

happened. Your daddy gave him the chance to take care of it. Leland Murry arranged for Martin Murry to get another name, then sent him packing with nothing but that, told him Wilkes County and surrounding counties were off-limits. With a new name, he could make up his own history, and he became a revenuer down in Alabama. I think it was on purpose, with the intent to eventually get back at your family. He's simmered over this for years. Through the ATU he heard about the Murry still being found not too long ago. It must've rekindled hard feelings. He somehow finagled it so he was assigned here."

This must've been what Daddy had talked about when he said Leland Murry had shown Mama some respect right after she died. Martin Murry had been disowned on account of her. I couldn't think of a thing to say.

He finished with, "From the way he makes it sound, none of his family liked the idea of somebody taking what they thought was theirs, and theirs alone."

I said, "We've heard about it all our lives. Right, Merritt?"

Merritt raised his prosthesis. "This is on account of them."

Mr. Reardon sounded surprised. "How'd that happen?"

Merritt said, "They run us off the road one

night. My arm got broke, then infected. Had to be taken off."

I said, "They got ahold of our cousin, branded him. Put an *M* on his chest. They also burned our uncle's house down."

Mr. Reardon said, "That house that caught fire a few months back, just down from your place?"

We nodded.

He said, "I'm wondering now if most of this was all of his doing."

I said, "Ain't a one of 'em ever not cause some sort of grief around here."

Mr. Reardon said, "That will hopefully improve. Especially now."

I said, "I guess he's the reason Daddy got caught too."

Mr. Reardon shook his head and said, "No. That wasn't him."

Merritt's chair scraped the floor, maybe an attempt to kick me under the table, his way of saying, *See? It was you all along.* I went still, my hands knotted in my lap, head down, and I waited for Mr. Reardon to say so.

He said, "That would've been because of your uncle."

I exhaled.

Merritt, his voice sounding doubtful, said, "Uncle Virgil?"

"Yep. He showed up at our office one afternoon,

yelling about the Murrys, pounding on my desk. He was so lit we could smell it coming off him. After he left, we kept an eye on him, thinking he'd lead us to something. Sure enough, he went to that still site not too long after he'd been in. We were about to nab him, but he got spooked. He took off through the woods, and although we waited for him to come back, he never did. But now we had the location, so we hung around, knowing someone would return. It ended up being your father."

I remembered how I'd felt watching them take him away while I hid. Uncle Virgil had bragged how he'd taken care of it. He sure had, knowing it had to have been his fault Daddy was caught. But all he'd worried about was if Aunt Juanita could tolerate him if he went to jail. I felt some-what vindicated, finally.

I said, "What's gonna happen to Martin Murry now?"

"He'll go to jail for a long time. He's been straddling the fence as a revenuer under a fake name. Plus, running liquor. That's serious."

Martin Murry had said to me, *You can't run in both directions,* and he'd been doing that very thing himself.

Mr. Reardon said, "I ought to let you know, I spoke to your father about what's been going on here. I asked him to tell me about Martin Murry, and he gave me the same account of what took place with your mother and what he and Leland Murry agreed on. He also said you never did act the same after you saw your mama die. Said he'd tried to understand you, and probably didn't do such a good job."

I had to blink fast. Aside from Mrs. Brewer, I'd never imagined anyone else trying to understand me, much less Daddy.

I said, "I ain't ever forgot it"; then I said, "Wait here."

I got up and went into the green bedroom and got her picture. I returned to the kitchen and held it out.

Mr. Reardon stared at it for several seconds. He said, "You favor her. She was quite the legend around here; so I heard from your father."

"Yes."

And I meant it for both parts of his comment.

He said, "Well, that's about all I know. Do any of you have any questions?"

Merritt and I looked at one another. It was so much to take in, but I did have a question.

"What happened to our daddy's car?"

"It was taken as evidence."

He retrieved his hat off the table, stuck it on his head, and stood. We got up and followed him to the front door.

Before he went out, he said, "We'll keep doing what we can to clean up the county here. Keep an eye out for me, will you?"

I said, "I sure will," only I didn't intend it in the way he meant.

After he was gone, I said, "Wow."

Merritt said, "No wonder we didn't know Martin Murry."

Mrs. Brewer said, "Shoot. I wished I didn't know not one soul in that family nohow."

We stayed with Mrs. Brewer another week, and then went back home. In time, I allowed what the Murrys had written inside our house, whether Willie, Royce, or maybe Martin Murry himself, to be painted over. We went back to making the Sasser shine, using Mrs. Brewer's still at first, and hauling it in her car like she'd suggested. Sometimes we used the truck, but we had to be careful because the back end sinking too low might create suspicion. Merritt said Daddy had told him once that Troy Dalton could fix the suspension on just about any vehicle that would hold it level even when loaded down.

I said, "But he'd have to have it a few days, and then we wouldn't have nothing to drive."

He said, "Maybe we could get us a new car."

"Maybe."

School went on as usual, and the saga that was Cora and Willie became the talk among students, especially after Cora got Homecoming Queen, and Willie, of all things, Homecoming King. It was bizarre how he was changed by Cora's influence. Even his clothes were different, penny loafers now instead of the Wearmasters, sweaters tied around his neck. He didn't spare me a glance, and it was like he was afraid I might notice him.

Every now and then I'd see Nash Reardon in town and I'd always throw a hand out the window, wave, and give him a thumbs-up as if I approved of what he was doing. I also went in to see him for no other reason than to keep him from coming out to check on us and maybe catch something going on. Times were changing. There was talk that one day brown liquor would be sold legally in Wilkesboro and North Wilkesboro, managed by the government. Wilkes County citizens weren't quite ready for that though, and kept voting to delay the permit of what was called a regulated Alcohol Beverage Control store. This was good news for us, and we continued to build on orders, while keeping Mr. Lewis, Mr. Denton, and others supplied.

After a while my fear of being caught at the Big Warrior subsided and we went back to using it, the dings and dents in the side a reminder of my time in the woods with Martin Murry. Being at the old still site brought back the past. Sometimes I'd get to thinking so hard about working with Daddy out there, I would swear his voice echoed through the trees. Then there were times I was sure someone lurked nearby. It was always the idea of it being a Murry that haunted me, and I'd get scared enough to abandon the site, no matter what point we were at. This irked Merritt to no end because we had to start with new mash all over again.

"How we ever gonna save enough for another car if you keep wasting the corn we're buying? That's twice now."

"I can't help it; geez, Merritt, do you want us to get caught?"

"No, but ain't nobody ever showed up. Ain't ever been a sign of a soul. You're just spooked is all."

I had to hope it would get better as time went on, this jumpiness I had. It caused internal turmoil, and made it difficult for me to manage that other thing, what Mrs. Brewer called "the monster." It felt like one, the roaring inside me like some horrible beast, urging me to eat, eat, eat, then give it the relief it wanted. I hated it, and loved it. I obeyed it at times and ignored it at others, and that made it rage louder and longer.

Mrs. Brewer got to where she hovered over me like a bee over a flower, maybe seeing something I couldn't.

I finally had to say, "I'm fine; it ain't all that bad anymore."

She folded her hands in front of herself, and sniffed. She didn't believe me, and the worry lines on her brow deepened.

She said, "I'm only wanting to help you, child."

I didn't admit how uneven my heartbeat had become, even as I lay in bed at night, or how unsteady my legs were, as unreliable as balancing on toothpicks. I didn't talk about how sore the insides of my cheeks were, the burning from my chest into my stomach, the odd way my lower legs and ankles swelled. I tried to do as she wanted, eating when she fixed food and brought it over. She took hold of my hand one time, frowned at the scrapes on my knuckles, which were from my own teeth from pushing my fingers down my throat. I pulled my hand away.

"That's from stacking wood crates."

She only shook her head.

Daddy came home in the late spring of 1961, almost unrecognizable, gray, sad-faced, thin as a scarecrow, and wearing the clothes he'd had on when he was caught. They were clean, but hung on his frame, flapping like curtains at an open window. It was good he was home, but strange too. I was seventeen, and Merritt fifteen, taller than me by almost a foot. Daddy wasn't so keen at first on knowing about our shine operation, while I was itching to tell him how I'd just hauled a hundred gallons into Winston-Salem two nights before.

He said, "So, tell me, Jessie. What do you want to do?"

This was puzzling.

"What do you mean, what do I want to do?"

"I been thinking. Had plenty of time for that, and such."

He gave me a sad little smile.

Merritt said, "Hey, Daddy, watch this."

He showed him how good he'd become at using his hook, twisting it and going around the kitchen picking up this and that.

He said, "I even learned how to pitch left-handed. I ain't as good as I was, but I been playing with some of the boys from school. I do all right."

Daddy said, "That's fine, Merritt. You've been working hard at it; I can tell." Then he turned back to me, and said, "I might've been wrong forcing you into something you never wanted to do. I can see that now."

"If you mean making shine, I do like it."

"You don't need to pretend just because of what happened."

"I ain't pretending. Ask Merritt. Ask Mrs. Brewer. They'll tell you it was my own decision. I ain't so bad at it either. Maybe not as good as Mama, but I reckon I could be, one day."

Merritt nodded, but Daddy held on to his guilt tight, like I held on to my own shame.

He gestured toward me, and said, "You look like you been locked up."

Mystified, I said, "What?"

His hand dropped by his side, like it took too much strength to hold it up.

465

He said, "Pale."

I shook my head. "I'm fine, just working a lot is all. Daddy, I made a haul over to Winston-Salem."

"You ought not work so hard; slow down some."

"I'm fine!"

Merritt said, "She ain't neither; she's puking in the toilet all the time."

"No I ain't!"

He said, "I can hear you, even when you turn them faucets on, Jessie."

I felt cornered. Mrs. Brewer could help me explain if she'd been here, her kindness, and softer words would've made it all right. I wasn't up to arguing. It had been a late night, and Daddy had only come in just this morning, at the crack of dawn, using his old key.

"I'm fine. I am."

The two of them swayed, like they were pitching about on the deck of a ship, but it wasn't them. It was me. I placed my hand on the back of a chair, steadying myself.

I said, "Really. I am."

Epilogue

A few days later we went to Big Warrior and I explained to Daddy how we'd transferred the materials from Blood Creek and rebuilt it. I was panting by the time we walked in, but if they noticed, they said nothing. He went over to the still, knocked on it, and smiled at the smell of the mash fermenting.

Daddy said, "I sure have missed that. Why'd you decide to move it here?"

Merritt acted like he didn't know, but I said, "I figured they wouldn't come back after they'd caught you, and destroyed the still that was here. Mostly though, because it was Mama's favorite place."

"That's mighty good thinking on your part, Jessie. Don't know that I could've been that smart."

His words filled me, but not the way food did. In a good way, because I didn't want to get rid of them, I wanted to hang on, hold them close. On the way home the three of us crammed into the front seat of the truck, and rode with the windows down, sweet mountain air filtering through.

Mrs. Brewer had come over and cooked a big

welcome home meal, and while we were all sitting around the kitchen table, I said, "I'll make a run into Charlotte in a day or so."

Daddy said, "I gotta tell you. You do sound just like your mama."

More words to cling to.

After I helped Mrs. Brewer clean up, Merritt and I showed him the money we'd saved, going to all the hiding places, and counting as we went.

He said, "You hear anything out of your uncle Virgil?"

We shook our heads. "Nope."

He said, "Just as well, I reckon. He acted the fool most of the time. That agent said he came in there drunk and they followed him. It's how they got me."

It was like he wanted me to know he didn't blame me for what happened. I brought up about wanting to buy a running car.

I said, "We got more than enough saved here. There's a '57 Ford that might work out good if nobody buys it before we do."

Daddy said, "I'll go look at it with you."

We went the next day, and Daddy again was full of praise for my good eye. We bought the car and I drove it home while he and Merritt followed.

He said, "It's your car, Jessie. What will you call her?"

I knew right away. "Lydia, after Mama."

It caught him by surprise, and I thought his eyes shimmered. Well, it was all right, because my own vision blurred. The next evening I prepared to go to Charlotte, and Merritt and Daddy helped me load her up. These cars, well, it was easy to think of them as family members, and I already had a special attachment to this one.

Daddy said, "We got to get Troy to make some adjustments, but she'll take right much, even now."

When we were finished, surprisingly, Daddy hugged my shoulders, his fingers kneading my bones, as if he was verifying for himself my physical state, buried underneath layers of clothing. I was always cold, even though it was almost summer.

I leaned against him and said, "I'm happy, Daddy."

I wasn't lying.

I got in the car, and went down our drive. At the end, I stopped, adjusted the rearview mirror, and saw him and my brother, side by side like they were framed for a photograph. Before I headed out, my fingertips touched the edges of Mama's picture on the dash, right where I could see her, like she was going along with me. I headed for Charlotte, winding around the familiar curves of Shine Mountain, smiling at the completeness, at how it had come full circle.

• • •

Over the next year, I gained a bit of notoriety when I got tangled up with a few agents, but they could never outrun Lydia. Daddy got Troy Dalton to do the work, and she could go like a rocket. My driving got better and better, and every now and then, I'd see some agent in my rearview, trying once again to catch me, then simply giving up.

Daddy said, "Maybe you ought to take it on over to that racetrack some of them boys is using. Bet you could win."

The back roads through the hills and hollers were enough for me.

Merritt and Lucy Morris became practically inseparable, actually that entire group of kids he'd taken up with ever since he'd played Captain Hook became his new crowd, while I realized I preferred being alone. I wasn't into what the other girls were, the dances, the boys, the dreams of being Mrs. So and So.

Mrs. Brewer had gotten to where she moved a little slower, said her legs bothered her, but other than that, it was me she fussed over, always trying out some new concoction I had to drink.

She was at our house often enough Daddy said, "You ought to just move in."

We thought he was only kidding until he got to building a little room off to the side, just for her, and old, scraggly Popeye. She sold her house in town, tried to give Daddy half the money, and he acted insulted by it.

"I ain't taking no crotchety old woman's money. How you think that's gonna make me feel?"

I remembered my own refusal over not taking money for particular reasons, and when I raised my eyebrows he gave me a sheepish grin. They got along good, and I noticed he was the only one who could make her actually laugh, which usually made me laugh because she sounded like an owl hooting.

I continued to fight the battle against my internal demon, winning some days, losing on others. Mrs. Brewer flitted around me, urging me to eat, always watching with a worried look, always telling me to fight the monster.

I patted her hands, and repeated what I always said: "I'm fine."

The event was unexpected. My heart vibrated, a spontaneous thing I paid no attention to as I drove Lydia fast around a curve. The odd trembling quickened, and within my chest came an unfamiliar pressure. Light-headed, I gripped the steering wheel, intent on working through it like before. I focused on the sunlight slanting across the trees, turning them so green and sharp it was like they'd been struck by lightning. The tires squealed, then became the cry of the gulls at the seashore from long ago. The scent of sour mash filled my nose; I heard Merritt laugh, and watched Daddy cradling Mama. I'd always been her daughter, and I'd become his too, bound by their love, but also by the moonshine that flowed in our veins. A sense of relief, happiness, and peace came over me, one of lightness, the sensation of being free. My gaze locked in on Mama's picture, and at how her face appeared to . . . shine.

Wilke Journal-Patriot,
September 18, 1995

An unsolved mystery may have been settled earlier today after the discovery of a vehicle thought to be owned by eighteen-year-old Jessie Sasser, missing since May of 1963, was uncovered in a remote area known as Switchback Holler, near the popular Moravian Falls. Construction of new condominiums planned for vacationers and tourists is underway, but was halted shortly after a bulldozer, operated by Tim Wheeler of Wheeler Construction, uncovered the 1957 Ford. Soon after, skeletal remains were discovered inside and the Medical Examiner was brought in. The remains have been sent off for positive identification and cause of death.

Local law enforcement in 1963 were unable to determine the circumstances around Miss Sasser's disappearance, although speculation it was because of an old rivalry between the Sassers and another family by the last name of Murry has circulated among locals over the years. The Sasser family, infamous decades ago for their highly successful moonshine operation here in Wilkes County and beyond, competed against the Murry family until the members of the latter moved away to an undisclosed location. Some locals said it was in deference to Miss Sasser, who gained notoriety even among revenuers with the Alcohol Tax Unit originally dispatched for the sole purpose of shutting down the illicit still operations that peppered the hillsides back then.

Aside from the discovery of remains, the vehicle also revealed hidden compartments, and crates of broken jars under the back seat, fitting the history of such pastimes. Because of the folklore around Miss Sasser, news of the findings brought many locals out, including Miss Sasser's father, Easton Sasser, 75, a retired auto

473

mechanic, and her brother, Merritt Sasser, aged 49, currently employed as a teacher at the local Pine Tops High School and a coach for the high school baseball team, despite the loss of his right arm, in what he called "an unfortunate accident years ago."

As the car was pulled out of the ravine, a quiet hush fell over the group of spectators as father and son approached the vehicle together to each place a hand on it.

Author's Note

A ll writers joke about characters telling them
what they want to do and we're to just
follow along. It happens with every book, but I
can honestly say when I began this story *I hadn't
planned on writing about an eating disorder
(ED)*. I spend a lot of time contemplating what I
view as important public issues, and I will sometimes land on a possible topic as I did with this
novel. I'd written the scene where Jessie Sasser
was frustrated with her father's lack of response
to her persistent questions about her mother's
death. Then, as so often happens when beginning a story, I was stuck. I sat back and thought,
okay, she's verbalized her frustrations with him,
how might she show this through her actions?
Within seconds, I wrote the scene with the peach
cobbler, how she kept eating, and couldn't seem
to stop.

At first, I went along with the idea Jessie's
low self-esteem would simply be tied to weight
issues. That was different, fresh and new from
my other characters in my previous novels, who
were all, in their own way, strong, resilient, and
essentially healthy-minded despite the trials and

tribulations I put them through. Jessie declared herself different almost immediately. First, it was the overeating. Then, she took over my keyboard and pounded out the first incident of purging. And there it was. My main character was going to suffer from an eating disorder.

What did I know about eating disorders? Nothing. It goes without saying I spent some very intense weeks studying about bulimia, and anorexia. I learned that, similar to autism, EDs can't be defined absolutely in black and white. There is a spectrum of disordered eating, and some individuals display behaviors associated with both anorexia and bulimia. Some have distorted visions of their bodies. Some may binge and purge twenty times a day, while others twice a week. Many think they are controlling it. They get good at hiding what they do. Very good.

I used sensitivity readers to see if I was portraying this disease accurately. I thank them immensely for opening up to me, and what I was trying to show: the origin of the behaviors, the suffering, the longing for normalcy, the signs that things have reached a critical point, and what happens when the health of an individual is severely compromised. I owe them a debt of gratitude. The true intent of my Author's Note, however, is to provide links to resources where those suffering from an ED and their families can

476

get help. There is always help. Please seek it if you or a loved one is at risk or suffering from an ED.

https://www.nationaleatingdisorders.org/

https://www.womenshealth.gov/mental-health /mental-health-conditions/eating-disorders

https://kidshealth.org/en/parents/eating -disorders.html

Discussion Questions

1. At the age of four Jessie witnessed her mother's brutal death. As time went on, Jessie came to her own conclusions as to what happened. Do you believe Jessie was destined to become self-destructive because of what she saw, or was it because she couldn't get the answers she sought?

2. Jessie grew to hate making moonshine, and this put her at odds with her father. Do you think his reasoning to stay silent was justified?

3. Merritt, Jessie's younger brother, didn't remember their mother's death, and couldn't relate to Jessie's sorrow or her intense dislike for what he viewed with pride, a family legacy. What did you think of Merritt and Jessie's relationship? What did you think of how he treated Jessie?

4. Jessie's "best" friend was Aubrey. Do you think she was ever concerned for Jessie's well-being, or did you find her mostly selfish and self-absorbed?

5. The time frame is 1960, and eating disorders were not well known. Despite lack of public

awareness, Mrs. Brewer, the school nurse, recognized it. If she could have known Jessie at a younger age, do you believe her herbal teas, support, and advice could have helped Jessie battle "the monster"?

6. Jessie's other family members, Uncle Virgil, Aunt Juanita, and cousin Oral, were each responsible in their own ways for creating discord. Of those three, who did you view as the most harmful to Jessie?

7. The leather journal Jessie's father kept with their family's moonshine history, as well as her mother's picture, became critical and important items to Jessie, giving her a better sense of belonging and understanding. These inanimate objects held such significance for Jessie. What do you think is the reason for this?

8. Fire is a component used in various major events in the story. Why do you believe the author chose it?

9. What did you think of the ending? Given Jessie's behaviors, did this seem like the most likely outcome?

Books are
produced in the
United States
using U.S.-based
materials

Paper is
sourced using
environmentally
responsible
foresting methods
and the
paper is acid-free

Books are
produced using
top-of-the-line
digital binding
processes

Center Point Large Print

600 Brooks Road / PO Box 1
Thorndike, ME 04986-0001 USA

(207) 568-3717

US & Canada:
1 800 929-9108
www.centerpointlargeprint.com